THE EINSTEIN POSSE

Laren R. Winter

ISBN: 154114919X
ISBN 13: 9781541149199

CHAPTER ONE

On the day one of my special education students died I was sitting in a school meeting counting the holes in ceiling tiles. I was up to two hundred twenty-five counting the holes in those tiles. These tiles were the same style as the ones I looked up at as a boy in the bedroom my dad built for me. The tile was manufactured somewhere in the early '60s. I counted them as a kid just because I wanted to see how many were in each ceiling tile. I am counting the holes today because I am bored silly listening to Ms. Reba Bennett discuss Scott Dumas again. She is his third grade teacher and is continually frustrated with him from the sound of her comments. I have wondered why she is even teaching. She almost always seems upset with her students. I get a headache the day before when I know we have an IEP meeting with her involvement. These Individualized Education Plans are to help kids achieve. Reba Bennett doesn't seem to act like they can be successful. Two hundred twenty-six. Two hundred twenty-seven. Two hundred...

"Scott Dumas isn't making progress in my class," said Reba. "He has trouble staying on task and the individualized education plan doesn't work. A lot of the day he just stares into space!" Reba looked at Scott's mother.

Reba was on a roll today. I was trying to tune her out, but her voice was harsh. I was beginning to see purple spots instead of the holes in the ceiling tile. Shawn Peebles, her principal, should get rid of her. The rumor is she has many complaints against her, and, yet, she stays on.

What happened to her anyhow? I wondered. Reba had been two years ahead of me in school here in Rua Springs and in my older sister's class. Reba was a cheerleader and the football homecoming queen her senior year. She dated the quarterback, Charlie Prewitt, and Reba and Charlie were considered the king and queen of the school. They were the beautiful people who had the rest of us in awe. They married right about graduation and were expected to succeed brilliantly. Of course, they didn't.

After three children, Charlie, the high school football star, started roving. My older sister filled me in on all the juicy details. His numerous affairs with other homecoming queen types crashed and burned the marriage. Reba had gained lots of weight and is like her earlier homecoming queen self in name only. She struggled with being a single parent, but she did manage to finish college in elementary education. Reba came back to Rua Springs and has been a teacher here ever since.

"We need a new plan. This one doesn't work." Bennett exclaimed.

We all looked at her waiting for her idea of a new plan.

"I'm trying very hard to help Scott succeed, but he just doesn't seem to care." Reba held out her hands, palms up, showing she was at a loss as to what to do.

Two hundred twenty-eight...I observed Reba Bennett's face as I would an act at a carnival. In high school she was the petite, cute, bubbly, smiling girl whose presence was everywhere. Even the teachers fell all over themselves to be near her. Now her hair was platinum blond. Her face was round and bloated, and she wore way too much makeup. At five feet two inches, she probably weighed in at over two hundred pounds, so she was about as wide as she was tall. Life went downhill after high school, not an unusual occurrence for some high school standouts.

The door from the middle school's conference room banged open. "She hung herself!" cried Tiffany Little, a middle school student.

"Miss Little, what are you doing here?" asked Bennett. "We're right in the middle of an important meeting. This is not the time or place for your stories."

"But, it's true, Ms. Bennett! I just..."

"Tiffany, please leave now. We..."

"It's Patsy Anderson!"

"Out right now or you'll..."

I came out of the fog at that moment and jumped up from the table. "Patsy?" I asked.

"How dare you interfere in my business here," Bennett barked at me. "You come back here with your big doctor's degree and think you know everything and are better than us. Some of us stayed here in our hometown and contributed to its growth. You didn't."

I had lived in New Mexico and had just returned to Colorado last July. So, she was right that I hadn't been living here for many years. My name is Marc (short for Marcus) Thomas, and I'm the school psychologist here. I'm thirty-six years old and a widower.

Her words stung, though, and I wanted to lash out, but now was not the time. "Tiffany, tell us what happened," I said in as calm of a voice as I could. Inside I was turning to ice and began to shiver.

"They found Patsy hung in the boy's locker room," said Tiffany, as tears ran down her cheeks. "Jerry Coleman, the custodian, came to the office. The high school principal said to bring you, Doctor Thomas." Tiffany was hugging herself and beginning to hyperventilate.

I reached for Tiffany as she was leaning forward and falling into my arms. "Let's go," I said quietly to her. We moved out the office door and all the others followed except Reba Bennett. She stayed seated for awhile, and began stuttering unintelligible words in a whine that sounded like a drowning hippo. Her face was a red/purple shade that looked like a Halloween mask of horror.

We were all quiet, except Reba, as we made our way to the boy's locker room in the high school athletic building. Reba was still grousing about being interrupted by Tiffany and Patsy Anderson.

"How dare Patsy do this to me," she grumbled as she waddled along behind us. No one thought to tell Reba to go back to her classroom.

I was in shock and trying to understand. I reached back to my experience and training in order to deal with the crisis. I knew something about Patsy Anderson's family even if I had been gone for fourteen years. Her dad and mom, Clive and Vivian, and I were in school here together. We weren't really close, but in a school system of only seven hundred and fifty students in pre-school through twelfth grade, it was a small community. Patsy's parents divorced right after she was born so it was just Patsy and her mom now. I thought back to my sophomore year when Patsy's dad, Clive, decided I needed a lesson about respecting elders. He was a year older than me, but I had recently won the quarter mile place on the track team that he had had for two years. When I came out of the shower he threw tough skin liquid on me and laughed with his buddies. The coach was standing nearby and didn't do a thing. He just grinned and said, "It's just a rite of passage, son." I've never forgotten the humiliation of that moment and the days that followed.

As we entered the locker room, Darnell Claussen, the high school principal, met us at the door. He was sweating profusely and had tremors in his hands. His voice was gravelly and hoarse as he said, "Doc, I need you to take charge of this situation with students and teachers. It will explode on us shortly."

He led us around a bank of lockers to where Patsy Anderson was hanging on one of the pipes that ran through the ceiling of the room. She had used a jump rope to hang herself. The rope was hanging over the pipe and had been knotted around her neck. An overturned chair was laying on the floor beneath her body.

Beyond all the locker room smells of sweat and dirty clothing I could smell the stench of Patsy's release of her bowels. Her eyes were part way open with the glassy stare of the dead. Reba Bennett started crying then. She was right beside me and was not quiet about it. Darnell spoke to her.

"Stop it, Reba, right now! You don't have any reason to be here so go back to your classroom." Her crying became a whimper.

I felt my breakfast coming up fast. The toast and eggs I had only two hours ago were making a comeback. I felt the darkness begin to devour my soul as I looked at the purple, bloated face of Patsy Anderson. I had spent a half of an hour with her just last week during our weekly meeting, as I had for several months. She was qualified for special education services as gifted in math and special needs in reading. Rua Springs schools were missing both the elementary/middle school counselor and school social worker now. The school system had me working with regular education students for counseling issues. There was almost no extra time in my weekly calendar and my load was already maxed out. I started seeing Patsy at the beginning of the school year, because she couldn't concentrate in class and was showing signs of depression. She had always been a good student but had been withdrawing into herself.

"Sheriff Montes is on the way," said Darnell. "The faculty and students will be texting even though we have a policy against it. Rumors and panic will crush us. They'll probably hear the sirens anytime now."

"I'll begin the crisis management plan and start setting up small and large group meetings," I said.

My eyes locked each of the people who were with me in the IEP meeting only minutes before. The special education director, George Novak and Ellen Chavez, the special education teacher for Scott Dumas were probably in shock like me. I vaguely wondered about Scott's mother. She was sitting in the meeting with us and we raced out leaving her behind. Was she waiting for our return while staring at the gray surplus file cabinets that stood like guardians at the edge of the room? My thoughts of Scott's mother faded as I glanced at Patsy. Dead.

It was difficult to swallow. My brain was seizing up. Seeing her hanging from that pipe was beyond all of my understanding. Was it really her? Why would she do this? Or did she? Was it an accident? I've dealt with lots of horrible things in schools, but this is one of the most gut-wrenching. She is/was a beautiful, compassionate young lady. Tears were at the edge of my eyes. I was struggling to hold myself together. I wanted to sit down, scream, cry and curse 'til I was hoarse. Why would God allow this to happen? Or, is there even a God? As a lapsed Episcopalian, I was having trouble believing in any kind of faith in a loving, caring God. The fundamentalist Christians will burst out of the walls of the school now. I can't dive into the God thing now; I have to be a professional here. I can't be a normal, hurting person. Play the part until I can let loose. Later, yes later.

CHAPTER TWO

EMTs, with sirens blaring, showed up a short time later. Bad news would spread like the plague through the school consuming everything in its path. The sheriff's "death" squad and Sheriff Montes himself showed up at about the same time. Lane County was a good-sized county in Colorado, and it was covered well by the sheriff and his deputies. He must have been close by to get here so fast.

"Hola, Marc. Arrepentido quedar con usted esta manera," spoke Sheriff Steve Montes as he came up beside me. (*Hi, Marc. Sorry to meet up with you this way.*) "Esto es malo, verdadero malo." (*This is bad, real bad.*)

Steve and I had grown up together and had a close friendship. When I moved back home he asked me to be a consultant with the sheriff's department. I accepted, but this was the first time something happened on my turf.

"Sí, Steve. Es verdadero malo," was all I could get out. (*Yeah, Steve. It's real bad.*)

"Okay," the sheriff said in his deep voice, "I need everyone out of here except my team and the EMTs. Move on out now so we can do our job."

I looked at Patsy Anderson one last time and turned to go out with the others. Reba Bennett was held up on each side by George Novak and Darnell Claussen. She was beyond any color of white. Her face was totally drained of color with a pasty look. Her eyes were large and dull, sightless. They had a hard time dragging her short but heavy body from the room. I don't imagine any of us looked much better though.

Darnell Claussen helped put Reba on a bench in the gym outside the locker room. The cool fall air woke me up from what I had just seen inside.

"I just hope to hell other kids don't start killing themselves now. Once one does it, others follow," said Darnell in his principal's voice. "We don't talk about suicide here, Doc. So, don't get into it with anyone. I don't want an epidemic of suicides going on now."

I knew his comments and logic regarding suicide were antiquated. One suicide didn't start others. The school needed to listen to students and pay attention to comments, however small, about self-harm. A plan needed to be in place that closely monitored students with recent loses, family problems, social isolation, loss of interest in their usual activities, etc. We really needed to talk about suicide prevention and intervention with students, faculty and parents. A detailed plan was a must. But I had already had that discussion with him. He didn't want to hear it. If we don't talk about it, then it won't happen, he believed; head-in-the-sand trick. Retirement couldn't come soon enough for him as far as I was concerned. His thinking caused more harm than good.

When we reached the high school I could see kids standing at the windows. From a distance I imagined I could see the faces of every middle schooler peering out the windows, too, but the high school blocked their view of what was happening. The schools were set up on the four points of the compass; north, south, east, west. The schools were situated on a large plateau. They sat above the town of Rua Springs which was down and to the west. The high school was on the north end and was the oldest of the buildings. The middle school was on the east. The elementary school was on the west. The preschool, the newest of the buildings, was on the south. In the middle was a large open space area with benches scattered around. Aspen trees had been planted as had various forms of vegetation. There were also beautifully sculpted and welded art forms. Sidewalks moved in and around the area. It was called Roark Park, named after a local boy who had died in Vietnam in the '60s. Dad grew up with him, but they served in different places in Southeast Asia.

Behind the high school was Gomez Gymnasium which held the locker, weight, and gymnastic rooms. To the north of that was the building trades and vo-tech building. The football field sat up above the schools to the south on an area that was carved out of the mountain above the plateau. Behind the middle school was its gymnasium and locker room. It was just called the middle school gym. The elementary school shared the middle school gym. All of the schools were far enough away so as not to crowd each other, but they were close enough that a person could walk between them. Walking did take time, though, as I knew, since I moved amongst the schools daily. It wasn't a normal school psychology job. In fact, it was far from it. But, it worked for me.

A low level cacophony of voices greeted us as we moved into the high school and to the common hallway. The noise was humming from each of the classrooms. Some teachers and students were standing in the hall. I knew this was the way it would be today and for the days that followed. I could almost hear the texting going on from cell phones even though it was a big no-no. All bets were off today.

"Get these students back to their rooms," exclaimed Darnell Claussen. "Teachers, get some order now!" he hissed at those teachers who were close by the entryway. "I want everyone where they should be second period. I'll make an announcement shortly over the P.A. system about our situation here!"

Situation? I yelled to myself without a sound. Is this what he thinks this is? A situation? Patsy Anderson just hung herself, and this is a situation? Too bad for Patsy's situation, huh? She's dead, you coldhearted dirt bag! I had to gain control of myself. I knew I had to be "on" now to keep many others from losing it. Darnell had his job, and I had mine. He sure wouldn't be sharing any empathy with anyone about this "situation".

"Doc, let's go to my office so we can figure out what I need to say," Darnell said through gritted teeth. We moved quickly to the main office. Mrs. Neeley stood up behind the counter as we entered.

"Is it true Mr. Claussen? Is someone hurt?" Mrs. Neeley said in a weak voice.

"Not now, Mrs. Neeley! Just stay here and do your job and keep people out of the office. Doc Thomas, Mr. Brighton and I will be in my office."

"But, the phones are already rin…"

"Just answer the phones with your nice, polite voice and say school is in session and everything is under control," quipped Darnell.

We moved to his office. Gerard Brighton, the high school counselor, was already seated in the office. Brighton had been around forever and was known for doing nothing but shuffling papers around and setting up classes for students. The only "counseling" he did was telling students they were too dumb to go to college or do anything productive in life. He was here when I was in high school. He also told me not to go to college, because I was not smart enough. When I moved back here this fall with a doctorate, he told me in the hall one day that he always knew I would do well. I wanted to punch him in his fat gut, although I didn't. With a big smile I thanked him and moved on.

"Okay, let's figure this out," sighed Darnell. "Doc, let's go with the Rua Springs School Crisis Guide you have worked on. I know it isn't in place yet, but you've explained the need for it, and I've seen what you have. So, let's run with what you have."

When I had first arrived in Rua Springs last July to begin my new position, I discovered the school district didn't have anything in writing about what to do if a crisis occurred.

I brought the idea to the school superintendent and the three principals plus the director of the preschool. They discussed the idea and asked me to begin work on it. But since the school district hadn't had any crisis for awhile they didn't believe there was any hurry. What I told them at that first meeting was that we needed a guide that was in writing so we could respond quickly to emergencies and crises. I let them know that the goal was to make the schools safe and secure by emphasizing prevention. That would be done by teaching a culture of respect for what might happen. Since I was an Eagle Scout, I hammered in the "be prepared" motto with them. I said we needed to address all the vulnerabilities and hazards we might encounter in our schools. Not really trying to scare them but just being clear with them, I told them that without a plan we were asking for disaster and chaos. Hmmm...I *was* trying to scare them.

Throughout that first meeting I outlined a possible team of people who would be key players in any crisis. Depending on the crisis we needed the principals, a rep from the teachers, mental health professionals like me, the school counselor, the school nurse, and school social worker, if we had one. We also needed the campus security officer, a parent rep, and a front office communication person. Within the crisis guide would be several key areas, which included everything from crisis response team personnel identification with roles and responsibilities to equipment that might be needed; health/mental health referrals. All of that information was almost more than the administrators could handle. They fell back on the "old traditional ways" that had always worked. But, they still wanted to see what I could do with it. And so, the work began. I already had a manual

I had used in a school district in New Mexico, so we had an outline. I just had to pull the people together. We had just begun writing the crisis guide for Rua Springs schools when we had a real crisis.

"Okay, we have already begun the 'First Hour Needs' of our crisis plan," I began. "The sheriff, EMTs, and coroner are already here. We need to contact the superintendent, wherever she is, along with the other two principals and the preschool director. Since the middle school counselor is on maternity leave and the social worker resigned because of illness, I'll call the professional counselor and the marriage and family therapist who have offices in town. The school nurse is at the elementary school today; we'll need her here. The chief of campus security was already at the boy's locker room, so he knows what has happened. The parent and teacher reps need to be contacted. I'll get with them. Patsy's mom has to be notified by Sheriff Montes before any communications go out. I'll keep in touch with him. The team needs to have cell phones on. Our first announcement will come from you, Darnell, but we can't really say what is going on yet. The windows of the classrooms on the north side of the building had a nice view of the sheriff's cars and the EMT van. I'm pretty sure word about something happening here is out, so we have to move quickly. There are lots of moving parts here so we all need to hold it together." I looked at Gerard Brighton, the high school counselor, when I said the last part. He wasn't known for keeping any secrets.

"Sometime today, after official word comes from the sheriff, we will have to initiate the proper phone tree and emails to teachers, students, and parents. The phones will get red hot in no time so we have to have a recorded message put together with information we want shared. Oh, I forgot-- school board members. We need to include them at least initially. Superintendent Espiñosa will handle that. Her communications director will handle all correspondence. Also, the school needs to stay open throughout this evening. It will be a long day and night. We will need to have the crisis counseling available from now on. Tomorrow and in the following days we'll want to be available for individuals, groups and classes. Hopefully, those two mental health professionals can be available soon." I stopped and looked at the Darnell and Gerard. Their looks were blank as if they had totally zoned out of what had happened and what we needed to do. Shock? Denial? Fear? Probably all three and worried about their jobs at the same time. This would be a dark stain on their records. "So, shall we move forward?"

"I want as little said as possible," whispered Darnell. "Don't want a scene here. No one talks about suicide. We don't use that word in this school. Until we know more from Sheriff Montes, his team, and the coroner, we don't share anything. Doc, you hang around here to deal with any trouble that shows up."

I must have missed something. He acted as if I hadn't said a word. It was a total discount of our crisis plan. I looked around to see if I had been transported to the *Twilight Zone*. Where was Rod Serling when I needed him?

"Gerard, you just...just...well, you know, just do what you would regularly do."

I knew what that meant. Gerard was to stay in his office and out of the way so he didn't cause more problems.

"Doc, the new crisis manual," continued Claussen, "I kind of hoped we wouldn't need it so soon. We never had a manual and plan before and didn't need it." He was saying that since I developed it I would be to blame for any failures. I said to myself, *How will this work?!*

"I'll make an announcement now that everyone is to be in class and working hard." And with that Darnell was up and out the door.

Gerard gathered his girth, rose from his chair, shrugged his shoulders at me, smiled his monkey smile, and left. He hadn't said one word the whole time. Man, it was going to be a long day with long days to follow.

Things in the outer office were humming tighter than a banjo string. Semi-quiet chaos reigned. I heard Mrs. Neeley on the phone saying everything was fine and no need for concern and no, they didn't need to come get their child. Darnell was at the public address system getting ready to make his announcement. I waited by the door that went into the nurse's office.

"This is Mr. Claussen speaking. I want everyone to calm down now and remain in your classes. There is no reason for alarm or concern. Everything is under control. There is no danger to anyone. Continue with your regular schedules."

As soon as he finished, a parent stormed into the office demanding to know what was going on. "I got a text from my daughter saying something happened, and I saw the EMT truck and sheriff's cars here. My girl better not be in any trouble here or you will regret it."

Carl Aimes was in dark blue coveralls smeared with oil. On his left breast pocket it read Carl's Auto and Welding. On his feet he wore large black work boots. He was about six foot four tall with broad shoulders. Carl had red hair and a crew cut. He had a broad forehead that came down to thick red eyebrows, which ran all the way across his face. Behind plastic glass frames, with plastic side covers, like welders wore, were his beady, small dark eyes that seemed to be a long way apart because his nose was large. It looked like it had been smashed across his face. Smudge covered various parts of his face. I was certain I heard *Dueling Banjos* playing somewhere around him. Oh, oh, is that a smile?

"Just hang on, Carl," said Darnell. "Tiffany is fine and in class. There is no danger here. We have it under control. Just an accident. Go on back to work, Carl."

"Like hell I will!" exclaimed Carl. "Something bad happened here otherwise Tiffany wouldn't have sent me the text."

"Well, Carl, Tiffany shouldn't have sent a text from school anyhow. She knows the rule about no cell phone use."

"I don't care about your rule! I'm taking her home now." With that, Carl rushed out the door and started hollering for Tiffany. "Tiffany? Come on now, let's go! I'm taking you home!" Teachers stuck their heads out their classroom doors to see what was happening. "Now, Tiffany!" I had walked out in the hall next to Carl to tell him it would be faster if we looked up which room she was in and just called the teacher to have her sent to the office. "Who are you? I don't know you. Tiffany!" Carl yelled louder.

"Carl, I'm Doctor Thomas, the school psychologist. I help with the students here."

"I don't care if you are Dr. Seuss. You are in my way."

With his size and demeanor, I wasn't about to put anything to the test. "I'll get her teacher and room number for you, Carl." And with that I went back inside and asked Mrs. Neeley to find out where Tiffany was this period.

Mrs. Neeley was on the phone trying to get a word in edgewise to what someone on the other end of the phone was saying. "Yes...No...No...I'll get...No need to...Yes... Mrs... I under..." I leaned over the counter and she covered the phone with her left hand. "Yes, Doctor Thomas?"

"Can you get me Tiffany Aimes's schedule for this period?" I quietly asked.

"Hold on. Yes...Yes...No..." She laid down the phone and I could hear some lady on the other end ranting about something I couldn't quite make out. "Here we are. Second period. Mrs. Adams in English." She picked up the phone again. "Yes...No...Okay...Ah..."

I walked out into the hall as Carl was continuing his rhythmic chant for Tiffany. "Tiffany, girl, get down here. Tiffany. Tiffany." With a drum I could have been his backup rhythm section. Tiffany, ah, ah. Tiffany, ah, ah. Maybe I should ask Carl if he was interested in starting a new chant group. Tiffany, ah, ah. Tiffany, ah, ah. Okay, maybe it wasn't a good time to ask.

"Carl, Tiffany is in Mrs. Adams's English class. Let's walk down and get her." I looked back into the office. Mrs. Neeley was still on the phone and Darnell was nowhere to be seen. I moved off hoping Carl would follow me. The high school was built like a "T". The long part of the T was a wide hallway with flower beds set in brick rectangular structures. In between the flower beds were metal benches with backs. Each bench had a companion bench backed up against it. The benches each faced banks of lockers built into the wall. Doors to classrooms were dispersed evenly along the way. There were skylights in a vaulted ceiling that provided natural light throughout the hall. I led Carl down the hallway and to the left. Mrs. Adams' room was the second on the left. I knocked on the door. Mrs. Adams approached, looked out the glass window, and opened the door slightly.

"Yes?" she said. "What is it?"

"Tiffany Aimes's father is here for her, Mrs. Adams," I shared in a low voice. Carl had been quiet all the way down the hall. He stood behind me trying to look into the classroom.

"I'm taking Tiffany home now," blurted Carl. It was loud enough I was certain that everyone in class had heard him. I was pretty sure Tiffany was turning every shade of red by now and was totally humiliated.

Mrs. Adams was jolted, as was I, by Carl's voice. "Just a moment, Mr. Aimes. I will get her for you," said Mrs. Adams quietly. She closed the door behind her as she went back to her class. A few moments later Mrs. Adams opened the door, and she and Tiffany came out. I could see that Tiffany had her backpack held in front of her. Her eyes were downcast and the embarrassment was apparent. She didn't say a word. Carl took her backpack from her and grabbed her right hand. Mrs. Adams looked at me, shook her head, and went back in her classroom. The door closed behind her.

"Mr. Aimes, you will need to sign Tiffany out back at the office." He looked at me, turned around, and pulled his daughter back toward the main office. I stood there for a moment, realized I was the only one left, and started the long walk back to the school office.

The room I used at the high school to see students was also the nurse's office. I was able to use it when the nurse wasn't here. There was one nurse for the entire school body of seventy hundred fifty students. Her main office was in the elementary school, which was where she was today. As I walked in to the outer office, Mrs. Neeley was standing and speaking with several parents who were asking to take their kids out of school. The phone was still ringing. Darnell had emerged from his office and was trying to calm the parents. I stood off to the side realizing that this was the calm before the storm. It was time to plan for the storm.

Up until now I hadn't allowed what had happened to Patsy Anderson to occupy my thoughts. I could feel the adrenaline rush that came from a crisis. I knew it would kick into high gear soon. Anyone who says a crisis like this doesn't provide a high isn't being truthful. As sick as it sounds, the high takes hold, clarity occurs, and a person is ready for action. It is probably like working in an ER. The rush is partly why we do this kind of work. There are some periods of boredom, but working as a school psychologist in a school system provided varying degrees of a high. This was the beginning of the rush and the high I would ride for awhile. Then, the crash would come. It would come later when my body signaled it was time to let the sadness, anxiety, and darkness come. I had ridden it many, many times. It was never any easier. No matter how much training I had, I always had to come off the mountain top and deal with the grief and sorrow of something like this. Keeping it purged was something I wasn't good at. Who do caregivers lean on?

CHAPTER THREE

The day progressed with several parents coming to get their kids. The phones continued ringing. The lid was not quite staying on. More rumors had to be squashed without actually lying. Kids were showing their confusion and fear. I had students asking to talk saying they were nervous. They didn't seem to know much just that something had happened and they were wondering what. I had to tell them that they were okay and that everything was being taken care of. Some were angry that we wouldn't tell them anything; others were scared. They wondered if the school had been attacked or something. Still others wondered if there was a bomb somewhere on the school campus. I assured them that none of those things were true. The tension of the morning rose with every tick of the clock. At about lunchtime the lid came off.

The sheriff called Superintendent Espiñosa first and then called Mr. Claussen. Patsy Anderson's mom, Vivian, had been notified by the sheriff and the department's chaplain, who happened to be my cousin, Katherine Hanson, an Episcopal priest. The scene in the locker room was a possible crime scene so it was still off limits. Now it was time for another Claussen announcement. This time more of the truth. I knew Superintendent Espiñosa's communication person would be setting things up for teachers, parents and the community. Hold on to your hats, boys and girls, we are in for a bumpy ride.

"May I have your attention please. This is Mr. Claussen." His voice boomed out over the loud speaker system in the high school. "We know this morning has been difficult for many of you because you are wondering what might have happened here at school. There has been a lot of concern and, of course, many rumors floating around. We had to wait to make sure we had allowed several things to be accomplished. At this time we can tell you what has happened. We want everyone to remain calm and respectful. As I said earlier today, no one is in danger. There is nothing wrong with any buildings here on campus. Nothing is going on in any of the other schools where you might have younger brothers, sisters or other relatives."

There was a long pause. I watched Darnell step back from the microphone and take a deep breath followed by a drink of water from a glass he had in his left hand. I could almost hear the total intake of air as everyone held their breath. The entire building seemed to inhale as if holding its breath and waiting. All the oxygen was temporarily suspended.

"It is my difficult and sorrowful duty to have to tell you there was an accident here at school. There has been a death. I am very sorry to say that Patsy Anderson, a junior here, has died."

Deathly quiet took charge, hung on, wrestled for superiority. It won for a second, two, more. But, it lost.

"Oh, my God!" I heard someone say in grief from down the hall.

"No way!" said another voice.

"It can't be," cried another voice.

Then there was utter silence again. Life was snatched from of the building. It stood empty, dead, and totally cold. I tasted the grief in my mouth and waited. It was bitter, vile.

"Noooo," whined a female voice. It was Mrs. Neeley. Tears were streaming down her face.

That was it. The building came to life again almost as if everyone let out a deep breath while saying to someone and no one, "Thank God it wasn't me. I'm still here, alive. I escaped that brush with death."

"Let me have your attention again," choked Darnell into the mike. "We know this is a terrible shock. We need to continue on with our school day. I know this will be difficult, but it is important to do so. Order and structure needs to remain. We will keep you informed. Once the sheriff concludes his investigation we will know more. The school will remain open this evening for those who need to just gather or talk to someone. We are here for you, and we will all get through this together. Teachers, we will now break for lunch as we need to keep up our strength."

That was the announcement. In a very flat, but clear voice, Darnell had said what needed to be said. Was he too cold? Who knows? How do you make an announcement like this anyhow? It can only be harsh, brutal, shocking, and devastating. Who can comprehend the death of a student? These adolescents are invulnerable, invincible. Death can't touch them. They are smart and worldly. And yet their developing brains can't totally grasp the fact that one of their tribe is gone. It just can't be true.

In a state of total shock, the school emptied for lunch. I stayed in the office area in case of total meltdowns by teachers, staff, or students. It stayed pretty quiet during the thirty minute lunch except for Mrs. Neeley quietly sobbing and blowing her nose into one tissue after another. She knew all the kids by name and was a second mom to many of them. Several teachers came to the office lounge area with their lunches. Some didn't leave their rooms choosing to be alone with their own thoughts. I could hear some of the teachers in the lounge speaking quietly about what a horrible thing this was. It was tragic. It was unbelievable. This would certainly make it hard to teach for awhile. Someone wondered aloud how Patsy's mom was doing. Huh? Did I hear that right? How was Patsy's mom doing? From personal experience, I have an idea how she is doing. She is in complete shock! When death occurs people say the dumbest things. Instead of saying nothing at all people ask insane questions, because they *believe* they are supposed to say something. Anything! Just fill the silence! There is always a need to cover up grief with hurtful or meaningless and non-thinking words.

Then, I heard someone say, "She is safe now in the hands of Jesus. It was His will. Praise Jesus." I wanted to run into the lounge and vomit on someone.

The students silently came back into the building. Their shoulders were slumped forward, and eyes were downcast. They shuffled along as if they had aged ten years in thirty minutes. There are always kids who want to lighten up the horror of the situation with clowning around and making inappropriate comments. Funny, huh? Somewhat like the teachers without the clowning around. "Shut up, Bobby! Just shut up!" I heard a small girl yell at the adolescent male walking beside her. "You are so stupid!" I looked forward to more volcanic eruptions as the reality of Patsy's death became more apparent. Everyone would deal with this in his or her own way.

The five stages of grief by Kubler-Ross were interesting, but nobody just goes through stages one to five and is done. Some will shut down totally for years. Some will shut down for awhile and then come unglued. Some will continue to talk their way through the pain. Some will cry. Some will laugh. Some will just jump to the anger stage and stay there for who knows how long. Some would need lots of hand holding and hugs, and some will become physically ill. And some will become depressed and need medication. There is only one healthy way through this, and that is to go through it. The adults don't do it any better than the students. The school would become an ER trauma unit where triage is done just to keep functioning. The goal now is normalcy; that is way out there, though.

The afternoon classes began. Several more parents came to pick up their kids wanting to keep them close to protect them from something bad happening to them. The belief that goes with death is that it might happen to them somehow. It is like a contagion that has to be avoided. I walked the halls trying to provide a calming presence to anyone who saw me. Many of the students meet with me regularly because of being qualified for special education services. Some were qualified because of academics, which included being gifted in a subject area. Others came because of an emotional/behavioral problem. Since I entered classrooms, with the permission of the teacher, to bring students to my office for fifteen minutes to thirty minutes, the other students knew who I was. They knew I wasn't a teacher or an administrator. As a school psychologist I held a very unique position in the school. I gave no grades or punishment. I listened, assessed, assisted, and supported. I didn't judge them. I was their confidant and best cheerleader. So, the students were mostly friendly to me. I knew some of their families since I had grown up here. However, I always knew I was an adult and, thus, a foreigner and never would be part of their tribe. I was an outsider; trust was something to be earned, and even then it might not come.

Two girls came into the office. One had her arm around the other while the girl held her stomach. The girl being held reached up with her right hand and wiped tears off her face. "What is it, Veronica?" asked Mrs. Neeley. "Don't you feel well?"

"Carlie was crying in class, and Mr. Wilcox asked me to bring her down to the office. Maybe we can, like, you know, talk with someone."

I was standing nearby. "Would you two like to come in here, and we can sit down and talk if you want? I'm Doctor Thomas, the school psychologist." I pointed into the nurse's office. "I know you don't know me, but I'm a good listener." The two young females came into the room. I entered and closed the door. They stood holding each other all scrunched up like they had been totally emptied. They looked ill and nervous.

"Have a seat either on the chairs over there or on the nurse's table here." I touched the padded table behind me. They chose to sit together on the table. "We can just sit here together, or you can talk if you feel like it. Sometimes words just aren't available. That's okay." I sat on one of the wooden chairs across from the girls. The silence settled in. I could almost smell the sadness emanating from the girls. It was time to just "be".

"Ah... she was sort of a friend of ours, Patsy, I mean," uttered Veronica softly.

"Yeah, she...," began Carlie, but stopped, wiping more moisture from her cheeks.

"Would you like to talk about your friendship with Patsy?" I asked quietly. I waited for them to continue on their own time. Time moved. One beat, two, more.

"Well," said Veronica, "we've been in school with her since elementary school. You know, we, ah, knew each other and did some stuff together sometimes. It kind of, ah, changed, though, here in high school. It's just, ah, sort of, ah, different."

I waited for more, but they both remained silent. I spoke. "I would like to hear more about your friendship with Patsy if you would like to tell me."

They looked at each other and then down at the floor. "Patsy was always kind of quiet when we were in elementary school. Carlie and I," Veronica looked at Carlie, then back at me, "we always tried to include her in things. Since she didn't have a dad and we did we invited her over. We had sleepovers, watched movies together and did outdoor things. She said funny things sometimes. We like Patsy's mom, too. She acted more like a sister to Patsy and to us. It was neat. Her mom worked all the time, so Patsy was at home a lot by herself she told us. I guess she liked it because it was quiet. She---"

"She did okay in school," said Carlie, interrupting Veronica. "Patsy studied hard while Vee and I just wanted to have fun and laugh. Patsy was easy to be around, too. Some girls aren't. They act stupid." Carlie and Veronica both laughed at some unspoken memory.

"Patsy always acted grown-up even in elementary school," Veronica offered, as she jumped back in the conversation. "I wanted to be more like her. She was always kind to me even when I got mad at her." Veronica looked off into the distance seeing something only she could see. We all stared ahead silently and waited. They, like me, probably hoped this would all just go away so we could start the day over. The sounds of the building hovered around us, breathed on us, and came and went like fog in the silence.

"We were always friends," muttered Carlie, "but things started to change even in middle school. Vee and I always had lots of other friends, and we started to hang out with other girls. Patsy was still quiet and kept to herself a lot. Sometimes other kids made fun of her." Carlie hesitated, coughed twice, tried to go on, but tears started tumbling down her cheeks again. She let them roll quietly. "I made fun of her, too, when other kids did. Everyone laughed at what I said about her." Carlie choked back tears. I handed her a box of tissue that was on the floor beside my chair.

She took out several, blew her nose and tried to speak again but had difficulty getting any words out.

Veronica held Carlie close, like a child. Carlie laid her head on Veronica's shoulder. Veronica swallowed, holding back her own grief. "I laughed at her, too. I just wanted to be liked by the other girls." It was said so softly I leaned forward wanting to hear. "Patsy was nice. This can't be true, can it?" Veronica looked at me not really wanting an answer. Her face was twisted into a painful smile; controlling her emotions was becoming increasingly more and more difficult. I wanted to reach out to both girls and hold them close to keep the anguish they were experiencing from moving any deeper into their souls. That wouldn't happen, of course, but perhaps I needed them to hold me as much as they needed to hold each other. I wouldn't cry now, but it took all my strength to hold back my own desire not to scream seeing the pain these two girls were experiencing.

In child-like voices the two girls told me about the difficulties Patsy seemed to be experiencing due to starting special education. Patsy didn't really confide in them about it, but they could tell she didn't like standing out because of it. She told them about being teased more because of being in a gifted class. Patsy already seemed odd to other kids, because she was so quiet and kept to herself. However, with the new special education help, Carlie and Veronica knew it became merciless at times. They had seen it and had even taken part, but Patsy always forgave them and seemed to understand.

Every day in middle school provided more craziness for all of them. They said the boys became more dorky and acted more immature, but they still wanted to be around them. Carlie and Veronica had each had a series of boyfriends in middle school. Patsy didn't. During middle school they spent some time together on weekends just hanging out at one of their houses. They watched movies and listened to music. Carlie and Veronica talked about boys and athletics and complained about school work and various teachers making up all sorts of crude names for the teachers and the boys. Patsy didn't talk about boys, didn't do athletics but did smile at some of the names they came up with for the teachers and boys. Patsy laughed at the name for the history teacher. He was "stool brush" because of his mustache and chin whiskers. The English teacher was "bubble butt" because she had a large behind. Another teacher was named "Shrek" because of a big head. Patsy seemed to be interested in the athletic adventures and the volleyball, basketball, and track stories the other two girls told. They told Patsy she really needed to try out for the teams, but she never did.

"I think Patsy started to change a lot last year in tenth grade," expressed Veronica. "She told us she was still teased about being in the gifted program. We knew it hurt her, but she didn't show it much."

"Yeah, but Patsy smiled more last year," interjected Carlie. "We still met up sometimes on weekends and listened to music and she was just, ah, like, strange, smiling and moving to the music. Very weird for Patsy."

"That's right Patsy was, well, I guess happier maybe?" Veronica added. "She was always the same, but now she was, ah, you know, smiling a lot?" Veronica looked at Carlie as if the answer to Patsy's life would suddenly be revealed in Carlie's face. The two girls continued to stare at each other.

"A boyfriend?" they both asked together.

"We asked Patsy if she had a secret boyfriend some-where," said Veronica. "Patsy never said, no matter how many times we asked."

The room resettled into silence again. Once again the school sounds entered into our space, crowded us, asked for its attention, and demanded that we hear it and acknowledge that it was there.

"This year Patsy was more and more unhappy. We didn't speak to her much and didn't get together at her house or ours. She was here but not here. Patsy went out of her way not to talk to us. She turned around and went the other direction when we saw her in the hall. I tried to ask her what was wrong, but she just moved away. I even yelled at her one time a few weeks ago and wanted to know what I had done wrong, but she never spoke." Veronica said all this in a painful voice, filled with sorrow. "If I had known, I could have helped," she cried. "Why wouldn't she let me help?" Large tears streamed down her face. Veronica was now being held by Carlie. They clung to each other in a deathlike embrace as if fearing if they let go, they would crumble into dust.

I heard all that these two girls had said and remembered my time with Patsy over the past several weeks. She didn't really tell me what was going on either. I knew she was in more and more pain as the weeks progressed, but what was actually behind it was a mystery. The dilemma was that Patsy was up and down. She would be happy at times, almost dreamy, but then darkness descended upon her at other times as if it was choking her. Patsy talked some about her gifted class for math and her special needs class for difficulty with reading. It was clear she didn't want to be in them and wanted out, but she's given up trying to fight that. I worked on engaging Patsy, but it never seemed to click. She was never unfriendly or rude, though. Patsy was gentle and kind, but also haunted. I realize now that I was working harder than she was. She was just there, but wasn't, as the two girls had said earlier. Whatever finally happened in Patsy's life, it sent her into the abyss. What was it? What could I have done differently? Were there signs I missed? I felt guilt. Was she so depressed that I should have intervened earlier? I didn't know. I may never know.

The afternoon moved on tick by tick. After my time with Veronica and Carlie, the school seemed to settle into a place of fragile numbness. It seemed if anyone moved wrong, spoke wrong, breathed wrong, the roof of the school would crash in on everyone. A few teachers stopped in to see if we had any other news about Patsy. We didn't. They didn't say much beyond that, keeping with the fragile and haunted look of everyone else. Students changed classes in subdued semi quiet.

Before school ended this seemingly endless day, Mr. Claussen announced again that the school gym would be open for people to gather if they so chose. I expected the two mental health pros from town to arrive anytime.

As daylight became twilight and that became nighttime, students and some parents and teachers came to the gym. I was there with Liz Chavez, the professional counselor and Mason Bishop, the marriage and family therapist from the area. We decided that adorned with name tags we would simply move around the gym and enter into conversations where we might be needed. The students gathered in groups of friends, as did parents. As I moved around the gym, I sometimes heard softly spoken conversation occurring. I didn't expect to be invited into many, if any, conversations. Our plan was to just be available. I did notice that a few ministers from town showed up and were moving around speaking with various groups. Hopefully, they were keeping their beliefs to themselves, but I doubted that. What better place to spread not only hope, but also fear and terror of hell and damnation. The word "suicide" was being spoken here and there. Preachers were their own breed of people. Some were okay, but some were there to pontificate. My cousin Katherine, the Episcopal priest, wasn't here. I figured I would see her soon anyhow.

The evening moved on with a few people coming and going from the gym. Everything was orderly. Some people just needed to be near others to know that they were not alone now. Several students clung to each other like Veronica and Carlie had done in the office earlier today. Tears were seen in some locations. Mostly, people had a questioning look on their faces. The question of, how could this happen here? It was as if some sacred rule had been broken by a member of the tribe. "How dare Patsy do this to us," some seemed to say to themselves. "This isn't allowed here," said others. "We don't have bad things go on here." I knew that wasn't true at all. Many other bad things had happened at this school and in Rua Springs. Conveniently, some people forget those times with "selective amnesia".

It wasn't all about Patsy, however. It was a shattering of what had developed over time in any school and community in regard to keeping the darkness at bay. The longer it is held off the more secure and complacent people become. That is what everyone wants, not a death too early. When something like this occurs, the reality of the world comes back full bore and slams into boys, girls, men and women like a tsunami at full height. Temporally all is lost. After some time the water recedes, the land dries and rebuilding occurs. We say to ourselves, "Well, that was interesting. Okay, now, what's for dinner, and when's the next football game?" Move on everyone! Cell phones and text messaging takes place, new movies are watched, humans fall in lust and love, and the next crisis is in some other place. We say, "Whew, I'm glad that didn't happen here."

By 9:00 p.m. the school was empty. I thanked Liz and Mason and asked if they could help us out again tomorrow. They said they would. The chief custodian locked up behind me. We said good night and all headed to our cars. I looked at the stars and the waning moon coming up and tried to figure out what just happened. The stars and moon didn't have any answers.

CHAPTER FOUR

When I arrived home I was emotionally and physically tired, and spiritually empty. This day had lasted a year. Once again death was at my heels. I parked in the driveway to the left of the garage doors so I wouldn't block Dad's or Grandpa's doors. After locking up I wearily walked to the side garage door, entered, and moved through the garage to the kitchen door. Opening the door I entered into the kitchen and heard laughter off to the right in the living room. The room was a large area with a vaulted ceiling and skylights. It had an oak floor so the rubber soles of my shoes made a swishing sound as I moved into the room. Sunny, Dad's golden retriever, and Kong, his corgi, raced over to jump up on me and get their loving. They each had a few years on them, but usually acted like two-year-olds. There was no better greeting. Dad and Grandpa were sitting in their respective reclining rockers smiling at the forty inch Sony television perched on the teak table across from them. It was the end of the Colbert show on Comedy Central. They watched it most nights, lapping up the jokes about the buffoons who ran the country no matter the party affiliations. I moved to the sofa to experience the end of the show. Maybe it would take my mind off the death of Patsy.

"Son," said my dad as I entered his realm of vision.

"Hi, Dad." I lay back on the sofa hoping to escape the pain my entire body was experiencing. "How you doing, Grandpa?" I asked my grandpa who had his rocker laid out for his comfort. He was laughing at something Colbert said about congress. I didn't expect a response from him. It wasn't a time to interrupt the two most important men in my life. This was their sacred time, their church sanctuary, and it was sacrosanct. The preacher was on and interrupting was punishable by extreme pain: flogged, drawn, and quartered.

"And in other news Congressman Rob Sturges officially said he hadn't touched those twelve prostitutes. He just went there to talk. His wife wouldn't listen to him anymore, and he needed oral stimulation. Those were his words, not mine." Colbert stopped and looked at the camera, pinched his lips, rolled his eyes. "Hmmm…I guess his twelve prostitutes certainly gave him some much needed oral stimulation."

Grandpa laughed his wheezy laugh for several seconds, slapped his right hand on the arm rest, and farted. Whoa! *Blazing Saddles*. That was his comment on politicians. I felt sorry for his rocker. Dad smiled. What a household. Three generations of males under one roof and no females to maintain order and provide rules, structure and good manners.

I had moved back to my hometown in July of this year. It was something I thought I would never do. I figured I was gone, and that was it. Why would I go back? But, the last two years of my life had been worse than hell, whatever beyond hell is. It was lower than Dante's nine rings. I needed to be with my dad and, by extension, my grandpa.

Two years ago my wife, Lilly, had been murdered in her car. She was on the way home from working her job in the ER where she was a PA, a physician's assistant. A drunk driver with five prior DUIs killed her. He murdered her, and he is still out walking around. Actually, he was probably still driving around. We had lived in New Mexico for many years. I knew it had one of the worst DUI stats in the country. Offenders are still out there driving around with five, seven, nine DUIs in New Mexico. I just didn't think about it ever happening to us. It did, though; broad daylight, no snow, rain, nothing. Clear blue sky. Mr. Five DUIs ran head on into her going fifty miles per hour. He walked away. Lilly lived seven days on life support, and I had to pull the plug. I died, too, that day, still breathing but dead. It was impossible to grasp what had happened. The days blurred into total numbness. There were no emotions except anger. I fantasized every way possible on how to kill the guy who killed, no, murdered my wife. There were murders with guns, knives, bow and arrow, ropes, pipes, poison, cars, strangling, barb wire, bombs, hammers, chain saws, circular saws, cattle bolt shot, and on and on. Fantasizing how to kill him ate me alive. Of course, I was already dead so what did it matter? I tried counseling, went to grief support groups, spoke with ministers, took pills to sleep and pills to wake up. And I drank. Nothing helped. I was nothing without Lilly. We had been married for twelve years, and she was dead and gone. Why go on?

Dad called me last spring. There was an opening for a school psychologist at the Rua Springs schools. His final comment was, "Son, it's time to come home." I applied and got the job, and here I am living with my dad, Bret Thomas, and my grandpa, Herman Thomas, both of whom had also lost their wives. My mother, Marie, died ten years ago from a brain tumor. It started slowly and then was out of control. She was in hospice a short time and then gone. Lilly and I visited her a few times before she passed on. My grandmother, Katherine, died twenty-five years earlier of a stroke. It was quick. I was a kid then and tried to make sense of it and couldn't.

Now, Patsy Anderson. The first time I met with Patsy at school I was shocked at the resemblance to my wife, Lilly. They could have been sisters. Of course, there was no connection. Lilly was five foot six with short auburn hair and blue eyes. She was shy and very gentle. Compassion could have been her middle name. There was a deep well of knowledge, but pain was behind the smile sometimes. She had an old soul as if she had felt and seen things the rest of us hadn't. Patsy was also five foot six with short auburn hair and blue eyes. She was also very gentle and shy. Pain was behind her smile and soft voice, and she was old beyond her years. When I was with Patsy I always felt I was with Lilly at a younger age when I hadn't known her. The desire to hold Patsy and keep her safe from harm was strong. Of course, I never let on to Patsy, always remaining a professional. Now, she is gone, too. If there was some kind of God out there I figured He/She must have gotten fired for being AWOL.

"Bad day at school today," my dad was saying to me. I shifted back to the present. Cobwebs were clouding my sense of location. I mentally shook them off to try to focus. I didn't want to let go of Lilly or Patsy.

"Yeah, it was," I was able to say in a constricted voice. I looked off to the right where my dad was sitting, waiting for more. It didn't come. He was watching a muted commercial on the television. I wasn't surprised he knew about school. He heard everything but didn't reveal much. My dad hadn't changed significantly from my earliest memories. He always wore Levi's and western rough out boots along with his work shirt. It said Rua Springs Hardware above his left breast pocket with his name, Bret, under it. Dad's face had a few creases, but he still looked younger than his sixty-three years. He had a dark complexion, from our Native American relatives, with long black hair, gentle brown eyes, and a straight Roman nose. He had a strong chin and oval face, which now had a day's worth of beard. Dad wore oval-shaped black metal framed glasses. When standing he was about six foot tall, not muscular, but certainly sinewy. I looked like my dad in a younger version and without the glasses. We were definitely father and son. On the other hand, there was my grandpa, Herman.

How we were ever related to Grandpa I would never know. He was about five foot four inches tall and looked like a gnome. He always wore brown lace-up high top leather shoes with gray work pants, gray work shirt, and a gray jacket. On his head he almost always wore a gray fedora; it seemed to be glued to it. He probably even slept in his hat!

Under his gray clothes I knew he always wore long-handle white underwear year round. His hair was pure white but hidden by his fedora, of course. His face was covered with a full white beard and mustache. His eyes were blue above which perched thick white eyebrows. His nose was a button and since I had never seen his lips I didn't have a clue what they looked like. But, there was always a rascally, impish look with a twinkle in his ice blue eyes.

It seemed Grandpa knew something about the universe, both good and bad, that no one else knew. He challenged it, begged it, pleaded for it to "bring it on," and he would just smile at it. Grandpa worked fifty years as a baker and loved every minute of it. At least that was how it seemed. Two of my childhood memories of him stood out. One, he always smelled like fresh baked bread. It was a comforting smell. The second memory was about a time when I was visiting him and my grandmother down below, and I told him about a kid who was bullying me at school. He looked at me and said, "Life is tough, get a helmet." I didn't know what that meant for a long time. Now I do. Grandpa hadn't retired until after my mom died, and he and my dad decided on new living arrangements.

My dad has owned and worked in the Rua Springs Hardware store since before I was born. We originally lived in the house behind the store. That was where I grew up. After my mom died, my dad did something he and mom had talked about for years. He built their passive solar dream home, moved out of the house behind the hardware store, and expanded the store to include the entire house. It doubled the size of the store. It wasn't a chain hardware store, but it had almost everything anyone needed. I always loved all the hardware things and had worked there in middle school and high school.

Now, the three of us males sat in this incredible home my dad built to honor my mother. It had windows all across the south part of the house. It was one level, and dad had a large sunroom where he grew all sorts of plants and vegetables year-round. The back of the house was partially earth bermed, except for the garage, so there weren't any windows on the north side. The one-level home held the garage, kitchen, living room, dining room, sunroom, utility room, and three bedrooms with baths. The roof was metal with south-facing photovoltaic panels across the entire south pitch of the roof, except where skylights were located. Dad had the house almost off the grid. That was the dream he and mom had together, and now my grandpa and I shared it with him.

"There are lots of stories and rumors floating around town now," stated my dad. "Patsy's mother is surely having a bad time of it. There have always been crazy stories about Vivian Anderson. I hear them at the store. Some people can't believe she never remarried after her husband left her when Patsy was just a baby. That was a long time ago. Viv has always kept to herself. That's okay, though, she can do whatever she wants, and it is nobody's business. Now she is by herself, and I know how hard that is."

My dad wasn't a big talker so that was quite a lot for him to say. I could feel his sadness through his reflections. Even though he didn't show a lot of affection and express emotions, I always knew he had a heart filled with empathy and compassion. The television was off now and as my dad stared off into eternity, my grandpa was busy reading his bible and mumbling to himself. Once every decade he went to the Southern Baptist Church. Now, he often sat around either reading from his bible or quoting scripture out of context. My mom had told me many years ago that Grandpa had gone to a seminary for a couple of years as a young man but dropped out to open his bakery and get married. Grandpa did do the biblical bread and wine thing, though, as he would make bread and then come home and partake in unusual great wines like Thunderbird, Ripple, and Pink Catawba. He worked hard to get the communion service down correctly so he had to try it over and over and over. Once in awhile I knew he was still working on it here at age eighty-three.

"You had anything to eat, Son?" asked Dad. "There's still some baked chicken left over if you want. Your grandpa wanted to finish it off, but I got him in a neck hold and held him away." Dad snickered at his own joke. His dry humor was one of his trademarks. I pictured Dad holding Grandpa around the neck swinging him around the room. Grandpa didn't reply but was saying something about the fiery furnace of hell.

"I'm not really hungry, Dad. Thanks, though."

"Okay, I imagine this has been a tough one for you. Kind of hard to think of food."

"I was just getting to know her; Patsy, I mean. We had met together once a week over the last couple of months. I still can't believe it. It just doesn't make any sense. These never do, though. I missed seeing something. That's what really bums me out, Dad. How was I so out of it with her? I feel like I totally missed things with her."

"Son, you're not God. That job's already taken.

"Yeah, well, God missed something here, too, if there is even a God. What kind of God would allow this?"

"I know where you are with God, Marc, and I won't argue with you. I have a tough time making sense of this, too. We'll figure it out in time."

Time wasn't going to help me figure this out. I didn't tell Dad that, though. We let each other believe what we needed in trying to get along in life. He still went to church and even sang in the choir. It worked for him but not for me.

We sat through the 10:00 p.m. news on channel seven coming out of Denver. After getting through several murders, corrupt state leaders, the state's and nation's budget crisis, and loss of jobs, there was finally some good news from the weather. It was going to be sunny tomorrow and about sixty degrees. No rain in sight. Then back to more bad news in sports. The Broncos and Nuggets both lost. If the Rockies had been playing and had lost we would have had a triple. Great. Tomorrow was going to be difficult at school. The news of Patsy's death would be all anyone would be talking about at school and in town. I headed to bed at about eleven.

Sleep wouldn't be visiting much tonight. She didn't come around much anymore. The invitation was always open, but I guess she neglected to open the invite. Someone did send the dreams, though, even though they weren't invited. They showed after a few minutes. I couldn't keep my eyes open. I knew if I succumbed the dreams would show. They had for the past two years.

Lilly walked toward me from the hospital entrance. She was waving to me. Her sunlit smile brightened up the street and surrounded her. A goddess. A miracle of creation. My breath caught in my throat. I started to raise my hand and yell out to her, "I love…" Lilly was driving away from the hospital. She was smiling as usual. I could see her coming toward me, waving. I lifted my hand to wave back and yelled, "I love…" Lilly was crushed back into her seat with the steering wheel pinning her. Her face was smashed and distorted with blood streaming in rivulets from her nose and cuts. I stood in front of the disintegrated car and looked down at her. She smiled at me and lifted her hand to wave. "I love…"

I sat up in bed taking in deep breaths, sucking in oxygen as if I couldn't get enough. Beads of sweat stood out on my forehead, but I was incredibly cold. Ice cold. Deathly cold. The dream was always the same. It didn't vary. Lilly… Gone two years now except in my dreams.

The minutes passed and my breathing and heart beat decreased. I stared up into the semidarkness not wanting to close my eyes again. One eye closed and then slowly did the other did. Peace. No, there wasn't peace. Patsy Anderson was walking toward me. She lifted her hand to wave. Her smile lit up her oval face, so it was golden. "Hi, Doc, I just…" I walked toward her and lifted my right hand to wave. Patsy walked toward me with her head down. She stopped, looked up at me with a sad smile, and started to wave. "Hi Doc, I can't…" I lifted my right hand to wave. Patsy was hanging by the jump rope in the locker room. She opened her sad eyes, looked at me and started to wave. "Doc, it was…" I lifted my right hand to wave. Patsy.

Again I sat up in bed trying to catch my breath. My heart was pounding like a bass drum. It felt like a heart attack was coming. Beads of sweat were on my forehead, but I was so cold, ice cold, deathly cold.

It was still dark, but I moved my legs over the side of the bed and placed them on the floor. I laid my head in my hands. Sleep was over for this night.

CHAPTER FIVE

B leary-eyed, I stumbled down the stairs toward the smell of piñon coffee brewing in the kitchen. Dad was sitting at the table reading the *Denver Post*.

"Mornin'," said Dad. "Grab a mug of coffee. It's your piñon beans from New Mexico. Great stuff! I'm hooked now."

"Morning, Dad." I moved to the counter, took my mug off the hook where it hung under the counter, and filled it with brew. "What's your day like?"

"Same ole, same ole. Order of plumbing supplies coming in today. We're going to rearrange some of the household cleaning products and make room for some new household LED lighting. We started with a small display of those lights, and they practically ran off the shelves. Time for the big league." Dad still lit up like sunshine when he talked about his hardware store. He loved it.

"Sounds like a busy day for you. Grandpa helping you out?"

"Oh, yeah, Pa works every day. The customers love him. He entertains them with lies, half-truths, and more lies. He seems to have "knowledge" of everything. Where he gets it, I don't know. He doesn't seem to repeat himself with stories. Of course, he always has to throw in some scripture about products. How he makes those connections is beyond understanding. You know, like 'You are the light of Christ; use LED lights' and other strange blends of scripture and hardware."

"Well, it's good that he's still able to provide comic relief for you down there. He sure has more energy than I do." I sat, sipped my coffee and watched the birds devour the seeds in the feeder outside a front window. As the weather person said last night, it would be a Colorado blue sky day today. I finished my mug of coffee and stood. "I'm off for a ride before I have to head to school. It'll just be a short one today, since I need to be there early to see what has happened overnight."

I was already dressed for biking so I moved through the door from the kitchen leading into the garage and took my Cannondale Quick4 bike off the rack where it was hanging. I rolled my bike out the garage side door, put on my Gitmos Atom bike helmet, added my Oakley sunglasses, stuck my ear buds in my ears, plugged them into my iPhone, set it to Pandora radio and saddled up. I was ready for the one thing that brought me any sort of serenity; mountain biking.

My route this morning would be a ten-mile ride I had set up on my dad's land and the open space forest land my dad's thirty acres backed up to. A fall chill had wrapped its tendrils around everything and I plunged into its grip as if I alone could break its hold. I stood up on my pedals and pumped my legs hard moving up the incline behind the house. There was an old logging trail that began on dad's land, which moved through the ponderosa pines toward the remains of an old log cabin about six miles in. I had Pandora radio tuned to ZZ Top's hard-driving rock as I pounded my legs like pistons, up and down, up and down, moving up inclines and up the trail, weaving through the pines. Limbs fanned out over the trail, and I had to continually duck, so I didn't have my head taken off. I moved in and out of the sunlight coming in from the east. I probably didn't need to wear my Oakley's in the dark of the forest, but I figured if I was going to crash and burn I might as well look good doing it. I smiled to myself feeling the lactic acid burn build up in my body. What a rush. It hurt so good.

I reached the old cabin and stepped off my bike for a break. My legs were almost numb, rubbery. I snagged my water bottle and started chugging it, letting it dribble down my chin. My only thoughts were of standing in the middle of a forest, being alone, feeling pain and exultation while ZZ Top blasted out any memories of anything and everything. As my breathing calmed, I decided to shut down Pandora and remove my ear buds. I let the sounds of the forest come at me. They quietly whispered their musical stories in my ears. I closed my eyes and let them dress me in their serenity.

The ride back was longer as I added a couple of miles over the ridge before I came back to the old trail and then headed home.

After a quick shower and some toast and a banana I kneeled down and said good-bye to Sunny and Kong, hugging them around their necks. They looked at me with sad eyes and seemed to ask why they couldn't come also. "I wish I could just hang out with you both today but school calls. Stay here and relax." I stood and headed for my Toyota truck. Dad and Grandpa had already left for the store. They always started early and worked late. I was sure Grandpa was already entertaining customers. What a trip.

The drive to school took about fifteen minutes. Dad's home was south of Rua Springs about five miles. It was off the main highway about a mile to the east stuck back in the woods. You couldn't see it from the highway, since the house was up from it. There was a dirt road coming down that wound in and out of the trees so being careful was a must. Grandpa drove an old Jeep CJ-5 that he thought was a race car. There were several raw places on the body of the Jeep that had kissed trees and not in a loving way. I could see the tree scars on my way down.

It was an uneventful drive on a beautiful day. I wanted to just keep driving. The school would be in the "day after shock" mode which I was sure would be wearing off. I parked in the lot close to the high school, locked my truck and headed in. I knew I would have another full day at the high school and would probably not make my scheduled appointments at the other three schools. Hopefully, fingers crossed, there wouldn't be a crisis at the other schools today. Other faculty and students were making their way inside. Everyone seemed subdued. I said "hi" to several students and a couple of faculty. Some said hey or just nodded their heads. Other students looked at me like I had three heads, wondering who I was to talk to them and invade their space. Adults! Ugh...there "otta" be a law! Some of the guys were pulling up their jeans so they covered their boxers. The school didn't allow the "baggy pants, gangbanger, I'm sexy look" per the dress code. I have never figured out how they hold them up, let alone walk in them. It's a scientific miracle! One pull and oops! What have we here? Your boxers need washing, bud. Stains are in? Oh, I wasn't aware of that new hygiene rule. The girls like it? Why are they laughing right now?

After going on my brain rampage, I calmed it down and with a serious face entered the building. Kids were huddled outside of classrooms whispering to each other. Some were holding hands and had their arms around each other. Teachers with straight faces marched around the halls hoping to catch some guy trying to feel up his girlfriend or vice versa. The hormones raging in the high school and the middle school made it tough moving through the buildings. The scent and the hormone ooze just filled the air. It was like walking through a blizzard. I'm glad I was never a teenager!

"Jeffery, keep your hands to yourself. Remove them from Tara now!" Mrs. Levitz, the Home Ec teacher, was on the job. "I've warned you about this before. Don't test it."

Jeffery and Tara looked like they were ready to rip each other's clothes off. This was nothing but torture for them. The air was fogged up with their panting. Life wasn't fair. I had always enjoyed the hallway drama in schools. It was very entertaining. Every emotion possible was displayed in living color. In the midst of death there was still life to hang on to.

The students and teachers entered their classrooms, and I strolled into the office. Mrs. Neeley was busy as usual. The phone was ringing. She answered the phone and continued her keyboarding. Darnell Claussen came out of his office.

"Hi, Doc. Good to see you. I've set up an assembly for second period today in the gym. The school board president, superintendent, and I met last night and decided we needed to have a small remembrance time for Patsy today. It will allow some time to say a few words about her and let everyone know we are all together on this. Patsy's mom won't be here. She's having a really rough time of it. Marty Dawson, the school board president, Qui Trang, a friend of Patsy's, myself and Mickie Lucero, the school body president will say a few things."

My antennae went on high alert. Marty Dawson was the school board president, but he was also the pastor of the Community Bible Church and a rabid, outspoken evangelist. He made it no secret that he wanted the school to be a Christian community and follow those values. It made it pretty tough on those who were not Christian. We had Muslims, Buddhists, Jews, and those who believed nothing. I hoped he kept his mouth shut today, but I had my doubts.

"May I have your attention please," said Darnell into the microphone. "During second period this morning we will meet for an assembly in the auditorium to remember Patsy Anderson. Several people will say a few words about how they remember Patsy. Please move in a quiet and orderly fashion from here to the auditorium when the bell rings. Let's remember with pride who we are here at Rua Springs High School. That's all for now."

The first period dragged by for me. I sat in the nurse's office and worked on some WISC-V results I had recently completed with a student. The Wechsler Intellegence Scale for Children is the IQ assessment I use to assess academic levels for students. It is one of the determining factors for being qualified for special education services. I remembered that Patsy Anderson had taken the WISC-IV before I came and had qualified for services. It uses normative age comparison and ten subtests. Its results show a student's IQ anywhere from 40-160.

I had administered the WISC V to a seventeen year-old girl named Brenda for a three year reevaluation of her special education services. I was looking for a global estimate of her cognitive ability. It would generate a full scale IQ score which I derived from different sources.

Brenda is in a regular eleventh grade classroom and receives special education services. The results of the WISC-V for Brenda's cognitive abilities showed that she scored in the low-average and average range. With Brenda's full scale IQ of 89 compared to her academic achievement, Brenda didn't show a big difference between her ability and her achievement levels. In other words, I tortured Brenda with all this and found out she still needs special education help. I learned what I already knew. Brenda has difficulty with attention and focus and these cause her great difficulty in attending to her required tasks. So, she has trouble working independently. Many reminders to keep on task and focused are needed. The end result is that Brenda meets the criteria for an educational learning disability. I'll meet with Brenda's IEP team and to help finalize her plan.

Reading through all Brenda's results temporarily took my mind off Patsy Anderson. My eyes were glassy and I was bored silly. No love lost between me and testing. It is necessary but almost too cold and impersonal for me. It probably had to do with IQ tests I had taken growing up I was always just average. It was easy to fall into the "average" thinking about self and not feel smart enough at times. I shook my head back and forth to clear the cobwebs. Geez. I'm glad I don't have to do this stuff all day long.

At 8:45 a.m. I was saved by the bell signaling the end of first period. I locked up my laptop and papers in the nurse's office and moved out of the office toward the exit and on to the auditorium. It was a solemn experience.

Some kids around me were whispering to one another and mostly everyone was well-behaved. I could only imagine the thoughts going through everyone's minds right now. I knew some would be grieving silently. Some would be more confused than ever and even afraid. And, I knew some wouldn't care at all. If they didn't really know Patsy, and they were still planted in their shoes, moving, taking in oxygen, and letting out carbon dioxide, then why should it matter to them? It got them out of class for a period so that was cool. It wasn't that they were uncaring, they just had better things to keep their minds occupied. Maybe they were thinking of a recent movie or being with their girlfriend or boyfriend or maybe looking forward to that toke during lunch break.

After everyone filed into the auditorium and finished squiggling into their seats, Darnell stood up from his seat on the stage. There were several people on stage with him all sitting in chairs behind the podium. The superintendent was there as was Marty Dawson, the school board president; Mickie Lucero, the school body president; and Qui Trang, one of Patsy's friends from the gifted program. Darnell cleared his throat into the mike. The noises hadn't stopped completely so he cleared his pipes again.

"Ah umm, can everyone hear me?" He tapped the mike. *Boom, boom, boom!* "Okay, let's settle down everyone." The room quieted. Well, sort of.

"As we all know, we lost a special member of our family here at Rua Springs High School."

Darnell seemed to choke up from his words. My mind jumped to Patsy being lost and said to myself, *Well, if she is lost we should be able to find her.* I knew what he meant, but Patsy wasn't lost; she was dead. Okay, maybe I need to get off her being lost.

"Yesterday, Patsy Anderson, one of our eleventh graders, passed on."

Oh, oh, now Patsy has passed on. Yeah, I know it is what we say without using the "D" word. We have a hard time saying dying, death, and dead.

Darnell continued, "We all are in deep shock about this occurring."

No, I thought, *some are in deep shock and some are in shock, but for sure not everyone is in deep shock.* I know it is important to be inclusive, so I guess we are all in deep shock.

"Funeral arrangements have not been completed, so I can't give you those details yet. When I know them, I will pass them on. Let's all continue to remember Patsy's mother during these difficult days. We want to support her however we can."

I knew that very few would probably reach out to Vivian Anderson, during this time. Vivian was in my class when I was in school here. I didn't know her well, but we were friendly. My plan was to contact Vivian soon. It will be a very difficult conversation.

Most people don't know what to say to someone grieving. It is hard being silent, though, with someone who has had someone die. So, silence is filled with "mind-noise". We are really uncomfortable and almost afraid the death will rub off on us. Death in America is a billion-dollar-a-year business. The idea is to keep us removed from it as much as possible. We view a body that doesn't look anything like the person looked. They are embalmed and look plastic, all painted up, so how they really look won't offend our senses. That would be too raw and real for us. "She looks so nice, doesn't she?" people say. They comment on how peaceful the person looks, how great the person's hair is fixed, or on the lipstick color. Give me a break! She or he is dead. She isn't there. What we see isn't real. It's done so we aren't uncomfortable. We pay so we don't have to feel the primal, gut-level reality of it all. We're sophisticated twenty-first century humans not from the dark ages. Keep us away from pain, won't you? Just make sure we feel comfortable.

"At this time we will have some others say a few words about Patsy," Darnell's tone was appropriately funereal. He sat down and Mickie Lucero, the student body president, stood and walked to the podium. I had seen Mickie in the hallway, but had never spoken to her. She was average in most ways. She was of average size and looks. She was someone you would walk right past without noticing her. The thing that set Mickie apart was that she was a born politician, according to comments I had heard from other students. Her life was about campaigning for something in a leadership role. Always.

"Good morning, everyone. I am also very sad that we have lost Patsy."

Oops, Patsy is lost again. Okay, concentrate.

"I didn't know her well, but this is a horrible thing for all of us."

Hmmm...don't want to be uncomfortable here because it is a horrible inconvenience.

"I have always heard good things about Patsy, and, I know she will be missed. I want us all to remember her for the good person she was and be happy with those memories. Our student council will meet to decide how we can remember her in our school yearbook and other ways. Maybe we can all wear yellow ribbons for a day or two. Remember to tell any of us if you have ideas for a scrapbook, a bulletin board, or something like that. We are all here to serve you. Thank you for your time."

Was this a political speech from someone running for reelection? Interesting. I have to quit being so negative. She meant well, I think. Didn't she? Mickie stepped back from the podium, turned around, and went back to her seat. Darnell stood and moved to the mike again.

"Now, one of Patsy's friends from the gifted program, Qui Trang, will say a few words."

Qui stood and walked to the podium. She wasn't as tall as Darnell or Mickie so she had to move the mike down to use it.

"Hello, I am Qui Trang and I have known Patsy many years."

I knew Qui from the gifted program. She was a tiny Vietnamese girl who was quiet, reserved, and very intelligent.

"Patsy and I were friends here at school and also out of school, and she was one of the best friends I have ever known. She was quiet and very gentle. She never hurt or bothered anyone. I will miss her terribly.

"Patsy and I originally met, because we were placed in the gifted program together. It was wonderful to be together because we had lots in common. I live with my mother just as Patsy does. I mean did." Qui stepped back from the mike to gain control of herself. "Uh, well...Patsy was my sister. We weren't from the same parents, but we were still sisters. The gifted program was good for us for awhile, but Patsy began to have a difficult time recently. She didn't like being different. Patsy told me kids teased her about being in the gifted program. It hurt her. She didn't want the attention. None of us do. We just want to be normal. Remember, we have feelings, too.

"I want to play a song that Patsy listened to over and over. She said it helped her get back up when she felt so down. It's by Coldplay." Qui leaned down and turned on a boom box and let the music enfold our minds. It was a song entitled *Fix You* about trying to succeed and feeling like a failure, loving someone, and having that person try to help them succeed.

I looked around the auditorium. There were blank looks by many, but some were wiping away tears. The emotional level had cranked up several notches. The lump in my throat was large. I swallowed. The music played on.

"Patsy talked often about needing to be fixed. She said she was flawed and something was wrong with her." Qui hesitated and then quietly spoke. "I'm sorry I didn't know how much pain she was in. I thought I did, but I didn't, not really." Qui was crying now. "Tôi s nh b n, Patsy. (*I will miss you.*)"

I had tears in my eyes. I heard others sniffling around where I was sitting. Qui's words were from her heart. She exposed her spirit to the school.

Once again, I knew some of Patsy's stories but not enough. I felt my guilt constricting my chest. Why didn't I know? After a long silence that became uncomfortable for many, Qui turned around and walked back to her chair and sat. She folded her arms around her chest. Qui looked very small as if she had shrunk from what she was before. Nobody moved for an eternal amount of time. Then, Marty Dawson rose from his chair before Darnell could get up and introduce him. Marty was about five foot six. I knew he wore raised heels to make him appear taller. He always wore a shiny, dark blue three-piece suit with a white shirt and narrow black tie. Marty looked like a pimp wanna-be. His hair was a light brown color all slicked back with grease. He had lots of hair so it stuck out on the sides. The light reflected on it just like his zoot suit. Marty had a high sloping forehead. His eyes were brown and bulged like a bug. His skin was very pale, like an albino. I'm sure he was well-liked as a kid, very popular. Well...maybe not.

After reaching the podium, Dawson stammered in the mike. "Good morning everyone. I know you all know who I am so I won't take time with that. One of God's children has gone on to greener pastures and we mourn her."

I already knew that he would be giving a sermon. He would have a come-to-Jesus meeting. It was a great place to proselytize, and he wasn't going to miss this chance even if the school was a secular place and off limits. He didn't care and tried to get away with it.

"And I saw and behold, a pale horse, and its rider' name was Death, and Hades followed him. Revelation 6:8."

Hmmmm...not a bad start for old Marty. I think he was quoting from the King James Bible. And I didn't think he was talking about Clint Eastwood in Pale Rider, *though.*

"And I heard a voice from heaven saying, 'Write this: Blessed are the dead who die in the Lord henceforth.' Revelation 14:13." Marty stepped back and raised his arms and in a booming voice exclaimed, "Blessed are those who wash their robes, that they may have the right to the tree of life and that they may enter the city by the gates. Outside are the dogs and sorcerers and fornicators and murderers and idolaters, and everyone who loves and practices falsehood. Revelation 22:14."

There was a collective gasp from the auditorium, but before any of us could take a breath, Marty charged ahead and was back at the podium pounding his right fist on the top.

"Patsy Anderson!" Marty vehemently called out as if he was trying to get her attention. "Don't you know that your body was God's temple and that God's Spirit lived in you? If anyone destroys God's temple, God will destroy him; for God's temple is sacred, and you are the temple. 1 Corinthians 3:16-17." He paused for effect and in a calm voice said, "I can't say I knew her, but suicide is a sin and can't be undone. She has sinned!"

The auditorium erupted with several cries of "What?" and "No way!"

"It was an accident!" Superintendent Espiñosa and Darnell both jumped up at the same time and moved toward Marty. They were speaking to him in what looked like heated voices. Marty stood there with the look of an angel and smiled radiantly. He had completed his task of spreading the word of God.

I was sick to my stomach. Even though I expected Marty to do something, I would never have considered anything this extreme. It was possible that Patsy killed herself, but that wasn't determined yet. Now, Marty had started a raging firestorm. Students and teachers were out of their seats. Darnell was at the mike telling everyone to quiet down. No one was listening.

I was thinking this might become a rave, and I would soon see bodies being passed around above the crowd. Teachers were trying to calm their classes and get them moving out of the auditorium in an orderly way. It wasn't working. People were moving every direction walking over others and trying to get out of their row of seats. I heard kids cursing at other kids.

"You prick, get off my feet!"

"What the hell are you doing, you dog shit?"

"Quit grabbing my breast, you pervert!"

"Hey, you jerk off, quit pushing me!"

And on it went. I had an aisle seat so I was up quickly and standing in the aisle trying not to get stomped on. Pandemonium! And then…the auditorium was empty except for some who had remained seated staring off into space as if the world had ceased to exist.

CHAPTER SIX

The third period was soon to begin when I returned to the office. Students were still in the hallway speaking to each other in hushed tones. What they were thinking now I could only imagine. Marty Dawson had done his job and stirred up a hornet's nest. I'm pretty sure that was one of his goals, besides getting converts. Some of these students probably went to his church so were used to his rants and were probably scared to death of going to hell because of wrong behavior. And, they may even be pretty good at quoting scripture, but may not have studied the bible enough to know that it does not ever call suicide a sin. That part was made up somewhere in church history to terrify people. Nothing new there. The church was good at terrifying people. After Lilly died, I continuously read the bible, as well as a slew of other sources, to try to find answers. I knew the bible pretty well even though it didn't give me any answers. At least, not the ones I wanted. So, I knew Marty was full of it, but the damage was done.

The office was crowded. Several kids wanted to see the school nurse. She was coming over from the middle school. Other kids wanted to call home because all of a sudden they forgot something and wanted to talk with their parents. Mrs. Neeley was holding down the fort in her usual grandmother-ly way. She would speak to them calmly and gently and help them reach some sort of equilibrium so they could go back to class. She did more counseling than I or anyone else ever did at school. School office managers were often like that. They, and the custodial staff, held everything together.

The principal wasn't anywhere around so I went into the nurse's office to catch my breath. I hadn't seen the high school counselor, Brighton, since yesterday. He had probably gone home sick already. Crisis? What crisis? Oh well, he didn't do anything when he was here anyway so it was good to keep him away from students as much as possible. Mrs. Neeley called out to me as I was moving toward the office door.

"Doctor Thomas?"

I whirled around in time to see Mrs. Neeley coming out from behind the counter toward me. "Hello, how are you doing?" I asked her.

"Well, considering what happened with Mr. Dawson's bombshell, I guess I'm holding up okay." She looked around and quietly asked me, "Did Patsy really commit suicide? I just can't believe she would do that. It is all so very sad. I feel like I have lost a family member."

"We don't really know what happened yet, Mrs. Neeley. Sheriff Montes and the coroner are still working on it, I imagine."

"It is just impossible to believe. We haven't had a suicide here for many years. Most everyone has already forgotten that one. A young boy killed himself with an overdose of his parent's pills because his girlfriend broke up with him."

"Yeah, I remember my dad telling me something about that." We both looked off into the past for a moment hoping to see something that would help comfort us now.

Mrs. Neeley turned around and told some students she would be with them shortly and to be patient. "Sorry, Dr. Thomas, most of the time I feel like a carnival juggler and balls are dropping all around me."

"You're great, Mrs. Neeley. You have the hardest job in the whole school. No need to apologize. I couldn't do half what you do. I would be jello for sure."

Mrs. Neeley looked down at her hands, squeezed them together, drew them apart, and then began to knead her dress with her right hand. "Well...thank you. You're very kind. I needed to tell you that Mr. Claussen wanted you to go around to the classrooms and just see how everyone is doing. He is meeting with the superintendent right now. That Marty Dawson does more damage in his school board president position than I would have ever imagined. I still can't believe he ever got that position. It is just criminal is what it is. Oh...sorry to complain. Anyway, if you would be present in the classrooms, he would appreciate it."

"No problem. It was my plan, too."

"Okay, I better get back to these students." With that Mrs. Neeley went back behind the counter and started listening to the students complain about headaches, stomachaches, and heartaches. She kindly gave her full attention to each one of them. I smiled inwardly and moved out into the hallway.

I stood at the door of the junior English class that Patsy had been attending. Miss Falhaber saw me and came over to the door. She was an unfortunate looking woman. She was stooped over giving her the appearance of a hump. She wore a light blue sack dress with black lace-up shoes. Her face was wrinkled and narrow like an axe head. Gray hair was pulled tightly back in a bun at the back of her head. It looked like she was trying to stretch the wrinkles out by pulling her hair. I wondered if it was hard to speak being so pinched. On her long, hooked nose she had perched a pair of large brown plastic reading glasses. Miss Falhaber looked over the top of her glasses at me with her dark brown eyes.

"Marc Thomas," she said in her strong deep voice. It was anything but feminine. Not a bass but close.

"Miss Falhaber," I responded and swallowed. She had been my English teacher here long ago. She had been here as long as anyone can remember. This was her marriage and her family. No one really knew her history, but kids cruelly made up all sorts of stories. I had, too. She was too ugly to have a husband. She was gay. She was a nun who ran away. Her parents abandoned her in a snow drift, so she was an orphan. She didn't really have parents, after all who could have birthed her?

Her hair was a little grayer and her stoop was more pronounced, but her eyes still shone with intensity. I had a love-hate relationship with her when she taught me English. She was a no nonsense taskmaster. Her thesis was that without knowing proper English for speaking and writing, the world was lost. Language was life-giving. If you couldn't speak or write properly, you would be handicapped. I really tried while in class with her, but drifted off in adolescent brain dysfunction always hoping to be transported to another reality. I never was, and she always caught me.

"Mr. Thomas," she would say loudly to the entire class, "I'm wondering if you would get back in the seat you are hovering above and give us the answer to the question I just asked." I didn't even know what the question was. I had transported myself elsewhere and missed the question.

"Uh, I'm, uh, I don't think I can answer the question, Miss Falhaber."

"And why is that?" she would say. Before I could respond, she would charge on.

"Mr. Thomas doesn't seem to take English seriously, class. He must think we are all here to dream dreams about his parents always taking care of him and just being Peter Pan all his life."

I would stare down at the scratched top of my desk and hope that it would come alive and fly me away. Others would shift around in their chairs with a sigh of relief that she hadn't caught them dreaming. She did believe in "equal opportunity" for all so no one was immune. I am sure, though, my humiliation seeped out of my pores and provided a huge stink to everyone around me. However, she was the best English teacher I ever had. Love-hate was our relationship.

"I'm sorry to interrupt your class, Miss Falhaber, but I'm checking in on classes today to see how everyone is doing. This morning has been pretty tough."

"Mr. Thomas, I mean Doctor Thomas," she smiled one of her rare toothy smiles at me, "I would be honored to have you come into my class and see how they are doing."

"Miss Falhaber, you are one of a kind, and I'm glad to know you." We both smiled knowing that our respect for each other was sacred. I stepped into her classroom for the first time in a long, long time. For a moment I flashbacked to many years ago when I sat where these students now sat. Their faces were replaced with the faces of my own high school classmates. Life was simpler then, it seemed. What would I have done if I knew what was coming? There were so many changes for me and my classmates. College, marriage, kids, divorce, jobs gained, jobs lost, new homes, death, wars, disease... I was invincible then, just like these students sitting in front of me. The world out there is exciting, wonderful, ready to be taken, experienced, owned. Patsy's death is only a bump in the road, there to be overcome and conquered. Death won't win. It can't. Can it?

"Hello. My name is Doctor Thomas, and I'm the school psychologist." I knew many of them knew me or at least of me. Word spreads quickly about the resident "shrink". There are always jokes about being analyzed while lying on a couch. They looked at me vacantly. "I'm checking in with classes to see how everybody is doing with Patsy's death. I know Patsy was in class with you. This can be a hard time. I'm here to listen now or we can get together another time. I'll listen and you can talk, or we can just sit together."

A hand went up at the back of the room. A young girl I didn't recognize. "Did she really kill herself?"

"Becca!" hissed the girl on her right.

"Well, that's what was said today. Did she?"

I hesitated and waited for the room to quiet. "We really don't know what happened to her yet. Everything has to be carefully evaluated."

"You mean like CSI?" said the same girl in the back of the room.

"Yes, like CSI."

"Then why did Pastor Dawson say that about Patsy?" asked a boy off to the right on the front row.

"I don't know and can't speak for him," I said. The room was quiet for awhile. Then a girl about half-way back asked, "How is Patsy's mother doing?"

"I'm sorry, but I don't really know. I will see her soon, I hope." After answering the question I realized I didn't know when I would see her. I wasn't even sure she was here. Maybe she left town to get away from the media attack that was surely on her doorstep by now.

"Do you know when her funeral will be?" asked a boy from the back.

"No, I don't believe it has been arranged yet. It will probably be at St. Mary's Episcopal Church. I was told she attended there."

The room was quiet. I let the silence roam, take us where it wanted. The students nervously moved in their chairs, looked at each other, and then around the room. The silence hovered. I knew it was probably oppressive for everyone, but I let it season. Finally, I broke the spell.

"There will be lots of rumors going around, both good and bad. I want to encourage everyone not to get into those conversations. They are not helpful. I'm sure you all have memories of Patsy. I hope you will share those with one another. I would like to hear them, also, if you want to tell me sometime. I'm here to help, so if you or someone you know needs to talk just spread the word. Miss Falhaber will take care of you. She did me when I sat where you sit a long time ago and had some hard times." I stopped and looked around the room. "Thanks for your time, and thank you, Miss Falhaber, for letting me visit."

"You are welcome, Doctor Thomas," Miss Falhaber said with that tiny smile of hers. I nodded my head at her and left her room.

The day progressed for me with my time in other class-rooms, specifically the classes that Patsy had been in this fall semester. The questions were about the same in all classes except for one boy who asked if I thought Patsy was going to hell now. I told him that I really couldn't answer that question. Politically, I couldn't get into that kind of ques-tion at school. But, personally I wanted to yell out that Patsy certainly wasn't going to any hell that I knew of, because it was lived here on earth so she was already beyond that. I couldn't open that door, or I would have a horde of angry parents on my doorstep.

The thing is, school psychologists, just like other pro-fessionals, can't share their own religious beliefs at school. Remaining neutral is often a brutal undertaking because of the extreme religious views that are often spoken by stu-dents and parents, and even some teachers. The desire to pick up and shake some people takes lots of will power to overcome. Stress, anger and anxiety for school psycholo-gists? Never! Remember the Barney song? *I love you, you love me, we're as happy as we can be.* Yep, that's us, always smiling and happy at school. There is another Barney song version where Barney is singing, *I love you, you love me, we're as...*

He is cutoff by a shotgun blast. *Shut the hell up, Barney!* See, that's what we would really like to have happen at school sometimes because of some of the imbecilic statements that are made.

During the afternoon three male students came to see me in the office. I didn't really know any of them as I hadn't seen them as special needs students so had no previous contact.

"Doctor Thomas, can we come in and talk with you?" asked the first young man.

"Certainly, come in. Have a seat." Like the two female students I had seen yesterday, these three sat together on the exam table. As soon as they were settled in and I had shut the door and sat on the chair facing them, I asked, "What can I do to help?"

They looked at each other and then around the room. I knew it took a lot of guts to come see me. Finally, the lead young man started off, "Well, we're all just...well, we sort of knew Patsy. Not well, but, you know, we were in class with her so..." His words trailed off.

I waited until I was sure that he was finished then said, "Yes, I know this is really difficult. Maybe we should start with names since I haven't met you yet."

"Er... I'm Spencer Vaughn," answered the lead young man.

"Hi, I'm Anthony Yankowski."

"I'm Jimmy Tuttle."

"Thanks, it is nice to meet each of you." I said. I hesitated, then spoke, "This is tough for me, too, since I knew Patsy, not as a classmate like you, but it still hurts." The room was quiet except for the outside noises from a living school in progress.

"Yeah, Doc, it does hurt," said Spencer Vaughn quietly.

"Yeah," said Jimmy Tuttle.

"Whatever we talk about in here is private, confidential, just amongst us. Sound okay?" I sat back and waited. The room was heating up with so many bodies in a small space. The young men all had red eyes, as if they had been crying. Spencer's eyes were the most red. He was the first to speak.

"We've all been in school with Patsy our whole lives. This is pretty unbelievable." Spencer stopped, took a deep breath, and moved on. "Do you think she really did this to herself? I just can't believe she would do this." He really didn't want an answer to his question so I didn't interrupt. "She has been pretty down lately, catching a lot of crap from some of the school bullies about being in special ed, mainly the gifted program." Spencer hesitated, took a couple of deep breaths again and sat back against the wall.

Anthony picked up where Spencer left off. "Those guys and some girls really make fun of the gifted kids. I know they are just jealous, but it must hurt those guys. We've jumped in a few times and told 'em to back off. They just laugh and walk off."

"Those cretins don't even have a brain to start with!" said Jimmy, with some venom. "Patsy hadn't been talking much with anybody. I've always got on good with her, but she just sort of disappeared." Jimmy looked out the window and stared off into eternity.

"I can't believe she is gone. It's just not right. Not right at all." Spencer spoke with tears in the corner of his eyes. "How can we go on without her? I just don't know." Silence surrounded us again. I let it hover, settle, take us.

I had some thoughts rumbling around. "Patsy must have been hurting a great deal lately from what you've said." I didn't expect them to respond. "Do you suppose there was something more bothering her?" They just shrugged their shoulders. I waited a moment and then said, "Being in the gifted program is really hard for those students sometimes. It's not easy being set apart from others like that. They just want to be normal." I realized I was probably saying more than these guys wanted to hear. "You're welcome to come and talk anytime you need to."

"Thanks," said Spencer. "I guess we better go back to class. Mr. Keiffer will expect us." The three young men pushed themselves off the table, stood and started for the door. I stood as well and shook hands with each of them as they departed. At least they didn't try to be all macho about Patsy and keep it inside. It was a start.

The final bell rang and the school day ended. I said good-bye to Mrs. Neeley, picked up my tote bag, and headed out of the building toward my truck. A few teachers and students said variations of "have a good night" as I passed them. I said variations of "see you later" to them.

Not wanting to head out to Dad's place just yet where the silence would be pretty lonely, I decided to go by the hardware store and see if Dad and Grandpa wanted to go out for some dinner later. I needed some rays of sunshine and pick-me-ups. I could always count on them to help.

The fall sun was still high in the sky and the day was still warm at about seventy degrees. It was a beautiful Colorado blue sky day in the foothills. I drove with my windows down letting the warm breeze run its gentle fingers across my face. It was a serene, tranquil feeling. I mirrored back the day as I headed down the hill toward town.

Marty Dawson had certainly provoked controversy at the assembly this morning. If it was his goal, he succeeded. A barrage of comments, questions, and rumors would be flying high around town now. Some would be in hushed words and some would be street corner evangelism. It couldn't be stopped. I figured I would catch up with Sheriff Montes soon to see what was up. It certainly looked like a suicide when I saw Patsy hanging from that pipe yesterday morning. Was it only yesterday? The world had stopped and started several times since then.

I reflected on my earlier conversations with Darnell about teaching the students about suicide. It would be preventative and necessary. The young people needed to understand it just like they are taught about drugs and sex. Unfortunately, Darnell nixed that preventative training. Now the lack of information would come back to bite us on the butt from students, teachers, parents, etc. Schools are torn apart by people like Darnell and Marty Dawson by inaction or insane words. That's life in a school. It is a mini community within a larger community. The school is part of the hive. The hive lives and breathes because of all parts of the hive. Schools contribute their energy as a tendril to every other tendril.

The student questions today were not unexpected. They were normal for a crisis like this. The three young guys who came in to talk this afternoon provided me with further insight into Patsy's life. Beneath the surface there were pods of students who naturally came together. Each pod had a specific task. Some were for the good and some were not. It was not unusual to hear about the bullies taking out their own lack of abilities on the gifted and other special needs students. They temporarily made themselves feel bigger and smarter by putting down anyone who was different. The tension was always there among factions just waiting for the right spark to set something off. It took a lot of maturity and compassion to cherish differences rather than be afraid of them. Those three guys were on the good side. I hoped they could hang on. But, I wasn't exactly sure what to make of them. It made me curious to know what their relationship with Patsy actually was; maybe just lifelong friends. I was glad Patsy had friends who cared.

As I reached the bottom of the hill I turned left on Hettie Road, which was the main street of Rua Springs. It was the first street named in Rua Springs by William Houghton, the founder. Hettie (Henrietta) was the oldest daughter of William and Rua Houghton. The town was laid out like any old mining town. Structures were built down a main area and then moved out from there in a way that fit the geographic terrain of the area. Buildings on Hettie Road kept the look of its history with a Victorian and old mountain town feel. As the town grew, buildings were built behind other buildings with a road in between. The streets were put in haphazardly since, originally, there wasn't a plan.

My dad's hardware store was a block down on the right. As building ebbed and flowed in town history, the hardware store location was where it had begun in the late 1800s. Land around the store was purchased and developed so there was space for parking, lumber, and different types of building materials housed under various roofs. The store itself was a large three story structure with a rustic mountain look. Behind the main building was the house I grew up in that Dad added to the business. I was able to park on the street in front of the store. I pulled in, rolled to a stop, shut off the engine, put up the windows, and stepped out of the truck. I debated locking it up, but figured since I had my school backpack inside I needed it to be safe. I clicked the button on my keychain and the doors locked. There were lots of vehicles on the street and in the parking lot, so I figured the store was busy.

Upon entering the store I heard clapping off to the right in one of the aisles containing paint. As I reached the aisle I looked around the corner. Grandpa was doing the moon walk back and forth in the aisle singing M.C. Hammer's song *U Can't Touch This*. He was a wild sight to behold blending Michael Jackson and M.C. Hammer, the rapper. Have you ever seen a gnome in a gray fedora do the moon walk and rap at the same time? Clapping and cheering continued to erupt from customers. He continued to moon walk as he sang. I saw Dad at the other end of the aisle with a huge grin on his face bobbing his head up and down. I guess we had two choices: Be totally embarrassed by Grandpa's behavior or else enjoy him and join the fun. We enjoyed him. After all, neither one us could moon walk and rap at the same time. No one can touch Grandpa's act.

Oh yeah, the town knew Herman. Come to the Rua Springs Hardware store and listen to Hammer and buy one, too.

Moving out and around to the next aisle I walked to where Dad was standing on the other end of the moon walk aisle. "Getting any paint sold today, Dad?"

"Yep, lots of sales today even with the entertainment blocking the aisle." Dad laughed in his big way as he watched Grandpa. "I don't know this for sure, but since he retired and started helping here at the store, I think business has increased. He does bring people in even if they don't buy."

I couldn't help but wonder what it was like to have a dad like his while he was growing up. My dad wasn't anything like his dad. Physically Dad was totally different looking, like his mother rather than his dad. Dad's sense of humor was dry but really awesome. Dad was quiet like his mother, probably because with Grandpa around no one could keep up with Grandpa's energy. Even with his small stature he took over a room. You can't touch this is right!

"Dad, I figured I could hang out and help you here until closing and then maybe we can go out to dinner. What do you think?"

"Excellent idea, Marc! How about Mabel's down the street?"

Mabel's was an old style country café, which had been around forever. It had gone by different names throughout the years, but Mabel Ledbetter had been the owner since before I was born. The food was about the best in town, so I was already salivating.

"Sure, I can always go for Mabel's cooking. Grandpa loves all the young waitresses so I'm sure he will approve." I stood by my dad listening to the sounds of the old store. The scraping of leather soles on the pine floors engaged my hearing. Murmuring of voices throughout the store sounded like a low hum penetrating and strumming on my eardrums. The sounds ebbed and flowed in a twilight dimension. Comfort…the hardware store sounds had always been that; a place of safety and comfort.

By six o'clock Dad had closed down the store. The employees had gone home or wherever they went after a day of work. Some of them had been with Dad for many years so I knew them pretty well. Good-byes were said and just Dad, Grandpa, and I remained. After Dad locked the front entry door he led us to the backdoor, set the security alarm, closed and locked the door, and we headed toward Mabel's.

Like many of the buildings on Hettie Road, Mabel's had a rustic mountain look. The front façade was made of wood and painted in bright colors. It had two floors. The first floor had square, rectangular, and round tables of various sizes spread throughout. The floor was wood plank. The ceiling had wood beams over which wood slats were laid. There was a large stone fireplace in the center of the room. Chandeliers hung from the ceiling. The walls were pine tongue and groove. The second floor was similar to the first floor except it held a bar at one end and tables for large gatherings at the other. It also had a stone fireplace in the center.

As we entered Mabel's the drone of voices surrounded us. It was busy tonight. A high school girl I recognized from one of the classes I had spoken with today greeted us. Mabel used high school students for much of her help. She offered them a good wage and all the love she could share with them. Dozens and dozens of young people had been blessed by Mabel's mentoring. She could be credited with turning around the lives of many who might have lost their way because of parental divorce, violence at home, drugs, or gangs. Mabel always had a waiting list to come work for her.

"Good evening and welcome to Mabel's," the girl said cheerfully. "How many in your party?"

"There are three of us," spoke my dad.

"Very good," she said, smiling big at us. "Hi, Doctor Thomas. Thank you for coming to our class today. It is a very sad time for many of us." I could see why Mabel had this young woman at the front greeting people. She was a star.

"I'm glad I could be helpful," I responded to her. "Tell me your name again."

She pointed to her name badge, "Charity. I'm Charity Bumgardner."

"Yes, hi, Charity."

Grandpa weaseled his way between Dad and me. "I'm Herman, Charity." Out of the corner of my eye I could see him winking at her.

Charity blushed and said, "Yes, Mr. Thomas, it's good to see you again. Well...let me show you to your table."

"Don't pay any attention to him," my dad whispered to Charity. "He likes to think he is a lady's man, but he's harmless."

Charity smiled back at my dad and said, "Yes, I know he is. He is cute, though," she giggled.

We had reached our table. Charity placed three menus on the table and said a waitperson would be with us shortly. We all thanked her and watched her walk away.

Grandpa was mumbling as he watched Charity. "If I was only ten years younger."

"Pa, if you were ten years younger you would still be seventy-three and that young lady would still be about sixteen. You would still be an over-the-hill old fart." We all laughed.

Quietly, we each studied the menu salivating at all the incredible choices.

"Well, would you lookee here. The Thomas men have graced us with their presence."

Our three heads popped up, and we were thrilled to see Mabel herself. As usual, she was a presence. Who knew how old she was, but she was still beautiful. At about five foot eleven, she was tall and slim. She had long gray hair tied in back with one of her many Native American clasps. Her face was only slightly wrinkled with large, I've-got-a secret brown eyes staring out of her round, metal rimmed glasses. She had high cheekbones, a narrow nose, and full smiling lips. Mabel. She always wore Levi jeans with a lady's western shirt. Around her neck she had her trademark purple bandanna with her squash blossom necklace hanging between her ample breasts. Her waist held a silver concho belt. Highly shined black western boots finished off her outfit. Mabel's employees wore similar outfits that she purchased for them. But, she was the only one to wear the purple bandanna. Everyone else wore red, black, yellow, or blue bandannas. Purple was her color. No one copied that.

Grandpa was out of his chair in a flash wrapping his arms around Mabel. Since he was short and she was tall, his head fit perfectly between her bosom. He was nosing around in there as Mabel patted his head.

"Hello to you, Herman," swooned Mabel. "It is always a pleasure."

She jiggled her shoulders. I didn't imagine Grandpa could survive in there for very long without coming up for air. Suffocation couldn't be far off. I could see the headlines now, "Man suffocates between breasts! Homicide or Suicide?"

Slowly, Grandpa removed his head from Mabel's chest. Above his white beard, his cheeks, nose, and forehead were bright red. His eyes were glassy and his breathing abnormal. But, what an angelic look he had on his face. He had died and gone to heaven. Or was that to Mabel?

"I'll be your server tonight, gentlemen," Mabel was saying. "Only the best for you handsome males! So, what can I get you?"

"I think Pa has already had his dessert, so he'll probably eat lightly," Dad joked.

"Ha, ha, my son, the comedian."

We studied our menus seriously as if we were getting ready for a final exam. I ordered first. "I would like the fried chicken, Yukon mashed potatoes, the carrot and broccoli casserole, fluffy biscuits, and I'll finish it off with your famous chocolate pie."

"I'll have the same except make mine the prime rib instead of the chicken," said Dad.

"How about you, Herman? We have a new supply of prune juice that is slightly cooled. That should do ya." Mabel was grinning from ear to ear.

"You know, Mabel, my pipes are running just…"

"Enough, Pa. We don't need that information right now."

Grandpa was laughing his wheezy laugh. We all joined in.

"You got me, Herman! No prune juice for you, old boy."

Still laughing, he finally ordered. "I want a bowl of your famous chili with some fried okra on the side. I'll end with your lemon meringue pie."

"Strange order, Herman, but you got it. See you boys in a bit." Mabel headed toward the kitchen with our orders.

We settled into the atmosphere of the place. I hoped Grandpa would control himself and not make a scene. He had a habit of doing that. Funny though he is at times, I usually want to crawl under the table when he takes off. I'm sure Dad often feels the same way, but he'll never say it. Growing up in this town my grandpa was discussed frequently because of his exploits. It was certainly more embarrassing then than now but still difficult. Where does he get all that energy and wit? I'm worn out every day, and I'm the grandson! Go figure.

After a time the hum of the voices around us took on individual spaces. Most men, women, and children were talking about the same thing: Patsy Anderson. My separation of the voices took on a sense of voyeurism. They spoke. I peeked. Most of the voices were either excited or depressed. I felt my emotions rising and falling as I rode their voices. Up and down I went as I focused in on one voice and then another.

"Isn't it incredible what she did," said an excited male voice. It was almost as if he was thrilled and awed that this had happened in town. He gathered energy for his life from it.

"This is the saddest thing ever," said a sorrowful female voice. "I have just cried and cried since I heard," she continued.

My rising and falling emotions continued. Dang, I can't keep this up. I began to feel choked and claustrophobic Time to jump off.

"Hey, Dad, tell me how your day went. It looked busy this afternoon."

"I think we had a good store day, Son. Lots of customers who actually bought something even in the bad economic times. We're hanging in. It's picking up each day so that's positive. Folks are getting into more of the remodeling kind of projects, so some bigger ticket items are selling. Recently, it has been appliances and bathroom fixtures. Lumber, too." Dad stopped and looked around Mabel's café. "Seems like more people are coming out to eat, too."

A dark shadow came across Dad's face. I knew that look; barely controlled anger. He had served two tours in Vietnam in the Special Forces. He came back with a rage toward national leadership for their lies and deceptions that simmered under the surface. It never came out on anyone else, but the immorality of our government ate at him all the time.

"The crooks in government get rich and the rest of us just try to survive. These are just good hardworking American people around us here, Marc. They don't deserve the pain they are in because of those thieves." He shook his head back and forth as if he could dislodge the anger and hurt.

"Gentlemen!" cried Mabel as she came to our table. "What are these long faces for? Wipe them off and get ready for your feast!"

All three of us brightened. No matter what, Mabel could always cheer us up. One of her teenager waitpersons carried our plates on a large tray behind Mabel. He sat it on a webbed top surface that opened to hold the tray. Mabel sat our food in front of each of us and stood back with a huge smile on her face.

"What are you waiting for? Dig in!"

We were practically drooling over our food as we began. No one spoke. It was time for simple pleasure now. No interruptions from suicides, crooked politicians, or anything else. Time to become pleasantly miserable.

After savoring every bite and loving our dessert we paid, hugged Mabel, and headed out. We walked back toward our trucks. Nighttime had joined us. The first stars were coming out, and a soft breeze tickled our faces.

"I think I will join BBA," muttered Grandpa into the welcoming darkness.

"What?" Dad and I said simultaneously.

"You know, one of those 12-step groups."

"BBA?" I said to Grandpa.

"Yeah, you know, Bloated Belly Anonymous."

"I think you mean Overeaters Anonymous," Dad said.

"Nah, I mean Bloated Belly, because that's what I have. I don't overeat."

"Huh...okay." I knew it wouldn't do any good to debate this.

I reached my truck and told Dad and Grandpa I would see them shortly. They walked around to the back where Dad always parked. After unlocking the cab, I scooted in, cranked it up, turned on the headlights, backed out, put it in drive, and began the ride home.

CHAPTER SEVEN

After a rough night's sleep having a variation of the same dreams I always have, I awoke at 5:30 a.m. with the alarm. I was groggy and didn't feel any more rested than when I went to bed. After suiting up for my morning ride, I headed toward the kitchen where I heard the rustling of paper. Dad was at the table drinking his java and reading the *Post*.

"Anything good in the news?" I asked.

"Nope, unless you want to read about murders, rapes, bankruptcies, and foreclosures."

"Why do you read it every morning if that's all there is?" I wondered aloud.

"Oh, you know, it's just a ritual. Drink a cup of strong, black coffee, have some fruit and toast and read the paper. It just starts a day."

Dad had the same ritual for as long as I could remember. I wasn't going to challenge it.

"I'm off to put some miles on my bike so see you later today."

Dad just grunted, and I walked toward the garage door. I figured today I would take a trail that wound up around the mountain behind Dad's house. It was about a fifteen mile trip up and back. After leaving Dad's land, it entered the open space park, opened up, and was pure wilderness. It would be easy to get lost in there if I didn't know the way. No music today. The sounds of the forest were what I wanted. I put on my helmet and gloves, hopped aboard my Cannondale and began. Soft, early morning light led the way.

Parking in the lot I always used, I locked up my truck and walked toward the high school. I figured I better check in here before anything else. My regular schedule was greatly backed up. It was feeling more and more burdensome. I had been in the middle school, where my main office was, only briefly over the past few days and needed to reschedule some assessments and meetings. It was hard enough to keep up and, really, I never did. Being a school psychologist was almost an impossible job. There were too many kids and too many problems.

As I entered the high school and the main hallway, I could see groups of students leaning against lockers waiting for the first period bell to ring. I was about to enter the main office when I heard what sounded like a stack of books dropping. They slapped the floor with a loud *smack!* Everyone turned to look toward the other end of the hall.

A beat of silence and then, "You fucker!" a high voice screamed. Several voices could be heard laughing and jeering. "I'll get you, fuck head!" yelled the voice again.

Teachers were coming out of their rooms now as I quickly walked toward the commotion. Adults were converging on the scene.

"What's this about?" I heard Miss Falhaber say above the din. "That's quite enough, boys!" she said sternly.

A young boy I knew from the special ed program was leaning over picking up his books. Two older boys were in Miss Falhaber's headlights and she was ready to make mincemeat out of them.

"You boys better talk fast or you will be out on your tails before you can say boo!" The other teachers and I stood back to watch this play out.

The taller of the two boys started to speak while trying to wipe a smirk off his face. "It wasn't us," he whined. "He musta walked into an open locker or something. We didn't do nothin'." His smug face said it all. He and his buddy were innocent and nobody would say differently. If someone did, someone would pay.

"What about you, Mr. Owens? What do you have to say?" questioned Miss Falhaber.

"Nothing happened, Miss Falhaber. I just dropped my books." He had filled up his book bag and was rising from the floor.

She looked each of the boys in the eyes. They wouldn't look at her. With hands in their pockets they shuffled their feet around as if they could get a better grip on the floor before it fell out from under them.

"Get to class then. You're already late." Miss Falhaber turned around, saw me standing nearby, gave me a small nod, and was gone.

The students and teachers vanished as if nothing had happened. The only sounds were the scraping of chairs and papers in classrooms. It never changed. The bullies denied everything and got away with abuse much of the time. Usually, bullies at school were bullied at home by a parent, sibling, or relative. They did to others what they were "trained" to do. I shook my head to clear the scene and walked back to the office.

"Call for you from the elementary school, Doctor Thomas," stated Mrs. Neeley, holding out the phone to me. "Something going on there."

I retrieved the phone from her as I came around the counter. "Hello, this is Doctor Thomas."

"Doctor Thomas, this is Lisa Guerrero, the office manager here at the elementary school."

I had met Lisa when I first arrived at my new position here. She was also new, so we discussed our new jobs together back in August. Lisa was young, probably in her twenties, but seemed very efficient.

"Hi, Lisa, how you doing over there?" I already knew that was a dumb question. She didn't seek me out like this unless there was a crisis.

"I'm fine, but Mrs. Purlee, one of the kindergarten teachers, is asking for you. A student is telling her he is going to kill himself."

"I'm on my way. Let her know I'll be there in a few minutes." A kindergarten kid saying he was going to kill himself?

Oh, boy. These kids today hear too much. He didn't think this up by himself.

It was only a short walk across Roark Park, the common area to all four schools. The day was now overcast and cold. It was spitting corn snow as I marched toward the elementary school. I didn't bring a jacket today; dumb move. This was Colorado, and I should know better. Anything was possible. We were socked in by low hanging clouds. Just a short distance down in Rua Springs it could be sunny.

A few minutes later I entered the elementary school. It always smelled like little kids here. "Children smell" was always unique. Body smells. It's not the same here as in the middle and high schools; not the same hormones exploding yet. Not totally contaminated yet by life? That wasn't true, though. Some of these kids had it really rough. Too much evil had already entered their lives. A five-year-old boy threatening to kill himself?

Turning to the right after entering the building I went straight into the elementary office. I always checked in at the office to "officially" be on-site. Being a school psychologist meant I was always a visitor in someone else's territory. I asked permission to be there. That was protocol, and I honored it.

"Good morning, Lisa," I said quietly as I entered her domain.

A small girl was sitting in a chair by the principal's door, which was closed. She was crying and trying to keep her nose from dripping on her dress. It was a losing battle. The girl looked up at me and started crying more. I gave her a big smile hoping to offer some assurance. It didn't work. I removed some tissues from a box on Lisa's desk and gave them to the young girl. She held them in her hands but didn't use them. Oh, well.

"Good morning, Doctor Thomas, I think." Lisa gave me a weak smile. She was a small woman with long black hair, sad brown eyes, a round face and a straight nose. Her coloring showed her Latina ancestry. "Mrs. Purlee is waiting for you down in her classroom."

"Thanks, Lisa. That's where I'll be." Mrs. Purlee's room was at the end of the hallway and to the right as I left the office. Young children and teacher's voices mixed together as background noise as I moved down the hall. The adult voices stood out as they called out assignments and children's names.

Mrs. Purlee saw me through the window of her door and came over to open the door for me. I entered her room. All the children looked up and stared wide-eyed at me. It was a normal occurrence when I came into a classroom. They always looked like an alien had just landed in their room. *I come in peace,* I said quietly to myself.

"Thanks for coming. Sorry to take you away from the high school. I know it has been very difficult there." She hesitated and glanced back at her students. They wilted under her glare, put their heads down and continued to pretend like they were working. She turned her head back toward me. "Jeremy Skubik is the boy sitting by my desk. He is usually very quiet anyhow, but this morning not only was he quiet, he was also crying. When I asked him what was wrong, he said he was sad and wanted to kill himself. I tried to get more information from him, but he just said he was sad. That's when I asked for you. Do you have some time for him?"

"Sure, let me see if he wants to come with me to my room." I walked over to Jeremy, squatted down on my heels so I was at his level, and introduced myself. "Hi, Jeremy, I'm Doctor Thomas. I come to listen to kids sometimes when they are sad. How would you like to come to my room and talk with me?" I knew that we wouldn't talk much about why he was sad, but maybe he could communicate with me about his sadness with the sand tray or other therapeutic toys in my office. Unlike some school psychologists, I actually had an office that I could set up for working with young children. "My room has lots of toys and fun things that you would probably like. Let's go there, okay?"

Jeremy looked up at me with his large, wet, blue eyes. "Okay," he said in a small voice so quietly I almost missed it.

I reached out my left hand and he put his small right hand in mine. His hand was so tiny it almost felt as if nothing was there. Standing up, with our hands clasped, Jeremy scooted out of the chair and stood up beside me. I had to lean over to the left in order to keep his hand in mine. We walked slowly toward Mrs. Purlee. Stopping in front of her, she stooped to Jeremy's level and gave him a hug.

"Jeremy, Doctor Thomas is a really good person. He will take good care of you. He has a wonderful room you will love. You go with him for awhile, and he'll bring you back in a little bit. Okay?" Jeremy shook his head up and down as a sign that it was okay. Mrs. Purlee whispered to me that she had called his mother to let her know what was going on. I nodded, and Jeremy and I left her room.

Walking across the common area outside I made small talk about the cold and corn snow. I asked him if he liked snow. He shrugged his small shoulders in answer. We entered the middle school where my main office was located and then entered the outer middle school office. Mrs. Chang is the office manager in the middle school. She said hello to us in her gentle way. She was one of the daughters of the couple who owned the China Wok Restaurant in Rua Springs.

"Mrs. Chang, I want you to meet Jeremy. He has come to visit us from the elementary school."

"Welcome to our school, Jeremy. It is very nice to have you visit us." She stood up from behind her desk, stooped down and shook hands with Jeremy. He tried to give her a small smile, but stopped and looked down at his shoes.

"Jeremy and I are going into my room for awhile," I said to Mrs. Chang. "See you soon."

I showed him to my room which was around the corner from the main office. We entered and I closed the door behind us. I stood with him in the middle of the room and let Jeremy look around.

"Jeremy, if you see something you want to play with that's okay. Just go ahead."

Kids "speak" through their play. I had a sand tray with lots of small figures to use in the tray like different people, animals, trays, fences, buildings, and much, much more. There were several trucks, action figures, small soft balls, colored paper with colored pencils, and a portable white board on which kids could draw. The teachers teased me about just playing all the time. They loved my room and wanted to come in and "play". With time, I knew I would have more teachers trust me enough to want to talk. It took time to develop that trust, but I knew it would come because teachers have troubles also.

For quite awhile Jeremy just stood and looked around the room. I didn't want to break into his silence, but I needed to bring up his sadness. I sat in one of the two chairs in my room.

"Jeremy, Mrs. Purlee told me you are sad and want to kill yourself. Could you tell me about that?" Jeremy didn't answer. "Lots of children are sad when they come into my room, and they show me about their sadness with some toys in the room. Do you think you might want to show me?" Jeremy didn't move for a few seconds and then went to the sand tray.

Jeremy stared at the sand tray for a moment and then eyed the shelves around the room, which held all the miniature figures that could be placed in the tray to silently develop a story. The sand tray itself was nineteen inches wide, and twenty-eight inches long and three inches high. I had made it out of oak and painted the bottom blue to depict water and sky. The sand tray size was based on the field of vision of what could be visually seen without turning one's head. Thus, a person's field of vision became the world. The tray was filled with very fine white sand such as found on beaches in Florida. I ordered my sand from a business there that sold it for sand trays. As Jeremy looked around I could tell he was starting to develop his story for his world. He sat on a stool in front of the sand tray that was there for the little ones to use.

Silently, Jeremy began to place miniatures into the sand in various places. Then, he would stand back, consider his story, and reach in and move some of the figures before he added more. Slowly, he was telling his story to himself. I began to see some things that probably represented his sadness and talk of killing himself. It was his story. I couldn't tell his story for him, so I kept quiet and observed. I needed to remind myself again that kids speak through play and the toys (miniatures) are their words. Finally, Jeremy stood back from the tray and turned his head to look over at me. It was his silent way of saying, "Here's my story."

Jeremy had placed a forest of trees spread throughout the middle of the sand tray. He had used pine trees with snow on them. Around the middle of the line of trees he had put a waterfall with lots of shiny stones around it. Off to the right of the forest was a house with a terrified woman standing in front of it, one hand out pointing forward. In front of the woman Jeremy had dug a hole in the sand and placed a black wooden coffin in the hole. Its lid was up. Inside the coffin was a dark-haired princess with a sparkling crown on her head. She was sitting up. Around the hole which held the coffin were several buckets of red flowers. Sitting close to the house were a police car and a hospital van. It had a red cross on its side.

On the lower left side of the sand tray Jeremy had dug a hole and placed a small brown coffin in it. Beside the coffin on the rim of the hole sat a small boy. Jeremy had placed a fence around the boy and coffin. There were no other miniatures on that side of the sand tray. Toward the bottom of the tray Jeremy had built a small town. It had houses, cars, trucks, kids playing, balls, a jungle gym, and small animals. A blond prince charming and a king with a sword and armor were standing on a hill nearby overlooking the town.

At the top of the tray Jeremy had placed a Jesus figure right in the center. A cross was placed in front of the figure. Its back was to the entire scene below. Behind Jesus a darkly-dressed evil sorceress was holding a magic wand pointed at the back of Jesus. Just in front of the evil sorceress was a wall all across the width of the tray. Whoa! I had to be careful here and not jump to conclusions. Several moments passed.

I began to ask Jeremy about his story. "I'm really impressed, Jeremy. Can you tell me anything about it? It is really wonderful what you have done here." I waited. He would or wouldn't.

"See, everyone is happy." He pointed at the town. "Really tall, tall hills." Jeremy showed me the mountains. "The princess was kilt because she was sad." He pointed at the princess in the coffin. "Her mom is sad, too." Jeremy stopped and then continued. "The bad witch is keeping out the good man who wants to help the princess. She's very bad and scary, so he can't." He tentatively touched the Jesus figure. Jeremy looked on without speaking.

"What's this over here?" I pointed to the boy on the left sitting by the coffin.

Jeremy looked at it. Then, quietly he said, "He's sad, too."

"Do you know what he's sad about?"

After a few moments of silence Jeremy said, "Kids are mean to him and he's sad. When he's sad he wants to go away."

"Jeremy, do you think the boy really wants to go away? Or, maybe he thinks he is supposed to go away when he's sad?"

"Yeah."

That was about the end of the story for Jeremy. I told him it was a great story and I hoped the boy knew he didn't have to go away when he was sad. Maybe then the boy could tell someone he was sad and together they could make a happy story. Jeremy said okay. We had spent about thirty minutes together and I figured his mom was probably here by now. I told Jeremy that his mother might come to see him and asked him to wait here a moment while I went to the outer office.

A blond-haired woman was sitting in a chair in front of Mrs. Chang's desk. Mrs. Chang nodded toward her as I came in.

"Hello, you must be Jeremy's mother. I'm Marc Thomas, the school psychologist."

"Oh…hello…yes, I'm his mother, Cheryl Skubik. Is he okay?" Her voice shook, and her eyes were terrified.

"Jeremy and I just spent some time together. He's a very nice young boy. Jeremy's been sad today and talked about hurting himself. I'm glad Mrs. Purlee called you."

"Oh, my God!" Jeremy's mother put her hands to her mouth as her eyes got as big as saucers. "Oh, my God! I did this. Oh, my God!"

"Did something happen today, Mrs. Skubik?"

She removed her hands from her face and put them between her knees, still shaking her head back and forth. "I shouldn't have said anything. I just shouldn't have." She hesitated as if debating with herself whether she should confess something horrible. "Jeremy asked me about the girl who died. He was there when I was talking to my neighbor about Patsy Anderson. Later, he wanted to know what happened to the girl. I didn't think. I just didn't think. I told Jeremy that the girl was sad and she had killed herself and that sometimes sad people did that." Guilt was streaming from

Cheryl Skubik's pores. "I had no idea what I had done. My God! Why did I say that?"

"Mrs. Skubik, Jeremy just needs you to love him now. He needs to feel safe, and you can reassure him. Why don't we go see him now?" She stood and followed me into my office.

As soon as she saw Jeremy she rushed to him and held him in her arms. "Oh, Jeremy, I love you. Everything will be okay now." They held each other for a moment. Finally, Jeremy spoke.

He looked at me and asked, "Can I show my mom the story I made?"

"Sure, Jeremy. You show your mom." I closed the door behind me as I left the room.

The middle school principal, Mac McDougal, was waiting for me by Mrs. Chang's desk. Mac was a large muscular man who had played tight end for some college on the east coast. He still looked solid in his light blue shirt and red tie, but gravity was taking its toll. Things were sagging around the middle in his khaki pants. He was moving toward "dunlaps" disease. It dun lapped over the belt. Mac had a granite-like face and a lopsided wide nose that looked like it had been broken a couple of times. His eyes were almost black they were so brown. He had a wrinkled short forehead topped off with a buzz haircut that came close to his large eyebrows. Mac had a gravelly voice, probably from yelling so much at the students. I don't think I had ever seen him smile. There surely was a fun giggly boy in there somewhere. Then again...maybe not. I have to admit Mac didn't have many problems in his school. And, I did respect him.

"Marc, I needed to give you a heads up on a student here." Mac didn't do greetings and salutations. He disliked small talk and hated wasting time. "Something's up, and I'll probably need your help. Remember that kid who came in a couple of weeks ago from a small town in eastern Colorado? The one in treatment foster care? His dad killed his wife in front of the kids, a boy and girl. Dad went to prison, and the kids went into foster care first, but had severe behavioral problems so graduated to treatment foster care. Donny Packerd is his name. His sister went somewhere else. Anyway, Donny has developed a following of other wanna-be thugs, male and female. Rumors of some gang stuff going on here at school is in the works. We need to stop this in its tracks now." Mac stopped, took a breath, then another, scrunched up his face tighter than before, and breathed out slowly.

I jumped in before Mac could wind up again. "Yep, I have seen him a couple of times since he arrived because of his emotional needs."

I didn't like labels, but Donny has qualified because of his special needs. Donny had behavioral problems, but couldn't be qualified as EBD, emotional behavioral disorder, because of his family background. He exhibited social, emotional or behavioral functioning that departs from what is appropriate according to the norms of his age group and culture, and it adversely impacts his academic progress and social relationships. To qualify, Donny had to do this frequently in school and in another place, but because of his abusive and violent home he can't be qualified as EBD. He is extremely smart, according to his records, but he has failed most subjects since being placed in foster treatment care. Donny is now a year behind. According to what Mac said, Donny was now being pumped up to a leadership role either by his own desire or because other students needed an antihero. These had to be kids looking for power, security, friendship, and a family substitute. It could be a bad storm rising.

"I don't have anything solid yet, so stay tuned." Mac turned around and went back into his office and closed the door.

I looked at Mrs. Chang. She looked down at her keyboard and went back to work. School office managers knew more about what was going on in schools than anyone else. Mrs. Chang heard it all, like a priest hearing a confession might, but kept her mouth shut. She gave out no advice or penance.

CHAPTER EIGHT

Every Friday the high school finished off with a pep rally in the gymnasium to kick off the nighttime football game. Tonight the game was here at home against St. Margaret's Catholic School out of Denver. Both teams were two wins and two losses and trying to get above fifty percent in the win column. After a couple of classroom observations, I was able to continue with the assessments I had begun. Toward the end of the final period I walked over to the high school from my middle school office, so I could attend the pep rally. As a new member of the school community, I wanted to participate in the life of the school.

Sitting off to the side with other faculty and staff, I was able to watch the high school students file in and find a place to sit in the bleachers. I could only hope this assembly wouldn't turn out like the fiasco with Marty Dawson a couple of days ago. That's all we would need to send everyone over the edge. It had been a brutal week with Patsy's death starting it off. The days right after a death like this are critical for everyone. We did what we could to manage things and try to provide a normal environment. This is only the beginning, though, because the horror of it will begin to sink in with the days and weeks to come. And Patsy's funeral tomorrow would bring about the reality of the truth. There was no way around it except through it.

Students almost always flocked together in their own little groups. They were further tentacles from the main school tentacle that was part of that larger community group. Each of these little groups fed the larger group which fed the larger group, etc. It fed on the good and the bad, but it did feed. As with a human body, cancer and disease were part of the growth. It was interesting for me to watch the groups arrive.

There were rules about where to sit in gatherings like this. A student had to sit somewhat close to his own age group. Trying to move up or down in an age group would have consequences, some subtle and some not. There were identities to protect and having an identity was at the top of the list for an adolescent. According to Eric Erickson, who was influenced by Freud, there were eight states of psychosocial growth during a person's lifespan. The one I was watching in the gymnasium today was the adolescent stage of "identity versus role confusion." They may have missed something during earlier psychosocial growth stages, but they had another chance now.

The very most important stage is the first stage "trust versus mistrust". If an infant doesn't develop trust in this first stage, it could be much more difficult to trust up to the age of four years old. After that, it could be impossible to trust anyone, thus the potential to develop an antisocial personality or a psychopathic/sociopathic personality. As my mind flashed this information, I couldn't help but marvel that any of us made it to some sort of "normal" place in life.

These students future psychosocial growth depended on what they did with their lives now. They aren't children, and they aren't adults. Not only is their prefrontal cortex of the brain not fully developed, their reasoning is illogical. In fact, it is almost impossible to expect an adolescent to think logically. They are continually searching for their own particular identity and struggle with that through social interactions and moral development. These kids are working to separate themselves from family and are trying to strike out on their own. It takes hard work and lots of wrong turns are made. Thus, role confusion shows it ugly face.

So, these would-be adults finding their groups and a place to sit are part of the journey. Will they make it or not? Time will tell, but chances are they will get lost a few times during these years. I watched them gather in groups that made a statement about their identity.

Over there were the jocks, the ones playing in the football game tonight. In another place were the other jocks divided up by individual sports. Another group was made up of the elite, attractive and "rich" girls and boys. In another spot was a group of adolescents who came from a lower level of the economy. They couldn't get into the other elite group, because they didn't have the money. Another group was made up of the academically successful girls and boys. They were the "brains" who made straight A's and others thought were total losers with a couple of loose screws. Another group had the bad boys and girls. They were known for being troublemakers, drinking and drugging, and having no morals. On the surface they seemed very proud of their identity and worked hard to maintain it. I knew differently, though, since I had talked to some of these kids. They also dressed in an extreme manner to flash their different identity. Although, all within this group dressed the same! Jocks had their letter jackets; cheerleaders had their outfits; rich kids had the flashy clothes and cars; and the so-called bad kids had their hats, shirts, pants, shoes, and jewelry. Gangs were not tolerated here at Rua Springs High School, but the truth is that I am watching all these gangs gather right now. Darnell Claussen would hate my logic.

Off in another corner I noticed other groups. These were the "sped" kids. The special education kids who were in the gifted program and had other special needs. The gifted students all sat together. I recognized most of them. The other groups held a variety of kids receiving special ed services. They have what we call "exceptionalities". Think about it. These groups are trying to find their identity and they get stuck in the "exceptional" group. It's a punch in the gut when they just want to be in normal groups. They aren't allowed to just be normal. Then there are the one-person "groups" sitting here and there in the bleachers. They don't believe they belong anywhere. Others stay away from them, because these kids seem to have a sign on their forehead that says "Nobody Here". And then there are the physically impaired students who are in wheelchairs or crutches and can't make it up into the bleachers. They don't want to have their own group either, but they do, lifelong. Interspersed between these physically impaired students and the other group of special needs kids are the hearing impaired and the visually impaired.

I watched the gifted group for awhile. This is the group of which Patsy Anderson was a member. Like many students here today, Patsy didn't belong to just one group. But, this group seemed to be the most difficult for her from what her friends told me. I watched these kids and wondered about what really happened to her in this group and possibly to others in the group. I zeroed in on a familiar face. It was the Owens boy who had "dropped" his books in the hall this morning; another gifted student who had been bullied. Hmmm...interesting.

"Good afternoon, everyone." I recognized Darnell's voice. He was standing in the middle of the gym floor speaking into a microphone. He does love his mikes. "As everyone knows, this evening we have a football game against St. Margaret's. I'm going to turn this over to Coach Gibson now, so he can get this rally going."

"Who's gonna win tonight?" bellowed Gibson into the mike.

"We are!" yelled the students.

"Who?" screamed Gibson.

"We are!" The gymnasium vibrated with the voices rebounding off the ceiling, floor, and walls. I felt like I was locked inside a metal garbage can and someone was beating on the outside.

"We are the Rua Springs Wildcats! Wildcats rule! Wildcats rule! " The cheerleaders were out on the floor in front of the stands now.

"Wildcats rule! Wildcats rule!" screamed the students.

"Wildcats stalk! Wildcats stalk!" the cheerleaders yelled.

"Wildcats stalk! Wildcats stalk!" the students yelled.

"Wildcats kill! Wildcats kill!" the cheerleaders yelled.

"Wildcats kill! Wildcats kill!" the students yelled.

My head ached, my ears hurt, and my teeth were even vibrating. Maybe my teeth could pick up some far-off planet's signals. I'm sure glad we are preaching nonviolence to these kids. A peaceful world is best. Right? Except, of course, when athletes are turned into "killers" on the field. I was an athlete. We didn't really kill anyone. Or did we?

"Let's have the football team up here now!" Coach Gibson hollered above the cheerleaders. The team was sitting in the front row of the bleachers. They stood and swaggered toward the coach. Most of them wore letter jackets with large "RS" letters on the top left of their jackets. They stood facing everyone with grim looks on their faces. Their legs were spread and their hands were placed behind their backs. Man, these guys are huge! What are they eating? Surely not growth hormones or some such thing. Nah, they wouldn't do that to their bodies. Well...maybe.

"Okay, the marching band will play the fight song now," ordered Gibson.

I guess his unsaid words were: *or else suffer the consequences.* The band, which had just entered the gymnasium doors, began marching in while playing the fight song. It hadn't changed, but, it did sound updated with new instruments. The gym was rockin' now. Most were standing, singing the fight song, stamping their feet and clapping their hands. The energy in the place was reaching mania; mass hysteria. If someone told them to jump off a roof now, they would get in line.

I noticed not everyone was into the school spirit. The groups of one were still sitting gazing off into space. Some of the gifted kids weren't up for it. They were leaning back on the bleacher seats behind them with their arms crossed, unsmiling. I wanted to ask them about it the next time I saw them. Maybe they would spill, maybe they wouldn't.

The fight song ended, the band started up a Sousa song and marched out of the building. The cheerleaders followed as did the players. The pep rally was over. The energy was seeping away, and the students were coming down from the rush. They moved in groups out of the gym. I joined them.

After gathering my book bag from my office, I spoke with Mrs. Chang for a few moments about the pep rally and the game tonight. We both hoped for a win. The middle school was empty except for the custodial crew beginning their cleanup. Another day of picking up after the students. They would have it shining for Monday. I moseyed out to my truck, unlocked it and jumped in. Time to head home for some relaxation before the game tonight. Dad, Grandpa and I always went to the games together. Before I moved back, they had always attended all the sporting events. They were die-hard Rua Springs fans. I couldn't wait to see what Grandpa wore tonight.

The stands were filling up as we exited the ramp that took us to the stadium seats. The "home" side of the field was behind the Rua Springs sideline. The wooden seats were bolted to the cement stands and were actually quite comfortable. We brought seat pads for our boney butts. After a few hours on the wood our rear ends became numb; thus, the pads. Above the seats were the announcer booth and places for the media. Anyone could sit on this side of the field, but most of the visiting team fans used the bleachers on the far side. Those were the regular wooden seat bleachers common to football fields. We placed ourselves in the general area where we always sat; creatures of habit. We knew most of the people around us from previous games. School colors were all around. Purple and white coats, hats, sweatshirts, scarves, pom poms, and those small purple and white triangular pennants.

And then there was Grandpa. He didn't go for the color scheme. Grandpa had on his trademark gray fedora, but this one had "RS" on the front of it. I wasn't sure if he sewed those letters on or glued them, but somehow they stayed on. Instead of his gray jacket he wore a gray hooded sweatshirt with a large "RS" painted across his chest. This really did look like he painted the letters on with a paintbrush.

The two teams were introduced. The captains called the toss of the coin, they shook hands, and ran back to their respective sides. Rua Springs lost the toss so they were kicking off. And the game began. There was a lot of that "hey you, take da ball and run up the middle." What kind of guy takes the ball and runs right into 2000 pounds of solid muscle that is trying to smash you into oblivion? "Here, you take the ball dude and…" "Are you totally insane? I'm not running up the middle again!" Wheee!

The game went back and forth with the radio announcer, who thought he was Dick Enberg, trying to give a play-by-play. Many fans around us had their radios on for the play-by-play.

"Number thirteen, George Mecklenburg, is back to pass again. He's being chased out the pocket running to the right. Oh my, what a hit by number 90, Grady Vargas. That boy must weigh 300 pounds and he's only a junior! What a play by Vargas. He can really run for a big guy. It looks like Mecklenburg is hurt. He isn't moving. Oh my, this will be a disaster for the Wildcats. Anthony Yankowski is the second string quarterback, but he hasn't had much playing time this year. Maybe Yankowski, number 9, can connect with Spencer Vaughn who was Mecklenburg's favorite target. Vaughn has dropped three passes so far which is very unusual for him."

The mention of Yankowski and Vaughn reminded me of my conversation with them recently. I couldn't help but wonder how they were doing. Vaughn seemed pretty slow and out of rhythm on the field tonight. The game was at a standstill as the Wildcat staff and volunteer doctor checked on Mecklenburg. Finally, an EMT van pulled into the open end of the stadium and followed the track around to where Mecklenburg still lay on the field. They brought out the stretcher, carefully loaded him up, and placed him in the back of the van. An EMT jumped in the back with Mecklenburg and the back doors closed. The driver loaded himself into the van, cranked it up and they drove around the track and out the entrance. After a few moments they fired up the sirens and hit the road. The crowd was on its feet in stunned silence.

The wanna-be Enberg radio announcer was still talking. "Oh, my, our thoughts and prayers are with George Mecklenburg. I will keep you posted on any information about him. I did notice his parents rushing out of the stands toward their car after the EMT van showed up. This has to be a terrible shock to them. Oh, my."

After a few minutes of near silence, the players were on the field pounding one another all over again. The Rua Springs players were more and more violent in their play trying to punish the St. Margaret Saints for what they did to one of their players. Payback time. Of course, several penalties were called on the Wildcats for all sorts of infractions; roughing the passer; unsportsman-like conduct; personal fouls, etc. When the Wildcats were on offense, Yankowski was nimble enough to stay away from Grady Vargas, number ninety. But Yankowski acted like he was running for his life most of the time. He tried passes to Vaughn, but only one of three was caught. Vaughn was definitely having a bad night.

The energy of the game ebbed and flowed. Back and forth the ball went without either team scoring. With about three minutes to go in the first half the Wildcats finally mounted a sustained drive. They made it to the five yard line and fumbled. Oh, my, is right. The Saints began the long haul to the other end of the field. *Boom, whap.* Harder and harder they hit each other. It was a duel to the death.

Grandpa was on his feet jumping from foot to foot. He was ready to stroke out but somehow held on.

"Blood makes the grass grow. Kill, kill, kill!" he bellowed.

The crowd around us was staring at him with wide eyes. The game was momentarily forgotten as he became the central focus.

He stood up on his seat and yelled, "Rock 'em and sock 'em and hit 'em in the knee! Rock 'em and sock 'em and make 'em go wheeee!" He leaned his head back and began his outrageous wheezy laugh. "Go home, pack up, we're gonna make you give that football up!"

Others were on their feet now as Grandpa led the cheers. His energy was contagious.

"Rock 'em and sock 'em and kick 'em in the knee!"

Some kid nearby yelled out, "Kick 'em in the nuts!"

Grandpa plowed on, "Go home, pack up...!"

The crowd was going berserk with Grandpa leading the way. Dad and I tried to act like we didn't know him, shifting away from him. No good. Everyone knew. Oh, my! It was a heck of a game.

Halftime came, and the game was scoreless. I told Dad and Grandpa I would grab us some sodas and popcorn from the concession stand. Fans were making the move to bathrooms and junk food. The concession line was several deep by the time I arrived. A slew of voices were intermingled, all in conversations about the game and Mecklenburg's injury.

Waiting for the line to move forward I heard loud voices off to the right behind the concession stand.

"Well, look who we have here, boyos! It's one of the genius brainiack nerds!" Sinister laughter followed. "Let's give this freakazoid an IQ drain!" More brutish laughter.

"I wouldn't try that if I were you mister hebetude, torpid, obtuse, blunt head," a strong voice said from the darkness.

"Huh?" said the leader. "What did he say?"

"I said I wouldn't try anything, or you will regret it, you brainless camel face."

"Grab him, Skater's!" There was a shuffling of bodies, a smack, and then, *ufff* as air was forced out.

I had heard enough. As I sprinted around the corner of the building I shouted, "Hey!"

There was a rustling of cloth and the squish of rubber-soled shoes moving at warp speed. Arriving at the poorly lit space behind the concession stand, the only face I recognized was Arnold Purdy's. His leering grin disappeared into the darkness. The space was empty. Only the sour smell of angry energy remained. Arnold Purdy: I hadn't had the honor of his presence in my office, yet. I knew of him from high school whispers. He was an oversized teenager who physically cleared the space wherever he went. The word was that even Darnell was afraid of him. Purdy seemed to live on the edge of violence, never quite tipping into expulsion from school. His nickname was "Skater," because he had a knack for skating out of trouble. I sensed I would see Mr. Purdy again. A shiver rolled up my back, cold and menacing.

Walking back to where Dad and Grandpa were sitting I was lost in thought when I reached them. They both looked at me like I had received a head transplant.

"What?" I wondered aloud.

"Uh, Marc, what happened to the soda and popcorn?" queried Dad.

It finally hit me. I had forgotten to stop at the concession stand on the way back. "Uh oh! Something came up and I totally forgot." I turned around and hurried down the steps.

Toward the end of the third quarter the Wildcats finally scored with a field goal. The score remained three to zero the remainder of the game, and the Rua Springs Wildcats were finally above 500 on the win/loss record for the year. Grandpa had continued his cheers and chants throughout the game. He was still jazzed as we left the stadium. If someone would take him, he would have hopped in the back of a truck and screamed and yelled with the teenagers as they drove up and down the main road in Rua Springs. Instead, he had to hang with two party poopers. Boring!

Arriving home, Dad said he felt like some music. Grandpa, who finally looked totally exhausted from his evening out, and I placed ourselves in the easy chairs arranged to the side of Dad's grand piano. He was a brilliant pianist who simply played for his own soul-soothing. He really didn't care if anyone listened to him or not. We listened. Boy, did we listen. Who would pass up a free concert?

Many years ago Dad had purchased a 1925 Model M Steinway Grand Piano. It was a five foot seven grand with a gorgeous satin cherry cabinet and a matching concert bench. It was an original, including the ivory key tops. It was worth a bundle of money, but that was totally irrelevant to Dad. He told me he had always wanted a Steinway grand and a customer was selling it cheap. The customer's wife performed on the grand, and she had recently died, so the man wanted someone who loved to play to have it. They made the deal and here it is. And, what an unbelievable sound Dad produced with it. He and the grand became one when he played.

Dad began playing Pachelbel, *Canon in D.* I closed my eyes and joined with the sound. It surrounded, clothed, and painted us with pleasure. The chair molded around me and I separated from earthly pain. Following that, Dad moved directly into Beethoven's *Für Elise.* I drifted on a stream of vapors between consciousness and sub-consciousness. Without stopping, Dad segued into Dvorak's *Symphony Number 9 in E Minor.* I floated, soared and moved beyond the sound. After death and rebirth I breathed silence. The chair was beneath me, and I was in solid time. Dad sat with his hands in his lap and his head down. Grandpa was asleep snoring lightly, his head down and chin on his chest. He still had on his fedora with the RS letters on the front.

Dad stood up, stretched, and smiled at me. "Night, Marc."

"Night, Dad, sleep well." I stood and trailed Dad back to our rooms. Grandpa would awake sometime in the night and find his way to bed.

CHAPTER NINE

I awoke from my usual disturbing dreams thinking about Patsy. I reminded myself that her service is today. It would be a very difficult day for many, including me.

In the kitchen, Dad sat reading the Saturday morning paper and sipping coffee. I hooked a finger in my mug, added some hazelnut creamer from the fridge, and filled my cup.

Silently Dad and I enjoyed our coffee and perused the news. I usually didn't read the paper except on weekends. Today's news seemed similar to past weekend news. The economic news was bleak as usual. Crimes continued to take place. There was an interesting story about a lady who saved animals from domestic violence in homes. Usually, it was children who needed to be saved, but this lady had the idea of taking pets out of homes also. She had rescued several pets which were abused along with spouses and children; an uplifting story.

"I will take the dogs for a hike today, Dad. They need a romp in the forest and so do I."

"Sounds good, Marc. I wish I could go with you, but I need to open the store and get things running before I take off for Patsy's funeral."

The service will be held at the Episcopal church with my cousin, Katherine, officiating. Dad sings in the choir and will be a part of the service.

"Grandpa is still sleeping so I don't imagine he'll want to go to the service."

"Hi, boys. I'm up and at 'em." Grandpa entered the kitchen in the same clothes he wore last night to the game. "Nope, I don't go to funerals anymore. Everybody in my age group has already died, so I've had all the funerals I can take. I'm even going to miss mine when it comes." He filled his coffee mug and sat down at the table with us. "I had a hard night, a real hard night." Grandpa shook his head back and forth as if he was carrying a heavy burden. "It must have been all that Viagra I took." After a few beats he looked at us to make sure we caught his humor. With a huge smile he slapped his knees and began his wheezy laugh. Funny man. Dad and I couldn't help but laugh with him.

Dad and I had some fruit and toast as we worked on the paper. Grandpa sat slurping his coffee. He poured it out of his cup into a saucer and drank, I mean slurped, from it. Part cat? Maybe, but definitely weird.

"Okay, gentlemen, I'm going to work." Dad stood up, put his cup and plate in the sink, snagged his keys, and headed for the door to the garage. "Marc, see you at the service. Pa, I'll see you...well...when I see you. Come on down to the store if you get bored." And he was gone.

"Grandpa, I'm taking the dogs on a hike up behind the house. You're welcome to come if you want." I stood up and, like Dad, put my plate and mug into the sink.

"Ha! What a jokester you are! I'm staying right here so you and those two hairy creatures go wear yourselves out." *Slurp, slurp.* Weird!

After attaching a fanny pack that also held a couple of water bottles, I loaded up on dog biscuits, grabbed their leashes and asked the dogs if they wanted to go for a walk. What a dumb question. They were already all over me when I put on my pack. Leaving through the front door we went around to the back of the house and began the climb up to the ridge. There was no trail up this route so we were just bushwhacking. Sunny and Kong were already running ahead of me bouncing from smell to smell and barking like the whole world needed to hear them.

"Hey, we're here! Did you miss us?" they barked.

The trees were cleared behind the house to make a defensible space in case of fire. Since the house was earth berm it backed into the mountain. Dad had taken advantage of the terrain. The mountain was stair-stepped similar to a staircase. The area that backed up to the house was flat for about fifty yards, then there was a steep incline which held boulders and ponderosa pine. It stepped up one more time, had a flat area, and then it was nothing but steep forest all the way to the ridge above.

Reaching the second step of the incline I stopped to catch my breath. The dogs were barking in the distance.

The soft sounds of nature's movement massaged my senses. The sunlight of early morning was sifting through the tall ponderosas painting light and dark images on the earth. Ethereal figures danced around me daring me, touching me, questioning me. I stood unmoving, quieting my breathing, communicating with the dancing shadows. Here I was free of the world. By invitation, I stepped forward to the climb ahead.

Reveling in the clothing of the mountain's terrain I climbed slowly skyward for several minutes. A small spring was sharing streams of water with the craggy face of a large boulder. Springs were in many places in the area and were the origin of the naming of Rua Springs when it was born. The moisture from this spring dripped to the ground below sinking into the soft loam of dried pine needles, leaves from aspen trees, and moist soil. The dogs were greedily lapping at the dripping water, occasionally looking up at me and giving moist smiles. This was their heaven and mine, too. Contentment covered me.

Here there was no time, only eternity. My legs pushed down and up as I steadily rose. The burn in my legs spoke to me of life, existence. I am. Ahead Sunny and Kong were climbing toward the ridge somewhere up above. They had slowed, panting with tongues hanging out the sides of their mouths. They wouldn't give up, though, just as I wouldn't.

My thoughts had remained clear, empty, but images of Patsy began crowding in as the pain in my lungs and legs grew with the climb. An image of Patsy hanging by the jump rope in the boy's locker room flashed into my consciousness. It was bright, clear, and harsh. The emotional pain of the image joined with my physical distress and a breath caught in m throat. I stopped, inhaled deeply, and pushed the air slowly out. Inhaled again, pushed air out. Why? Why did Patsy do this? Or, did she? That thought sent an icy shiver through my body. What if? Would someone want to hurt Patsy? But, why? The shadows danced around me, challenging me now. It felt menacing somehow. I pushed onward hoping to regain the earlier contentment. Suicide? Maybe.

Suicide in adolescents was at an epidemic level. Why? It had never entered my thoughts as a teenager. My search for understanding netted an abundance of information, but it still was difficult for me to understand at a primal level. Who would do that? I knew and I didn't. What I did know was that suicide was the third leading cause of death in adolescents fifteen to nineteen. I also knew that an adolescent killed herself or himself about every two hours in our country. Suicide claimed more lives than disease or just plain old natural causes. It was beyond shocking to me. I understood and I didn't. Suicide often followed depression, but that wasn't all there was to it.

Patsy was depressed from what I know now, but it had to be more than that. Substance abuse, anxiety, and attention deficit hyperactivity disorder also have joined with depression according to research that I had read. Stressful events can trigger suicide attempts. Were there other stressful events for Patsy that I missed and that she didn't share with anyone else? Possibly. Impulsive adolescents are more apt to try suicide. I would have never viewed Patsy Anderson as impulsive. Before, I didn't believe Patsy was socially isolated, but that may have been a mistake on my part. Now, it seems she was moving in that direction. I didn't know of any violence in her home or of any psychiatric hospitalizations. And, her friends didn't make any reference to Patsy talking about hurting herself. Again, what did I really know about Patsy? Maybe not so much, and that caused me guilt and gut-wrenching pain.

If I had asked the right questions of Patsy would she have told me? Should I have questioned her about her eating habits, sleeping patterns, drug use, how she got along with her mother, social relationships, exercise habits, mood changes, etc.? I believe we had talked about those things because it was normal to do so. I must have missed it all. I failed Patsy. Tears came to the corners of my eyes. They blurred my sight as I stepped over rocks and down timber. My body felt leaden now. Moving upward was almost more than I could physically endure. I was filled with burning anxiety. It was sour tasting and coated my mouth like a rotting substance I couldn't purge. Tugging out a water bottle from my fanny pack I flipped the top open and poured water into my mouth hoping to spew out the rot. I finished one bottle and grabbed the second, drinking greedily. I forced myself to spit, trying to cleanse myself. My mouth remained as dry as desert sand. Looking upward I didn't know if I could move, the pain was so severe.

The barking of the dogs snapped me back to the mountain. It provided a healing spirit that I drank in, gulping in the comfort it gave me. I forced a step forward, then another, and another. The mountain joined me, and I climbed upward, pushing my bruised spirit on. The trees became farther apart and more sunlight flooded my view. I could see the ridgeline above me. Sunny and Kong were walking beside me now sensing that we should reach the ridge together.

Standing on the ridge a short time later the three of us looked about us in amazement at the wondrous views. We remained silent looking in all directions, as I took snapshots with my eyes. Snapping and saving. Snapping and saving. Eventually, I sat and unzipped my pack to find dog biscuits for Sunny and Kong and a power bar for myself. Sipping water and chewing on a chocolate bar, my body finally began to cool down. The dogs were lying beside me snuggled up waiting for more treats. We stayed there silent, unmoving. Time expanded, continued.

Then it was time to leave the mountaintop. As someone once said, "A person can't stay on top of the mountain and survive. They eventually have to go back to their lives down below. I had to go down. Patsy's funeral was waiting.

Slowly, I picked my way down through the rocks, boulders, and timber that I had encountered on the way up. Different muscle groups were asking to be noticed now. I moved more and more quickly as I descended, testing, probing, challenging the mountain and myself. On the verge of recklessness, I pushed myself on. The dogs jumped over the uneven terrain racing each other toward the bottom. Kong's short legs moved in a blur matching Sunny on the way down. What Sunny jumped over, Kong went under and around. I followed at a poor third in line. The breeze fanned my senses more intensely as I raced onward.

Sunny and Kong were barking happily, waiting for me at the space above the house. I slowed, sucked in air, and leaned over and placed my hands on my knees, waiting for my breathing to slow. With Sunny and Kong at my sides, I moved down and around to the front door. They were ready to sleep contentedly the rest of the day. My day would not continue like theirs. I locked my mind into what loomed ahead; having a lobotomy seemed easier.

CHAPTER TEN

St. Mary's Episcopal Church was located a block west of Hetti Road in Rua Springs. It was originally built in the 1880s, but a fire gutted its wooden structure in 1923. Following the fire, it was rebuilt exactly like the original church so as to keep its historical look and feel. It was wood framed with a high vaulted ceiling rising to about twenty-five feet at the center beam. Wooden cross beams held the walls together. The outside wooden siding was painted yellow, which according to town history was William and Rua Houghton's favorite color. The front of the church housed the bell tower, which still worked, and a large white cross, which was above the bell tower on the front ridgeline of the wooden slate roof. Several wooden steps in front ascended to the large two-door entrance. On either side of the steps were metal railings, which were finally added in the 1980s because several elderly people had fallen off the steep steps going down and broken various bones in their bodies. Attending church is dangerous.

It wasn't until an injury lawsuit occurred that the church was forced to break with history and put in the railings. Following that, to meet ADA requirements, the church added a wheelchair accessible ramp, so disabled folks could get into the church. The only problem with that was that the wheelchairs had to be rolled to the very front of the church right below the lectern because there was no room at the back. They complained because they didn't want to be in the front where everyone would watch them. It was easier to be anonymous and hidden in the back. Besides, during boring sermons they could catch some shut eye without anyone noticing. In the front, they were continually heard snorting and snoring, much to the amusement of those in attendance.

The entrance led to a small narthex or entryway, which then led through more doors to the nave of the church itself. It was filled with rows of wooden pews that looked like Moses had built them. Recently, cushions were added so the earthly and non-spiritual bottoms didn't go to sleep along with the wheelchair crowd. The main aisle went straight down the middle of the nave toward the altar. There were also aisles on both sides of the nave. Since the church was built in cruciform style, it had a transept that provided more seating off to the right and left arms of the building. The walls inside the church were painted white and held the fourteen Stations of the Cross, also called Via Dolorosa. They were hand-carved by an artist in the early 1900s. Since I had grown up in this church I knew the Stations well. The scenes of horror stayed with me. Some people loved them and said they provided an awesome spiritual experience. I thought all they showed was the brutality of people toward one another. Let's see now. So...your God was killed and came back to life? Interesting. I don't know of any other gods who have been killed and came back. Have you ever known anyone who came back from the dead? I didn't think so. And, because of all this, you now know you'll get eternal life? Hmm... So, now I should be grateful that my wife, Lilly, has received eternal life. Yeah, right. How do I know that? Oh yeah, faith. Un huh, yeah. So these stations are a spiritual experience? Not for me. All they show is pain.

The altar sat like a huge coffin three steps up from the transept. It was all white like the walls of the church. There were huge wooden chairs covered in burgundy cloth to the left of the altar. Now these were the comfortable chairs, the thrones! Too bad the common folk didn't get to sit in them. Off to the right was the alcove that held the choir loft.

I had parked about a block away from the church. Cars were lining both sides of the street and the church parking lot, on the north side of the church, was filled to capacity. Entering, I could see that the only seats left were almost at the back. Everything else was filled. Maybe I should have come in a wheelchair.

Stepping over several pairs of legs and excusing myself I sat almost exactly in the middle of the pew. Sitting in the pew? Sounds yucky. The organist was playing dirge music quietly. Dad had shared with me that someone had recently donated a huge new organ to the church. I could see it down front on the left below the choir loft. Dad said it was a Legacy Series Phoenix Opus 77 model. He knew what that meant. I didn't. It had lots of pipes, pedals, and keyboards. *Chop Sticks* would be fun to play on it, I imagine.

I spotted Dad up in the choir loft. They were in their purple and white robes and so looked pretty classy. There was a vacant spot where Patsy had probably stood with the choir. They were acknowledging her absence. Gazing around the gathered people I could see lots of people I knew: Students, teachers, and others. I noticed the group of gifted students sitting together. Other special ed students were with them also. There were many folks I didn't recognize. From the back I had a decent view of lots of people.

Behind me I could hear more bodies trying to get into the church. Extra chairs were placed on the ends of each pew to add more seating capacity, but those were filled already. Both inside and out, there was standing room only now. A large number of people came to remember Patsy. I wondered how Patsy's mother, Vivian, was doing. I could see her sitting in the left front row with a couple of women sitting on either side of her. I didn't recognize them. A horrendous time for her. I knew, because I went through it. It brought it all back to me like a fist punched into my stomach. Actually, this is the first time I had entered a church in over two years.

The organ music stopped, and I turned to the right to see the crucifer holding the cross, acolytes and lay Eucharistic ministers standing at the ready. I imagined Katherine, the priest here at St. Mary's, was standing behind them. Processional candles were lit, grim faces were put on, prayers books and service bulletins were open, the congregation was silent. It was time to rock and roll.

"I am Resurrection and I am life, says the Lord. Whoever has faith in me shall have life even though she die." Katherine's strong voice came from the narthex of the church and the procession began. "And everyone who has life, and has committed herself to Me in faith shall not die forever."

I could see Katherine now. She was wearing a purple chasuble over her white alb. Originally, a poncho was worn by a priest in cold churches to keep them warm. It was just an article of clothing. The poncho became the chasuble and a beautiful vestment, of which there were many colors, to be worn during different seasons and services. As usual, the church took something and made it part of the glamour. Katherine's chasuble was purple and used for funerals. The significance of purple was that it was the color of royalty. There was also a mix of penance with it so it represented Jesus as royalty and also having done penance for all. At the top of her chasuble I could see her white stole that was hung around her shoulders.

Katherine was carrying a silver urn in her hands. It was all that was left of Patsy, and it was jolting; burned down to nothing but ash. Lilly was cremated, also, so I knew exactly what the contents inside of that urn looked like. I had spread Lilly's ashes in the mountains in a favorite place we liked to backpack in New Mexico. Her ashes were bone white and I had let them sift through my fingers as they flew away with the wind. Gone.

"As for me, I know that my Redeemer lives and that at the last He will stand upon the earth. After my awaking, He will raise me up and in my body I shall see God." The processional party moved toward the front of the church as Katherine spoke. "I myself shall see, and my eyes behold Him who is my friend and not a stranger. For none of us has life in herself, and none becomes her own master when she dies. For if we have life, we are alive in the Lord. So, then, whether we live or die, we are the Lord's possession. Happy from now on are those who die in the Lord! So it is, says the Spirit, for they rest from their labors."

I would have to see if Katherine really believed this stuff that she was saying. Of course she did or she wouldn't be a priest. Or, would she? Maybe she had to say these things, but inside she didn't believe all of it. I doubt if she would tell me, but she might. Even priests probably needed someone to talk with about how to justify all this faith verbiage.

The procession reached the transept of the church and the steps going up to the chancel and the altar. Katherine had finished the reading and placed the urn containing Patsy's ashes on a stand at the foot of the steps. After genuflecting, they all proceeded up the steps and to the chairs on the right. The crucifer placed the cross in its holder, and the taper bearers placed their candles in the stands at both ends of the altar.

The congregation remained hushed, somber. Seeing the urn sitting on the stand was probably beyond jarring for many folks. I would also surmise that a few of the people here today had never before attended a memorial service. That is extremely rough, to put it mildly. The anxiety, grief, fear, and stress of those in attendance today was so intense that it was palpable, tangible, with a life of its own. It felt like I could grab it and feel its essence.

Katherine walked to pulpit. "We are gathered here today to remember and celebrate the life of Patsy Ruth Anderson." I could see Katherine taking a deep breath seeking her own inner peace. She continued, "The Lord be with you."

"And also with you," expressed the congregation.

"Let us pray." Katherine continued with the rite of the service.

Prayers were said. Scripture was read. Words were spoken between the priest and congregation, similar to a badminton birdie floating on the wind. After the gospel was read by Katherine, she stepped to the pulpit again.

"Patsy's mother has asked that I share a few words about Patsy. There are no appropriate words to express our loss or to achieve an understanding about why this has happened. Today will possibly not answer our questions. It may even bring up more questions and pain. My hope is that by gathering together we, as family and friends of Patsy and Vivian, may somehow together discover some peace." Katherine hesitated, picked up a glass of water, sipped, put it back down, and continued.

"I have known Patsy for several years. I watched her mature into an incredible young woman who was very talented. She loved people. She continually gave to anyone and everyone. Patsy was a shining star in our midst here at St. Mary's. She attended the youth group, sang in the choir, helped with the Sunday school for preschoolers, visited the elderly who couldn't come to church, and helped me with church services."

Katherine stopped, looked down, and gripped the sides of the pulpit as if she was trying to stay on her feet. Her words brought on more tears in the congregation. I could hear people crying openly, noses being blown, sniffling, shuffling of feet on the wood floor, and other sounds of grief and sorrow that were almost more than I could handle. I choked back my tears using all my will to hold up.

"My words today may be empty and hollow for you. I honestly wish I could watch Patsy walk through the door down there and tell us it is all okay." Heads shifted toward the back as if Patsy might just walk right in. "I also know that Patsy is okay. She is safe, and she is at peace now. You may ask me how I know that. It's a good question. I know it because of my faith. I only have my faith to keep me going. Faith is all I have in a time like this. I have faith in knowing Patsy is with Jesus and pain-free. Whatever happened to her and whatever sorrow she had is now gone. Please hang on to your memories of Patsy. She lives on with each of us in her own special, beautiful way."

Katherine stepped from behind the pulpit, walked down the steps and over to Patsy's mother. Kneeling down, Katherine put her arms around her, brought her close, and they both wept. Tears were running down my face. I didn't care. I didn't agree with what Katherine said about having faith, but it didn't matter. Only memories of Patsy mattered. The church was overflowing with salty, wet tears. It sounded like we all might be consumed by the pain. Students were hugging each other. Adults were sitting with arms around one another. What a loss. What a tragic, terrible loss.

With difficulty Katherine arose and stepped back up the altar. There would probably be no communion, because the majority of the people didn't attend St. Mary's so wouldn't take part. The choir stood and the organist/choir director approached and stood in front of them. The choir director began to hum and sway back and forth. The choir then began to move back and forth together, humming a song along with the choir director. With a start I, and everyone else, realized they were humming a Bill Withers song, *Lean on Me*. It was mind-blowing. No songs from the Episcopal hymnal today! Incredible! Was this really an Episcopal church? Singing a cappella they began, continuing to sway back and forth, back and forth. It was a perfect song about having pain and having friends there to lean on.

The congregation was still shocked. Mouths were hanging open. Mine was, too. This wasn't the church in which I grew up. In fact, it wasn't like any church I had attended.

The choir concluded, stood quietly for a few moments and then sat. The congregation was stunned! Who would have guessed the choir would have sung this today. Dad hadn't said a word to me. I was as shocked as everyone else. And then it began.

One person in a wheelchair up front started clapping. Two ladies in wheelchairs with blue hair high-fived each other and joined the clapping. After a moment of disbelief, people in different parts of the congregation stood and joined in. The entire congregation was on its feet clapping now. It was thrilling, awe-inspiring, as if the noise itself brought us higher and God lower, touching hands with the essence of eternity. It was the most incredible experience I had ever had in a church and maybe anywhere. Patsy was here, bringing us all together. We were changed, never to be the same as before. I quietly said a thank you to her and felt her smile embrace me. In death, she gave us life.

When the clapping had subsided and people sat, Katherine and the processional party walked down to the urn with Patsy's ashes. Standing beside it Katherine continued the service.

"Give rest, O Christ, to Your servant, Patsy, with Your saints."

The congregation responded from the Episcopal Book of Common Prayer, "Where sorrow and pain are no more, neither sighing, but life everlasting."

"You only are immortal, the Creator and Maker of humankind, and we are mortal, formed of the earth and to earth shall we return. For so did You ordain when You created me saying, 'You are dust, and to dust you shall return.' All of us go down to the dust, yet even at the grave we make our song Alleluia, alleluia, alleluia."

"Give rest, O Christ, to Your servant Patsy with Your saints, where sorrow and pain are no more, neither sighing, but life everlasting," the congregation replied.

Katherine stood behind the urn and spoke, "Into our hands, O merciful Savior, we commend Your servant Patsy. Acknowledge, we humbly beseech You, a sheep of your own fold, a lamb of Your own flock, a sinner of Your own redeeming. Receive her into the arms of Your mercy, into the blessed rest of everlasting peace, and into the glorious company of the saints in light. Amen."

The Lord's Prayer was said by everyone and Katherine picked up Patsy's ashes and began the long walk out of the church. Katherine stopped and took Patsy's mother's hand and lifted her up to join her on the way out of the church.

As Katherine walked, she spoke an anthem. "Christ is risen from the dead, trampling down death by death, and giving life to those in the tomb. The Son of Righteousness is gloriously risen, giving light to those who sat in darkness and in the shadow of death."

Everyone, including me, was focused on Patsy's mother. She was totally broken, shattered, only a shell of her former self. Her eyes were wide and unseeing. Her color was gone as if emptied of life along with Patsy. I couldn't imagine how she could even put one foot in front of the other.

Katherine continued with the anthem until they were out of the church.

After a time, Katherine reentered the church and gave the dismissal. The service was over. St. Mary's had a columbarium to hold ashes, but I guessed that Patsy's mother had other plans, so her ashes wouldn't be kept there. Silently we all exited the church. The Colorado blue sky was still there where we left it before entering the church. Sounds of the village could be heard around us. A car horn honked. A baby cried somewhere in the distance. The shuffle of feet and the rustle of clothing nearby tickled my hearing. People spoke softly to one another as they moved away from the church and toward cars. Vehicles started and drove away. The sounds of life. We were all still alive; changed, yes, but still here. Patsy was a memory now, gone, but not. I walked around the side of the church to its office. Katherine was there.

CHAPTER ELEVEN

B ehind the church was a recently built office, classroom and day care structure that congregants of St. Mary's had constructed. My cousin was instrumental in the growth of the church in recent years, and that made it possible to finance this new structure. I had visited Katherine here once soon after I moved back to town.

The structure sought to maintain an historic look like the main church, but it was built environmentally friendly. It had a metal roof with solar panels catching the energy from the sun with lots of southern facing windows for passive heat. Dad had served on the building committee to design the building so had pushed for the solar features like he had on his home. It was a beautiful building and even had the outside yellow color which matched the church. However, the multiuse building was stucco, not wood like the church. Dad told me the church was looking to the future and had plans to add solar panels to the church building before long. The old and the new coming together. Why didn't other churches do this?

After entering the building, I moved through the entryway doors into a hallway that went down the middle of the building. The office was just off to the right. An older lady was typing on a keyboard behind a desk. I knew her name was Bertha something. Her last name escaped me. Bertha looked up and smiled angelically at me. She wore large red-framed glasses on her moon-shaped face. Her nubbin of a nose barely held her glasses up. Her blue eyes shone brightly through her thick lenses. Bertha's short hair was gray and fixed nicely in a tight perm which was actually quite attractive in an odd way.

"Hello, Doctor Thomas. It is good to see you again!" She acted like my new best friend.

"Hi, Bertha, it is good to see you, also. I'm here..."

"Wasn't that a beautiful service? It was so uplifting, don't you agree?"

"Well, uh..."

"It was probably the most wonderful funeral service I've ever attended, and I have been to a lot. Hundreds! I love to go to funerals. The angels are there, don't you agree?"

"Well, um..."

"The flowers in the church open all my senses to God's love for me, and the words are so comforting. I read the burial service at least twice a week just to remember how much I love those words. Aren't they just wonderful, Doctor Thomas? I've asked Mother Katherine to have burial services more times per week just so those who love it can come and feel the presence of God around us. We don't have to have a body there. We can just pretend. Isn't it a wonderful idea, Doctor Thomas?"

Mother Katherine? Was Katherine called mother here? Burial services twice a week and just pretend there's a body present? Where did Katherine find this lady? Is she an escapee from a mental hospital? In a separate reality?

Bertha was still talking, "...but, I'm not sure about that song the choir sang. They should have sung a wonderful hymn from the hymnal like *The Old Rugged Cross*. It would have been much more uplifting than that "leaning on the pea" song. Don't' you agree, Doctor Thomas?"

"Well, er, I don't think it was about leaning on the..."

"Bertha, my cousin Marc and I are going out for lunch now." Katherine had come out of her office and saved me from Bertha, whatever her last name is, lover of funerals. "It is Saturday, Bertha, and you don't need to be here working. Why don't you go home now?"

"Do you think there are anymore funerals in town today, Mother Katherine? I would love to attend one or two more before I go home."

"I don't believe there are, Bertha. It is a slow day for funerals." Katherine took me by the arm and led me out of the office.

"Who is that lady?" I asked Katherine

Katherine put her finger to her lips to hush me as we went out the front doors of the building.

After a few steps forward on the sidewalk, I couldn't hold back any longer. "That was totally weird, Katherine. Unbelievable! Is she mentally challenged?"

"Bertha is actually a very good secretary, Marc. She is very strange, I agree, but she is the best I've ever had."

"I'm not sure that says much about church secretaries then."

We continued walking past the church to High Street, which was the street in front of St. Mary's.

"Bertha had a strange upbringing, Marc. Her dad owned a funeral home in Arkansas. Bertha grew up helping him with all aspects of running the place and I mean all aspects."

"You mean..."

"Yes, I mean she assisted her dad with everything. When she was a teenager her dad was arrested for necrophilia and went to prison. He was having sex with dead bodies, Marc, and Bertha walked in on him."

"My God!"

"She was so traumatized that she was picked up walking down the street that night in a tiny nightgown. Evidently, Bertha was mumbling about an angel lying on top of the dead bodies, so the police went to check. When they confronted her dad, he confessed, telling them he just wanted to comfort the dead on their journey. Bertha went to foster care until she was old enough to move out on her own. Her dad, Tiny Butt, is out of prison, but she has never seen him since that night."

"What? His name was Tiny Butt? No way!"

"Yes, way. His real name was Jimmy Tom, but he was a giant of a man, and everyone called him Tiny."

"Unreal! So, that means Bertha's last name is Butt? Bertha Butt?"

"You're a winner, Marc. You got it in one."

We had stopped walking. This was one of the wildest stories I had ever heard. Bertha Butt?

"You know, Katherine, in the early 1970s a guy by the name of Jimmy Castor Bunch wrote a song called *Troglodyte*."

"Yep, I sort of remember. I would have been in elementary school."

"Yes, well, in the song he talked about Bertha Butt, one of the Butt sisters."

"Our Bertha Butt doesn't have any sisters, Marc."

"Okay, well, maybe Jimmy Castor Bunch knew her dad, Tiny Butt, and…"

"I doubt it, Marc, but who knows. Anyhow, now you can see why Bertha loves to go to funerals. It is where she finds some sort of peace. It was all she knew the first years of her life so she has sought out jobs in funeral homes and churches. She has been "released" from every job in her past, and you can see why. She's bizarre, but I trust her."

We began walking again. I was trying to take in all that Katherine had told me. Shaking my head, trying to clear the macabre images, I walked beside Katherine down to Hettie Road.

Looking down at Katherine, I am always amazed at how small she is. She is about five foot two with an athletic body. Katherine has long, straight brown hair that comes to her shoulders. She has high inner eyebrows, large brown oval eyes, pronounced cheekbones, upturned nose and a wide chin. Katherine is quite attractive, but most important is that she has a face that is very trustworthy. People naturally want to talk with her, because they know she cares about them. Katherine is two years older than me and was in my older sister's class. They didn't do much together, but Katherine and I did. She has always been my favorite cousin. Katherine's mother, Lenore, is my dad's older sister. She lives in San Diego with her third or fourth husband. Or, maybe she's divorced again. I never really liked her much. Lenore was always loud and argumentative so I stayed away. She and Dad get along okay but don't talk much. Occasionally, Lenore blows into town and tries to dominate everything and everyone. Dad puts up with her, and Grandpa just ignores her. She's very self-involved.

My cousin, Katherine Hanson, certainly is nothing like her own mother. She is gentle and loving, and she is a great listener. The other difference between Katherine and her mother is that Katherine is gay. Supposedly, Aunt Lenore almost stroked out when she found out that Katherine had a female partner. Growing up, I never really thought about Katherine not dating or having a boyfriend. She was just so much fun to be around because we talked, played music, hiked, biked, and skied together. She was always my best friend. Her mother ragged on her mercilessly about getting a boyfriend, so she would be with a man and, thus okay. It didn't seem to affect Katherine outwardly, but I'm sure inside it was hard to stomach. Nonetheless, Katherine never bad-mouthed her mother.

Katherine's dad, Bentley, walked out on Lenore when Katherine was in high school. I always wondered how he lasted that long. I liked Uncle Bentley, but he never said much and was kind of a recluse. No one seemed to know where he was or what he was doing. He had just vanished. Probably wanted to keep his sanity intact before it was all gone. Nowadays, Lenore's treatment of those around her might verge on domestic abuse.

After getting a degree in social work from the University of Colorado, Katherine worked as a case manager in a drug treatment center. She had always been a very spiritual person, so I wasn't surprised when she felt God's call to ordained ministry. Katherine was a member of the Episcopal Cathedral in Denver and always active in the life of the church. With the approval of the vestry, she attended the Church Divinity School of the Pacific in Berkeley, California. After receiving her Master's of Divinity, she was ordained deacon and then priest through the cathedral. And, she stayed on there for several years. Five years ago she came back to Rua Springs and St. Mary's Episcopal Church and thus made the journey back home.

Little did anyone at the Cathedral know, or the Episcopal church itself, that Katherine was already in a relationship with her partner, Lexie Montaine, before, during, and after seminary and ordination. It wasn't spoken of publicly, but Katherine's family certainly knew about it, as did others. The church had the military's version of "don't ask, don't tell". The Episcopal church didn't condemn homosexuality. In fact, they spoke about gay people being loved and accepted as much as any straight person. The truth was, the church didn't actually want their priests to be gay. Too late, Bishop Boys, gay priests were alive and well in the church, but of course, they really didn't want to discuss it much. Hmmm... double standard? We just love having all you gay people in our church! Can't you tell? Praise Jesus!

Since I had arrived back in Rua Springs last summer, I had spent lots of time with Katherine and Lexie. Their home was about twenty miles out of Rua Springs on the way to Denver. Lexie commuted into Denver where she was an architect in a large firm. Katherine and Lexie were down-to-earth people and wonderful to be with. We laughed and cried together. I cursed God, and they praised Her. I said there probably wasn't a God anyway, and they spoke of the "God experiences" they regularly experienced. We hugged, and we said we loved one another. And we did. It was always a gift to be around Katherine, as I was now.

A health food café and store called Wild Weeds Organic Café and Market was our destination. It was located on Hettie Road just on the north end of town. We entered Wild Weeds and turned right toward the café. To the left was the market part of Wild Weeds that housed all the herbs, food, vitamins, bakery, and floral products. There was a table for two by the front windows, so we snagged it. The café was doing a brisk business with several customers taking advantage of the free Wi-Fi that Wild Weeds offered.

Katherine and I went up to the counter and ordered lunch. I selected the meatless quiche with a cup of their home brewed dark roast coffee. Katherine ordered the barley soup with a can of cream soda. Both of us had trouble resisting their Wild Weeds original brownies so we each added one of those, too. No, they weren't those pot-filled brownies we sampled in younger days. Actually, Wild Weeds could probably get a Colorado license to sell medical marijuana and really do up those pot-brownies right. Nah!

After moving our purchases off the trays and onto the table we sat and began our healthy feast. Neither of us spoke for a few moments, enjoying the taste of our food. I was thinking about Patsy's memorial service when Katherine spoke.

"So, Cousin, what did you think about the service?" She smiled at me with her "I know what you're thinking" look.

I put down my fork, dabbed my mouth with the paper napkin, leaned back in the chair, smiled, and said, "Do you really believe that stuff you read at the service?" I showed her my radiant "let's get down to it" grin.

"You know me well enough to know that I certainly believe it. I know you have to ask but come on. How can you?" Katherine smiled angelically.

"Yeah, yeah, I know. It's just...just... those words at the service don't explain why Patsy died. We all got together and spouted words about where she is now and how she had no pain and all that bunk, but it didn't help me at all. And, Katherine, don't bring up Lilly's death here. I'll never understand something so horrible, nor will I understand how come Patsy may have hung herself off that pipe in the boy's locker room. What kind of God allows that kind of pain to occur?"

Katherine looked at me with sadness in her eyes. "Marc, I don't have an answer to your questions. I don't understand it either. But, without my faith in something beyond all this," she held both of her hands out, palms up, "I don't have anything at all. I know we don't believe the same way and that's okay. It always has been that way with us since we were kids. I have to hang on tightly to my faith right now because I am also angry that Patsy is gone." She looked around the café and then back at me and shook her head once, then again. "I'm not without feelings in this. It hurts like heck. I wake up at night with a deep pain in my soul. I have screamed at God for answers, but She doesn't answer. You don't have a market on this confusion and anger, Marc. The difference is that I have to lean on my faith or I will be consumed by sorrow. You do it your way, and I'll do it mine."

We sat silently, looked at each other, and then glanced around at the other activity in the café, hoping it would help us escape from something. Reality? Maybe.

"I know you hurt, Katherine. You help other people through these hard times, but I know you also feel it deeply. There is a fine line between where we each are right now." I stopped and thought about everything I missed while seeing Patsy at school. "I thought I knew Patsy, but I missed everything, Katherine. How could I blow it so badly?" I looked into her eyes for an answer. The answer wasn't there, but her love was. It provided some relief from the sadness.

"Marc, you know I spent a lot of time with Patsy just like you did. She was in the youth group, helped all sorts of people, sang in the choir. We talked a lot about life. I knew she was sad and wrestling with something lately, but I missed it, too. I missed it, Marc. It wasn't just you. I question myself morning, noon, and night. Why didn't I know? How did I allow this to happen? See, we both are wallowing in our grief trying to understand. I know God is crying now. I just know it. God doesn't stop bad things from happening, but She is always here to comfort us."

I looked out the front window trying to find some answer out there somewhere in the distance. There was nothing written in the clouds, no voice coming from the sky. People walked down the sidewalk and drove back and forth on the street as if things were normal. Really, what is normal? I heard laughing from some part of Wild Weeds. A man nearby was talking on his cell phone quietly. Someone else was frantically texting someone. An older woman was reading a newspaper. The smells of food, flowers, herbs, and candles bombarded my nose. Quiet music played over the store speakers. I didn't see God here anywhere. If God allowed Patsy to die and didn't stop it, then what good was God? What did God really do? So, God created everything and then walked away and watched it crumble, not intervening at all? Is God just some wild concept in our minds to keep us from going totally off our rocker? Something horrible happens, and we say "Thanks God, for comforting me even though the world collapsed around me?" Get real!

The silence stretched. Each of us was into our own thoughts struggling to find some sort of meaning in all this. We had finished our meals and were sipping our drinks, winding down after eating. However, I wasn't ready to finish this conversation yet.

"When Lilly died, I wrestled God everyday begging for answers. You know my story, but something I haven't spoken to anyone about is what I did discover. Each day I searched for answers in healthy and unhealthy ways. I didn't find anything in my talking with people or in my reading for a long time. The pain was brutal, but I kept at it. I was obsessed in finding anything that would give me any sort of understanding and peace. Often, I felt like I was studying for comprehensive exams or researching for a dissertation. I read Aristotle, Plato, Kant, Descartes, Dante and others looking for something. Anything! They were interesting, but they really didn't help. I journeyed down into Dante's nine circles of hell and up through his eight levels of purgatory and on to paradise. I wanted a paradise, any paradise, but it wasn't to be." I hesitated, realizing my voice was rising, and my words were coming faster. Talking about it brought up all the pain and rage again. People nearby were looking at us with questioning looks.

Katherine waited, not interrupting me. She nodded to me to let me know she was listening and still with me, no matter what. I knew I couldn't shock her with anything I said no matter how outrageous it was. No one was better at just "being" with another person than Katherine. This was all selfish on my part, but I rushed forward.

"Finally, I researched everything I could on church history, spirituality, religion, heretics, violence, and corruption. I imagine you already know all this, but a lot of it was new to me. And, I found something that began to unravel some of the questions. Not much, but I've hung on to it." After a pause, "What do you know about Albigensianism and Mithraism?"

After a soft cough into her right fist, Katherine looked at me and smiled. "Actually, I know quite a bit. I studied some of it in seminary and then more on my own. And, I can probably guess where you are going with this. But then again, maybe not. Continue." She leaned back, put her forearms on the table, clasped her hands, and nodded again.

"Okay, this all goes back before the time of Jesus according to religious history. It is said that celebrating the light and fire by striking flints together brings Mithra out of a rock wearing the Phrygian cap holding a dagger and torch light. That cap is the red conical cap with the top pulled forward. It was like a priestly cap for the Phrygians. Mithra is a judicial figure, an all-seeing protector of truth and the guardian of cattle, harvest, and water. The birth of Mithra is celebrated on the winter solstice. The roots of Mithraism go back to Zoroastrianism, a Persian religion that was very popular about 390 BCE in Greece. Mithra was in the role of a deity and equal to the sun god. Its priests were Magi. Remember them?"

Katherine nodded, "Yep, the same magi who supposedly visited Jesus in Bethlehem when he was born."

I continued with the history, as Katherine listened and affirmed my story as I plunged forward. Mithraism, in the Roman empire, was popular with many of its emperors and the regular populace. It had seven sacraments, the same as the Catholic church, which included baptism and communion with bread and water. Mithraism also believed that after death they would live in bliss waiting for the judgment of humankind. The wicked, the rejected, and the non-baptized would be destroyed by fire, and those accepted into paradise would live with Mithra forever. And, just like Jesus later on, Mithra would ascend to heaven, at the close of all time, after Mithra's messiah brought salvation to all those who were saved. A chariot of fire was used to ascend.

"But," I said, "Paul confuses everything by mixing up the Jewish messiah idea with the Hellenistic Greek concept of Christ. Paul mixed these two up like he was beating eggs, and the result was the theology around the sacrificial nature of the Christ of Christianity."

"Interesting!" whispered Katherine. "But I'm still waiting for your great 'aha' from your 'grief walkabout'. This isn't news."

"I'm gettin' there. I'm gettin' there," I said in my best Brooklyn accent. Katherine giggled, and I gave a harrumph.

"The new kid on the block, Christianity, following mixed-up zealots like Paul, ripped off Mithraism and Judaism, and began a new gig in the religious world. Sure, they were hunted, and they hid out for a few hundred years because following the man Jesus was against the law, but they hung on and grew. Mithraism began to take a backseat to the upstart Christ followers.

"The cannibalistic elements of what is called Communion/Eucharist, and the imagery of the blood of Jesus washing away sins and granting eternal life, just like Mithra, all come from the merging of Judaism with Mithraism. The transformation of Mithra into a ram or bull preceded the eating of his flesh and blood. This parallels the death of Jesus and His rebirth, and Jesus telling his disciples they should eat and drink His flesh and blood to wash away sin and thus gain eternal life."

Drinking my now cold coffee I thought again how bizarre Christianity really was. It stole from anyone and everyone. And look at what it has become. There is almost nothing original about it. Same song, sixteenth verse.

"Hang in with me, Katherine. I'm processing this as I go along, since I have never spoken it before. So, Cousin, how am I doing?"

"Grrrreat!" She always loved to do the Tony the Tiger thing. Coming from this tiny woman it was definitely a hoot.

"Meanwhile, back at the ranch…" I raced on. "Constantine, the emperor in 313 AD, ruled that December 25 was the birthday of Jesus. He used the same day as Mithra. And, he made Christianity the official religion above all others and moved Judaism's Sabbath day, which literally means Saturday, to the Mithra 'Sun' day as it is the day of the Sun. Thus, Saturday, the Sabbath of Judaism, was abandoned in favor of the Mithras Sun-day. Cool, huh?"

"Yeah, really cool, Marc. I'm sure you are working toward a connection here."

"Patience, patience, dear priestess cousin of mine."

Trying to pull all these things together seemed easy for me when I was in hyper-drive after Lilly's death. I though it made sense then. But formulating the history into coherent sentences was much harder than I had ever imagined. I continually put off writing anything down because maybe I really didn't want to see it on paper. If it was purged from me and became external, it might heal segments of my brokenness. Then maybe I would lose Lilly, and I never wanted to let her go. Perhaps it was too frightening a leap to put it out there because the grief would make sense, and I would have to move on. Did I want to move on? Part of me did and part didn't. But Patsy Anderson's death unleashed a flood of emotions and memories for me, and it was time to unload it on someone I trusted.

Katherine was twiddling her fork, deep in thought. Time moved slowly as we both existed separately but together. I closed my eyes and let my senses explore. This was where I wasn't sure I could put my thoughts into words. Katherine solved it for me.

"Let me see if I can further translate history for you, Marc. I believe what you are heading toward is dualism: Light and dark, yin and yang, good and evil. The Christian Church has tried to stamp out dualism from the beginning. Except they have never let go of the God and Satan battle, which is curious. Am I on target here?"

"Yes, the good and evil part is where I delved in order to make some sort of sense of the world."

Katherine continued, "Another religion, Manichaeism, was a major Iranian Gnostic religion from the third to the seventh centuries. The word Gnostic means hidden. Manichaeism stands out because of its elaborate cosmology describing the struggle between a good, spiritual world of light and an evil, material world of darkness. They believed that as human history went forward light is gradually removed from the world of matter and materialism and returned to the world of light where it came from in the beginning. And Manichaeism used the name Mithras as the name of one of their deities. So, we have our connection between what you shared about Mithras and now Manichaeism in religious history. Mithras was adopted into Manichaeism just as Christianity adopted Mithraism and Judaism. So, we have two religions paralleling each other for several centuries. And, you can guess who didn't like the parallel."

"The Roman Catholic Church," I said.

"Yep, the Catholic Church was devouring everything in its path by any means possible. Manichaeism was just one of many heretical sects that the Catholic Church was out to get. Dualism was the culprit and the Church was brutal about crushing all of them. Albigensian, better known as Catharism, was a name given to a gnostic, dualistic religious sect that appeared in the langue d'oc region of France where the Cathars were. And it called itself a Christian religion, so you can just imagine what the Roman Church thought of that. They had to keep Jesus, the man and the God, on stage and dualism didn't work in their favor. The Cathars were heavily influenced by the Manichaean beliefs from the past so now we have our next connection in our sequence. Mithra to Manichaeans to Cathars."

I picked up the story from there telling Katherine that my research showed that the Manichaeans in the West had died out in the seventh century, but the dualistic thinking hadn't. Those Hellenistic Greeks who influenced Paul had the belief that a person was born and the soul of the human was always trying to escape the material body. Thus, the two were separate. Several centuries later the Cathars said that within a human being was a spark of divine light. That light, or spirit, was held captive by the corrupted physical body of humanity. There, we connect all the way back to ancient history. According to Cathar belief, the world had been created by a deity who was identified with Satan. Humanity was trapped in a defiled world created by another god, a usurper, and ruled by his debased minions.

"So," I said to Katherine, in a hollow voice, "What if there are actually two gods. A god of light and a god of dark; good and evil. One is the supreme being and dominator of the so-called heavenly part and the other is the supreme being of the earthly part. The god of light that the Christian church always prays to cannot actually do anything here on earth. He/She doesn't control it, the dark one does. Everything that goes bad on earth, like Lilly being murdered by a drunk driver, and Patsy, perhaps being so desperate she killed herself, were just normal things in the dark/evil world. The dark lord, no pun intended here, allows and even promotes evil happening. Things are out of control and always have been."

"You know I'm not going to agree with you on this, Marc. I do understand that it might give you some relief and understanding but having two gods doesn't work for me. I can't live with it. My faith won't allow it, and it doesn't comfort me at all. The one true God is still omnipotent. She just doesn't interfere with what She created. It is humanity that is faulty and not because of some dark lord corrupting life. God allows us to screw up but also invites us back, hopefully having learned something from the past experience. The light of Christ is within us, and we can choose it." Katherine paused, looking at me to see if I was getting any of this. She took in a deep breath and blew it out.

I knew we weren't going to agree. That was okay, though. I thought about her words and tried to make sense of them and her own battles with the church. As a woman, she was treated as a second class citizen by the church. As a priest, she wasn't any better off. As a gay woman, she knew the Church still had extreme prejudices. And yet, she didn't back down and somehow miraculously kept her faith. She has more guts than I do.

"What I don't get is how you put up with the church's 'good ole boy' system that has been in place forever." I worked my napkin into torn up pieces. Plunging ahead I said, "The church has been corrupt. It has lied, cheated, stole, killed, promoted celibacy and then didn't follow it and ripped off its entire structure from other religions. You know as well as I do that from the beginning the church has covered up its messes in order to develop the God, Jesus, Holy Spirit thing. It was created by males. You call God 'She,' which must piss off the Church royally. How can…"

"Marc, enough. We've had this discussion many times. It works for me. I'm doing what She, God, called me to do. But, it's on my terms. I've never said I buy into everything. I certainly don't think scripture was written by a golden pen from some Santa Claus guy in the sky. But faith and having something good to believe in helps me to help others. People are crying out for something to hang on to. You are too, by the way. The world is crashing down around us, but I'm not giving up. There is still a lot of good out there. Look what happened at Patsy's service. Didn't that do anything for you?"

I wrestled with my napkin some more. It was obliterated. I knew Katherine was right. Patsy's service did move me. It brought me to tears. And it did temporarily help ease the pain just as it probably did for many other people.

"Yes it did, Katherine," I said quietly. "I just don't understand this, though." Why Lilly? Why Patsy? I knew Katherine understood what I meant.

After several moments of silence we both stood knowing this conversation was over for now, but not forever. We would have it again. At least I had put into words what had helped me grab a gnarled hand onto something, anything. Were there two gods out there somewhere? One good, one bad? My journey had led to this point, but I would probably never know.

We walked back to St. Mary's parking lot where my truck was parked. Katherine said she and Lexie were driving down to Denver to take in a new Meryl Streep movie and do some shopping at Costco later this afternoon. Katherine and I hugged, said good-bye, and she headed back to her office to lock up. We made plans to get together next week. I stepped into my truck, cranked it up, and headed home.

My afternoon plan was to play my new Yamaha acoustic guitar. I had played very little after Lilly died. Once I moved back home, I purchased the new Yamaha to add to my collection. My calluses were building up again. Dad and I were even working on some jazz music together. Besides the great classical music he played, he was also outstanding with the jazz pieces and various other types of music. We were getting pretty good and making plans to add percussion and horns. He knew some folks who might be interested.

CHAPTER TWELVE

Sunday morning I stumbled out of my room and toward the smell of coffee. It had been another bad night of nightmarish dreams about Lilly and Patsy. The difference in last night's dreams and prior dreams was that Lilly was fading and Patsy was becoming dominant. My dream last night began with Lilly driving toward me and waving at me. I was lifting my hand to wave back when her car disappeared. Instead of Lilly waving at me, it was now Patsy. She was standing at the other end of the hallway, which was dimly lit. Patsy started moving toward me but not really walking. Floating was the more correct word. The image changed to Patsy hanging by the jump rope from the pipe in boy's locker room. She was looking down at me and speaking, but I couldn't understand her. I awoke in a cold sweat trying to shake off the image.

I felt like I was losing Lilly and was worried I wouldn't remember her in my dreams. Even though the dreams had horrendous scenes of Lilly being killed I felt myself struggling to hang on to a picture of Lilly. In an insane sort of way I didn't want to lose the gore. Sick.

Entering the kitchen I wasn't surprised to see Dad there drinking coffee and reading the paper. I was surprised to see Grandpa leaning against the sink with a steaming cup of coffee in his hand. He had on a sweatshirt that I hadn't seen before. Of course it was in gray. The front said, "*I found God!*" in large letters. When he saw me looking at him, he turned around so I could see the back. It said "*She was hiding behind my recliner!*" He turned back to face me and started laughing his wheezy laugh. What a way to wake up! There was only one place the sweatshirt could have come from: Katherine!

"Morning Dad, Grandpa," I mumbled as I headed toward the coffee pot.

"What do you have planned today?" Dad asked. Before I could respond, Grandpa jumped in.

"Me and Charlie Forman are driving over to see Vera McKesson."

My head popped up and my mouth dropped open as I looked at Grandpa. Charlie was eighty-two years old and Vera was eighty-seven. Unbelievably, all three still had licenses and were still driving. And, they had all gotten into texting on their cell phones and were burning up the cosmos with messages to each other. Grandpa, Charlie, and Vera texting? Who would have thunk?

"Uh, Grandpa, do you think it's wise for you and Charlie to drive anywhere together? I mean, uh, remember what happened the last time?"

"We've got it covered, Marc. Charlie and I talked and made a deal not to get into arguments while one of us is driving. We know it's unsafe."

I'm sure I looked like a deer caught in the headlights. "Unsafe? Unsafe? You two are a danger to society when you are on the road together. It always ends in a disaster!" I knew my voice was rising, but I couldn't help it.

Herman and Charlie were well-known around the county for the crazy accidents they got in together. Grandpa was bad enough by himself, but together they were a menace! The last time, they were parking Charlie's 1962 Plymouth Fury on Hettie Road to go into a sporting goods store. They were arguing about where to park and before Grandpa could get out of the passenger side, Charlie somehow put it in reverse and got his foot caught on the accelerator pedal with it mashed to the floor. The Plymouth screeched backward across the road and glanced off a light pole. Grandpa was dangling out the door with one foot in and one out while hanging on with one hand to the door handle. He was screaming, and I'm sure cursing, his lungs out during the ride. It was a miracle that no semis, motorcycles, baby strollers, or three-legged dogs were in its path. They didn't speak for two weeks after that. Thank God no one was hurt! The time before they were on a forest road in Grandpa's jeep and while yelling at each other, Grandpa ran off the road into a ravine. The jeep had to be winched out. Unfortunately, it wasn't wrecked so Grandpa could still drive it. Grandpa and Charlie weren't hurt, but they didn't speak to each other for several days. Those old farts acted like they were an old married couple. They always "kissed" and made up.

"Charlie and I have already decided to visit Vera, so we're going. I'm driving this time, so we'll be safe."

Amazed, Dad and I looked at each other knowing it was no use. We had had this conversation many times before. Each time Grandpa went out we expected a phone call telling us he was dead or had killed somebody. I guess we'll keep waiting. Clear the roads folks, here they come!

"What about you, Marc?" asked Dad.

"I need to catch up on some report writing for school. Things have piled up over the last week."

"How about after I get home from church you and I head into Denver and do some carousing? There's a hardware and tool show at the convention center I want to check out."

"Sounds like a plan, Dad. Hopefully, I can wrap up some of my paperwork this morning."

I settled down on the living room couch with Sunny and Kong at my feet. Picking up my coffee cup from the end table I slugged down some dark roast piñon. Through the windows I could see what a beautiful day it was. I wished that I was out there sucking in the mountain smells rather than sitting here forcing myself to do what I didn't want to do. Once again, I had to admit to myself that I really didn't like writing reports. I would rather be in the "trenches" with the kids. But, a great deal of my time as a school psychologist is spent writing reports. I know they are necessary, but I always grit my teeth and force myself to sit down and put things on paper. Even after all these years it seems like fingernails on a blackboard. Screeeeech! Ahhhhh!

One of the most recent trends in schools is called Response to Intervention, RTI. Believe it or not, RTI is matching the amount of student resources to the degree of student need and then matching the precise nature of student need to their instruction. Then, we use this student data to maximize their learning so we can tell whether what we are doing is working. We used to call it "individually guided education" (IGE) way back

Okay, I know RTI is an improved model so I can't boohoo it. There are some new beliefs that support it that at least have moved schools into the twenty-first century. I thought about some of those beliefs, "*All children can learn. Educators are responsible to teach them. Parents have a great deal of knowledge about their children and should be partners in the education system. Teachers and parents deserve the resources necessary to meet the educational needs of children. The best educational strategy is the one that works; the response to intervention approach evaluates effectiveness frequently.*" Yes! Pump fist into the air! We actually have checks and balances to see if the kid is truly making progress. How about that! Twenty-first century stuff! I had worked myself into a frenzy. Education in America drove me crazy. Why did I even care? The kids!

So, I'm reviewing our team RTI plan for a third grader named Benito. The problem is his oral reading fluency. The team created a plan to help him during second grade, set baseline data for his level of fluency, wrote an action plan, figured out how to measure it, and let it roll. I'm a new member to the team since I wasn't here last year when Benito was in 2nd grade. Another role I have with Benito is working with him on his anger. And really, who wouldn't be angry? He gets frustrated because he can't read. Benito escapes by whining, wiggling, asking for breaks, and trying to redirect his teacher to conversations unrelated to the lesson. Actually, I think he's a really cool kid. He tells great stories about all sorts of things. Of course, he tells the stories while he should be reading. Huh. Maybe what he is supposed to be reading is junk anyway. Now, now. School is fun! Isn't it?

Benito received Reading Recovery instruction the second semester of second grade. And, he has received additional help targeted at fluency and phonics this year. The analysis of the team was that incentives needed to be provided to Benito for his reading efforts, so he would be able to sustain his reading for longer periods of time. The team realizes that he has not read enough to become a fluent, accurate reader with comprehension. The goal for Benito is that by January of fourth grade, given passages from fourth grade reading curriculum material, Benito will read seventy words correctly in one minute with five or fewer errors. He will succeed. I'm sure of it.

Benito's story is all too common. His parents are first generation immigrants from Mexico, and since they couldn't really read English, he had no opportunity to read it either; nor were stories read to him in English. Benito came into second grade way behind his peers in reading skills. I really like Benito and his parents. They practice their English skills on me, and I practice my Spanish skills on them. We've all developed a pretty good relationship. But Benito is still catching up and it is tough for him. So, he does his "shuck and jive" moves and tells incredible stories to act out his anger and frustration.

Believe it or not, Benito is lucky. His parents and the team all support him in this. RTI plans don't always work like this. If the team is in disarray and the parents aren't involved, it can all lead to further problems, conflict, and acting out. Remember, kids can learn, but only if they have the support to do it.

The rest of my morning moved slowly along as I plowed through some WISC-V's and Woodcock Johnson IV's Cognitive and Achievement assessments I had completed. I also wrote up a few of my classroom direct observations and caught up on my session notes. Even though I didn't like doing these, I still made sure they were complete. This was about the kids, not me, so I always kept my focus on how we were going to help them succeed.

By noon Dad was home from church and we were making lunch to take with us on our drive into Denver.

"No bad news from your grandpa yet?" Dad grimaced as he spoke.

"Not a peep. Maybe he and Charlie won't push the world off its axis today."

"Dream on, Son, dream on."

"Yeah, Dad, I know what you mean."

We headed out to the garage, locked the house door behind us and crawled into Dad's Toyota Tundra truck. Dad backed us out and pointed the truck toward Denver.

On our return from Denver, Dad and I were discussing the new power tools he wanted to add to his store. He was mentioning the various brands, pros and cons, when both of our cell phones started beeping. A text message was coming through. Removing my iPhone from my holster, I read the screen: "h/c drunk fighting fr lwn. hp qt".

"Oh, Christ!" Dad exclaimed. He rarely cursed, but his pa brought it out at times. "Herman and Charlie are drunk and fighting on Vera's front lawn," he read from his cell as he tried to keep his eyes on the road. "Vera wants us there ASAP."

We were about ten miles out when the text came in. Dad stomped the pedal to the floor of the truck. The big V-8 engine screamed, slammed us back in the seats, and accelerated like a rocket. If I didn't know better, I could imagine that our faces were turned into putty and pushed flat into a death mask smile or grimace, as the case may be. Dad was mumbling to himself about what a total imbecile his pa was. Barely under control, I heard Dad adding a few more foul words. This was totally uncharacteristic of him, except when it came to Grandpa.

Dad rammed the truck in park when we arrived in front of Vera's place bringing it to a sudden halt. It was dusk so not totally dark. I could make out three images moving around not far away. We both bolted from the truck leaving the doors open and the *bing, bing, bing* of the keys still in the ignition. The sight was both comical and tragic at the same time.

Grandpa and Charlie were lying on the ground barely moving. Charlie had Grandpa in a headlock as the two senior citizens moved back and forth in slow motion. It looked like two gnomes practicing prime-time wrestling one move at a time. Charlie was totally bald and clean shaven, otherwise they could have been twins. One would move and the other would follow. Nearby, I spotted some empty bottles of Thunderbird. To finalize the scene, Vera was standing over them with a broom in her hands, swatting them every few seconds.

"Stop! Stop! You drunk morons!" Vera was a tiny woman herself so fit in the gnome category just like Herman and Charlie. Her voice came out as a squeak. "Stop!" *Bam, bam* with the broom she went. Her effort with the broom wouldn't have harmed or even disturbed a fly.

Dad was on the two men in a flash. "Let go, Charlie. That's enough now." Dad brought both gnomes to their feet as he grabbed them by the coat collars. They hung on his arms like bags of trash. "Grab Grandpa, Marc, and get him in the backseat and buckle him in. I'll bring Charlie."

We half walked, half dragged our charges to the truck and strapped them in. They both smelled like rank vinegar and sweat. Neither said a word. We walked back to Vera and sat on either side of her on the stoop.

"Those old coots drink and act like little boys in a pissing contest. It is always about nothing." Vera quieted and shook her head. After a few deep breaths she spoke. "I don't know why I even have them over. Of course, they are really cute and funny most of the time. Then, they bring out the bottle, slug it down, laugh, cry, and always fight." She halted, stood, said good night, and disappeared into her house.

For a lady eighty-seven years-old, she still looked and acted about seventy. Dad and I stood, trudged back to the truck, and plopped ourselves in the front seats. Dad cranked the starter, and we headed for Charlie's home. The old coots were asleep in the backseat.

As we pulled away from Vera's house I realized she lived next door to Patsy Anderson's mother. My vision narrowed and I tasted grief like dry ashes in my throat. I couldn't help but wonder what Vera knew about Patsy's life, if anything.

Or maybe Vera knew less than I did. I decided I needed to return to Vera's place and ask her about Patsy. Maybe she could help me understand. Looking at Patsy's house I saw dim light coming from behind a front window. I would also visit Vivian after I talked to Vera to share my condolences.

Dad pulled up in front of Charlie's tiny bungalow and my vision cleared as we came to a stop. Time to deal with the present.

After carrying Charlie into his place, we tossed him on his couch, locked his door, returned to the truck, and headed home. At home, we carried Grandpa in, tossed him on his bed, closed the door and returned to the living room. Dad sat on the piano bench and began to pound out his frustrations with some dirge music on his grand. I flashed on *Phantom of the Opera*. Dad's face was dark, angry. I listened for a few minutes, stood, and went to bed. Another interesting day.

CHAPTER THIRTEEN

My morning routine changed somewhat today. Instead of a bad night of sleep with the same dreams, I woke up earlier than usual feeling only halfway bad. Grandpa wouldn't be seen for most of today. He would pay the price. Again.

I decided to ride my bike up past the old cabin to get more miles in. The coffee would have to wait today. The morning light was just making a presence in the kitchen when I entered. Dad wasn't up yet so I left him a note that I was out riding and where I was headed.

Saddling up on my bike, I adjusted my helmet and secured my iPhone in its holster. It was always safer having the phone with me on these rides. I wasn't in the mood for any music except from nature therefore didn't have my ear buds connected. It was a gray fall day with a touch of moisture in the air. The dawn light was throwing a kaleidoscope shadows and muted colors around so it made it hard to gage the trail's contours and danger areas. The soft breeze was cooler than usual, hinting at the late fall snow coming soon. I was glad I dressed for it with long sleeves and long pants. Higher up it would be even cooler.

The trail I was riding was the one I had hiked a few days before. A few miles up was the old cabin that was at the edge of Dad's property. Leaves from the aspen trees were covering the trail, and the fall gold of the aspens was racing toward the end. The nights were much colder now so the leaves were saying good-bye to their lifeline, and gently floating to the ground. My bike tires were making a crunching sound as the dried leaves were shattered into mulch so they could become part of the rich nutrients for the forest soil. It would feed and nourish the Aspen trees, and they would offer their catkins in the spring and grow their leaves after the catkins had done its pollination dance with nature.

I rode past the old cabin and turned left on a rarely used trail that went around the back of the mountain. The terrain was rough, washed out in many places. The fall chill felt good on my face as I pedaled through the thick ponderosas so close that it seemed they were jumping in my way. I weaved in and out with my handlebars almost touching the brown bark of the pines at times. The forest was thick here. Rays of early morning sunlight filtered through the tops of the trees and dropped strange shadows of dark and partial light on the trail. I continued to push my legs hard following the remains of what I thought was a weak game trail. I had ridden this trail before, but it looked odd, spooky, and not recognizable today. Shadows looked like ghost figures stepping out on the trail in front of me. Some looked so real I was sure a person was standing there, but when I flashed by, the images shifted left, right, and up into nothing. I rode on.

It looked like another Monday at school as I watched students and faculty trudge into various buildings. Of course, this included me. I stopped at my office in the middle school first to get ready for the day. First on my schedule was a social skills training I was conducting with a third grade class. I chatted with Mrs. Chang a moment to see how she was doing. She worked weekends at her parent's restaurant, so she filled me in on how the business was doing. It was doing well, as usual. All of her family worked hard. They were a good example of a close family and provided a work ethic that was missing for many others. Mac McDougal, the middle school principal, was in his office with the door closed. I could hear his loud voice going after some kid. A weak "yes, sir" or "no, sir" could occasionally be heard from a small voice when Mac paused. I expelled a breath. It was only Monday!

The walk across Roark Park was quiet and serene after leaving the middle school. I was tempted to just sit on one of the concrete benches and let the day pass by, listening to the birds flitting through the trees. Clouds moved silently across the blue sky, and a slight breeze softly touched my clothing and skin.

The elementary school was warm and smelled of cleaning solutions as I entered the front entryway. There was the normal hum of children and adult voices sweeping the halls. Lisa Guerrero, the office manager, was in her usual location.

"Morning, Lisa."

"Good Morning, Doctor Thomas. How was your weekend?" She was always so bright and cheery that no matter what my mood she lifted me up.

"Not too bad. Patsy's service was difficult for me. I'm sure it was for everyone, though. Otherwise…"

"Yes, I was there. It was a nice service, wasn't it?" She seemed to run out of air.

"Well, it's good to see you, Lisa. I'm working with Mrs. Hashemi's class on social skills again. Last week kind of upset our schedule so I'm trying to get caught up."

"They will be glad to see you, I know." Lisa smiled. A teacher was bringing a young boy into the office and neither looked happy. I waved at Lisa, turned around and entered the main hallway. Turning left, I walked toward Mrs. Hashemi's classroom. It was comforting to be here with the school sounds touching my auditory senses.

Before I reached the right room I could hear the voice of Reba Bennett booming out of her classroom. That voice wasn't comforting. I hadn't seen her since the morning Patsy Anderson had died. The last I saw of her, she was shaking and moaning as she was led away from the boy's locker room. Today, it sounded like she was back to normal. I could visualize the children in her room cowering in their chairs, shaking from fear. Scott Dumas was still in her class, and I imagine she was still trying to get rid of him, poor kid. Too bad, Reba, ain't gonna happen.

Standing in the door of Mrs. Hashemi's classroom I waited there until she saw me. She stopped what she was doing, smiled at me, and came to the door.

"Welcome, Doctor Thomas! Thanks for being with us." She turned to her class and said, "Doctor Thomas is here, class."

The kids began bouncing in their seats. "Hi, Doctor Thomas!" the voices of the third graders exclaimed.

It was always nice to be welcomed into a class. After being around for awhile now, the children were getting to know who I was. They knew I wasn't a teacher, and they also knew I had a really neat room over at the middle school. Whenever I took a child to my office, they all wanted to go. I knew it was the things in my office and not really me, but that was okay.

I walked to the front of the class. "Good morning, everyone! We are going to continue our lesson about *Getting Along With Others* that we began two weeks ago. Does anyone remember what we talked about the last time?" I knew asking a question provided an opening for the children to jump in with just about anything, but it was a chance I took.

Several hands went up throughout the room. I was always amazed at the amount of energy put into raising a hand. They were practically jumping out of their chairs while waving their hands around. I pointed to a boy in the back.

"We, er, we talked about getting along with others," said the boy.

"Yes, that is correct, Simon. What did we say about getting along with others, class?" I pointed at a girl in the middle who was jumping around so much I wondered if she was on fire and trying to stomp it out.

"We said we needed to respect others and be fair even if they were different."

"Yes, Brianna, that is correct." I hoped her name was Brianna. Names were pretty easy for me to remember, but I did make mistakes. They always corrected me pretty quickly if I was wrong, but she didn't correct me. "What else did we talk about?"

I pointed to a girl in the front.

"We talked about what it was like to be unhappy and not feeling liked."

"Very good, Ashley. Okay. I'm going to give you a worksheet you can each write on in your pod groups." Mrs. Hashemi had her class sitting in pod groups of six children each, so I used those pods as groups to do activities. I walked around the room handing out a worksheet entitled "Benefits of Getting along with Others".

When everyone had a copy I spoke, "What I want you to do in your groups is to explore the different benefits of getting along with others. Write those down on the top part of your worksheet. Remember last time we talked about benefits like not being left out of games and having more friends. Those are the kinds of benefits I want your groups to explore. Then, on the bottom part of your worksheet explore different behaviors that help us get along with others and write those down. Those are things like don't lie and tell the Truth. After awhile we will discuss these all together and make a list on the board. Okay, start exploring."

I walked around the room listening to each group and asking questions. They all worked well together and came up with great examples while sharing personal experiences. The "caretaker kids" were easy to spot. They put their hand on a shoulder and said nice things. Of course, there were the children who hung back trying not to share much about themselves. I didn't pick up any major problems though.

With about ten minutes left, I brought the class back together and the groups shared a few things that we put on the board. Mrs. Hashemi wanted to leave the benefits on the board for awhile to remind the kids. I said good-bye to the class, thanked Mrs. Hashemi and started walking back to my office.

"Doctor Thomas?" came a woman's voice.

I turned and saw Mrs. Frazier, a fourth grade teacher, coming toward me. "Hi, Mrs. Frazier. How are you?"

Trudy Frazier was a tall, gangly woman probably in her forties. She had blond hair cut in a bob, a narrow, longish face with blue eyes, a long straight nose, and narrow, thin lips. She wore khaki slacks with a denim light blue blouse buttoned to the top. Trudy Frazier wasn't exactly feminine, but not masculine either. Standing in front of me, I could tell by the look on her face that she was in a lot of pain. She was pinched and barely hanging on with worry lines across her forehead and between her eyes.

"I'm not doing too well right now. I was....was wondering if I could speak with you sometime." Her eyes dropped toward the floor probably from embarrassment.

"Sure, I would be happy to speak with you. Any time better for you?"

"This is very hard for me. I've never talked to anyone about personal things before. I...just...I just don't know what to do."

"We'll talk, okay. Soon. Do you have any breaks this afternoon?"

"About two? My class is at music then. I'll come to your office."

"Sounds good. I'll help however I can."

She nodded to me, turned around, and walked toward her room. I watched her for a moment then turned and moved toward the front office. People would probably be surprised at how often teachers want to speak with a school psychologist. It's not all about the kids. The adults have troubled lives also. I couldn't imagine what was going on with Trudy Frazier. Something painful, that's for sure. It took lots of courage to even ask me for help. I only hope I can.

Midmorning I was out on the playground doing a direct observation of a second grade girl. A team was working with her on several academic and social issues. I would conduct an intelligence test and several other assessments before we met as a team for her IEP. Part of what I often did with assessments was observe children in various situations like the playground, classroom, and lunchroom. It all depended on the reason for the referral. This girl, Nico Gabriel, looked like she had just drunk two cans of Jolt. She was a whirlwind running full out around other children and playground equipment. As I watched Nico move toward a group of girls she looked like an NFL running back. She knocked two girls down and just kept going

"Nico!" yelled a teacher's aide, "Nico, stop right now!"

Nico didn't stop. She looked like her eyes were almost closed. Her hands were straight out to her side like airplane wings. "Nico Gabriel!" yelled the aide. That aide and another teacher were racing after Nico who was still imitating an airplane and an NFL running back going up and down. The goal posts were in sight! Nico would score!

Both ladies reached Nico at the same time. Nico didn't score. Each grabbed an arm and lifted her up. Nico was so into the groove of running that her feet kept moving even off the ground.

"Nico! Stop! Stop now!"

She looked up in wonder at one woman and then the other. They put her on the ground and started pointing at her first and then the girls Nico knocked down.

I had seen enough to write up my observation. From the other information I had received about Nico we were probably looking at ADHD characteristics. Of course, only an M.D. can make the ADHD diagnosis, so we could only describe characteristics and possibly recommend a doctor's involvement to see about a diagnosis. It was sad, because her hyperactivity was interfering with her academic progress. But, she certainly was entertaining. Humph. Maybe I should put that in my observation and see what happens.

A group of kids were lined up waiting to get on swings. I watched them trying to own their space. It was a battle as a great deal of pushing was going on.

"Get your dick outta my ass!" screamed a young boy.

Huh? I stopped in midstep wondering if I had heard correctly. A teacher raced over to line of kids and straight for a young boy with bright red hair. Behind the young boy was a young girl smiling at the teacher. I looked at the boy and then the girl and figuratively scratched my head. Okay, so if it was the boy who said 'get your, etc. etc.' and the girl was behind him in line then how could she have had the right body part? Interesting! Maybe kids were made different now-a-days. Oh well...

"Doctor Thomas!" panted a middle school girl as she ran up to me. "Come quick. Mr. McDougal wants you. It's an emergency!" She leaned over and put her hands on her knees to catch her breath.

The out of breath girl and I ran back to the middle school and into the office. I was breathing hard and trying to slow down my heart rate when Mac McDougal stormed in.

"This is bad, Marc. I knew something was in the wind, and here it is."

"What's going on?" I asked, breathing heavily.

"Come with me. I'm trying to keep a lid on this." His face was grim. His jaw muscles were twitching rapidly, and he was clinching his fists at his side. "It's in the boy's bathroom."

Mac, with me following in his wake, hurried out of the office and down the hall toward the boy's bathroom. So far the hallway was quiet, so whatever it was hadn't made the school "news" yet. The middle school chief custodian, Mr. Oakley, stood outside the door of the bathroom. He nodded his head as Mac and I entered. Mr. Piño, the middle school football coach and science teacher, sat beside a boy on wooden chairs that must have been brought in to the bathroom recently. The boy was large enough that he could have been a high school student. Middle school was very tough for boys because the girls were outgrowing them at a rapid pace, and the boys sometimes didn't begin their growth spurt until later in high school. This boy was an exception though. This boy was staring at the floor with an angry look on his face. Pieces of gray duct tape were scattered around the floor.

Mac leaned over and whispered to me, "Mr. Oakley, the custodian, came in a short time ago to clean up and heard muffled screaming noises behind a stall door. He opened the door and found the boy duct-taped to the toilet. His pants were down and he was on his knees with his head above the toilet. His private parts were spray painted red. He had duct tape across his mouth and eyes, and someone used quite a bit of duct tape to wrap him up and bind him to the toilet."

"Oh, God!" I mumbled.

At the beginning of the year I had met both Mr. Oakley and Mr. Piño. I had only said hello to them a few times since then. Mr. Oakley seemed like a nice guy, did his job, and kept a low profile. Custodians faded into the background in school and were often invisible until needed. Mr. Oakley was a small man with a burr haircut. He was quite plain and really nondescript. Mr. Oakley didn't stand out; the invisible man.

Mr. Piño was a large Hispanic man with a kind face and a deep voice. He did stand out because of his size, as he was probably six foot four and about 275 pounds. His dark features were movie star handsome so the kids seemed to want to be near him. He was a big teddy bear.

Mac was speaking, "Mr. Oakley cut off the duct tape and paged me on his school cell phone. I asked Mr. Piño to help us. His aide is handling his class. I've also called the sheriff's office. This may be a crime of unlawful restraint and sexual abuse. I'm not sure, though. His mom has been called. No dad on the scene. I need your help here with this boy. His name is Aaron Lepowitz. He's a seventh grader. Unfortunately, he has been on my radar this year. He is making a name for himself being a school bully."

Walking over to Aaron, I kneeled down in front of him. He continued to stare and the floor. "Aaron? I'm Doctor Thomas, the school psychologist. I'm here to help you." Aaron looked down at me, which was a start.

"Yeah." Aaron said abruptly with force.

Aaron looked directly in my eyes. "I will get them," he hissed.

I stood almost falling backward. Aaron slowly stood. Mr. Piño slowly removed his hand from around Aaron's shoulder.

"Doctor Thomas is a good guy, Aaron. He'll make sure you are okay. He will take you to his office until your mother arrives," said Mac quickly.

Aaron looked at me with anger that startled me. Mac opened the restroom door and checked the hallway both directions. He held the door as I led Aaron out and to the right toward my office.

Once inside my office I closed the door behind us. Aaron had never been in here before, so he stood in the middle of the room and looked around at the various things I had on the shelves and table. I let the silence hang for a few moments before I spoke. "Aaron, it's okay to just sit and wait for your mother or you can explore my room. We don't have to talk unless you want. Your mother should be here soon. I'm here to help you and just listen. I'll do whatever I can to help you get through this."

Aaron sat in a small chair beside me. All the chairs were small, so I was on his level. He tapped his left foot on the floor and took hold of the chair seat with both hands. The silence stretched. I didn't expect him to speak. I was wrong.

"I didn't see anyone, but I will find out who did this," said Aaron through clinched teeth. His adolescent voice was changing so it was part boy part adult male. His warning was clear. I waited. "Someone shoved me into the restroom and taped my mouth and eyes. No one spoke at first. Then, someone whispered in my ear, *This is for Patsy, asshole.* I don't know any Patsy." Aaron glared at me challenging me to contradict him.

Patsy? My mind whirled. Who was Patsy? Why did someone go after Aaron? The only Patsy I knew was Patsy Anderson. I couldn't connect this. This was the middle school not the high school where Patsy was.

We sat with the quiet. I couldn't imagine the terror he had just experienced. Aaron didn't seem traumatized though. He was all anger from head to toe.

After a soft knock on my door, I stood up and opened it to Mac McDougal. "Aaron's mother is here." I nodded. Mac stepped back and let her into my room.

She ran to Aaron and folded him into her arms. Tears were running in rivers down her cheeks. I closed the door and stood silently. These times were always gut-squeezers for me. It was hard for me to see and feel the depth of their pain, and I worked hard to stay in control. Tightening my jaw, I hung on.

Finally, Aaron's mother wiped her tears on her sleeve and stood back from him. "Are you okay, honey?" She didn't wait for an answer. "What happened? Are you hurt?" Her questions began pouring out. I handed her a box of tissues.

"Mrs. Lepowitz, I'm Dr. Thomas, the school psychologist." She reached out her hand and shook mine in greeting.

"What's going on here, Doctor Thomas? All I've been told is that Aaron was involved in an incident and I needed to come."

"Why don't we sit down?" I suggested to her. She sat where I had sat with Aaron before, and he sat beside her. I pulled up another small chair and sat. I hesitated. Not knowing what to say. How do you tell a mom her son was duct-taped to a toilet and his private parts spray painted red? And in school where he was suppose to be safe? This was new to me, and I've seen a lot. Unreal!

"Aaron, is it okay if I speak with your mom about what you told me?"

He shook his head okay and looked straight ahead not making eye contact.

"Mrs. Lepowitz, Aaron was going into the boy's restroom and someone shoved him in, grabbed him from behind, and put duct tape over his eyes and mouth. He doesn't know who did it. They put him in a bathroom stall and taped him to the toilet." I left out the pants and paint part for now. This was hard enough to share.

"Oh, no! Oh, no! My God! Oh, dear God! Why? Why would someone do this?"

"I don't know, Mrs. Lepowitz. I really don't know." She wasn't blaming the school yet, but that might come. I was preparing myself for the blast.

"Oh, Jesus! Aaron, oh Aaron!" She took him in her arms again. "Why? Why?"

"I'll be here to help you and Aaron whenever I can. The sheriff's office has been called because we need their input. They may be here already. You will want to stop by the ER and have them check Aaron for any burning from the tape being removed." I couldn't say anything about the legal part, if there was one. "You are welcome to stay here and talk." I looked at both of them for a moment. "Aaron, I'm always here for you, so we can get together again, if you want. Just let me know."

Mrs. Lepowitz looked at Aaron for a few seconds. "Aaron," she said through clenched teeth, "we will get whoever did this to you. Count on it!"

Aaron looked up at his mom and gave her a chilling smile. He actually smiled!

They stood. I leaned forward and put out my hand to Aaron. He looked at my hand and walked past me without shaking hands. Controlling myself and feeling like a complete hypocrite I said, "Aaron, I'll be here for you. Or, if you want to talk with someone else out of school, I understand. I can help you with that, too."

There wasn't any reason to review everything that happened. It was not time to relive the horror or say sweet things about how I understood how hard this was for him. I didn't understand what he had been through, so saying I understood this was total bunk and unprofessional. The truth was I wasn't sure what I felt for him.

There was a knock on my office door. I opened it. Mac was there with a deputy sheriff standing behind him. "The deputy would like to speak with Aaron for a few moments."

"Aaron, are you okay staying a few more minutes to speak with the deputy?" I asked

Aaron just glared at me defiantly.

The deputy shrugged his shoulders and walked past me into my office.

Leaving the room after the deputy entered, I waved back at Aaron and his mother, closed the door behind me and went to the outer office. Mrs. Chang and Mac were both looking at me. I shrugged. What could I really say?

"There has not been a peep from anyone about this," stated Mac. "It is as if whoever did this was invisible." Mac placed his arms across his chest. His anger was a seething caldron that looked like it would explode out of him at any moment. "This was well-planned, devious, and evil as hell! Pardon me, Mrs. Chang." He looked toward her. She nodded, understanding. "I'm going to find out who did this to Aaron and our school!"

Heaven help those students, I thought.

CHAPTER FOURTEEN

Lunch was with the elementary school kids. Most kids liked having any adult eat with them, but since I wasn't a teacher, they liked me even more. It was about trust and word had spread quickly that I was a trustworthy, fun guy. I didn't dole out punishment like a teacher so I was mostly okay. Once a week I sat with a different age group of students.

Today I was with the fifth graders. They were at the beginning of that stage where they were okay with adults, but they were starting to question our sanity as they rightly should. The kids around me talked about the new songs they were downloading on their iPods. It helped me to learn what music they were into. The "tweens" as they were called, listened to music I had never heard of. I had to ask them who played it, and what they liked about it. Some kids were still using the word "cool" to describe their songs.

Others used the word "sweet," not as in a sweet taste though. Everyone was called a "dude." No dudettes? Hmmm...They also used words like omigod, scream, woo-hoo, and score. Kids! Entertainment, dude! Sweet! It's why I love this job.

After lunch I went back to my office in the middle school. More and more referrals were coming in, and it seemed impossible to keep up. I needed to clone myself. Nah, we don't need two of me.

My first appointment was with a seventh grade girl who was falling further and further behind in science and math and getting more and more frustrated; a deadly mix. She was already qualified for special education services. The team decided it was time to add psych services once a week. I joined the team and was supposed to meet with Jaylee Wright last week. Of course, that didn't happen because of Patsy's death.

I stood in the doorway of Jaylee's science class. Mr. Piño, who had helped out with Aaron earlier today, walked over to me. "Who do you need today, Doc?"

"Jaylee Wright," I answered. "Oh, and, Mr. Piño, thanks for your help with Aaron earlier."

"Yours too, Doc. I'll get Jaylee."

When Jaylee stood up from her chair and came to the door with Mr. Piño, I watched the other students in class. They were all staring at us. Confidentiality in schools? They all know if the school psychologist comes to the door of their room that someone is receiving some kind of psych services. It is already a label. There is no way around it. Might as well stamp their forehead. Kids can be very cruel about this. No doubt, the special education kids get attention from other students and some of it is not so good.

"Jaylee, this is Doctor Thomas. He is the school psychologist you met in our meeting a couple of weeks ago. He will spend some time with you each week. Okay?"

I stuck out my hand to Jaylee. She was gaining some height, so I didn't have to lean over. She lifted her hand to mine and we shook. "Hi, Jaylee, good to see you again. How about we go down to my office and see how your week is going? Sound good?"

She looked at me and then looked away. "Okay," she said in a singsong voice. It was a nice sound, like alto bells ringing.

We entered the outer office and I said hello to Mrs. Chang as we went into my office. "Sorry about the small chairs, Jaylee. Elementary students come over here, also."

"That's okay," Jaylee said.

She sat and looked around my room. It was always fun to watch their faces as they scanned my room for the first time; eyes big, mouth slightly open. Some had a look of wonder and others had a puzzling over what they had just stumbled into. Jaylee had the wonder look, like maybe this wouldn't be so bad.

I let the silence stretch as she searched each area of the room for...for what? Help? Magic? Healing? After a few seconds of silence, I finally spoke.

"Jaylee, do you remember what we discussed in that first meeting?"

She looked at me, studying me, thinking. "Yes. I have been frustrated in class because I have trouble understanding the math and science stuff. I just can't get it, and I've caused problems."

Good summation by her. It wasn't really complicated and maybe the two of us could talk about how and why the frustrations come out in class. "I'm sure it is frustrating to not understand what is going on. Maybe you and I can talk about it. You don't know me well, but I'm a good listener and our conversations stay just between us. It's called confidential talk, just you and me."

"You won't tell my teachers?"

"No, Jaylee, I won't." She was quiet for a time and then rose and stepped over to the sand tray. She began running her fingers through the sand, combing it, making rows like a newly plowed field.

"It is just so hard. I really try but can't get it." Her words trailed off. I waited. "Other kids make fun of me. They call me names that make me angry. Why do they have to be so mean?" Jaylee was sniffling now rubbing the back of a hand against her nose. I handed her the box of tissue. "They call me dunderhead and lunkhead and dunce." Hearing Jaylee speak about the abuse from some kids made me want to strangle them. "Finally, I can't take it anymore and I scream at them to stop. They laugh, and I'm the one who gets in trouble!" Tears were running down her cheeks. She swiped at them with tissue as if they were to blame and she would get them. "It's just not fair."

I wanted to hold her and tell her everything would be okay. That wouldn't happen, but I still hurt for her. Damn. The pain some of these kids have to go through. Some social skills training was in order for that classroom. Mr. Piño would approve it, I was sure.

Jaylee didn't say much more during the rest of our time together. I began some training with her on managing her anger when it arose. We didn't have much time today so didn't get far with it. What I wanted to say was, "Well, Jaylee, when they start to call you names just pick up your desk and drop it on them. That will stop them." I didn't say that. It was just my fantasy. I took her back to class saying we would meet again next week. Thirty minutes a week to help her with this? Who was I kidding? Sometimes I felt helpless in my job, and it all seemed futile.

Pain and anger didn't decrease for me because at two o'clock Trudy Frazier, the fourth grade teacher, showed up at my office. I had forgotten she was coming. My schedule was like a house of mirrors and a madhouse mixed together. Where am I? Who am I? Why am I here? They're coming to take me away ha, ha! They're coming to take me away ha, ha!

Trudy knocked on the door frame of my office. I looked up at her, temporarily startled. I'm sure my face showed it as she quietly said, "Oh, did I catch you at a bad time?"

Quickly rearranging my face into a smile, I stood and reached out to shake hands with her. "No, not at all. I was just lost in thought for a moment." This was all true, but I had forgotten about her coming.

"Are you sure? I can come back another time."

"Come in and take a seat." I pointed at the small children-size chairs. We both grinned. Progress. The first rule is to make a connection with the client. We just made that connection through small chairs.

"I'm right at home with these chairs," said Trudy brightly. She looked around my room taking in all the toys, games, drawing items, and the sand tray. "My, oh, my, Doctor Thomas. If I had known you had this much fun over here, I would have come sooner."

After a few beats a cloud of anguish came over her face. She looked at me for a moment and then dropped her eyes to the floor. Moisture was at the edge of her eyes. I moved the box of tissue closer to her letting her know it was okay to have tears if she needed.

"It's just...I don't really...you know...beginning this is very painful. I'm very embarrassed...humiliated. Other teachers say you are a good listener and trustworthy. I just didn't know where to go."

I wanted to say to her that it was okay but that would be very dumb. For sure, it wasn't okay. The pain was radiating off her in buckets. "Take your time, Trudy," I said softly. Brilliant! What a comment. What do you say in a time like this? Maybe—life sucks doesn't it, Trudy?

She opened her mouth to speak, stopped, tried again. "Things have not been good with me and my husband, Ronnie. This goes way back now. We are kind of ...existing together." Trudy took in a deep breath and closed her eyes tightly. She opened her eyes and looked at me seeking out trust. I nodded to her. "I have always been the initiator of sex in our marriage. Ronnie has often turned me down saying he was too tired. I always thought it was the woman who was too tired but not with us. It's him.

"We have two children, and he is a great dad. He helps around the house, provides part of the income, and doesn't harm anyone. After awhile, though, I have stopped beating myself up about not being attractive enough for him to want me and have just, sort of, become numb. We never have sex anymore." Trudy stopped, licked her lips, and blew her nose.

Listening to her speak, I had a bad feeling about what was coming. There were various scenarios and none were good. I sat on the edge of my small chair with my shoulders hunched over, tension building in my chest.

"The other night I woke up, and Ronnie was gone from the bed. I thought maybe he had fallen asleep in the living room watching television. Walking down the stairs, I saw light coming from under his office door. It wasn't quite shut, so I quietly pushed it open so as not to disturb Ronnie if he was asleep. Oh, God, I thought I was going to throw up." Trudy was biting down on her lower lip so hard I thought she would draw blood. It was taking all of her energy to hold herself together. Trudy was volcanic molten lava ready to explode.

"I swallowed my bile and looked again at Ronnie. I thought if I blinked the entire nightmare would disappear. It didn't." She swallowed, as if choking back that same bile. "Oh, God...Ronnie was sitting in front of the computer screen. His pants were down around his ankles. On the screen was a pornographic scene of two women having graphic sex. Ronnie was masturbating, and making mewing noises, and gyrating around in the chair. For a moment I was paralyzed, couldn't move, I was so stunned. When I came to, I quietly left the room, went upstairs to our bathroom, and vomited."

I thought she might vomit again right in my office. She was gagging back her visions. This wasn't my first choice as to what was going on, but it was close. I thought it might be child pornography. This was bad enough. She grabbed a wad of tissues from the box, blew her nose, again and continued.

"I didn't know what to do with what I had witnessed. I was appalled and yet hurt so much, because he rejected me for Internet sex. How could he do that? It isn't real? It is non-threatening, non-intimate, non-emotional sex. There is no commitment!" Her voice was raising, and I hoped nobody was walking past my door. "He was cheating on me with a computer screen! How do I compete with that?" Trudy held back her tears. I could tell she had made a deal with herself not to shed tears about this. Her rage was too deep.

"When Ronnie left for work the next morning I went into the office and explored his computer. He is so stupid he doesn't even have a password to lock it up. I checked his Internet history and discovered several porno sites he subscribed to that went back a long way. These weren't new sites. I looked at his Outlook Express and found dozens of emails to women where he discussed having sex with them. It was vulgar, filthy trash; things I couldn't even imagine. His fantasies were horrible." She stopped, drained, bent over with her elbows on her knees, and her head resting in her upturned hands.

Our time was almost up. It was too short, but I wasn't set up to do this kind of therapy in school. I would need to refer her out but let her know I was still here. I couldn't really see her here if she was in psychotherapy on the outside. That's the way it works in schools. Short-term crisis work was all I could do in situations like this. I had to leave her with something helpful.

"Trudy, I know telling me this was probably one of the hardest things you have ever done. I want to be able to get you in with someone I trust who will be able to help you. Talking with me was a major step. I know you'll have to tell this again depending on what you decide to do. Would you like the names of some therapists who can help you further?"

Trudy looked up at me and nodded yes. "I really need to know what to do now. I haven't confronted Ronnie yet, and the longer I hold this in, the more filled with rage I am. I know you don't have time to see me much, but I just needed to tell someone and get a direction to go. I'm afraid I will do something I'll regret, and I don't want to do that."

"Okay, Trudy. I do know Ronnie has a problem and needs help. When confronted he may admit it or deny everything and make light of it. This is serious, so no matter what he does, you need to take care of yourself and your children. This impacts all of you." I wrote down three names and telephone numbers and handed them to her. "These are not referrals. I can't do that, because it would be best for you to decide and make your own choice if you want to speak with someone else. If you choose to do so, I would say that you need to call each of them and see if any of them seem like people with whom you would feel safe. You interview them. They will need some details, but you decide."

After some final words and a thank you, Trudy left my office. Dang, I felt totally deflated, exhausted after hearing her story. I believed Ronnie might be a sex addict and needed help, but as a school psychologist I couldn't make that diagnosis. Also, because he was into porn didn't necessarily make him an addict. I loved the names that sexual addiction was now called. Calling it something like sexual dependency or sexual compulsivity seemed to take the sting of it away.

As I thought about everything Trudy had told me, I remembered a workshop I attended a few years ago. It was about the effects of sex addiction on couples and families. The thing that stood out for me, no pun intended, was that most couples didn't seek any type of help. They just suffered. The stigma of it was enough to play ostrich. There is a fear of others finding out, and that even with therapy, it wouldn't help. From meeting Trudy I believed she would seek help, but what about Ronnie? I might never know. They were in for a rough ride, that's for sure. And Ronnie hadn't gone blind yet, so...

I worked over at the high school on some assessments the remainder of the afternoon. The final bell rang. I gathered up my papers, loaded up my bag and said good-bye to Mrs. Neeley in the front office. I needed to go back to my office at the middle school so was heading for the door to the outdoor common area, when I heard someone yelling from down the hall. Turning around I saw a young girl waving her hands at the other end of the hall near the side entrance. Mrs. Neeley and some of the other teachers stepped out of their rooms.

"Something has happened," she yelled. The hallway was mostly empty, so her voice echoed off the walls and ping-ponged back and forth. "Something in the parking lot!"

A couple of the teachers and I hurried down the hall toward the girl. We all exited the building and moved quickly toward the parking lot. The loud cursing could be easily heard long before we could even see what was going on.

"God dammit to hell! Son of a bitch! I'll kill whoever did this! I'll kill 'em! God dammit!"

A large crowd had gathered in the center of the student parking lot. As we got closer, I could see that everyone was gathered around a large bright red Dodge Ram 4 by 4 truck.

At least I thought it was red. It was streaked with mud and dirt as if someone had driven it through a blizzard, rain storm, dirt storm and tornado just to decorate it. It sat high on seventeen-inch wheels also decorated with all colors of mud. Except those large wheels were flat. Huh? What? Flat as in no air?

Pacing back and forth in front of the truck was none other than Arnold Purdy. I recalled his sneer aimed toward me at the football game last week.

"Those fuckers! I'll kill 'em! Whoever did this is dead!"

He kicked the front bumper of the truck as if this was all the truck's fault. It was my guess now that this beautiful Dodge truck with a Hemi engine, looking like it had been to hell and back, was Arnold Purdy's. Of course, he may have rented it for the day or even stole it. Whatever the case, he was definitely entertaining the student gathering. Or, maybe it wasn't even his truck, and he did this every day after school...kind of like a school play!

Huddled nearby with scowls on their faces were the two students from last week who were laughing at the gifted student whose book bag had mysteriously dropped on the floor. They seemed to be disciples of Arnold Purdy. They could have been SS storm troopers the way they marched back and forth seething with anger and spouting foul words.

"We'll kill 'em!" They parroted back to Arnold. "Whoever did this is dead!"

There must be an echo out here somewhere. Maybe the mountains do that. Sheep. They were just sheep. Arnold is the leader here.

I pushed through the gathering of students to get closer to Arnold. By the looks on the student's faces I could tell they were loving the drama. Maybe blood would be shed! All right! This is great! This was a mob-like mentality.

"Hey, Arnold, what's up here?" I said as I stood in front of him.

He was a tall kid, about six foot two, beefy, but already turning to fat. Probably too much beer and starch. His brown hair was in a buzz cut as in a skinhead look. Arnold had yellow/brown beady eyes like a reptile. He had a long, wide, hooked nose with large nostrils. He had puffy lips on a moon-shaped face, which had zits all over it. Arnold wore camouflage colored pants and shirt with black lace-up boots.

"Who are you?" he snarled at me.

"I'm Doc Thomas, the school psychologist. Can I help in some way?"

"Yeah? So what. I didn't ask for a shrink!"

"I'm just here to see if I can help out. What seems to be the problem?"

"Problem? Problem?" he roared at me. "You're a problem! Yeah, you're a problem!" He looked around to see if his disciples and other students were watching. He needed to keep up his image.

I ignored his sarcasm. "It looks like you have some flat tires on your truck. I'm guessing this is your truck, Arnold. Right?"

"So what if it's my truck. What of it?"

"No problem with it being your truck. I'm just trying to see if I might help."

"Don't need your help! Don't need no one's help! I'll fix this on my own, and I'll fix whoever did this!" He glanced around again seeing if his audience was with him. Arnold hesitated, waiting for applause. None came. A small "yeah" came from one of his disciples. It was weak, though. Arnold was losing his crowd now as several students walked away.

"No problem, Arnold." I moved to the opposite side of his truck and looked down at the tires. "It looks like all of your valve stems have been cut off, Arnold." Someone had the stones to go after Arnold. Now that was interesting. Who would challenge him? I didn't have a clue...yet. "Would you like for me to call the sheriff's office? It is vandalism."

"Just stay out of this! I said I would fix it, pal!"

"Just for the record, Arnold, I'm not your pal." I began walking back toward the high school. "Have a good day, Arnold!" I lifted my right hand and wiggled my fingers. I couldn't resist. All of a sudden the voice of the boy Arnold and his crew had surrounded behind the stands at the football game last weekend came back to me in a rush.

The voice was speaking to Arnold, "I said I wouldn't try anything or you would regret it, you brainless camel face."

You will regret it, Arnold. Huh. Maybe this was payback. But, by who? I had a very strong gut feeling that we should all be prepared to see more of this. Oh, crap! A school war?

Behind me, Arnold began his chant again. "I'll kill 'em, god dammit!" His echoing disciples came back with their designated part. Most of the students had left. Show over.

Now that I had met Arnold Purdy face-to-face, I knew this would not be the last time we squared off. Icy fingers ran up and down my spine as I thought about that another encounter with Arnold. Not good. I recalled an encounter I had with a similar student down in New Mexico. I was involved in getting him suspended for bullying special ed students. He too was nothing but a thug with poor self-esteem who had to build himself up. I know, I know. It's not his fault. It was his home environment. Yadda, yadda, yadda. But, that kid and Arnold are still bullies and thugs.

The New Mexico kid was arrested after breaking into my home holding a piece of steel pipe. He broke into our backdoor one night. I was watching a movie in the living room, and Lilly was in the bedroom. The kid came at me with the pipe before I even noticed him in the room. I was just starting to stand when a blur behind the kid rushed into the room. Before I even realized what was going on the kid was on the floor, out like a light. Lilly stood there with a six-cell Maglite in her right hand. She was just coming out of the bedroom when she saw the kid enter the living room. Grasping the Maglite from the bedroom she came out and did her thing. Everyone should own a Maglite for protection...or have a courageous woman around!

I would need to watch my back now, I admitted to myself as I entered the high school. The school was dead. The only sounds were the sounds of vacuums cleaning up after another day of school, and my rubber sole Clarks squishing on the tile floor. A shiver ran through my body. I remembered one time as a teenager being in the school after dark. I tucked that memory away for now. Darkness still frightens me when I am in strange places. I froze up, expecting something horrible to happen. Too many horror movies as a kid? Maybe or maybe not. Time to get over to the middle school, lock up my office, and head home.

Driving down the school road into Rua Springs I made a decisión to drop by Vera's and Vivian's before heading home.

I didn't really want to see Vivian because I knew it would be very emotional for me. Her grief would still be so new that I didn't know what to expect.

Stopping in front of Vera's place it looked very different in the daylight. There weren't two gnomes wrestling on the front lawn dressed like Grandpa and Charlie for one thing. I shut off my truck, grabbed my keys and stepped out. Closing the door I looked up and saw Vera standing on the front porch.

"I knew you would be back and not to talk about Herman and Charlie," said Vera in a clear voice.

Joining her on her porch we sat in colorful metal outdoor chairs that had seen a few years, but they were still functional. "You knew, huh?"

She looked over toward Vivian's house. "I've known Patsy since she was born. There isn't much to tell really. She was one of the nicest young girls I have ever know. She helped me with chores even when she was a little girl. Patsy always wanted to help. She stayed with me sometimes when her mother was working late." Vera wiped her eyes with a denim shirt sleeve.

Stumbling with my words I quietly said, "I guess, er, you must have known her well."

Vera looked at me with a sad smile. "That's just it, Marc, I didn't." She shook her head slowly as if it took an incredible amount of energy. "I don't have any idea what happened with her. None at all. I'm as shocked as everyone else and I may have been one of the closest people to her most of her life."

I understood everything Vera said and at the same time I understood nothing.

We sat together in our own thoughts for a few more minutes listening to the wind blow through the trees and the birds singing in the branches above.

"Take care of yourself, Marc." And with that Vera stood, opened her front door, entered, and disappeared behind the closed door.

With a leaden feeling in my legs I stood, stepped off Vera's porch and cut across the grass to the Anderson front door.

Ringing the door bell I stood with my hands in my pockets like a man going to the gallows. I almost hoped the door would not open.

It did. "Yes?" said one the women I had seen with Vivian at Patsy's service.

"Hi, I'm Marc Thomas from school." I felt like I was being observed through a microscope. "I just wanted to stop by and extend my condolences to Vivian."

"She's resting and I don't want to disturb her." The gatekeeper protecting Vivian.

"Okay, I understand, just tell her Marc Thomas stopped by and…"

"Who is it Beth?" Vivian had stepped around Beth to see who was at her door.

"Hi, Vivian, I just wanted to say hello. I don't want to bother you."

"Ah, hi, Marc, ah, I'm not doing very well." Vivian ran out of words for a moment.

Her face showed every second of her agony, grief, and confusión. There were so many questions I wanted to ask her but I knew now was not the time. My questions were selfish. I wanted to know how I had failed Patsy. Wrong time, wrong place.

"Well, ah, maybe we can talk another time, Marc. I'm not doing very well."

Her words were clear. *I'm not doing very well.* I knew she was barely functioning. Any sense of sanity was a long way off.

"I'll check on you again, Vivian. I hope that is okay."

"Please do, Marc, I just can't cope right now."

And with that the front door closed. I stood looking at it for a second or more and then turned and walked back to my truck. Driving home I felt numb and selfish worrying about why I felt more lost than ever about understanding Patsy.

CHAPTER FIFTEEN

Dad and I had a tomato and cucumber salad and barbecued salmon for dinner. My job was the salad. I minced some garlic, thinly sliced a section of onion, and placed it in balsamic and red wine vinegar to set for a few minutes. Following that I washed and chopped up basil and oregano leaves. The cucumbers and tomatoes were next. Those were washed, the cucumbers sliced into coins, and the tomatoes into wedges. These were placed in a salad bowl and sprinkled with sea salt. Olive oil was mixed with the vinegar and I dressed the veggies. Not bad for an amateur chef. Meanwhile Dad had seasoned the salmon with a combination of miso and soy sauce. This was painted on top before going on the grill. It was like sitting in a five star restaurant when we began consuming our creations. It doesn't get any better than this.

We shared stories about our day. His was normal but busy. He knew Arnold Purdy's folks. He didn't call them trailer trash, but came close. Dad didn't get into bad-mouthing people. I, on the other hand, well, let's just say I have a hard time accepting the behavior of some people and have to keep my emotional responses in check. I don't always do it well and suffer the consequences.

Dad said the Purdy family had been around for several generations and hadn't changed much. Arnold's dad was foreman on a ranch nearby so came into the hardware store pretty often for materials. He was short, about five foot six, wore a large black cowboy hat, western shirt, blue jeans, and tall cowboy boots with his jeans tucked into them. He never smiled and always growled at anyone and everyone. Dad said he had a high pitched squeaky voice that was totally incongruent with his look. Dad also said Mrs. Purdy showed up in town occasionally. She, unlike her husband, was very tall, maybe six foot, and also dressed very masculine in cowboy-like garb and had a deep voice. As he described her face I realized where Arnold got his name "camel face". Dad said she ran the family and with her physical description I could see where Arnold got his looks. Not happy folks according to Dad. He had described them but hadn't put them down in any way. Where does he get all his compassion and empathy?

My mom had told me stories about my dad before and after his two tours of Vietnam. He was an angry, yelling, cursing maniac before and a pacifist, gentle man after. He rarely spoke of his time over there, so no one, including Mom, really knew what had changed him so much. Mom's guess was that all the pain, horror, and inhumanity of war made him face his own demons. Evidently, he did and won, unlike many vets who came back more angry and filled with rage than when they left. Mom said it was one of God's miracles. I guess it was, but what do I know?

Grandpa was still recovering from his night out with Charlie. Dad had seen him a couple of times gathering snacks to take to his room. Evidently, he looked like a walking corpse. Maybe he would learn? Nah! This is who he is. So, it was just the two of us for dinner. It was a gift to be with Dad. He was a good role model for me and a man of great wisdom. We had become wonderful friends since I came back and I really respected him. I am sure he respects me, also. He treats me as an equal. It is a fantastic place for a father and son to be.

After cleaning up the dinner dishes, Dad and I decided we would play some music together. I went to my room and retrieved my guitar. He played a few songs on the grand to limber up his fingers. I tuned my guitar with his help, fired off some chords and we were ready. We began with a few simple songs: *All of me, Summertime, Autumn Leaves,* and *How High the Moon.* From there we moved into some Charlie Byrd songs. We played *Bamba Samba* which was a tune Sherman Feller had written. He played Woody Herman's big band and Tito Puente and I joined him on it. For guitar it was a mix of classical and jazz made famous by Byrd. We moved on to a Pat Metheny version of *Two For the Road* by Henry Mancini. Finally, we finished with a Charlie Parker song called *Billie's Bounce.* I was still working on building my calluses so my fingers were feeling inflamed, and I called it quits. Dad played some other classical music to wind down.

I was probably smiling cheek to cheek as I looked at Dad. What a trip it was making music with him! All the world's worries disappeared for a brief period of time. I was at peace. I couldn't say that very often.

Dad was in the kitchen drinking coffee and reading the paper the next morning when I walked in. Thankfully, my dreams were tame so I wasn't consumed by them. I'm pretty sure the music helped.

"Morning, Son," Dad said, without looking up from the paper. "Sleep okay?"

"Not too bad for once. Thanks for the music last night. It was great fun for me."

"Yep, for me, too. We're sounding pretty good. It's time to get some others together and crank it up some."

I filled a mug with coffee and was ready to sit down at the table when I heard singing coming down the hall. "Youooooou move me!" Dad and I looked at each other with confusion written all over our faces.

Grandpa came waltzing into the kitchen. "Youooooou move me, really you do!" Sung in his wheezy voice it was like being bombarded with icy pellets.

"What in the...." Dad and I said at the same time holding our ears.

"Youooou move me, yeah, really you do." I hadn't noticed it before, but I now saw that he was holding a box of ex-lax to his chest as he twirled around the room.

"Pa, enough, okay? We get the picture."

Grandpa stopped, gave his wheezy laugh and pushed out the box of ex-lax toward us. "This, my friends, is my new best friend." He kissed the box. "For a man my age I need all the help I can get, if you get what I mean. But, with its help, I am a new young man. Wow! You wouldn't believe what happened this morning. Why, it was…"

"No! Stop, Grandpa," I yelled. "We don't need details."

Grandpa kissed the box of ex-lax again, winked at us again and turned to leave the kitchen. "I have a date. See you fellows around," he said in a Mae West imitation. Laughing his wheezy laugh, he waved and was gone.

Dad and I sat there traumatized with our mouths hanging open. "Uh…Dad, what just happened? Have we been transported to some far off new planet? Man oh man."

My dad just sat there moving his head back and forth as if trying to expunge the images. "Geez!" He stood and left the room. For some reason I had lost my appetite so I put my mug in the sink and went back to my room. Rain and sleet were coming down outside so biking was out today. I wasn't that hardcore. It was just a "gray-lady-down" kind of day.

CHAPTER SIXTEEN

Leaving for school, I could see that the day was one of those late fall days when it couldn't decide whether to rain or snow. So, it did a little of both. On the way, the clouds and sun danced with each other playing hide-and-seek. Every once in awhile the sun would shine through as if to say, "Aha, you beast, thought you would block me out, but I ran wide, faked left, and found an open space to do my thing." Then, the rain and snow would stop, the sun would shine, and I would put on my sunglasses pretending it was going to stay sunny. It didn't.

Pulling into the parking lot at school I saw Arnold Purdy's red Dodge Ram truck. It was in a different place, so he must have gotten new valve stems. Humph. He got some help somewhere. I parked away from his truck. Who knew what could happen to anything or anyone close to Arnold. I wasn't interested in finding out.

I had several appointments with high school students today. My mind sort of held out hope that I would catch up with my schedule. Not seeing the students I was suppose to see thirty minutes a week for psych services meant I was out of compliance. If the Department of Education in Colorado decided to pay a visit today I/we would be hammered. Shush! Don't tell anyone!

As I was walking toward the middle school, my iPhone beeped. A text message was coming through. I stopped, retrieved it from my side holster, and read the message. It was from Steve Montes, the sheriff. I hadn't seen or talked with him since the morning Patsy Anderson died. He wanted me to meet him after school at his office. I sent a text back that I would be there about four o'clock this afternoon. I mulled over what this could be about. Patsy? The middle school kid, Aaron? Arnold? I was tempted to call him and ask but decided I would wait. Maybe he just wanted to see me since we were longtime friends.

The morning began with me reviewing an assessment I had done with a second grade boy named Robert Pacheco. He was referred by both the school and his mother for an initial evaluation. He had shown difficulties in academic learning and with his behavior. Robert was currently in general education but, from the results of his assessments, that would probably change.

Robert's behavioral concerns, as related by his classroom teacher, were inattention, constantly moving around, easily distracted, and responding to questions with totally inappropriate answers. He does these behaviors throughout the school day in class, physical education, on the playground, and in assemblies. I couldn't help but wonder what his totally inappropriate answers to questions were. Hmmmm. It could be that the questions presented were dumb, dull, made no sense, had no connection to anything in life that is relevant to Robert, and maybe they are just plain goofy. I already like Robert! He reminds me of...well...me in the second grade. I have copies of my elementary school grades, and there are comments on them that say things like can't stay in his chair, and gives smart-ass answers to the teacher. Nah, they didn't say smart-ass, but it's what they meant. I visited the principal's office a few times because of my mouth. Anyhow, Robert is a great kid. I know, I know, Robert needs help so I can't praise him for his inappropriate comments. But, then again...

Several interventions had been instituted with Robert already. The teacher set up alternate seating for him near her. Now that really helps Robert! He already feels bad, and now his desk is right beside the teacher's desk. I mean really, how would anyone feel if they had their desk moved right next to the teacher. He already stood out because of his academic learning difficulties and now this! But, to be fair, he did get additional help with reading, study aids, and the opportunity to respond orally. Watch your mouth, Robert, or you will visit the principal's office! Okay, these are good things, right? Robert also gets positive reinforcement, frequent breaks, and private conversations about his behavior so he isn't called out in front of the whole class. Actually, this special ed stuff isn't too bad is it, Robert? Look at all the help you get! Lack of academic achievement pays! Maybe t-shirts could be made with that on it.

My part so far has been administering the Woodcock Johnson test of achievement for Robert. The WJ-IV, as it is called, measures a great many aspects of academic achieve-ment with a variety of brief tests. It measures things like reading, math, written expression, letter word identifica-tion, calculation, spelling, and passage comprehension. Robert is then measured against other kids his own age. The question I always have is where are these kids his own age located? They don't come from Rua Springs, Colorado. Yeah, I know we have to measure Robert somehow, but these assessments always bother me. It is an ongoing debate and the WJ-IV is only part of Robert's evaluation.

Robert showed up average in math, low average in broad written language, low average in broad reading skills, and low in written expression. My observations of Robert were that it is hard for him to put his thoughts on paper. He also can't get the punctuation and capitalization right most of the time, and he has trouble sounding out words. The bottom line is he sounds like a lot of students I was with in graduate school. Oops! I can't include that information here. Anyhow, Robert needs help and we will give it to him, thank goodness. Robert will qualify for special ed services because of the reading, written expression, and process-ing information difficulties. That's good. I look forward to helping Robert. He is a really neat kid and fun to be with. So, even in bad times, good can come from it. At least now we can get Robert "officially" qualified for services.

Later in the day I walked over to the high school to coun-sel with some of the gifted students. All seemed quiet when I entered the building. Maybe there would not be any crisis today. Who was I kidding? I thrive on crisis. I'm a junk-ie and like the rush. They need me when a crisis occurs! Boring WISC-V's, WJ-IV's? Never! No high off those. Death, destruction, mayhem in the schools. Yeah! They need school psychologists to pick up the pieces. Geez, what kind of a sick person am I thinking this way? Calmness, yeah, that's what I want in school. Peace and serenity, that's the ticket. Breathe in relaxation, breathe out tension. Breathe in...

"Hey, Doc, you missed the excitement," spoke Darnell, as I entered the office.

What! I said to myself. *I missed something? No, that's not supposed to happen!*

"Hi, Darnell. What did I miss?" I worked on a smile, but the muscles in my face kept working toward a "*No*". I felt like slapping my face around to make it behave.

"Well, after lunch the head cheerleader came back drunk. She was stumbling down the hall laughing and then crying about being dumped. First, Mrs. Neely went out to see what the ruckus was. She came back and told me that Bambi Madison was high on something and causing a disturbance. I went out into the hall, which, of course, was filled with students and teachers. Some of the students were laughing and pointing at her, and she was taking swings at them."

Darnell stopped and chuckled once and then realized what he had done. He put on a serious face, cleared his throat, and continued on. "By the time I reached Bambi, the cheerleader's coach, Misty Carnes, had Bambi wrapped in her arms and was speaking quietly to her. Bambi was laughing then crying about her boyfriend, Ryan Pennington, ditching her for another cheerleader. She would say she loved him and then yell she was going to cut off his balls and feed them to his new girlfriend. His new girlfriend, Portia Benetiz, is Bambi's best friend. Or, I should say *was* her best friend." Darnell hesitated, took a breath, ran his tongue across his teeth, and placed another stern look on his face. I could tell he was working very hard not to smile.

"Misty and I got Bambi down here to my office, and I called her folks. They both showed up about fifteen minutes ago and took her home. They, of course, blamed Ryan and Portia and even me for allowing this to happen. None of it was Bambi's fault. Someone must have forced her to drink that Scotch because Bambi didn't drink. They were outraged. If they only knew the stories about Bambi." Darnell stopped, ran his right hand across his forehead then wiped it on his pant leg.

I had a strong sense old Darnell was really enjoying telling this tale. I don't think he minded at all that the head cheerleader got brought down a few notches. Oh, how the mighty have fallen, he was probably saying to himself. He might have been the type who asked a cheerleader for a date when he was in high school, and she laughed in his face. Might he be holding a longtime grudge?

"I'm sorry I missed it. Too bad about Bambi. It is really hard to get dumped on by someone at any age." Darnell looked at me like I had three heads. Maybe I needed a mirror. I shrugged and went into the nurse's office to get ready for my afternoon schedule.

Qui Trang was in the gifted classroom and my first student this afternoon. I looked over Qui's file, so I was up-to-date. She was Patsy's best friend who spoke at the assembly the day after Patsy's death. I hadn't seen her since then. I left my office and walked down the hall to the gifted classroom. Entering, I glanced around and could see several students spread out around the room working on computers, writing in notebooks, and speaking with Arlene De La Salle, the gifted education teacher. Qui was speaking with Arlene so I made my way over to where they were in the back of the room.

Qui looked up and saw me moving toward her. She waved her left hand at me. Arlene had her back to me so she turned around.

"Hi, Doctor Thomas!" Qui said brightly. Arlene smiled and nodded.

"Good afternoon, Qui, Ms. De La Salle. How are you both doing today?"

"Qui and I were working on some advanced math problems. She is incredible with these problems. Very impressive!" Qui smiled, proud of her success, but always humble.

"I'm okay, but others are way ahead of me," said Qui quietly. "Ms. De La Salle is very helpful." Qui dropped her eyes to the floor. Taking compliments was difficult for her. Ms. De La Salle put her hand on Qui's shoulder and squeezed.

"Well, this work is beyond me. I had to take algebra over in college so that tells you my knowledge level." I looked at Qui and grinned. She smiled back. "Are you up for some time with me today, Qui?" I looked from Qui to Arlene for approval.

Qui stood, having received a pat on her shoulder from Arlene. "Yes, I'm caught up with the math for now."

"Let's go catch up then, Qui," I said.

We walked together out of the room and down the hall to my office. Upon entering my room Qui hopped up on the padded exam table that was part of the nurse's office. She tucked her legs under her and looked smaller than usual.

I decided that I would jump right in since our time was limited. "We haven't spoken since before Patsy's death, and

I wanted to see how you are doing with this." I hesitated, wondering if I should say anything about her words at the assembly. Pushing ahead I said, "Your words about Patsy and the music at the assembly were very special. Thank you."

Qui gave me a half smile, not one to expose a whole lot. "It has been very hard for me. I really miss her. Patsy was the first to accept me when I moved here. She didn't think twice about me being Vietnamese but others did. There are still those who are leery of me. They seem afraid. Look at me. I'm tiny. What could I do to them?"

I flashed on my dad's two years in Vietnam during that war. Somehow, he came back without fear and hate of the Vietnamese people. Many others didn't though and have passed the prejudices on. I will never fully understand what it is like being someone like Qui, but I know what she says is true.

"Patsy was a very special person, Qui. I miss her, too. You two were lucky to have each other. But, I know it was too short. I'm very sorry."

Qui looked out the window for a time quietly contemplating whatever was out there in the day's ethereal beauty. "Doctor Thomas, you know I am Buddhist. Patsy and I talked for hours about our religious beliefs. She wanted to know all about Buddhism and had even begun to share with me in rituals. I went to her Episcopal church sometimes, also. I know Katherine is your cousin and Patsy really trusted her, but she was searching for something. As close as we were I didn't really understand what she wanted."

Silence filled the room and embraced both of us for a moment. Qui seemed to radiate serenity. "Maybe you know this, but in the teaching of the Buddhism we will all pass on as part of the natural process. We must always keep in mind the impermanence of life even though we wish to hang on to it. But, Buddha says that death is not the end of life, it is only the end of the physical body we live in during this life. And, our spirit remains and looks for a new attachment to a new body and, thus, a new life." Qui stopped and looked directly at me. "Is it okay that I talk about this today? Since Patsy has died I haven't spoken to anyone about this."

"Of course, it is okay, Qui. I very much appreciate you sharing with me. I know some about Buddhism but not much, so this is a gift to me."

"Thank you. I want to share it with you so you will understand me right now. I may sound like I'm kind of cold and distant from Patsy's death, but I am not. Actually, I get scared and confused, because Buddhism teaches that we will be reborn after we die. This is a result of the past and the accumulation of everything we have done, both good and bad. And this cause and effect, called karma, is the result of past actions. I have grown up thinking I understand all this, but after what happened with Patsy, I am worried about her coming back. Did her suicide bring on negative karma that will hinder her when she comes back? You see, there is confusion in Buddhism about suicide. It has been said that if someone reaches enlightenment in life, then suicide is not a problem because they have already achieved all they need in life. But, if they haven't then their karma is impacted."

"So, Qui, you are concerned about Patsy's karma as a result of her suicide and how that impacts her next life?"

"Yes, that is true. Except, in Buddhism life never ends; it just goes on in other forms that are a result of accumulated karma. There is always impermanence of life so death should not be feared. Except I have a weakness. I do have fear. Fear for Patsy, for me, for my family." Qui drew into herself for a moment and sat quietly, possibly contemplating life, death, or maybe just what she wanted for dinner tonight.

"Do you ever have fear about death, Doctor Thomas?"

Oh, Qui, if you only knew, I said to myself. It sometimes has me by the throat and will not let go. I wouldn't tell Qui all of my own fears. It wasn't appropriate here. So instead I said, "Yes, Qui, I have a fear of death. Probably most people do."

"My parents told me after Patsy died that grieving is natural according to our belief, and that our world would seem empty and even desperate for a time. They also said that the bigger the personal loss the more a person will feel sorry for herself. My parents told me a story about a woman who came to Buddha. She was experiencing terrible grief as she carried her dead child. She begged Buddha to bring the child back to life. Buddha told her to bring him a mustard seed from any household where no person had ever died and Buddha would bring her child back to life. The woman searched everywhere for a house that held a mustard seed where no one had died, but it was in vain. She eventually realized that there was no household anywhere where someone hadn't died. The woman had learned about the universality of death."

"Qui, I know Patsy's death hurts a great deal. And we both know what the woman learned is correct. But, it doesn't stop the pain right now or prevent us from wondering where she has gone. I have to believe that Patsy will

continue to come back into this world and be the wonderful, giving person she always was."

"Yes, I am working on believing that. It is hard, though.
You know the idea is to reach nirvana at some point so the
death and rebirth can stop. Patsy probably has a ways to go."
Qui had moisture at the corners of her eyes. Silence again.
Our time was almost up.

I needed to check with her on something before we
stopped. "Qui, are any of the other gifted students saying
anything about Patsy? Does anyone ever speak with you
about her?"

Qui eyed me nervously, then looked away. I had hit a nerve.
Interesting. She shifted quickly from being comfortable with
me to acting like she would rather be somewhere else. "Things
are pretty quiet. No one says much," Qui whispered.

I pushed on. "It sounded like Patsy was having trouble
with some other students. Did you get that feeling?"

Wrestling with herself, it looked as if Qui was debating
whether to say something or keep quiet. She looked me in
the eyes and made a decision. "Patsy was having trouble
with Arnold Purdy and his buddies. I think he asked her for
a date several times, but she must have turned him down.
He was into calling her names and teasing her about being in the gifted program. There was a definite change in
her recently. I guessed that Arnold had increased his mean-
ness to her, because she was more down than ever. We still
talked and spent time together, but it was as if she was dying
inside. I was planning to tell Ms. De La Salle about Arnold
when Patsy..." Qui cleared her voice and waited. Her eyes
seemed to go hazy. She disappeared from the room.

"Qui?" For a moment she didn't react to her name.

"Ah, sorry. Yes?"

"I'm just wondering if something is going on with some students that I might be able to help with. Some of the gifted kids are getting picked on more. At least it looks like it to me. Maybe it is isolated though."

"Well, we are often made fun of and called names by some people. It's just part of it." Qui opened her mouth to speak but stopped.

She had a harder edge to her now. It seemed like the temperature in the room dropped. Her face changed from gentle and vulnerable to anger and rage. I knew then that we were done. I also knew that there was more to this. Sides were chosen. Something was up, and it tied in with Patsy. What?

CHAPTER SEVENTEEN

After the final bell, I loaded up my paperwork and walked back to my office in the middle school. After meeting with Qui, I had other individual sessions. Those went well, so I felt good about the day.

The middle school had emptied out. It was quiet as I entered, locked up, and left the building. The parking lot was mostly vacant of student cars. As soon as school was out for the day students fled like a plague had come calling. I unlocked my truck, hopped in, started it, and drove down the hill toward Rua Springs.

Reaching the intersection with Hetti Road I turned right toward the Lane County government offices, which included the courts, county offices, and detention center. The office of sheriff Steve Montes was located in the detention center section. Located a couple miles north of town, the entire complex was located on several acres of land donated by a transplanted rancher who wanted to help the community. The same rancher had provided a great deal of the funds to build the place. The story Steve Montes told me was the rancher who owned the ranch land came from New Jersey after his son was killed in a freak drive-by shooting. They never caught the shooter so when he bought the ranch he decided to help with justice by donating the land and helping to fund the place.

As I turned right off the highway into the complex, I was once again struck by the incredible beauty of the place. It was designed and built in consideration of the mountain terrain with minimal damage to the environment. Numerous ponderosa and aspen trees surrounded the complex, and the road to the parking area out front was lined with fir trees, planters, and old-fashioned light poles, like the old gas lights, which added a sense of history to the place that matched Rua Springs itself. The road to the complex was brick. The front was stucco with rock walls separating each section. It had large windows across the front outlined with bright colors.

The entire complex was shaped in a gentle curve built into the mountain behind it. On the left were the court rooms. The center held the county offices and the main entrance. On the right was the detention center, which held the sheriff's department offices and the jail. Each section had rounded glass atriums on the roof bringing in natural light. A road wound off to the right and behind the detention center where they unloaded and loaded prisoners. I knew the jail had an outdoor area for the prisoners, which was topped with razor wire. On top of the ridge behind the complex stood several dozen solar panels which provided all the energy. The entire place was high-tech.

Parking, I stepped out, closed the door, locked my truck and walked toward the front entrance. I wouldn't want some escaped judge stealing my vehicle, so I had to be careful. I wasn't real keen on spending time here, but Steve had asked me to be a psychological consultant for the sheriff's department after I moved back. I had agreed, but I didn't have much faith in the justice process since Lilly's death.

I stopped and looked at the complex. Behind its beauty it had a sense of shame, guilt, and pain. This is where court verdicts changed people's lives and where murderers, rapists, car thieves, home invaders, domestic violence offenders, drunkards, etc., came for a day or up to two years. Or, they passed through on their way to the Canyon City Penitentiary and possibly Supermax, a $223 million dollar complex known as the "Alcatraz of the Rockies". I shuddered at all this as I considered where Steve Montes worked and our lifelong friendship.

Steve Montes and I grew up together. His family had been here for generations, beginning back in the mid 1800s. Steve and I began kindergarten together and were immediately best friends. My early memories of Steve were of visiting his family's ranch. It was a homestead that had housed the Montes family from its beginning, even before Rua Springs was established. There were four generations of the Montes family on the ranch when I first met the family. Steve and his sisters and brothers were the latest generation. His parents, grandparents, and great grandparents were all there. I was scared to death of so many of one family located in one place, but they accepted me like another member of the family. They spoke Spanish in the home, so I learned to converse with them early on since I was there so often. His parents and my parents were good friends so Steve and I spent time together at both places. We were welded together.

Both Steve and I succeeded together and failed together, always there for one another. We got in trouble in school together, sat in the principal's office together, played sports together, double-dated together, and, together, got drunk for the first time. The day after our first drunk we were sick as dogs together, and our parents had no sympathy at all. We were required to do physical labor on the Montes Ranch during that hangover day. We even vomited together as our families stood by and laughed. Fortunately, it taught us an important lesson: Don't expect any kudos from our family if we did something stupid!

One of my funniest high school memories of Steve was about the convertible hearse he acquired. It was a '60s black Cadillac. Someone had removed the top. It probably wasn't done by a funeral home that's for sure. Can you imagine a convertible hearse carrying a coffin around? Not in reality but true in Steve's world. He built a pine box in the shape of a coffin, put it in the back, and drove around Rua Springs. But, that wasn't all. He had purchased an old leather flying helmet with ear flaps, goggles, and a life-size blowup female doll. Steve drove up and down Hettie Road in his hearse outfitted with his helmet and goggles, his blowup doll in the passenger seat, and coffin in the back. Needless to say, he made the news all the way down to Denver. He had kept the entire thing from me so I was as shocked as everyone. It was one of the most bizarre and funny scenes I had witnessed then or since. Most people enjoyed his humor. Some were outraged and wanted Steve arrested for something, anything! He was obscene, vulgar, immoral, a menace to society, un-Christian, un-this, un-that. Who did Steve hurt? Nobody! And he didn't break any laws. He made a name for himself that day that has stuck. Obviously, since he has been re-elected sheriff many times most people believe he isn't harmful to society. I'm sure he still has enemas out there, though. Oops! I mean enemies.

Following high school we stayed in touch but for the first time went to different colleges. I went to the University of Northern Colorado in Greeley and Steve went to Metro State University in Denver. I majored in psychology, and he majored in criminal justice. It was a huge change for us, and we had long conversations about it before we ventured off into the world beyond Rua Springs. Steve had always been interested in the world of criminals and read everything he could about the law and those who broke it. For a time, all he did was read books about serial killers. He leaned toward the justice side of humanity, and I leaned toward what made human's think and behave the way they did.

We set up weekend get-togethers whenever we could, but I lived on campus in Greeley, and Steve commuted everyday from Rua Springs into Denver to attend class. I wasn't home much. We still saw each other but began to drift apart as years went by. Steve graduated from Metro and first worked as a deputy sheriff in Jefferson County outside Denver and then back in Lane County as a deputy sheriff. After the longtime sheriff of Lane County retired and moved to Arizona, Steve ran for sheriff, won, and is now in his fourth term.

I stayed on in Greeley and went to grad school in school psychology. When I finished my Master's and then my Specialist degrees, I moved to New Mexico to begin my school psychology career. That was where I met Lilly. She was working as a physician's assistant in the ER when I came in after crashing my mountain bike during a race. She helped patch me up. We immediately connected, and I asked her out to dinner for the following week. Unbelievably, she accepted. We married a few months later.

Steve Montes and I occasionally spoke on the phone, and I saw him a few times when I came back to Rua Springs for family gatherings. Lilly and I had married and Steve had married a lady from Denver who had been a dispatcher for the Jeffco Sheriff's office when he worked there. He and his wife, Emma, had two children. Lilly and I had none. Life went on, the years went by, Steve and I talked when I came back for a family funeral, but otherwise Steve and I didn't have much in common anymore. I knew inside it was a loss for me, but I tucked it away. It was just the way growing up was. Right? And then...Lilly died.

Friends and family called to try and cheer me up after Lilly's death. I didn't want to hear from anyone. Steve called and kept calling no matter how much I tried to get him to go away. He listened and didn't try to give me answers to why this happened. I gave him nothing in return except drunken rants about evil in the world, the existence of God, and the unfairness of the world of criminal justice. It was all crap. Steve listened. I told him not to call anymore.

He kept calling. I cursed and cried. He kept calling. I raged at everything. He kept calling. My dad told me about the school psychology opening in Rua Springs. Steve said to come home. I did. He was the first person to come visit me as soon as I moved back. Our friendship wasn't dead after all. It just grew up.

CHAPTER EIGHTEEN

The entryway was a jungle of plants that loved the light from above. Steve told me they had the inmates nurture the plant life. The floor was brick, like the outside driveway. Soft light also came from light poles like the ones outside. Benches were scattered throughout the area with areas of running water and waterfalls. It was supposed to be a peaceful park-like area. It almost was; almost, but not quite. Most people didn't come here to achieve peace and serenity.

To the right and left of the park area were offices. In the center of the right set of offices was a large hallway that provided entry to the detention center. The large hallway on the left led to the courtrooms. I entered the right hallway and eventually reached the entrance to the detention center. After entering I walked to the front desk to let them know I had an appointment with Sheriff Montes. The young lady helping me checked her calendar on her desktop computer. She told me Sheriff Montes said to send me back to the jail as he was dealing with a problem there.

I thanked her and moved to the scanning machine in the hallway that led to the locked sally port that shut the jail area off from the front offices. Placing my driver's license, wallet, keys, cell phone, etc., in the tray by the retractable tray in the wall, a voice told me to step through. I moved through the scanner and came to the sally port. It hissed open, and the voice told me to step through. It hissed closed behind me. I was in a small hallway with a closed sally port behind me and another one in front of me. To the left was a bullet proof window with a grim-looking deputy sitting behind it. I thought I needed to hand him a boarding pass to get on the tram to get to the "C" gates, so I could make my flight. He didn't look like he had a sense of humor so I kept my mouth closed. After looking me over and comparing me with my driver's license picture, he told me to walk forward to the next sally port. It hissed open, and I walked through to the main area of the jail. Steve Montes was standing at the front counter.

"Bueno verle compañero viejo." (*Good to see you, old buddy*.) "Arrepentido tener que devolverle aquí." (*Sorry to have to bring you back here.*)

"No un problema. Usted sabe que adoro estar aquí." (*Not a problem. You know I love being here.*)

Steve switched back to English. "Ha, good joke, Marc. Don't worry. I'll let you out...maybe." He laughed at his joke. It was the same one he used the last time I was here when he showed me around soon after I had moved back.

"Yeah, well, it's an uplifting place," I said with a small smile on my face.

Steve's face became serious and then spoke. "We've had a near riot here today. It's just now calming down."

"If this is a bad time we can reschedule."

"No, no, this is fine. We have things segregated now so the bad guys lost again."

I didn't know whether to probe about the circumstances of today, but I was curious. "It sounds serious and since the head honcho is back here, well…"

"It started because of a couple of butt bandits."

The questioning look on my face must have told him I didn't have a clue what he was talking about.

He had walked out from behind the counter and was standing beside me now. "You know." He moved his hips forward and backward a few times. Recognition blasted into my head.

"You mean…"

"Yeah, you got it, that's what I mean. These two guys were brought in last night for drunk and disorderly and lewd behavior. They were picked up at the Night Owl Bar down on Hettie. That place never has a good clientele after ten at night. Anyhow, these guys were loaded and crawling all over each other disturbing the other high class, high IQ customers. That took some doing, but even they couldn't take it. The owner, Cap Townsend, called it in.

"This morning these two guys wake up from their stupor and start to go at each other again. Bad decision when all around you are another bunch of brilliant guys who had been brought in yesterday on other charges. As you can imagine, they didn't take kindly to these two displaying their sexual desires right in front of them. Not smart at all. Not at all.

"The other inmates jumped all over these guys and started pounding them into mush. By the time my deputies got there, pandemonium had broken out. Other guys in locked cells were cheering them on and stirring up more trouble. They were all eventually pulled apart and segregated in locked cells. We put the two guys in different cells and had the EMTs come and check them out. Nothing broken but several cuts and bruises. I just hope they don't try to sue anyone because of this."

I knew Steve well enough to know that he didn't care what people did sexually in private, but doing it publicly in his jail was not acceptable to him, which made perfect sense. There really wasn't anything to say to him. I just shook my head in wonderment and looked around the room. Other deputies were answering phones and typing on laptops. Inmates were yelling about changing the channel on the television. A weird smell of fear, anger, failure, and loss filled my nostrils.

"Okay, enough of that. Let's go in this room and sit." It was a glassed enclosed room where attorneys and visitors could meet with inmates. After taking seats, Steve looked at me with concern and spoke again. "I wanted to talk with you about Patsy Anderson. Some things have come up, and I need your insight and consulting skills."

It felt like a fist punched me in the gut. I really didn't want to hear what was coming. Clinching my teeth I waded in. "Sure, what's up?"

"A couple of disturbing developments came from her autopsy. Maybe you've heard some rumblings since her death."

Oh, God! I wasn't sure I could focus on this. Suddenly, I felt a chill, but it wasn't from the temperature of the room. It was a black dread that was freezing my brain. Disturbing developments? I didn't want Steve to go on, but I knew he would, and I knew I had to hear it.

He looked at me to see if I was ready for this. "There were bruises on her shoulders and a bruise on the right side of her face." He pointed to his right cheekbone. "The shoulder bruises would be consistent with someone grabbing her here." Steve reached across the table and placed both hands on top of my shoulders and squeezed. Removing his hands, he continued, "The bruise on her face could have come from someone punching her. None of the bruises would have been debilitating by themselves, but they were premortem."

Hearing Steve's clinical description of Patsy's bruises made me want to scream. It was cold and removed from Patsy, the young woman I had known. He was just doing his job, but it lacked all compassion. I wanted to shake him and tell him to remember that Patsy was a wonderful, caring, gentle soul who had touched my life.

"But, that wasn't all."

It felt like a chicken bone had caught in my throat. There was more? "There's more?" I asked weakly. The dread must have shown on my face.

"This is very difficult, I know. Sorry to have to share this with you, but you're on the inside at school, and I need your help." Steve looked at me with warmth and empathy. "This is tough to say, Marc, but Patsy was pregnant."

The floor dropped out from under me. I fell through into nothingness. My brain crashed, paralyzed. It seemed like hours before I came back, but it was only seconds. Pregnant? No! Who? My God, this changes everything. "Pregnant, Steve?" I said hoarsely.

"Yes, very early on. The death itself seems to be a suicide. We didn't find anything that pointed elsewhere, but remember, it was a locker room so there were dozens and dozens of fingerprints, hair samples and clothing threads. But, the bruises and the pregnancy lead us in another direction; Murder."

I choked not wanting to believe any of this. Who would murder Patsy? It was so outrageous I couldn't swallow any of this. "I just...really...I can't imagine who would want to hurt her. It makes no sense at all."

Again, Steve looked at me with concern. "Not to be harsh about this, but Patsy was having sex with someone. Any idea who?"

"Not a clue. I didn't even know she was dating anyone. Or, maybe she wasn't." Arnold Purdy's face invaded my space. Could he have...raped her? "Some students have said Arnold Purdy was bothering her. Maybe...I don't know. I just don't know. Otherwise, there are no rumors at all. Zero. Not a whisper." I glanced over the top of Steve's head. There was an oil painting of a peaceful mountain scene with snowcapped peaks hanging on the wall. I tried to transport myself into the scene to escape the implications of Steve's words. Again, I realized how much I really didn't know about Patsy. It was arrogant on my part to think I knew her. I didn't at all.

Silence filled the room. There were noises from outside filling some of the gaps of silence. I could hear inmates talking loudly in the module where they were housed. Someone wanted the television turned down. A deputy must have told them to zip it up as the voices lowered to a murmuring sound. The telephone rang at the front counter. Some "okays" were said and then silence. It seemed like the room was moving around me. I hung on to the edges of my chair trying to ground myself.

Steve's voice intruded into my consciousness. "Okay, I'll check on Arnold Purdy. We honestly don't know if this is a suicide or a murder. The case will remain open. There are just too many unknowns, but we are still looking. I need your help at school. If anything shows up, I need to know about it. I'm not asking you to reveal confidences from students or teachers. Maybe someone will say something outside of that, which will help us."

"Does Patsy's mother know?" I blurted out.

"Yes. I have spoken with her several times. She doesn't know anymore than we do. Her life has been ripped apart and she is barely surviving. All she does is cry when I'm there. This latest news has sent her farther over the edge. And we don't know squat. It is incredibly strange that even her own mother didn't have a hint of any of this. But, then again, I guess parents are the last to know. Patsy and her male friend took great strides to keep everything a secret. Or maybe he wasn't a friend. I just can't imagine anyone can be that secretive though. Someone has to know something. But, who? And, when will we learn anything? Maybe never."

He seemed to be processing things internally while speaking. It was almost as if I wasn't there. It was clear that he didn't like not knowing, and Steve was a bulldog in finding answers. I wouldn't want him after me.

"This is the worst, Steve. The worst."

"Don't be too sure, amigo. A young person died, and we don't know why. That alone is very troubling to me. The 'why' is out there, and it could hit us at anytime. Beware, Marc. We're flying blind right now, and I don't like crash landings."

Our conversation wound down. Steve reminded me that Saturday was his grandmother's birthday, and I was to be there at six in the evening. He laid out the food for the celebration: tamales, green chicken enchiladas, tortilla soup, chipotle salsa, and Mexican flan. I was salivating by the time he finished the list. The Montes celebrations were well known around the county. They celebrated everything and always had something cooking.

"Sorry to lay this on you, Marc. I know it is hard to stomach."

We shook hands and said our good-byes agreeing we would see each other Saturday. I left the jail reversing the process from my entrance and exiting through the two sally ports. The deputy pushed out the tray when I was out, and I collected my things and left the complex. Driving home I tried to put all the pieces of Patsy's life and death together and always came to a brick wall. I knew more now than before meeting with Steve, but I felt more confused than ever. I hate jigsaw puzzles and this was the biggest I had ever encountered. It felt like a dark-clouded depression was descending upon me again.

Driving home was about the same as when I left home this morning. It was still trying to snow or rain. Things were wet, and the sky was overcast and gray. It was getting dark and my headlights caused a glare off the wet asphalt. In a few weeks it would be bitter cold and that wet asphalt would freeze and cause accidents for some poor souls. When I lived in the New Mexico high country, a man from Texas driving a big white Cadillac skidded off the road near our place. The roads were extremely icy that day. I helped pull him out and afterward he said to me, "Y'all know how to drive on ice, so give me some tips." I responded that none of us know how to drive on ice so we all stay off the roads. He looked at me curiously, got in his car, and drove off down the road at a high rate of speed. I chuckled at the memory pushing back the darkness of my depression as I carefully made my way home.

CHAPTER NINETEEN

The next morning was a beautiful blue sky day. The rain and snow had cleared out. I was feeling tired and cranky because of the night visits from Lilly and Patsy. They were more unusual than ever. Both Lilly and Patsy were riding in Lilly's car. I waved at them when they passed me, but neither one looked my direction. My eyes followed them as they continued down the road leaving me behind. The dream shifted, and Lilly and Patsy were driving past me again. I waved at them, and this time they looked at me but didn't wave. They just stared at me and drove on down the road. The dream shifted again, and Lilly and Patsy were driving by me again. This time they waved when I waved at them, but they and the car evaporated right in front of me. I was left standing on a street all alone. The street was devoid of all life. I awoke and sat up quickly, feeling totally abandoned and alone. I felt sick. They were both gone now.

After greeting Dad in the kitchen, I loaded up to go for a morning bike ride to try to clear out the fuzz in my head before heading to school. Sunny and Kong were jumping up and down and whining by the kitchen door. They were ready to burn off the fuzz in their minds also. I hoped their dreams were better than mine. Dad said to take them along since they hadn't been on a run for several days. I stashed some dog treats in my fanny pack, filled another water bottle, and we were ready to rumble.

The dogs ran ahead of me, barking at the new day. Ah, to have that much excitement and energy about something so simple as being outside. I wish I could live their lives. They only worried about getting fed, petted, and loved and sleeping in their favorite places, like Dad's and Grandpa's recliners. They have comfort needs to meet.

Kong, the Corgi, ran off to the right like a speeding bullet. Those four short legs were powerful and fast. I saw a squirrel jump for a tree and climb up just far enough so Kong couldn't get to it. The squirrel chattered down at Kong probably saying, "Ha, look at you stubby big ears. You're not so tough down there on the ground are you?" Kong had his front paws up on the tree barking like a maniac. The squirrel chattered. Kong barked. Sunny, the Golden, looked at both of them like they were total nut cases. I glided by on my bike. Sunny stayed beside me as we moved up the trail toward the old cabin. Kong would catch up when he and the squirrel were done lecturing each other. Up above, I heard a couple of ravens cawing and clicking at all of us poor souls on the ground who couldn't fly like they could. I couldn't bark. Kong couldn't climb. The squirrel couldn't fly. The ravens had us all beat. And Sunny could have cared less. So, God, if She exists, does have a sense of humor.

Pushing myself hard on the steep incline, I tried to keep thoughts of school at bay. Strands of peculiar, disconnected occurrences filtered through my subconscious. I saw them as various strings of happenings that were totally unrelated. Except it didn't feel like they were unrelated. I imagined pulling on one string and everything jumps and reforms, but I didn't know where to pull. If it was a weaving of a story, it had a starting place. Maybe. Or maybe I just wanted a story that fit the events, and there wasn't a story at all.

During the ride home I could see that my bike was a muddy wreck, and I was, too. The moisture yesterday provided just enough to make mud amongst the rocks on the trail. Sunny and Kong looked like they had dived into a pigpen, but they were grinning from ear to ear. Do dogs grin? Why not! The muddier the better, I could hear them saying. Baths would have to wait until later. Dad would love me now!

The first part of my day was at the middle school. The middle schoolers were talking loudly at their lockers as I entered the building. Some were leaning into their lockers banging around inside. I would have been afraid to look into those semiprivate caves of theirs for fear of being crunched under a pile of unknown early teenage treasures. Screeches came from up and down the hallway where clusters of hormones fought for freedom. There were soprano voices and cracking male voices from those going through the change, mixed with high and medium squealing female voices. The sounds were of life's joys, pains, confusion, anger, and everything in between. Where else in the world could you hear sounds so sweet but in the hallway of a school? They were probably solving life's problems here better than the so-called adults in Congress. Maybe we should allow middle school students to solve the problems of war, health care, stock markets, and terrorism.

As I entered the office area, several students were crowding around Mrs. Chang's desk. One of them had left an assignment at home and was frantic and almost in tears. She wanted to call her mom or dad to bring it to school for her. The rest of the students were patting the assignment kid on the back saying soothing things and giving support. I always wondered why it took about five other kids to support the one who was in crisis. They worked the system in packs in middle school.

Mac McDougal called to me from his office, "Doc? Got a sec?"

I walked into his "man cave". Mac had a large oak library desk pushed up against the left wall. It had stacks of papers and files lined up in an orderly fashion across the back of it. Rows of pens and pencils were laying together with the tips all at the exact same distance from the back of the desk. He also had an old oak library chair at his desk. The walls and shelves were all orderly.

Posters about achievement were all framed the same and exactly mounted exactly the same distance from each other and the ceiling. One said *"Achievement: It is hard to fail, but it is worse never to have tried to succeed."* (Theodore Roosevelt) Another stated, *"Achievement: Optimism is the faith that leads to achievement. Nothing can be done without hope and confidence."* (Ralph Waldo Emerson). Bookshelves had books lined up exactly the same distance from the front of the shelf.

I had been in Mac's office several times, but I always felt like I had to march in and stand at attention, not breathing, until he gave me an exact order where to sit and when to do it. His office screamed control and order. A few characteristics of obsessive compulsive disorder were here. It was all a contradiction to being a middle school principal. These kids were hanging off the rafter's part of the time, bursting at the seams with energy. How do you keep order in this environment? But Mac did and the students seemed to respect him for the effort. He believed in them and, thus, they had inklings of believing in themselves.

"Shut the door and have a seat." After I was seated he continued, "Still no progress on finding out who attacked Aaron Lepowitz. Nobody seems to know anything at all. It has me totally baffled. The truth is, it has me tied up in knots."

Mac's face was turning red as he squeezed the arms of his chair. I hoped he didn't stroke out on me here. Starting the day that way wasn't on my schedule.

"Aaron is back at school and seems to be doing okay. He may even be angrier than he was before, if that is possible. His teachers are watching him closely and paying more attention to student rumor mill. Nothing! Zero! Usually by now someone is bragging."

I didn't know what to say to his comments so stayed quiet.

"Well, let me know if you hear anything, okay?" He looked at me with an intensity that almost took my breath away. It took all my strength to maintain eye contact.

"Sure, Mac. All has been quiet on my front, too. If one person did this, he is one cold person. If two or more did it, the chances of a leak are much greater unless they made a sort of death pact. Figuratively, I mean. Scary thought but possible."

Mac looked at me intensely for a few heartbeats. "Doc, do you think some kid like Donny Packerd could be behind this? I mean, he did have some horrible things done to him, and he has his following of thugs now."

I hesitated for a moment before I responded to Mac. I had thought the same thing about Donny. The kid had a very bad beginning. What would that do to him? I had some ideas. Those who are abused earlier may be more apt to become abusers later. "Well, Mac, I just don't know. I am seeing Donny next though."

Mac stood. The meeting was over. I stood and left his office saying hi to Mrs. Chang on the way out. The day had begun.

Donny Packerd was my first appointment. He was the student from eastern Colorado who was in treatment foster care in the area. I had seen him a couple of times since he arrived, and there were no reports from teachers about inappropriate behavior since our last session. In fact, he hadn't acted out in any way at all since he started school. Mac was worried about him starting something since some boys and girls had started hanging around with him. Supposedly, he was set up as the leader, but I had not seen any sign of it.

First period was science class for Donny so I walked down to Mr. Kite's room. Standing in the doorway, I caught Mr. Kite's eye from across the room. He nodded and I walked into the room to where Donny was working on a project with a couple of male students. He looked up and stared at me with a blank face. As if on command he broke into a big smile. It seemed like he could turn it off and on as needed.

It was now needed. My guess was that Donny knew how to play in the adult world very well. With his background it would fit. Adult, male authority figures would be the ones with whom Donny would shine. A la dear old dad. Donny would usually hold adult males in high places. Not because he respected them, but because of the harm they could do to him. At least that is what his mind had been taught. That would probably end at some point and he would act out his rage on males or maybe females. His dad killed his mom after probably dozens of household beatings. Donny wouldn't respect females at all, because his mom must have allowed his dad to abuse her. Twisted logic, yes, but it is where his thoughts might lead him.

"Hi, Donny."

"Hello, Doctor Thomas," Donny said happily.

"Are you ready to come down to my office?"

"Sure, absolutely! I look forward to seeing you."

The two boys sitting with Donny looked at me with disgust. I had intruded into their space. I didn't know them, but I could tell they didn't like me taking Donny away from them. Donny patted them both on the back.

"You guys hold the fort until I get back. Okay?" Donny's face hardened as he spoke to them. Then, it flicked back to the big smile, ready for the performance.

"Sure, Donny, whatever you say," expressed one of them. They both shook their heads in approval.

He was their god. They were his slaves. The relationship dynamics were very clear here. Dangerous. I mentally shook myself and led Donny from the room. As we walked down the hall, I noticed again that he was about my height and weight. He was pure muscle, sinewy with long arms.

Donny was always well-groomed. Today he had on nice gray slacks and a mustard yellow long sleeve shirt. His blondish color hair was cut short and set off his tanned skin and oval-shaped brown eyes. He had a short, narrow, upturned nose and full lips. Donny was definitely a handsome young man; a Pied Piper sort.

Donny said hello to Mrs. Chang. Mr. Polite himself. I could tell he didn't fool her at all. She had an internal detector that could spot a phony a mile off. She smiled knowingly.

When we were seated in my office with the door closed, I asked Donny how his week was going. A strange after-shave smell attacked my senses. I couldn't place it. Donny was probably shaving now; more physically developed than other middle school students.

"It's going fine, Doctor Thomas." Donny looked at me and then around the room serenely. Every time he had been in my office he had never once attempted to explore any of the things in my room. During our first meeting I told him it was okay to explore and touch things. Most students did some exploration. Not all, though, so Donny wasn't alone. He didn't present any curiosity at all and never asked questions about any of the items. Again, that was not unique to Donny, but it did enlighten me. Considering his background, I didn't imagine he had much of a childhood. Playing with toys and games were possibly not allowed. Donny and his sister would have learned to obey and follow strict rules. Submission to the abuser turned family members into stone figures. No talking was a common rule.

"Your teachers tell me you are doing well in class and that other students look up to you." I hesitated to see if

Donny would have a comment. He didn't. "How are things at your foster care home?"

"Things are fine there, Doctor Thomas. Everyone is very nice." Flat. Almost robotic.

These sessions with Donny were like pulling teeth. I had to watch myself from filling in the silence with my own comments and questions. Not good. I usually use the direct approach with students rather than just make making "nice".

"Donny, you've been through a lot with the death of your mother and your father going to prison. Do you ever feel like you want to talk about it?" The frontal approach from me but another question. "I would really like to help you with anything that makes you sad or angry." Silence.

Donny smiled at me and continued to look around the room. Just quick glances here and there. Enough! I moved my chair over to the sand tray and began moving my fingers through the sand.

"Did you ever have a sand pile as a kid, Donny? Or, maybe just a dirt pile that you liked to play around in?" I didn't expect an answer. Continuing on I said, "When I was a kid, we had this big dirt pile behind our house. I guess it was left there when the house was built. My older sister and I dug trenches, caves, and made little mud towns when we added water. It was really cool." I continued running my fingers through the sand as I looked over at Donny. He looked at me and smiled.

I moved some of the sand tray figures down into the sand tray and began to make a small town. Placing houses, cars, trucks, and people around, I set up a homestead that had animals, fences, and lots of trees. Out of the corner of my eye I could see that Donny was watching me.

"Sometimes I like to make a home and a town that is a perfect place. Everyone is happy." I stopped, took a couple of breaths, and continued, "Did you ever just want to have a perfect place that was safe, Donny?" Silence. "Sometimes it's okay just to want a safe place that is all yours where you can sort through all the sad feelings you have about things." Donny was listening. I could tell by his breathing that something had changed.

"There were times I would go out to my dirt pile and tell it all the troubles I was having at home and school. It was a friend that just listened. You know, Donny, you are welcome to use my sand tray to create a safe place that you can tell things. Maybe, it would be easier to talk to it than to me. What do you think?"

"Maybe."

Jackpot!

"Okay, think about it. You can make things in it and talk, and I'll just listen. I know there have been some very painful times for you. I'm not here to tell you that you are wrong about what you think and feel. They are your thoughts and feelings, not mine so I will never tell you they are wrong. Okay?"

"Okay." One word was better than none. I took what I could get.

Our time was up so I walked Donny back to his classroom. "Thanks, Donny, for your time today. I'll see you next week."

He gave a slight nod and moved to his desk where his two wide-eyed buddies awaited him. I was exhausted, because I had worked harder than Donny had during that thirty minutes, and that was not professional on my part. Spinning wheels use lots of energy.

CHAPTER TWENTY

I spent the rest of the morning at the preschool conducting behavioral assessments and playing music. Today I was following up on the BASC 3 (Behavioral Assessment System for Children) for two young girls. They were both beginning to act out in class so were referred. The teacher, parent, and child all complete a form that, when combined with the others, measures children for emotional and behavioral issues. The goal is prevention rather than intervention because if a child is showing early signs of emotional and behavioral problems we can begin work with them immediately. By waiting to discover these problems they increase, and, thus, an intervention is needed to stop a problem that might have been prevented. The two young girls were in the normal range and would be monitored for any change.

Several weeks ago I had also begun working with groups of preschool children with music. Yes, music. I bring my guitar to school and play and sing songs about feelings, relationships, and friends. Research has shown that music is great therapy for the little ones (big ones, too!), I join them weekly, we sing a song, and then talk about the words and what they mean. I show them the feeling or behavior with music. They learn social skills by interacting with the other children according to a song. Everyone is involved as it is all interactive. I love it! We conclude with some relaxation exercises done to my music. The kids have their own music classes, too, but mine are designed to teach and train emotionally. Maybe I get more out of it than they do, but I think it helps them also. Time will tell.

As I was walking across Roark Park from the preschool to the high school, I heard a siren coming up the road to the school complex. As I got closer to the high school I looked to the left and could see an EMT van turning left out of the parking lot driving toward Gomez Gym and the vo-tech building. The siren brought back memories of the EMT van coming to the gym and boy's locker room the day Patsy Anderson died. A sharp breath caught in my throat, and I temporarily froze. All I could imagine was that something horrible happened again. Oh, no, I mumbled to myself. My brain locked.

After what seemed a lifetime but was only a few seconds, I erased the terrible images from my mind and began to run toward the EMT van. The van stopped outside the gym and the EMTs hustled through the gym doors. Right on their heels I retraced those steps I had taken not so long ago into the building and to the boy's locker room. Young boys were scattered around the entrance of the locker room in various stages of dress. Some were fully clothed, and others had on part of their physical education shirt, shorts, and shoes.

No one had called me here, but like a magnet I was drawn to the locker room again. Inside I heard a boy screaming. The physical education teacher was standing back from a boy lying on the floor writhing in pain, crying, and yelling, "Get it off! Get it off!"

All he had on was his jockstrap. Moving over beside the teacher I asked him what had happened.

"He was getting suited up for class, and all of sudden I heard him screaming. I rushed out of my office, and he was lying on the floor like this." He stopped and watched the EMTs slowing taking off the jockstrap. "I wasn't sure what happened, so I didn't want to take any chances. I called the EMTs, and they were here within ten minutes."

I watched, like a voyeur, as they gently began to pull down the jock. The boy kept screaming. The other boys standing around the locker room were in a state of shock. There were no comments as they stood mesmerized, viewing the scene on the floor. They were quiet now, but I could only imagine what the stories would be later on. This poor kid would be the brunt of derisive jokes for years.

When the EMTs had pulled down the jockstrap exposing the boy's genitals, I could hear a collective gasp from everyone around, including me. My, God, I thought, what in the heck happened to him? His genitals were scarlet red with blisters around the entire area, including around his waist.

"Jesus!" snarled the teacher standing beside me. "What in the hell happened to him?" He spoke loud enough so the boys around the room and one EMT glanced at him.

The EMTs nodded to each other, and one of them leaned back and opened their kit. He withdrew a tube of salve, opened it, and began to gently spread it on the blistered areas. The boy's cries were down to a whimper now.

The other EMT came over to the teacher. "We've seen this before. Someone messed with his jock. We'll check it, but from the smell the likely culprit is a mixture of Red Hot, itching powder, juice from chili peppers, and possibly some other chemicals. It is all mixed together and rubbed in the jock. Not giving it a thorough check, he probably just shed his clothes and put it on. After a moment it began its work."

"How in the hell could someone even get to his jock? It is locked up with padlock, and he has the key. Jesus, what a disaster." The teacher had turned an ugly pale and seemed to rock back and forth. I hoped he didn't collapse. He sucked in a breath and spoke again, "What should we do now?" He looked like his safe, sane world had just cracked down the middle.

"It would be good to notify everyone to check their gear. They should take it home and wash it. Their jocks should be cleaned thoroughly, or maybe even buy a new one. The mix in this kid's jock has only a slight smell. Someone went to a lot of trouble to get the mixture right."

The EMTs went out of the room and within moments wheeled in a gurney. They gently loaded him on it, strapped him down, and pushed it out the door. The silence was like a bomb had gone off and broken our ear drums.

"Would you like for me to talk to your class for a few moments to see how they are doing?" I said, leaning toward the teacher.

"Hmmm…uh, yeah…that would be helpful." He seemed to have trouble moving his mouth. He was in shock. I decided to take control.

Turning to the remaining boys in the room I asked, "Can you go to the door and ask the other boys to come in?"

"I'll do it," spoke a tall, thin boy. He moved to the door of the locker room.

"Can you all just take a seat on the benches?" I asked the boys standing around the room. They quietly moved to the benches in front of the lockers and sat. The other boys came and found places to sit also.

Clearing my voice, I began, "This has been quite a shock, I'm sure. I don't even know the boy's name." I stopped hoping someone would tell me.

"Archie Deaver," said the tall, thin boy. "His name is Archie Deaver."

Something clicked in my memory. Quickly sorting through where I had heard his name I knew it had been recently. Where? Where was it? A blinding light flashed across my vision. Archie Deaver was a good buddy of Arnold Purdy. Was there a relationship between this happening and being one of Arnold's crew? What was going on here? Too many coincidences occurring. Random? Part of a pattern? My gut clenched at the thought of the latter. Escalation.

"I just want to let you know what has happened and what we need from you. Nothing is certain, but it looks like someone tampered with Archie's jockstrap. A mixture of things may have been rubbed into it, and it caused a burning reaction with Archie. We don't know how it happened, but we need all of you to take home your gym clothes, wash them thoroughly and maybe buy a new jock just to be safe.

The school will ask the boys who have gym clothing to wash their gear." I looked over at the teacher. He rocked back and forth still mute. His kingdom had been violated, and that was beyond belief for him. He needs to shake this off and deal with his students soon. They seem to have it more together than he does. Strange.

"Archie will be taken care of by our good medical help. Hold yourselves together on this." I sounded like I was full of bull. Hold yourself together? Come on, be a professional.

"You may have questions or just want to be quiet. I'm here to listen or just be with you. It's okay, either way."

The boys stared at the floor. Some were clinching their hands together. Others were shuffling their feet on the tile floor. The smells of the locker room were familiar to me. I guess universally all locker rooms smell the same. Since Patsy's death here the smell wasn't familiar like before. It was dark, foreign, frightening.

"It was pretty scary seeing him like that." A short red-headed boy spoke from the corner of the room.

"Yes, I know it was and probably still is. I was scared, too. Not knowing what is going on can be frightening. But, it is normal, so if you feel scared, you are just being a normal person."

At that moment the door to the locker room banged open and Darnell stormed into the room. "I just heard. What happened? What do we need to do?"

"We've been talking to the class." I pointed to the teacher to include him. He and I were buds now. "We were just talking about how scary it has been. But, these guys are okay and dealing with it." How did I know these guys were okay? They could be shattered inside, but I didn't see that on their faces. So, maybe they would be okay. Kids are tough, but we just didn't know what went on inside their internal world.

"Okay, good. Good. Doc Thomas will help you out." He looked at them, trying to look official but failing. Another crisis notch on his school belt couldn't be going over very well.

I turned back to the boys and asked if they wanted to talk more. They were clammed up before, but with Darnell here they hid farther inside themselves. Telling them they were always welcome to come and talk with me, I said goodbye and headed toward the door. I heard the teacher finally find his voice and tell them to get dressed and head to their next class. Darnell caught up with me inside the gym.

"This is criminally outrageous, Doc! Who would do such a thing?"

Even though I had some dark thoughts flipping around the back of my mind, I didn't want to feed the fire with speculation. "I don't know, Darnell. It seems somebody had something against Archie."

During my time in New Mexico I had seen several examples of cruelty toward fellow students. At the high school in New Mexico where I worked, the boy's locker room and gym were attached to the high school building. Some bullies grabbed a small boy when he was getting ready to shower and tossed him into the main hallway between classes. He stood naked pounding on the locker room door trying to get back inside. The bullies held the door closed so he couldn't enter. His humiliation sent him to the hospital with depression and suicidal thoughts.

Cruel behavior at school is a mirror of society so I don't know why we are ever surprised. We teach our children well. I wanted to say this to Darnell, but I kept silent.

When we entered the high school things seemed normal, whatever that was. Darnell wanted me to hang out for awhile in case there was fallout from Archie's incident. He called things like this "incidents". I could fantasize people saying, "Terrible thing about that 'incident' with Archie." Someone else would say, "What incident?" The first person would say, "You know, that incident where Archie got his penis and balls fried." The second person would say, "Oh, yeah, that incident." Interesting incident, huh?

The afternoon dragged on waiting around for some kid to come unglued about Archie's "incident" so I could jump into action. The thrill of victory! The agony of defeat! I needed something to happen, but it didn't. Maybe most students didn't care that Archie was attacked by someone. Perhaps they were thinking it was payback time. Too bad, Archie. Maybe you just weren't well-liked. Perhaps counseling will be in order to work on the rejection. Or maybe Archie would come back meaner than ever. It's not good to provoke a snake.

Later in the afternoon I left the high school and walked through Roark Park to the elementary school. I wanted to check on Trudy Frazier, the fourth grade teacher I saw last week, and Jeremy Skubik, the kindergartener who was talking about suicide.

I stopped in the office and said hello to Lisa. As usual she was bright and cheery.

"How are you, Doctor Thomas?"

"I'm doing okay, Lisa. You know how it goes, full speed ahead most of the time. How are things here?"

"The usual." She leaned her head toward two young boys sitting outside the principal's office.

Nodding to her I said, "Yes, things must be normal."

I said hello to the two boys. They didn't look anywhere but straight ahead and didn't respond. Mum is the word. Of course, when you are going to the guillotine there weren't many words left. I remembered the first time I sat where they were sitting as a young boy. A bully was pushing me around on the playground, and I punched him out with a right hook. That didn't go over well. I was punished by the principal and then again when I got home. I asked myself what's up with that? The bully gets away with bullying, and I get punished. I realized Lisa was watching me strangely.

"Well, I need to check on a couple of folks." I tried to re-claim some stability from my flashback. "See you soon, Lisa."

First I checked on Jeremy in Mrs. Purlee's class. Standing in the doorway she eventually saw me and came over to say hi.

"Doctor Thomas, what a treat. Who are you checking on today?"

"Hello, Mrs. Purlee. I just wanted to see how Jeremy is doing."

"Why don't we ask him?" She walked over to Jeremy's desk where he was beaming at me from across the room. Leaning down she said something to him. He jumped up and ran toward me.

Kneeling down on my heels, I caught him as he ran to me and gave me a big hug.

"Hi, Doctor Thomas! I'm glad to see you!" His face was in a huge smile with teeth showing.

"It's good to see you, Jeremy. I just wanted to say hello and see how you were doing." He hung on my left arm mov-ing back and forth.

"I'm happy!"

"That's great, Jeremy. I'm glad you are happy!"

"Can I come to your room again? I have some more stories to tell you."

"Let's check with your mother and see if it's okay."

"All right. She'll say okay."

"Good, Jeremy. I'll speak with her."

"Okay. Bye."

"Bye, Jeremy. It is good to see you." I stood up feeling fantastic. All it took was one little person like Jeremy being happy to see me and my day was made. What a great job!

I thanked Mrs. Purlee and walked the length of the hall toward Trudy's classroom. Her door was closed so I quietly opened it and stepped inside. Her students were working in groups on some project, and she was moving around the room checking with each group and sharing comments. I could tell the students really liked her, because they became animated when she joined their group and took hold of her arms and hands. Their smiles at her told it all. This was an important place for all of them, including Trudy.

She saw me by the door, stood, and showed a weak smile of her own. I stayed where I was and she joined me at the door, away from her students.

"I apologize for interrupting, Trudy. I just wanted to check on you."

Her face fell. I knew things weren't good. "If it weren't for these kids I would totally fall apart. This is the best class I have ever had in all my years. They keep me alive."

I waited. I didn't want to pressure her in any way by asking questions she didn't want to answer here or couldn't.

Chewing her lower lip she whispered, "I told him the truth of what I had discovered. He was outraged that I sneaked around and entered into his space. He made it sound like it was all my fault. Since the day after I spoke with you and I confronted him, we haven't said more than a dozen words to each other. Things are just...just, I don't know, frozen, numb, surreal. We don't even exist to each other. At least that is the way it feels." Trudy looked around at her class and then back at me. "I'm sorry to unload. It just feels like something died."

"I'm very sorry this is happening, Trudy. And I'm sorry for bringing it up here."

"No, no, it's okay. I'm glad you came by. Maybe we could talk again sometime?" It was a statement but also a question. I could see the extreme pain on her face. It looked like her face was caving in on her as we spoke.

"Yes, we can get together, Trudy. We'll work out a time." I wished I could remove all her hurt. It was coming off her in waves. Helpless, that is what I felt.

"Good. I better get back to my class. Really, thanks for checking on me. I do appreciate it." She turned and reentered her safety zone and came back alive.

Watching for a moment, I finally moved myself toward the door, opened it, and walked toward the entrance. Too much pain in the world. Too much. Another layer of it embedded itself into my soul.

CHAPTER TWENTY-ONE

Returning home after school, I had just sat down in the living room with a new book while Sunny and Kong jumped around at my feet when the phone rang. Feeling invaded from the ringing, I was tempted to just let the answering machine pick up. Ever since Lilly's death and the doomsday phone call I received about her accident, I cringed when the phone rang. Always expecting bad news, I tensed at the noise of the ringing. Nevertheless, I couldn't let it go. Maybe dad was in trouble. Or, something happened to someone from school. Or, someone died somewhere. Who cared where, just somewhere. My brain zoomed off in a dozen horrible directions. I had to know.

Picking up the instrument like it was a poisonous snake, I spoke, "Hello."

"Mr. Thomas?"

"Yes, one of them. Which one do you need?"

"Are you Herman's son?"

"No, I am his grandson, Marc."

I heard the woman breathing close to the speaker end of the phone. "Well, is Herman's son there?"

"No, my dad, Bret, is still at work. Can I help you with something?"

"I'm not sure but maybe. Yes, maybe you can help." She cleared her throat. "It's about your grandfather, Herman."

"Yes, I thought it might be." Gee, I'm a brain whiz now. How did I know it was about Grandpa? Duh. "Is he all right?" I had images of him being hurt or even dead. Dang!

"No, he is okay. Well, sort of okay, I guess. He and Charlie Noonan come over every week and do activities with the residents here. Oh, I forgot to tell you who I am. I'm Eileen Coulter at the Serenity Assisted Living Home." She stopped, and my mind was just catching up with what she said.

Oh crap, Grandpa and Charlie again. What are they into now? Activities at the Serenity Assisted Living Home with old people? They are probably older than a lot of the people there. Why hadn't I heard of their work there before?

"Grandpa and Charlie are doing activities with people there?" I must have sounded like a total fruitcake.

"Yes, they are here now. Things have kind of gotten out of hand. Can you come over and talk to your grandpa and Charlie?"

Good gad! What in the heck have they done? "I'll be right over." I didn't say good-bye. The phone was dropped in the cradle, and I sprinted for the door. Sunny and Kong raced after me, but I told them to stay. They looked as if I had beaten them. Flat ears and downcast eyes which seemed to ask how I could leave them again.

I leaned down and petted them. "I'm sorry. Grandpa has done something again." I kissed each of them on top of their head. "I'll be back soon." They didn't respond, just gave me the you're abandoning us again look. They really knew how to pull the emotional blackmail trick.

Cranking up my truck I backed out of the drive and headed back into Rua Springs. The assisted living home was in the south part of town a couple of blocks west of Hettie Road. I called Dad on the way to let him know that Grandpa was into something again. All he mumbled was something about that old man having had his last chance. He said he would meet me there as soon as he could.

As I moved on toward the Serenity Assisted Living Home I recalled a recent joke Grandpa had told Dad and me at dinner a couple of nights ago. A man took his elderly father to an assisted living home to check it out. The old man was placed on a couch in the entryway as the son went to speak with the administrators. As the old man started to tilt slowly to the left a nurse raced over and piled several pillows on his left side forcing the old man to sit straight up. The old man then started to tilt slowly to the right. Again the nurse ran over and piled pillows on his right side forcing him to sit straight up. The old man started to lean forward, and again the nurse raced over and piled pillows on his lap. About that time the son returned, not commenting on all the pillows and asked his dad what he thought about the place. The old man replied, "I guess it's okay, but they won't let me fart."

Grandpa laughed his wheezy laugh, slapped his thigh and then lifted up his left cheek and farted. Howling, he returned to his food with a contented look on his face. Maybe it was a story and statement about his ever being in an assisted living home as a resident. I couldn't imagine what chaos he was causing now.

The Serenity Home came up on my right as I reached the corner of Pine and Aspen Streets. It was an outrageously ugly structure with no resemblance to the historical architecture here. I had visited here a long time ago and remembered it looking like a prison. It was built with cinderblock painted gray and had a flat roof. It looked like someone had brought in gigantic blocks, like children's wooden blocks, and just stuck them together in a haphazard fashion. I expected to see razor wire around the top of the roof and guard towers on the corners. They weren't there, of course. Small windows were built into the cinderblock at regular intervals. These were probably individual rooms. The entire complex sat on about a two-acre plot of prime land. Dad had told me it was one of several dozen around the country owned by some eastern corporation.

Stopping my truck out front, I saw Grandpa's jeep parked a little farther down. I didn't see Charlie's old beater so I guessed Grandpa had picked him up on the way. It's a miracle they made it this far together the way they are always going at it. I locked up the truck and walked toward the entryway. Man, if this place could look any bleaker, I wouldn't know how. If I was a little kid I would feel like I was entering a haunted house. Of course, I'm a bigger kid, and I feel that way.

The front door had one of those large metal buttons you had to push to open the doors. It was made of metal and said Push on the front of it. There was also a numbered keypad that could be used when the place was locked down. What if a person was blind? What then? I followed directions and pushed the button. The doors hissed open. Entering, I stood before two more doors with the same large Push button on the right of the door and another keypad above it. I followed directions again. What would have happened if I hadn't followed directions? I didn't see a doorbell anywhere. I guess a person just pounds on the door hoping someone will hear them. I didn't imagine hearing was one of the stronger senses for people here, though.

The second set of doors hissed open and the music hit me like a sledge hammer. I would swear to God that the same woman was sitting at the organ playing the funeral dirge music. She must be 120 years-old! The last time I was here I figured she was a hundred years old, and here she was looking like a pruned corpse, playing the same organ and the same dirge music. Maybe they were making a movie like *Phantom of the Opera* or something, but I didn't see any cameras. Geez! If a person wasn't depressed when they came to live here they would be within fifteen minutes. She paid me no attention and continued playing. Maybe she was already dead and everything was just a recording and they just embalmed her and sat her there for effect. I watched her for a moment to see if she was breathing. Maybe. Maybe not.

Trying to clear my head of the scene, I sincerely hoped I didn't get trapped in here. Those doors better open when I'm ready to leave or I'll... What? I'll what? Have a panic attack? Walking up to the front desk all I could see was a lineup of old men and women in wheelchairs and walkers. A lady grabbed my sleeve and said, "Can I go home now?" I looked at her and pulled away. Another woman was screeching that she wanted her mommy. An old guy was trying to move his wheelchair, saying over and over, "Help me! Help me! I'm broken." I was shaken, already depressed, and felt bile come up in my throat. The smell of Lysol was overwhelming. But the smell of urine, feces, and vomit was also apparent. I was ready to run.

"Can I help you?" a woman questioned as she stood up behind the counter.

"Um...yes...I was called about Herman Thomas. I'm his grandson."

"Yes, Eileen said you would be coming. See that door over there?" She pointed to her left and my right. Double doors were at the end of the hall. "That's the activity and cafeteria area. Herman and Charlie are in there doing activities with some residents. Or, at least they call it that. Head on over. Maybe you can calm those old geezers down."

Walking between the wheelchairs and walkers I tried not to look at the men and women. It was just too painful to see these people like this. I moved quickly to the double doors and...yes...there was another large button that said Push. I followed directions, and the doors hissed open.

The scene before me was immediately branded on my eyeballs. Grandpa and Charlie were racing each other around the room like race car drivers on a track. The difference was they were each pushing a wheelchair with an elderly woman in them. Amazingly, the women didn't look afraid at all. In fact, they looked...drugged. Their eyes were blank. Maybe they were blind. Oops! I mean visually impaired. They certainly showed no emotion. These two old farts were running like school boys. Laughing it up, bumping into each other and charging ahead. There were several other people in wheelchairs sitting in the center of the room. Some were trying to clap and cheer, but it just took too much energy to get the job done. Things were done in slow motion.

When Grandpa and Charlie reached the other end of the room, they stopped and gave each other a high-five. Then, they walked to the counter behind them, put on their fedoras (Grandpa's was gray and Charlie's was black), and placed sunglasses on their face. I was so paralyzed I couldn't imagine what was coming next. Grandpa picked up a microphone from the counter, turned it on and began to sing as the two of them in synchronized movement leaned back and forth.

"I'm gonna get my motor cranked up and look for some adventure." Grandpa sang. My God. An old Steppenwolf song? Sort of.

Charlie joined Grandpa and together they sang, "I'm gonna love you and embrace you and make all your dreams come true."

Charlie took the mike and continued, "I like heavy thunder and rain."

Back together they both held the mike. The incredible thing was that they were singing a cappella, and they were quite good. Amazing. I stood there speechless...until dad tapped me on the shoulder.

"What in the heck are they doing?" dad hissed in my ear.

"I'm gonna love you and embrace you and make all your dreams come true," they both sang.

"Why didn't you stop them, Marc?"

"Well, I uh..." The truth was I was enjoying them. They were good!

"I'm stopping this right now," bellowed

Dad. "Enough of this, Pa! We're leaving right now! You two cusses have embarrassed yourselves again. I'm appalled."

"Lighten up, Bret. We were providing activities, which is what we do every week here. Look around you. Do you see anybody complaining?" I looked around at the people. No emotion at all. A really difficult crowd to entertain.

"Let's go. Now!" growled Dad. We followed him out of the room. Walking down the hall and toward the entrance, both Grandpa and Charlie were calling these people by name telling them they would see them soon. Most didn't respond, but that seemed okay with Grandpa and Charlie. They understood. Both of them touched the people, pushed back the hair on their foreheads, held their hands, spoke quietly in their ears, gave them hugs as they sat in their wheelchairs or stood in their walkers. This was a side to these guys I had never seen. They really liked being with these folks. I didn't think I could be anymore shocked than I was. But…I was.

"Patsy Anderson volunteered here, Marc," mentioned Grandpa as he stepped past me.

Stunned, I stumbled, caught myself from falling, and stopped. "She did?" I asked stupidly.

"Yeah, she was great with the old folks," smiled Grandpa knowingly.

"Well, ah, that's great. I didn't know that." Another important bit of information I didn't know about Patsy. When would the next surprise come next about Patsy?

The two sets of front doors hissed open as we followed directions and pushed the big button. We were outside in the clean Colorado air. Darkness had set in. I took in a deep breath. I had just had an amazing adventure and another shock about Patsy's life. I had a lot to learn from these old coots. Dad opened his truck door, stood for a moment, then walked over to me and smiled.

"They are really pretty good, aren't they, Marc?" He walked back to his truck, hopped in, started it up, and drove off.

Grandpa and Charlie climbed in the Jeep, cranked the starter and off they went. I stood by my truck staring off into the night as the Jeep's taillights receded into small red dots and then...nothing.

CHAPTER TWENTY-TWO

"Some news, Marc," Dad stated, as I came into the kitchen the morning after Grandpa and Charlie's visit to the assisted living home. I filled my mug with piñon coffee and sat down across the table from Dad.

He hesitated. I could tell he didn't want to share this news. Dad squished up his face and closed his eyes. "We are having company this weekend."

Uh, oh. I wasn't going to like this. "Who?" I quietly asked.

"Your Aunt Lenore called last night and said she is coming to visit this weekend."

Looking into Dad's eyes I checked to see if he was just kidding. He wasn't. "Oh great," I huffed. "Just what we need." I held my coffee mug with both hands looking at the brown liquid hoping to see some glimmer of hope for the weekend. Nothing.

"I'm going to Steve's place Saturday evening for dinner. It's his grandmother's birthday." Maybe I could just stay with Steve for the weekend.

"I'm not dealing with her by myself, Marc. So lose the idea of staying at Steve's."

Dad read my mind. He had seen me pull this many times when I was growing up.

"Is she really your sister, Dad? She's a total nightmare." This was an old discussion.

"I know, Marc. But, we're still family. I doubt if her own daughter, Katherine, will even want to see her, but Katherine will show up. And, Lenore made it clear she won't stay with Katherine and Lexie, because they are gay. So, she will stay here, and she can have my room. It's only for two nights. I hope."

"You hope?" I asked Dad. "She might stay longer?"

"No, no. She said two nights. But, she's known for changing her mind."

There it was. I looked at my watch realizing I didn't have time to take a ride this morning. I had lost my appetite, too. I picked up an orange, peeled it, savored each slice and tried to put Aunt Lenore from my mind. I lost that battle. My memories of her growing up were of a loud mouthed, sharp-tongued, sarcastic, bombastic hurricane with border-line personality disorder characteristics who caused chaos and bolted. The weekend would come too soon no matter what.

When I reached the school parking lot, I was confronted by an abundance of purple and white decorated vehicles. Beat North Park was written on the back windows of many vehicles.

The final game of the football season was tonight, and the energy level was ramping up. I could feel the buzz at school as I locked up my truck and headed to the middle school. It was an excitement that I remembered from my youth. I recalled the feeling from those days and the belief that the most important thing in life was the upcoming football game. Things were simple, straightforward. Life was out there to be experienced with abandon, and everything was right with the world. Not for all youth, though, I found out later. Football games had no meaning; only surviving did. I know, because I see what's behind the curtain with some kids and it isn't filled with the excitement of athletic events.

Mrs. Chang was at her desk collecting parental permission slips from seventh graders going to a museum in Denver today. The yearly trip was part of a lesson on Colorado history. I could have gone as a chaperone but couldn't take the time away from some yearly reviews going on. The IEP meetings never stopped. I loaded up some paperwork I would need for the day and headed to the high school. The high level chatter from kids going on the museum trip followed me out of the building. Anything was better than sitting in school all day, the chatter seemed to say.

Entering the high school, the excitement of the upcoming game filled the hallways. It was also spirit day because students were decked out in school colors. Mrs. Neeley was at her place in the outer office quietly typing on her computer keyboard. Loud voices were coming from behind the closed door of Darnell's office. Someone was getting reamed by Darnell. I caught snatches of conversation about clothing. A student must be with him.

Probably a dress code violation since the costumes today were pretty wild.

"Doctor Thomas, it is nice to see you!" Mrs. Neeley smiled at me, paying no attention to Darnell's harangue going on nearby. Her name should have been the Great Karnack, since she knew all the secrets of the school.

"Good morning, Mrs. Neeley! Good to see you, also. How are things today? Or, should I ask?" I nodded my chin toward the principal's office.

"Spirit days are always filled with energy. So, I expect things will be interesting. For some reason, the kids seem to think it is a time for experimenting with behavioral boundaries. They can't do a thing that I haven't already seen a dozen times. But, they do disrupt teaching." She sighed and shook her head as if to say, "kids will be kids".

"Well…I hope it doesn't get too wild around here today. You'll handle whatever comes, I know." I gave her my best smile and winked at her.

"Oh, you, just get to work now, or I'll dig up a problem for you," she laughed and went back to her keyboard.

I went into the nurse's office and settled in reviewing several new referrals before I started sessions with some high school students. I was considering what assessment plan would work for each of them since they were all behavioral concerns. My door was open, but I wasn't paying much attention to voices or phones ringing. Mrs. Neeley's knock on the door jamb brought me out of my reverie. I looked up at her and knew it wasn't good. My mind raced in all sorts of directions at once figuring the worst.

"The middle school just called. It was Mrs. Chang. She said Mac McDougal wants you over there right now. It is something very serious." Her face showed all the pain of her job during these times. It was a roadmap of school crises, and I hurt for her.

"Thanks. I'm on my way." I stood after putting files in my book bag. On the way by her I squeezed her shoulder letting her know it would be all right. She gave me a weak smile and walked back to her desk behind the counter.

Walking quickly, I reached the middle school within minutes. The hall was quiet as I entered the office. Mrs. Chang was at her desk, and Mac was standing in front of it. Their faces spoke volumes.

"Another attack in the boy's bathroom." Mac's face was granite hard. Someone had soiled his school again. The rage was pouring off him in buckets. I could almost smell it.

"What happened?" I didn't know what else to say, but this just sounded weak.

"The seventh graders were going to the museum today." I remembered the permission slips Mrs. Chang was collecting when I came in this morning. "The buses were loaded except one boy was missing by the teachers' counts. They waited for awhile and then came in to tell me he hadn't showed yet. He had turned in his permission slip so we knew he was here at school, but he hadn't arrived at the bus. We started checking classrooms first but then checked the boy's bathroom. He was there. The same trick with the duct tape was used."

My gut clenched, remembering what had happened to Aaron Lepowitz and his reaction to it. Mac told me that Aaron was out of school for a couple of days. His mother was making comments about a lawsuit against the school.

"Let's go down. We'll need your help on this, Marc." He led the way out of the office toward the boy's bathroom.

"This was as bad or worse than the last time. The boy's name is Billy Hartsell. Another kid who I've had several conversations with this year about his bullying. He was grabbed from behind, so he didn't see anyone either. His mouth and eyes were taped. Billy's pants were pulled down, and he was spray painted red all over his genitals and rear end. Then, he was duct-taped on his knees in front of the commode with his face over it." Mac gave a cold, clinical description of what happened to Billy, but his face betrayed the incredible pain and anger.

It was the same scene as before. Mr. Oakley, the chief custodian was standing outside the door. I nodded to him and he nodded back. Flat affect. Huh? The yellow bifold plastic cleaning sign sat in front of the door letting everyone know it was off limits. He nodded at us as we entered the restroom. Again, Mr. Piño was sitting with the young boy on chairs in front of the stalls. He was giving comfort, talking softly. The boy was crying, sucking in deep breaths as his shoulders moved up and down. I recognized the seventh grade boy, but he wasn't a student I was seeing. Pieces of duct tape littered the floor and this time I smelled the fumes from spray paint. Curious. Mr. Oakley and Mr. Piño on the scene again. How did they happen to be here?

Someone was acting well-planned abuse on young boys who were also known as school bullies. It didn't seem to involve any ritual so didn't fit in the ritualistic abuse category which involved other cult kind of behavior like masks, costumes, and animals. Is it a teacher? Another student? Why, though? The boys seemed targeted but by whom? It was so well-planned and vicious that it looked like part of some larger picture, but it wasn't clear at all. Keeping this quiet, again, was going to be almost impossible. If word of some sort of "serial" abuse happening here began, the school would be a ghost town. Fear and rumor mongering would spread like a pandemic flu.

"The sheriff's office has been called. They should be here any moment. I'm sending the buses on to the museum trip. Billy's parents have been called. Maybe you could just sit with Billy for awhile, Marc." Mac looked lost, vacant, unsure of where to go with this. This was all new to him. Unfortunately, I had seen something like this before. Although it was the reverse of what was happening here.

A few years ago several white students were targeting Native American males with what was thought to be ritualistic abuse. Young boys from the reservation were picked up after school as they walked home. They never saw the vehicle or who was in it. They were blindfolded, tied up, stripped naked, and placed in a field tied to a post. When the blindfold was taken off they saw that they were painted from head to toe in various colors with feathers tied on their head, arms and ankles. A group of people danced around them chanting words from a rap song about killing. The group was dressed all in black with black hoods, which had eyeholes.

They danced around the victim in a step that was similar to a Native American feast dance. After approximately a half hour, the ritual stopped, the victim was blindfolded again, taken by car to a major highway, and put out on the road. This happened to five different boys before someone saw a group of males pick up a young boy. This person followed them to the open area, watched the ritual begin, and called the sheriff's office. It turned out to be six white male students I had counseled at school for behavioral issues. They all thought it would be a lark to scare the boys and let the stories build. Needless to say, kidnapping and abuse charges were brought against all of them. It wasn't so funny then.

"Hello, Billy. This is Doctor Thomas, our school psychologist. He's going to sit with you until your parents arrive." Mac's words brought me back to the present. That memory from years ago hung on me like a shroud. Was this someone's idea of a lark? A joke? Payback?

Mr. Piño stood from where he was seated by Billy, squeezed Billy on the left shoulder, and walked past us toward the door. I sat where Mr. Piño had been seated. The chair was still warm.

"Hi Billy," I spoke gently to him. "I'll stay here with you until your parents arrive."

His tears continued. I handed him some tissue from a box I had picked up off Mrs. Chang's desk. He wiped his eyes but continued crying. This boy had been hurt badly. I'm not sure he would behave like Aaron did. The violation was more sexually humiliating than before.

"They said this was for Patsy."

I was so stunned at what Billy had just said that I could only stare. For Patsy again? What was going on?

"Hi, Marc." My head twisted around quickly. Steve Montes, the sheriff, was standing just inside the door.

"Thanks for coming so quickly, Steve." I had no clue the sheriff of Lane County would come in person, but I kept the shock out of my voice.

Steve came over and knelt down in front of Billy. "My name is Steve Montes, Billy. I'm the sheriff, and I came here personally to be with you." Steve halted, took a breath, and continued. "Your parents are in the school office right now. They are anxious to see you, but I need to collect information from you so we can find out who did this." He paused again. I could tell he wanted to reach out and touch Billy, but he wouldn't do that not after what just happened to him.

"I want to know if you can help me here. Just shake your head yes or no if you understand." Billy shook his head yes. "Okay, good. I have a deputy here who will come in and gather up this duct tape and take some pictures of this area. What I need for you to do is come with me to the office so you can see your parents. Sound okay?" Billy blew his nose on the tissue and wiped his eyes with another one. He nodded yes.

"After we see your parents, I want us all to go down to the hospital emergency room to check you over and get you cleaned up." I knew Billy's body was going to be checked by the ER doc and pictures would be taken. His clothes would be taken so tests could be run. Further humiliation was coming for him. My gut clenched as the coming reality collided with my desire to not have him hurt further. The pain train was coming.

"Are you ready to come with me, Billy? I'll be with you through all of this." Steve Montes could be a total hard-ass when necessary, but there wasn't anyone more gentle when it was needed. "May I take your hand, so we can walk to the office together?" Billy nodded yes and lifted his right hand. Steve softly took it. Billy stood, and looking like a totally broken young boy, unlike Aaron when this happened to him. Steve opened the door and quietly said something to his deputy as they stepped out into the hallway and were gone.

I sat for a moment too stunned to move. My mind couldn't grasp what had happened to Billy right here in the middle school bathroom. It was pure evil and it was loose in this place. The deputy came in and asked Mac and me to leave the restroom, so he could process the crime scene. With his words "crime scene", I grimaced and stood on legs that were made of rubber. I didn't feel my feet hit the floor as I left the room. Two middle school boys and two high school boys. There was a common link. They were all bullies. Would there be more? *Jesus*, I said to myself. I caught myself wondering why I had used the word Jesus. Did I really believe he could help? Or did I just use the word as an act of despair? Words we use in times of crisis are telling of something. I don't know what but something.

The office was empty except for Mrs. Chang when Mac and I arrived. The hallway had been eerily quiet on the way back as if everything and everyone were holding their collective breath.

"If this latest violence doesn't get out, it will be an incredible miracle," Mac murmured as we stood in front of Mrs. Chang's desk. "Marc, you have more experience with this than I do. What's next?" He looked at me as if pleading for some positive guidance. I didn't have any.

"They are escalating, Mac," I spoke bluntly. "He, she, or they are very well organized to pull this off during school without anyone knowing or seeing anything. That part alone is so unbelievable that I can barely grasp it. Someone may have done this before or seen it done and is reenacting scenes. Very pathological stuff going on." I quit talking and thought about what I had just said. Had someone seen this done? Had it been done to them? Done it to someone before? Sick, really sick. Who fit? I... For Patsy? Patsy Anderson? Bullies?

"We need to search lockers, desks, and book bags for duct tape and spray paint." Mac stopped, "But if we do that everyone will know something is going on. Maybe not...," He trailed off. "We should..."

Mrs. Chang's voice softly filled the room. "There have been stories of lots of drugs coming into our school. We have to keep everyone safe by not allowing that to happen. It's time we did a ..."

"School search! Yes, we can't have drugs here," Mac was beaming. "What do you think, Marc?"

"That's your area, Mac. I don't know the policy on something like this. I assume the policy takes into consideration school safety and this certainly qualifies."

"Yep, this is a safety issue. I need to call the superintendent." Mac bounded into his office.

"Good work, Mrs. Chang."

She smiled thinly at me as if to say, "Who me?" School secretaries and office managers always know more than anyone else. Their level of knowledge was way beyond mine. They saw and heard everything.

"Any thoughts on this, Mrs. Chang?"

She looked at me directly, held eye contact, and spoke, "Nothing. This is a dilemma for me, Doctor Thomas. I seem to always know but not this time. They are ghosts, and that scares me."

I swallowed, broke eye contact, and vaguely heard snatches of Mac's phone conversation with the superintendent. "Yeah, it really scares me, too." I stood for a moment saying nothing. Picking up a snow globe she had on her desk, I looked at the little boy and girl inside walking across a bridge as snow fell on them. Maybe they knew.

"I need to get back to the high school, so I'll see you in awhile." I set the snow globe down on her desk and watched the two kids covered with snow. I stepped out of the office and walked toward the front doors. This job...

CHAPTER TWENTY-THREE

E ntering the high school from the parking lot side, I was walking the length of the hall toward the front office. Classes were in session so student and teacher voices bombarded me as I passed classrooms. One room was showing a video with the noise level too high. The classroom door was open and I saw vague images of students at desks through the gray murkiness. They seemed to be concentrating on the screen at the front of the room. Or maybe they were all asleep. It looked like some history lesson on ancient Greece. Pictures of broken statues on the screen captured my attention. I hesitated just wanting to escape.

"Got any popcorn?" a low, husky female voice whispered in my ear.

My sphincter almost released. "Sh...oot! What the heck!" Miss Falhaber was standing beside me with her hand on my elbow.

"Good movie, Marc?" She had one of her "I caught you" smiles on her ancient face.

Slowing my heart rate and clinching my sphincter, I tried to act cool. "Oh, yeah, it looks pretty good." My voice broke like an adolescent going through puberty.

"I'll walk you to the office. Is that where you were headed? I'm going there too."

"Sure, sounds great. How are you doing?" I looked down at her thinking her bowed back looked more painful than before.

"I'm still enjoying teaching most days, but students and families have changed. Of course, I said the same thing when you were a student here, so what do I know. Basically, the kids are fun and want to learn. The problem is the parents. Yours excluded, of course. You always paid for your sins twice. Once with me and again at home. Kids are still kids. They just want to be accepted and have someone care about them. We try to do it here, but then they go home. I get one hour out of twenty-four. Not good odds." She trailed off whispering something under her breath.

There wasn't much to be said as a response so I kept silent. We moved down the hall until we reached the main office. Mrs. Neeley was at her command seat running the school. The door to Darnell's office was closed.

"Good to see you, Marc. Thanks for listening." Miss Falhaber looked tired.

"It was good to see you, too. I'll listen anytime." I squeezed her right shoulder as I moved by. She patted my hand with her left hand. I stopped, needing her touch. She seemed to need mine, also. The moment of intimacy passed. We withdrew our hands at the same time.

"Thanks for coming down, Miss Falhaber," said Mrs. Neeley, kindly. She had seen our moment of sharing and smiled at both of us. "I just have some forms for you to sign."

I stepped into the nurse's office but left the door open. Sitting at the desk I opened my book bag and retrieved some assessments that were conducted on a couple of new referrals. These evaluations were the Connors Rating Scales that the teacher, parent, and student all completed. It was used with these two students, because it gave us a screening of hyperactivity and gave a perspective of behavior from people close to the student. With a behavioral baseline for a student, we could monitor the results of interventions on their behavior as we progressed with a team plan. Combining all three of the Connors reports we could come to conclusions and then consider this information along with several other assessment instruments. I would do a classroom observation on these two students shortly. That information would be added to the Connors results.

Time passed quickly as I began to write up the Connors outcomes. My mind slipped a gear occasionally, and I would catch myself staring off into the scene of the horrific abuse of Billy, Aaron, and Archie. I wondered how they and their parents were doing.

The bell rang and I stood, stretched, and thought about the student I was going to observe. Right now I only had some information on paper and a picture of what he looked like in my head. Time to move.

Hallway chaos was in full swing when I emerged from the outer office. A multitude of voices at all levels surrounded me. Deep base and high squeals touched my auditory senses. Laughter, serious, secretive, and braggart conversations all caught my attention. I have always been able to keep track of several conversations at once to the detriment of my psyche. Who needs this gift?

Moving through the throng of humanity toward my intended classroom my ears and eyes locked onto two groups of students watching each other.

A male voice spoke "Hey, puke brain! Do you have a naked picture of your mother?" It was directed at one of the gifted kids I recognized from the gifted classroom. I slowed, shocked by the question. Did I hear that right?

The boy who was questioned stood with two other students. They all had smiles on their faces. The boy spoke, "No, I don't have a naked picture of my mother."

"Do you want one?" yelled the questioner. Stunned silence reigned for a beat, and then the questioner turned to his nearby audience and began laughing and hooting like he had made the funniest comment ever. He high-fived a buddy near him, and they did a fist bump as they roared with laughter. "Do you want one?" he hissed in laughter to no one and everyone again.

The only people laughing were this guy and a few of his crowd. Other students nearby were struggling to determine if they were supposed to laugh or keep quiet. The boy to whom the question was asked continued to stand serenely with a smile on his face. His friends did, too. No reaction at all. Geez, how did they stand there still smiling?

I was about to wade into this when the boy who had asked the question turned around and began to open his locker.

Kapufff! The boy staggered back from his locker screaming and holding his hands to his face. The sound reached my ears at the same time. It sounded like an air gun of some type had gone off. Paralyzed by the sound and the scene, I momentarily stood watching the boy fall backward onto the tile floor. It seemed to happen in slow motion. And then others began to scream.

"Ohooooo, ey ose!" He was lying on the floor with red paint covering his hair, face, and shoulders. His nose looked bent to the right. "Fuggg, sittt!" He screamed.

The hallway had erupted into a madhouse. Those who had already entered the classrooms rushed out to see what had happened. Insanity!

Finally, I unfroze and raced to the boy on the floor. Red paint was mixed with blood. I yelled at everyone to get back so we could have some space.

"Someone get Mr. Claussen and have him call the nurse and the EMTs! Now! Let's move!" I yelled into the tangle of students. Another teacher was kneeling by my side now.

"Good Lord! What happened?" he yelled in my ear.

"An explosion when he opened his locker," I hissed back. "Move these students back!"

"Ohmigod! Ohmigod!" screeched a young girl nearby. "We're being attacked!"

"Get her out of here!" I yelled at another teacher standing by her.

"Fugggg! I urt so muk!" The boy was writhing on the floor crying out in pain. "Hep ma! Hep!"

I didn't know his name, but I had seen him the other day with Arnold Purdy. I flashed back to the scene in the parking lot. He was part of Arnold's crew. Jumping scenes to the boys smiling before the explosion from the locker, I looked around for them. No sign. They were in the wind or else well-hidden by the mass of bodies.

"Hang on, we're getting help." I tried to offer words of hope to him. He continued screaming.

The teachers were having some success at moving students, but several wanted to stay nearby to witness the gore.

"What in the devil happened here?" Darnell asked. The school nurse was moving by him and knelt down by the boy. I stood and faced Darnell.

"When he opened his locker something went off and exploded in his face." I walked to the locker and looked in. "Paintball gun rigged to shoot when the locker was opened," Darnell was beside me peering in.

"Son of a bitch!" moaned Claussen so only I could hear. "Someone set this up so opening the locker door pulled the trigger. It looks like one of those Goblin Micro-launcher small paintball guns. It's like a small handgun. At close range these things really do some damage."

I looked at him with a curious expression.

He shrugged, "I do paintball games with some guys once in awhile so know quite a bit about models and so forth."

I tried to picture Darnell dressed like Rambo out in the woods. It didn't come.

"We're going to have to check every locker to make sure this doesn't happen again. And how the hell did someone get into his locker? All lockers have different combinations." Darnell looked like steam should be pouring out of his orifices. He and Mac should get together and destroy something. Maybe a sledge hammer to an old car would do it. Or, maybe a new car?

I checked out for a moment. Okay. Another one of Arnold's crew encounters violence. First Arnold's tire valve stems. Then, the jock strap incident with Archie. Aaron and Billy at the middle school. Now this. Things are ramping up. Smiling gifted kids. What's that about? My equilibrium was thrown way off today. The middle school this morning and now this at the high school. Connected? Don't know, but things are coming unglued at Rua Springs schools, and no one has a clue.

The EMTs pushed their way through the throng of students until they reached the boy on the floor. Darnell and I barked orders at the students to get in their classrooms. A deputy sheriff followed the EMTs in and began his work. No Sheriff Montes this time, but I was sure he probably already knew. The whole town would know soon enough.

Noise in the hallway had tapered off to whispers coming from classrooms. Darnell had stalked off after the EMTs left to make arrangements to check all lockers. I wondered if the paintball gun in a locker was a onetime event though. The deputy sheriff was still working the crime scene. I guess it's a crime scene, but I don't know exactly what the crime is. Deadly weapon use? Maybe. Are paintball guns deadly weapons? Could be under the right circumstances, like close range right in the face. Were paintball guns on the list of no-no's that couldn't be brought to school? I didn't know. The locker door wasn't injured so there wasn't defacing of property. The defacing was to a real human, like harm to "de-face". Ha!

The desire to do anymore work today wasn't in me. I sat in the nurse's office staring at the walls. I was drained. Numb. I reread reports several times and finally gave up.

Out in the hallway I heard the sounds of lockers being opened and closed. Claussen was doing his detective work. Lockers checked in the middle school and now lockers checked in the high school. I was afraid to go to the elementary school for fear of some hideous crime happening there.

The final bell rang, and students stampeded out of the building like a herd of cattle. The stories told about today would get bigger and bigger as the day turned to evening. There would be a lot of absences tomorrow. Parents would be freaked, scared, angry. Time to lock the doors, bar the windows, and stand guard over their kids. The airways would be crackling with phone calls, texts, and emails. Calls to Darnell and Superintendent Espiñosa would keep them up tonight. The school board would be harassed, and they would want answers yesterday. "Why can't you keep our kids safe?" parents would ask. "If you can't do it, we'll get someone who can! Get law enforcement over there and guard my kids!" Steve Montes would be yelled at for not protecting the schools. "Call out the National Guard. This is a terrorist attack!" some would say.

I stood at the front desk waiting for the school to clear out with my mind going in a thousand directions. There had been bad days at school before, but today was brutal for me emotionally. Two more students violated during school; two too many.

Leaving school I drove down the hill into Rua Springs. My brain was short-circuiting trying to put all the pieces together from the last couple of weeks. It felt like it had been a year since I walked into the boy's locker room and saw

Patsy hanging from an overhead pipe by a jump rope. Is any of this connected or are all of these things just unattached things? Some would say school has to be like an armed camp to keep these things from happening and to keep kids safe. What a disaster for kids to have to live this way.

As I was leaving town driving toward home, I remembered I had a haircut scheduled. I had driven right by, my brain fog so complete. I made a "u-ey", drove two blocks, and parked in front of one of my favorite character's shop. My barber, Frank Watatooka: who was also my godfather. Frank was full-blooded Cherokee. My family had Cherokee relatives from a couple generations back. He and Dad had grown up together and were close friends. They had served together in Vietnam where they shared a lot of history. But neither man ever talked about it. They had both survived, come home, and moved on with life. Frank never married, said all he ever wanted to do was cut and style hair. That was interesting considering his own hair, which he almost never cut.

Frank had long white hair pulled back behind his ears. His face was creased like a gully with water trails. Frank had a long forehead on a narrow face with an aquiline nose. His eyes were black onyx. He always dressed in western shirts, Levis and moccasins.

As I entered, Frank boomed out, "Doc! How's it goin'?" Frank had started calling me "Doc", instead of Marc after I had received my doctorate. He said it was an honor to call me that, so he would. He was clipping away at a young boy's shaggy hair. An older lady sat under a dryer. She looked up quickly and then back down at the magazine she was reading, going with the hum of the dryer rather than the talk.

"Hey, Frank. Good to see you!" I sat in one of his ancient chairs, hoping it wouldn't collapse on me.

"Yeah, from what I hear you're probably glad to have made it through the day," Frank winked at me. I knew Frank heard all the gossip around town and seemed to know about everything.

"Tough day, Frank," I yawned, sat back in the chair, crossed my ankles, and closed my eyes. *Walela* with Rita Coolidge and her sisters played in the background. Frank played various artists like John Huling, Carlos Nakai, Queen, Bryan Adams, and The Moody Blues. I was always entertained here.

"Doc, you ready?" I had dozed off. Frank was looking at me from across the room, holding up the multicolored cape to keep hair off my clothes.

I stood on wobbly legs and walked over to the barber chair. "I'm ready, Frank. Just trim it up all over. I'm getting shaggy."

Frank placed the cape over me and secured it to my neck. "Funny thing about hair, Doc. It keeps growing. Even after we're dead it keeps growing. At least that's what I've heard. I've worked on dead people's hair getting them ready for viewing but never after that. So, who knows?"

"Uh...that's interesting, Frank, I guess. Don't dig me up after I die to find the answer, okay?"

"Sure, Doc. No problem. But, what would you care if you were dead? You wouldn't know."

"Well...you look good, Frank! Business okay?" I hoped a quick change of subject would get us off the death talk.

"No need to be afraid of death, Doc. It's a natural part of life. You need to come to terms with it, embrace it. Know what I mean?"

"Just maybe not today, Frank. I'm not ready for it now. Bad day at school, and I'm wrecked." Frank and I had discussed death extensively since I had returned home. He had seen everything life and death could throw at him and walked away smiling. I, on the other hand, had seen enough for the rest of my life and wasn't smiling.

"Lots of rumors going around about happenings at schools, Doc."

I wondered what he already knew. Probably more than I did. "Bad stuff happening. I can't figure it out."

"Cutting hair, I hear things. Kids talk. Share conspiracies. They can't get enough of it. They think life is a movie or video game. Even when it is real it's not real." Frank worked on my hair. I could hear the snipping sounds of the blades coming together. *Snip, snip, pause. Snip, snip, pause.*

"Strange things being said, Doc. The middle school crimes are done by some freako sneaking in when everyone is in class and catching boys when they enter the bathroom. Of course, nobody knows why he isn't ever seen. Kids call him the 'phantasm' saying he can appear and then disappear at will.

"The high school stories are different. No phantasms there. There are stories about how this relates to Patsy Anderson's death. Some say an outside gang, maybe out of Denver, targeted Patsy because she wouldn't go out with one of them. Maybe they killed her. Others are saying it is all a gang thing at school and it is payback. Maybe someone at school killed her because she rejected him."

I recalled one of the students telling me about Patsy rejecting Arnold Purdy. Would he kill her for that? Maybe. There was certainly payback about something going on.

Frank went on, "The kids are confused about all this. They can't believe Patsy committed suicide, and they want to think someone offed her. Vague comments about the gifted kids behavior have leaked out a couple of times. Strange, though, they acted as if they wanted to protect them so didn't say much."

The gifted students were a unique group. Some had IQs in the clouds but struggled in school. Estranged is the word that comes to mind. Patsy seemed to think that way according to her friend Qui. They had certainly shut me out.

"All done, Doc! You're looking great!" Frank removed the cape, shook it out and hung it up, then began sweeping up my donated hair.

I stood from the barber chair, stretched and walked to the counter. Frank came over and put his hand on my shoulder.

"Watch yourself, Doc. There's some dark clouds over the schools right now. Don't let it inside you. It's dangerous to your spirit, and you can't afford it."

I looked directly into Frank's dark eyes; eyes like Dad's. Eyes that had seen too much pain and yet were still warm and caring. Both men knew me well and could see my battle with the descending gloom. They had seen worse. This was just a blip on the radar. But, dang, it seemed like a huge blip.

"Let me tell you a Cherokee story, Doc." Frank stopped, looked at me and began. "Mr. Bear invited Mr. Rabbit to dine with him. They had beans in the pot, but there was no grease for them, so Bear cut a slit in his side and let the oil run out until they had enough to cook the dinner.

"Mr. Rabbit looked surprised and thought to himself, 'That's a handy way. I think I will try that. So, when he started home he invited Mr. Bear to come and have dinner with him four days later.

"When Mr. Bear arrived, Mr. Rabbit said, 'I have beans for dinner too. Now I will get the grease for them.' So, he took a knife and drove it into his side, but instead of oil, a stream of blood gushed out and he fell over nearly dead.

"Mr. Bear picked him up and worked hard to tie up the wound and stop the bleeding. Then he scolded him, 'You little fool, I'm large and strong and lined with fat all over, and the knife doesn't hurt me. But, you're small and lean, and you can't do such things.'"

Again, Frank stopped and looked into my eyes. "Remember, Doc. You are not Mr. Bear."

I laid a twenty on the counter. "Thanks, Frank. I know the danger." Knowing and keeping it away were two different things though. Frank saw right through me too.

We said our good-byes; I left his shop and walked to my truck. The sky still was light, but darkness was coming on fast. It was that time of year. Days were shorter, and the temperatures were dropping. I figuratively wrapped my arms around myself to ward off the cold. Time to get home where it was safe.

CHAPTER TWENTY-FOUR

The dreaded weekend was here. Aunt (Attila the Hun) Lenore would be arriving at any time. Dad and Grandpa were both gloomy at breakfast this morning. I asked again why they didn't tell her she wasn't welcome here.

"She's family," they both said.

"How could she even be related to us?" I asked.

"I was there when she was born," said Grandpa. "She's related. I always wondered if your grandma was fooling around though," said Grandpa.

"She and I used to look like twins," lamented Dad.

She's related. Borderline Lenore, I thought. *Off her meds. Heck, she was probably never on meds,* I considered as I headed to school.

I was thankful that the school week was ending uneventfully. It had been a rough week. Billy hadn't returned to school. No one knew anything. Mac had tried to call his home several times, but there was no answer. He was off the grid. I had heard from Darnell that the paint ball kid, his name was Leroy Malone, did have a broken nose but he wasn't back either. His parents, a couple of backwoods rednecks according to Darnell, were threatening to sue the school. Great! Another possible lawsuit. Superintendent Espiñosa and the school attorney were trying to work something out with them. Good luck there!

The past couple of days had gone by quickly. I saw kids in the elementary school one day and was back in the high school today. I was almost wishing that school continued over the weekend. Almost. The students were antsy. The last football game had been Wednesday night with a nearby school. Why not Friday night? The reason was that the other school was out for parent/teacher conferences. Rua Springs had lost anyhow. They ended the season at .500. It was the last period, and I was a good kind of tired. My last appointment had just returned to class. Even though it had been a difficult week, I believed some good progress was made with several students.

Ba boom! The windows of the high school rattled. I felt the energy of the blast in my feet. Sonic boom? Bomb in the school? Oh no! No, no, no! I screamed silently. Mrs. Neeley and Darnell were already in the outer office. I met them there and we raced out into the hall.

"What?" cried Darnell. "What was it?"

"Don't know," I replied. My voice was low, hoarse.

Teachers were in the hallway yelling back and forth. Confused, scared looks were etched on their faces. Students were talking loudly from within the classrooms. Some of their heads were sticking out of doorways.

"It was a bomb!" screamed a female voice from down the hall.

"We need to evacuate!" yelled a nearby teacher at Darnell. Darnell had come out of his stupor and started down the hall. I stayed with him. "Back in the classrooms! Go back in! Let us check this out. Please! Please remain calm. There is no smoke so we are okay."

I wondered how he knew we were okay. Just because there was no smoke doesn't mean there wasn't a fire somewhere. My nerve endings were firing triple time. It felt like a band was tightening around my chest. *Got to get a grip,* I told myself. *Don't freak out.*

"What if we're under attack?" shrilled a young girl standing in a classroom door.

"We are not under attack!" yelled some male from inside the room. "Don't be a dunderhead, Sybil! It was probably a sonic boom."

A teacher came running out of her classroom. "The parking lot! A truck is on fire. We can see it out of our windows."

"Keep everyone in their rooms!" boomed Darnell to the teachers. We ran to the building doors that faced the parking lot. Darnell was on his cell calling 911 and the fire department.

Racing down the steps we could see a truck in the middle of the lot burning out-of-control. Heavy dark clouds of smoke were rising as the flames danced on every surface of the truck. The heat was so intense we couldn't get close. Cars parked nearby were being scorched. Paint peeled and windows cracked. Selfishly, I was glad my truck was parked elsewhere. Unfortunately, I recognized this truck. It was

Arnold Purdy's big red Dodge Ram. Good God almighty! They targeted his truck again. It was toast, and there would be hell to pay.

"Ahhhhhhhhh!" cried a voice behind us. "No way! No way! Noooo! My truck! My truck! I will kill them! Those fuckers will die! Die! Dead, dead, dead!"

Angry tears streamed down Arnold's face.

He tried to run past us into the flames. Darnell and I both grabbed him.

"Get your fuckin' hands off me! I'll kill you! You bastards! I'll kill you both! Let go of me! I have to save my truck!"

It took all our strength to keep him from running into the flames. "Arnold! Stop! It's too dangerous. It's gone, Arnold," Darnell yelled. He had moved in front of him. I had him in a bear hug from the back. Racking sobs came from Arnold.

"My truck," he whimpered through his tears. "My truck. Who would do this to my truck?" He was spent, limp. The life had gone out of him. He would have collapsed if we had let go of him.

The three of us stood there. Darnell and I held on to Arnold, watching the flames devour the truck. I was sick to my stomach. Way too far. This had gone way too far. No matter what Arnold had done in the past, this was beyond senseless.

Siren sounds bounced off the surrounding mountains sending a chorus of echoes at us and bombarding us with the cruel music of a tragedy in progress. Arnold changed from trying to pull away from us to hanging on to us like a broken person clutching to life. My emotions were jumbled, raw. All out war had been brought to Arnold and his crew. Whatever had happened, Arnold's total demise was the goal, and it had been reached.

The fire trucks could now be seen winding their way toward us. Behind them I could see a couple of sheriff's department SUVs close behind. We waited in silence as the fire trucks stopped, quickly brought out their equipment and dragged the hoses toward the burning truck.

Sheriff Montes stepped out of his vehicle and walked toward us. Another deputy was behind him. "Marc. Darnell," he acknowledged us first. "Arnold, I'm really sorry about your truck." Evidently, Steve somehow was acquainted with Arnold. I could only imagine those situations. Steve was going to speak with Arnold about Patsy. Maybe he already had.

"We'll need to process this as soon as the fire has cooled. This will take awhile so we'll have to make arrangements for students to leave school without impacting our work. It looks like some other vehicles are also damaged so they stay too."

"Let me know when and how we can release the students, Sheriff," said Darnell.

"Yeah, just hang on, and we'll set this up for you," intoned Steve.

"Arnold, we'll need to talk about this as soon as possible. Not right now but soon. Okay?" Steve stood in front of Arnold, waiting.

After some uncomfortable silence, Arnold was whisper quiet when he spoke, "Yeah, okay."

Time moved slowly until the students were released, and their vehicles could be maneuvered out of the parking lot.

I returned to the middle school and packed up my book bag and returned to the parking lot. The fire department was still working on hot spots with the vehicles. Steve was making calls to bring in klieg lights to continue work on the crime scene. Trucks don't usually light themselves on fire. They need help, so Steve was calling it a possible crime scene.

Arnold's mom showed up shortly before I was leaving. I could hear her ranting in Steve's face about who was going to pay for this and what she was going to do to him. This was the first time I had seen Mrs. Purdy, and I could see that my dad was right. Arnold looked like his mom, including the sneering facial expressions. Not attractive at all. I still felt a tinge of sorrow for Arnold, but watching him gear up to join his mom in the diatribe lessened my sorrow. He was bouncing back quickly.

CHAPTER TWENTY-FIVE

It was dinnertime when I arrived home. There were two cars parked in the driveway. The Prius I recognized as Cousin Katherine's. The other was a black Hummer. I parked off to the side of the road since I couldn't get in the driveway. Exiting my truck, I hooked my book bag over my left shoulder, locked up, walked to the Hummer, and looked in the driver's window. There was an Avis rental brochure on the passenger seat. Aunt Lenore! Who else would rent a vehicle that guzzles gas and looked like it belonged in a Mad Max movie. I shook my head and walked to the side door of the garage. Entering, I stopped to gather my strength before proceeding to the battlefield. A loud female voice could be heard above all the other sounds. Oh, geez, I would rather smash my thumb with a hammer.

"Get them away from me! What's wrong with these mutts? I hate dogs! No! No! Get away, you damn dogs! My white slacks are already coated with hair! Back off you mutts, or I'll kick the shit out of you!" Aunt Lenore screamed.

"Hey! Hey! You back off, Lenore! These dogs live here and are family. You don't live here! So don't you dare speak to them that way!" Dad was so angry spittle was flying from his lips as he yelled at her. I thought he was going to punch her.

"I will talk to them anyway I…"

"Like hell you will! Not in my house! So shut your face or else leave!" Dad was almost nose to nose with her. The cords in his neck were as tight as cables and bright red.

Standing in the doorway I watched all this unfold. Katherine stood by the sink with Grandpa, holding his hand. Their faces showed the horrible embarrassment of Lenore's behavior. They probably wanted to crawl in a hole. Wow! Welcome home everyone!

Kong and Sunny spotted me, gave up on Lenore, and raced over. I kneeled down and nuzzled both of them. I would have sworn they both smiled at me and winked. Huh. Silently, I was saying, "good job guys." She shouldn't have worn nice white pants here anyway. Maybe she'll decide to leave. She spotted me. Oh, oh.

"Marky, how good to see you!" Lenore left Dad and hurried toward me.

"My name is Marc not Marky, Lenore."

"Okay, Mar…c," She almost discounted my correction but caught herself. Lenore always tried to get away with calling me "Marky" like I was still a little boy. I challenged her on it when I was age six, and it has never stopped.

She tried to give me a hug. It was awkward, because I always felt like she was trying to grope me, so I resisted. And she always smelled like cigarette smoke and booze. I figure she drank on the plane from San Diego to Denver and maybe stopped for another hit on the way here. Those smells on top of her same old sickly sweet perfume made me want to wretch. I was sure she used embalming fluid as perfume.

Lenore was three years older than Dad. She had Grandma Thomas's height instead of being short like Grandpa. There was a time when she did look like Dad but not anymore. She looked worn, used up. Lenore had already had surgeries to do away with any wrinkles. I could see tiny scars.

Her overall look was of someone trying to stay young and failing. Lenore's hair was in a flaming bright red perm that was almost blinding. She was thin almost anorexic, starved. Covering her dark black eyes were blue contacts. It was clear she was working hard to not look like her family. Why was she so different? What happened to her? The stories I heard as a child, sneaking around the house listening to secret conversations, talked about her crazy moods. Up. Down. Crying about nothing, something, everything. Laughing inappropriately. Inability to keep friends. Crowding them. Smothering. Flings with men. Diagnosis? Medication was not mentioned that I heard. Maybe my grandparents couldn't get her to see someone. Maybe she did go, tried it, quit. "No talk rule" for this family. There was a purple elephant in the living room, and nobody acknowledged it being there.

"You still have that cap gun I gave you when you were young?" Lenore blurted.

What? I stumbled back on my heels in my brain. Where did this come from? "Uh...cap gun, Lenore?"

"Remember, I gave you a cap gun for your birthday?"

My memories of gifts from Lenore were zero. She was not known for giving anyone anything. She took. Selfish. Into herself.

"I don't remember it, Lenore."

"Oh...I was sure since it was a gift from me you would still have it for sentimental reasons." She looked crushed, betrayed. A look of hate crossed her look. *You'll pay for this,* I could almost hear her say.

The kitchen was silent for a moment. Gloom had settled over it, clutching at my throat. An alien force had invaded our home. Safe was now unsafe.

Shift. "Well...it is great being home! I've missed all of you! It's just that I am so busy, I can't get away," said Lenore. Excited. Bubbly. Shift.

"Let's eat! I'm starved." Grandpa was not his usual self. His tone wasn't playful or joking. His daughter must be an enigma to him. We never talked about Lenore. She never came up for any of us. Too painful? Even wild and crazy Grandpa Thomas had feelings. It was probably not a conversation I was going to have with him or Dad anytime soon.

We followed Grandpa into the dining room. Two large Papa Murphy's stuffed pizzas were laid out on the table.

"I picked these up on the way home from work. Figured we would all be hungry." Dad didn't meet Lenore's glaring look.

"Looks and smells great to me," exclaimed Katherine.

"I don't like pizza. You know that. Why did you get pizza?" Lenore was shifting again. Aggressive. Hostile.

Dad bit back an angry retort, "Lenore..."

"We all work hard, Mom. There isn't a lot of time to fix a fancy meal." Katherine, the daughter, peace-maker. "This will be great! Thanks, Uncle Bret, for getting them!"

Grandpa was already sitting, snagging a couple of pieces of pizza. "Ummm," He snorted, as he chewed off a chunk.

The rest of us sat and began to load up our plates. Dad had purchased salads, also. A plate of large cookies took center stage on the table. We all dug in; all except Lenore. She sat with her arms crossed and glared. None of us paid her any attention. Conversations took off in several directions with each of us sharing our day with each other. Our conversation was lively and friendly. The four of us got together often so we were comfortable with our talk.

Lenore finally realized we wouldn't play her game. She leaned forward to spoon out some salad on her plate and filled her glass with ginger ale. "I guess salad will have to do," she grumbled. We continued our conversations.

"Mrs. Grumbine died yesterday," shared Katherine. "She was in the assisted living home for years. She was ninety-eight years old. Can you believe it? I'm doing her memorial service at Zamora's Funeral Home Sunday afternoon. I loved visiting her. The stories she would tell. Raunchy! Wow!" Katherine was beaming.

"Me and Charlie saw her every week," Grandpa said, with a mouthful of pizza. "She was a doll. Yeah, her stories were raunchy. We loved 'um, me and Charlie. Of course, we told her a few of our own. She loved dirty jokes. Had a litany of them longer than Charlie and me combined." Grandpa's eyes clouded over. He stopped and swallowed, choked up.

He wiped his eyes with the back of his hand, chewed some more, and laughed one of his trademark wheezy laughs.

"Did you hear the one about the guy who had to go to the ER because his girlfriend stuck a wire up his dong?"

"Okay, Pa. It's okay. We don't need to hear that one right now," said Dad.

"It was one of old Mrs. Grumbine's favorites. She laughed till she cried every time... Humph."

"I went on an Alaskan cruise a few months ago!" Lenore was back again.

"That's great, Lenore. Can you tell us about it?" I really was interested but probably sounded like I was making fun of her.

She looked at me, squinting her eyes, wondering if I was serious. Lenore probably didn't have many friends. They wouldn't put up with her. She decided I was serious and really wanted to know.

Lenore spoke for thirty minutes about her trip. She went with some new male friend named Monte. As the story progressed Monte sounded worse and worse. He didn't measure up and was the only downer on the trip. When they returned home, Monte hit the road. Gone. Splitsville. Hasta luego, baby. Good riddance. Sounded like a good guy to me. Lenore had a new beau now named Pierre. According to Lenore he is fantastic. The love of Lenore's life. Huh?

"How about your love life, Marc? Got any 'honeys' on the side?" Wink, wink from Lenore. "I'll bet all the ladies are ready to jump your bones," Laugh, laugh.

Even though I felt invaded, I tried to hold my tongue from blurting out obscenities at her. "No, Lenore. I'm not seeing anyone." End of discussion. No it wasn't.

"How long has it been since Lilly died? Two years? It's time to get back in the saddle, Marc. There is life to live!"

I wanted to shove a large piece of pizza up her nostrils. The tension spiked in the room. For a moment it was electric as everyone watched and waited for me to pounce. Control. I have it. I won't stoop to her level. I didn't bite. She waited.

"Well...how about those cookies Uncle Bret brought us? They're huge!" offered Katherine. Grandpa already had one in his mouth. Lenore gave Katherine a look like it would burn the hair off her head. Katherine looked at her mom and didn't flinch.

"Uh, huh. Uge," Grandpa said, as he chewed. If there was a heaven, he looked like he was in it.

Dad, Katherine, and I stood and collected our dishes to take to the kitchen. Grandpa was inhaling the next large cookie and eyeing another one. Lenore looked like she couldn't believe we all abandoned her. I almost felt sorry for her. She traveled all the way from San Diego for a family visit, and this is what she got. Why did she even bother? It was this way every time she came. It was love/hate with Lenore and the rest of us. Conversations among her family members showed that everyone really wanted to include her. Unfortunately, Lenore pushed us away and then tried to jerk us back. She really did have a mental disorder. Probably borderline. Maybe bipolar too. Knowing that didn't draw me to her, though. Those days were long since gone by the entire family. Drive on.

After we had cleaned the dishes and readied the coffee for morning, we all adjourned to the living room. Katherine had brought her guitar, so Dad and I set up to play some music. Katherine was an outstanding guitarist. She was a natural. I wasn't. Lenore commandeered Dad's recliner. Grandpa lit a fire in the fireplace. In a few moments it was blazing. The sap from the ponderosa pine popped as it was heated. Table lamps sent soft light with dancing shadows into various parts of the living room. For a moment all of us watched the fire. A serene sense enveloped me as only the noise and flames from the fire worked on us. Sunny and Kong stretched out in front of the stone fireplace and closed their eyes. Grandpa rose from the hearth, petted both dogs and moved to his recliner. He sat and then leaned back with a smile on his face. Ambience at its best.

"I saw Frank today, Dad. We should have invited him and his bass guitar tonight." Frank was an awesome bass player and had played professionally with a couple of bands in earlier days.

"Having Frank here would have been great," sighed Dad. "I imagine he is busy, though." What Dad meant, and we all knew it, was that Frank wouldn't be caught dead or alive in the same room with Lenore. His disgust of her was well-known. She treated him like dirt as a kid. He tried to like her because he was Dad's friend, but she abused him mercilessly. Dad didn't know why, nor did my grandparents. The only possible reason might have been that Frank's family was poor, and they were Native American. Lenore never admitted anything. It was just what she did.

"What shall we play?" asked Katherine.

"Let's play some early Billy Joel tunes," suggested Dad.

"Yeah, Dad, let's start with *Piano Man*." And so we did.

Dad was high on our music as he rolled through *Piano Man* and into *Only the Good Die Young*. Katherine and I would follow Dad's lead on the piano and she would play lead and I would play rhythm. We followed those with *The Stranger* and *Just the Way You Are.* We stopped and stretched our fingers, feeling good. Music had always brought peace to our family. Lenore was clapping and asking for more. She requested *Captain Jack* and *Big Shot.* We rocked on.

Lenore stood, walked over to Grandpa and grabbed his hands, pulling him to his feet. As we played, she and Grandpa boogied. Laughing together, they did the funky chicken. I knew Grandpa could dance, but watching Lenore's graceful moves was a heart stopper. And I knew she had broken more hearts than I could count. Too bad. If only she could manage her life.

I played on, watching her. She seemed happy, content. We all were. After *Movin' Out* and *New York State of Mind,* we wrapped up. My fingers were almost raw but felt good. It didn't get any better than this. The rest of the evening was spent in quiet conversation, catching up. Peace for now.

CHAPTER TWENTY-SIX

The next morning Katherine arrived with her partner, Lexie, for breakfast. Lenore came in looking like she was going to a fashion show; hair immaculate, black pant suit with sequins, low black heels, pearl necklace and earrings, and silver bracelets. Everything looked expensive, but I didn't have a clue about fashion. Lenore ignored Lexie, not even a hello. Katherine and Lexie were used to Lenore's shunning. They had received the moralistic lecture from Lenore years ago and shrugged it off. Hearing a morality speech from Lenore was humorous.

All of us pitched in to set the dining room table. Dad had cooked up bacon, sausage, and scrambled eggs with chorizo. Grandpa had baked his famous gooey buns that added five pounds of fat for every one eaten. With jugs of orange juice and hot piñon coffee to wash down the chow we were ready.

"We're hiking part of the Colorado Trail in Pike National Forest today," said Katherine. The plan is a seven mile trek up Raleigh Peak. "Marc, Lexie, and I are going. Anyone else interested?" She already knew the answer. Dad and Grandpa were working at the hardware store. That left Lenore, and we all knew she wasn't going for any hike dressed like she was going to a big city dinner reception.

"Pa and I have to work the store today. Sorry we can't join you. You all have fun. It is late in the season for that trail but it should still be open, and the weather report is blue skies and cool breezes."

We all waited for Lenore to respond. Sounds of silverware on pottery plates, chewing of food and gulping of drinks filled the space.

"I'm playing tourist today and stopping by to see a few friends," giggled Lenore.

I didn't think she had any friends here, but what did I know.

"Sounds like everyone's day is all set," said dad through a mouthful of chorizo filled scrambled eggs.

Food sounds filled the dining room again. We were all alive and well and taking sustenance, getting ready for our day.

Katherine, Lexie, and I were tired after our hike and arrived home in the late afternoon. We had encountered some snow on the trail from a recent fall storm, but otherwise it was a perfect day. The Raleigh Peak hike wasn't very long or strenuous, but it was still nice to have a change of scenery. We had gone off the Colorado trail to explore the quarries near Raleigh Peak and that added some time and energy to our day. Lunch was fruit, cheese, trail mix, and Power Bars on top of Raleigh Peak. Even though we had packed our day packs with sweaters and rain gear, we didn't need them. The three of us talked about community things: church, school and, of course, Lenore. It was all low-key, just sharing information. We spoke softly to each other when we spotted a certain bird or animal. Three introverts on a hike gives a lot of time for introspection, and we each had several hours of that.

I cleaned up to ready myself for dinner with Steve Montes and his family. Katherine and Lexie already had other plans for dinner, so they were heading home. Dad, Grandpa and Lenore were going out to the China Wok Restaurant for dinner, so we all prepared ourselves for our night out. Aunt Lenore added a few choice comments about those of us who were not joining her for dinner. She couldn't understand why we didn't cancel our plans and come with her. What could we say? We told her we already had plans before we knew she was coming, but I had other words I wanted to say. I didn't blow my great day by jumping into the snake pit with her though.

Arriving at Steve's place I was again amazed at the hacienda the Montes family had created. All but one of Steve's siblings lived in their own homes on the Montes Hacienda. Each house kept the original southwestern adobe-look of the main house. It was the gathering place and at the center of the structures. The houses made a semicircle around the main house. Two large barns stood behind them.

Children were playing in a large park-like area in front of the main house. Several older youth were sitting on the large verandah near Grandmother Montes. Steve came out to meet me.

"Hola, Marc, gracias para venida. La abuela ha estado preguntando por usted." *(Hello, Marc, thanks for coming. Grandmother has been asking about you.)*

"Es bueno estar aquí otra vez, *Steve*, y estar aquí por los cumpleaños de su abuela. *"(It's good to be here again, Steve, and to be here for your grandmother's birthday.)*

"Vayamos vea a Abuela Bosques. Será estremecida." *(Let's go see Grandmother Montes. She will be thrilled.)*

Walking to the verandah, several of the children and young people said hello to me. We all knew each other from school, but none of them were on my "client" list.

"¡Yo tan soy honorado que vino, Marc! Mis cumpleaños son completos ahora." (I am so honored that you came, Marc! My birthday is complete now.)

"¡Los cumpleaños felices, la abuela! Parece maravilloso y nunca edad un poco." *(Happy birthday, Grandmother! You look wonderful and never age a bit.)*

"¡Qué diablo de pico de oro que usted es! Sé qué edad que miro tan se olvida sus mentiras resbaladizas. Por lo menos usted no ha cambiado su hábito de estirar la verdad." *(Oh, what a silver-tongued devil you are! I know how old I look so forget your slick lies. At least you haven't changed your habit of stretching the truth.)* She cackled and slapped her leg with her hand. We laughed together as I bent down and gave her a hug.

The evening was filled with great food and laughter. It was good to catch up with my second family this way. Everyone was doing well and the love and respect shown to one another was amazing. I flashed on Aunt Lenore and wondered how we added her to our mix. Who can guess about families?

Steve and I spoke briefly about the crazy things going on at school. He said he was suspicious about several things and was checking them out. My brain was fried from a long day hiking, great friendships, and incredible food. I couldn't fit all the school pieces together in my head, though. Brain fog. But I had a suspicion of how things might tie together and I didn't like it one bit.

I finally said my good-byes and walked with the embrace of the dark to my truck. Driving home, I moved slowly because of the large number of deer out by the road. A skunk skedaddled across the road moving through the beams of my headlights. What I didn't want to do was harm that guy tonight. Whoee! I caught a whiff of its lovely odor as I slowly moved past. Fog slipped in and out of my headlights having a mesmerizing effect on my senses. My bed was calling me, and I was listening.

The weekend was over and I was on the road to school. Aunt Lenore left Sunday morning still angry about what Grandpa had done at the China Wok Restaurant Saturday night. The story I heard Sunday morning was that when they had arrived at the restaurant, Grandpa had gone to the kitchen to visit with his friends there. The Chang family loved Grandpa and allowed him to help out whenever he showed up. Of course, Lenore didn't know anything about this so when Grandpa came out dressed like a waitperson and speaking like some version of the old fictional detective Charlie Chan, wearing round, black rimmed glasses and fake buck teeth. Lenore was totally humiliated.

The China Wok was filled to capacity that night so Grandpa was making the rounds taking and delivering orders. All the while, he was in his Charlie Chan act. And, to make matters worse, he told everyone that Lenore was his long lost daughter who had finally come to visit. Lenore's face was as red as her hair, she was so outraged. Dad thought she was going to have a stroke right then and there. He said he tried to keep a straight face but couldn't pull it off. She was so mad, she didn't even eat.

Dad and Grandpa told me all this after Lenore had stomped out of the house with her designer suitcase, jumped in her Hummer rental, and sped off toward the Denver airport. They were both laughing so hard, they could barely get the story out. I wasn't laughing as hard, but picturing it wasn't hard to do. Part of me felt sorry for Lenore, but she would turn the tables, if given the chance, and grind someone into the ground if they crossed her.

CHAPTER TWENTY-SEVEN

Parking in the school lot, I turned off the truck and sat for a moment watching students and faculty trudge toward their respective buildings. No one looked like they wanted to come to school this Monday morning. Last week was fresh in my mind. A few spaces away from where I parked was the scorched pavement where Arnold Purdy's truck had fried itself. Man oh man, I didn't want another week like that one. Please, no!

Checking in at the middle school office, Mrs. Chang was at her desk, fingers flying over the keyboard.

"Mornin', Mrs. Chang!"

She looked up at me, smiled, and said, "Good morning, Doctor Thomas." All the while her fingers danced on the keys. A multitasker for sure. "Your grandfather was a hit Saturday night at the restaurant. He makes all of us smile."

"Were you there?"

"Yes, I was helping out in the kitchen. He had all of us laughing so hard we were crying."

"Evidently, he didn't make Aunt Lenore very happy. She still wanted to strangle him on Sunday morning."

"He didn't do anything wrong at all. She was just too sensitive. Of course, she always has been." Mrs. Chang had known Aunt Lenore from way back, but she was kind with her words.

"Yeah, Lenore is…sometimes difficult," I offered.

"Hmmm." Mrs. Chang usually kept her true feelings to herself, so she wouldn't speak ill of Lenore.

My morning began with a divorce group for young boys. I had begun a group for second grade boys from divorced families a month ago. Parents had given permission for them to attend the group after the second grade teachers made recommendations. There were six young boys and none of them had missed a week yet. In fact, now they hounded me almost every day to come to my office for group.

The boys were very leery at first. They didn't know me and either their trust levels were zero or they were too trusting. Either too much or too little was a problem. A couple of the boys were totally flat in their affect. They had shut down completely. Another two had begun to talk about their parent's divorce. The remaining two were flying with either extreme happiness or extreme anger. All six of the boys had academic performance problems now. Their parents had given permission, but that didn't mean the parents had stopped acting like children themselves.

Divorced parents often times bad-mouthed each other to their children, dumped too many emotions on their children, used their children as go-between's, threatened legal action in front of their children, brought home strangers to spend the night, left their children with other caretakers too often, drank and drugged into oblivion, went into deep depressions, and a multitude of other things. The bottom line is that the kids were abandoned because the parents sling unhealthy behavior all over their children. How do you cope with life when your caregivers drop you off an emotional cliff?

So, week after week I watched these six boys try to survive another minute, hour, day without totally going berserk. And then, when the young people come unglued, the teachers and school system are blamed for not doing enough. What's wrong with this picture?

The boys and I were sitting on the floor in my office playing the "Talking-Feeling-Doing Game". Last week we had begun to explore feelings and values. The boys liked it so much they wanted to play it again this week, so here we were. Chris rolled the dice and landed on a yellow space, so he drew a "feeling" card. He read it to the group, "When Donna is sad, she wants to eat. What do you do when you feel sad?" Chris looked at the card and then up at me.

Most of these boys had never discussed their feelings before, so this was a major step for them. Of course, many grown men still haven't explored their feelings, so maybe these boys would learn early in life what made them tick.

"Well...I just...you know...kind of go to my room and play with my trucks," said Chris. He kept his head down, not looking at the rest of us.

"Chris, does playing with your trucks help you to feel less sad?" I asked

He looked at me with large eyes, startled that I wanted to know more. "I guess...sort of," he said quietly.

Harry was sitting next to Chris. He rolled the dice and also landed on a "feeling" space. He grabbed the next card and started to read, "Robin feels angry when someone teases her. When do you feel angry?" Harry didn't hesitate. "I'm angry at my dad for leaving us!" He blasted it out. The rest of us waited. I could see that some of the boys were stunned at the vehemence of his outburst.

"Have you ever told your dad you are angry at him, Harry?" I asked.

He looked at me for a moment and then his face fell. "No," he whispered. "I'm afraid he'll never come back if I tell him."

Other boys shook their heads, agreeing with Harry. It was a common theme. Fear of losing one or both parents keeps kids quiet, unable to really tell their parents how they feel.

We played for another twenty minutes talking about fears, courage, disappointments, and nightmares. One boy landed on a "doing" space and had to put his finger in his belly button. The others roared with laughter and put their fingers in their belly buttons, too. So did I! What a hoot! The boys were opening up some, but there was a long way to go. After taking them back to class, I realized I felt empty. Their stories drained me. They had so much pain, and I could only be a small way station of hope on a hard journey.

Later in the day, after sitting through two IEP meetings and a multitude of paper work, I left my office in the middle school and walked to the high school. The day was clear but cold. The temperature hovered near freezing, and I had left my coat at home. Dumb. It even smelled like rain, but I didn't see many clouds on the horizons. The weather could change quickly in the mountains so being unprepared was not a good excuse. The gravel crunched under my shoes. The small stones seemed to feel the cold also and appeared to cry out in pain as I stepped on them. I was going too far with this. Stones didn't feel. Did they?

After pulling open the hall exterior door, I entered. The door hissed shut behind me. Turning my head to look behind me, I thought the doors made a different sound today. Nothing there. Huh. I was getting jumpy. Maybe the school day had been too quiet. No problems. No crisis. It was easy to become jumpy because of the last couple of weeks at school. It was easy to fall into those PTSD behaviors. I was just waiting for the other shoe to drop. Not a good way to live. No one had told me I had eye tics yet. Maybe I was still okay. Tic, tic. Not funny.

The high school office was quiet for once. Even Mrs. Neeley was away from her desk. Where was everyone? Maybe they had had enough and had run screaming from the building. Too quiet. I looked in Darnell's office, but it was empty. The teacher's lounge down the short hallway to the right was deserted. Geez! I was getting spooked. I walked back out in the main hallway to make sure school was in session. Standing still, I calmed my breathing and listened. Yes, the classes were doing business as usual. Voices floated into the hallway from classrooms.

Walking back into the office, the first person I saw was Mrs. Neeley at her desk. How did she get there? Darnell was talking on the phone in his office. Huh? Maybe Mrs. Neeley and Darnell had been hiding in the bathroom together. Nah! I slapped my mind around trying to lose that visual image.

"Hello, Doctor Thomas!" exclaimed Mrs. Neeley.

"Uh...hi, Mrs. Neeley. How are you doing?" I grabbed the image of her and Darnell out of my head and deleted it. Press delete! Hopefully, my thoughts weren't showing on my face.

"This letter was left on the counter for you. Just your name typed on the envelope. I don't know who it's from." She serenely looked at me. Okay, she couldn't read my gutter mind. I was okay.

"Thanks, Mrs. Neeley." I picked up the envelope and looked at the front and back. Nothing but my name, Dr. Thomas, was typed on the front. Interesting. Why do people always look at an envelope as if it has more writing on it when it obviously doesn't? Invisible ink? Secret code? Nanoparticles built into the paper? Maybe the nanos were crawling up my arm now! Yikes!

The nurse's office was free, so I went in and made myself comfortable in the desk chair. Holding the envelope in both hands I stared at it for a moment before making the decision to open it. I didn't have a letter opener so I ripped open the flap. A single sheet of paper was inside. It was folded in thirds. I pulled it out and unfolded it. It was typed and had no signature. I began to read:

Dear Dr. Thomas:

I wasn't sure how to go to about this. But, things have gone too far now, and I need to tell someone. It wasn't supposed to be this way, but we let it grow beyond us. It needs to stop.

This began a long time ago, but Patsy Anderson's death brought it to a head. We believe Patsy was killed by others here at school, but we have no proof. You have probably noticed that some strange things have gone on recently. We have taken action against those we think are responsible. Someone needs to pay. At least that is what I thought until now. Plans are in the works for more extreme violence against some people. I can't be involved anymore.

I trust you, as do others, and I need your help ending this. There is a secret group here at school called the "Einstein Posse". I'm a member, as are several others. We meet every week at the old Bonner place. Please come there tonight and help stop this before it goes too far. Seven o'clock.

White envelope and white paper. I looked at it front and back and read the letter again and again. Secret group? The Einstein Posse? They thought someone killed Patsy. Who? I was guessing that the "strange things" were those things that had happened to Arnold Purdy and his crew and the boys in the middle school. Did they think Arnold and his group killed Patsy? Why? I knew about Patsy's rejections of Arnold. Was that enough to kill her? That seemed weak. Maybe there was a lot more unknown about that rejection. And where was the Bonner place? I had never heard of it. Dad would know. The Einstein Posse? Give me a break!

After school I drove to Dad's hardware store to ask him about the Bonner place. Entering the store, I saw Dad waiting on a customer in the paint section. He looked up and nodded. I heard Grandpa's wheezy laugh coming out of one of the aisles. He was probably telling someone a crude joke. I walked down the center aisle looking right and left. Grandpa was in a left aisle helping some older lady with light bulbs. They seemed to be flirting with each other. One would whisper something and touch the other's hand and the other would whisper something back and touch hands again. They reminded me of adolescents working up to the main event. For them, maybe the main event was just touching each other's hands. But, with my grandpa nothing would surprise me. What a Casanova my grandpa is! I slipped on by, smiling. No touching interruptus by me today.

Dad finished with his customer and walked toward me. "Hi, Marc. Everything okay?" His dark eyes bored into mine.

"Sure, Dad. A quiet day at school." I glanced around, feeling paranoid. Was someone listening?

Dad's eyes roamed to where I had glanced. Curious. Concerned. "Something's up, Marc. I recognize that look of yours."

I reached up with my right hand and pulled the unsigned letter from my left shirt pocket. Handing it to him I said, "This was left in the high school office for me."

He unfolded the letter and began reading it. His brow furrowed as he read. Like me, he turned the letter over looking for some sign as to who had written it. He read it again.

"I haven't heard mention of the Bonner place in decades." He handed the letter back to me. "When I was a kid I heard stories about the place being haunted. Grisly tales that scared the heck out of me. The stories had to do with old man Bonner back around 1910. He was a sheep rancher who was continually at odds with the cattle ranchers around him. His sheep went missing. They were found shot, sometimes gutted and hung from trees, heads cut off. Bonner called the law on his neighbors, but nothing ever happened. He didn't get any help so he decided to become the law himself.

"The story goes that he made plans to go after the cattle ranchers. But he made a mistake. He trusted his own family. Bonner had a wife and three daughters. Unknown to him, his oldest daughter was having a secret fling with one of the sons of a cattle rancher. She tipped them off. When he showed up one night, they were all waiting for him. He was armed with a shotgun, but the ranchers were waiting with rifles and pistols. They "convinced" him to drop his shotgun and go on home.

"Bonner was totally humiliated. He couldn't imagine how they had known and were waiting for him. The story goes that he was in a desperate mood and began on some of his homemade moonshine he made in his still out in his barn. His wife and daughters were also becoming more distraught the more he drank. He asked how the cattle ranchers had known. Finally, his wife told him about their oldest daughter.

"Bonner erupted, screaming, cursing, breaking things, yelling that his own family had betrayed him. He was trying to keep the family alive with his sheep ranching and this is what they did to him. Finally, he grabbed another shotgun off the wall and threatened to kill his wife and daughters. Everyone was hysterical. They begged him not to kill them.

He didn't. He got revenge on them by blowing his own head off."

The suspense of the story hung in the air. I could picture it all happening and could still feel the emotions of that fateful night. "Whoa, Dad!"

"Yeah. Quite a story. Who knows if that is exactly what happened. The ladies stayed on for awhile but couldn't keep the sheep ranching going. They drifted away to who knows where. The place has stayed empty since then. Old man Bonner is supposedly still shrieking around the place wanting to tell everyone how he was betrayed." Dad stopped. He took a deep breath and then another.

"When Frank and I were teenagers we decided to venture to the Bonner place to test our abilities with a haunted house. We went out there one summer night with flashlights and a Coleman lantern. At that time it was still in pretty good shape for an old log cabin. The windows were out and time had taken its toll, but the walls, roof, and floor were still intact. Frank and I tried to scare each other by yelling out that we had seen old man Bonner's ghost, but all we did was scream and then laugh about it. We stayed there for an hour or so hoping to find something, but the place was bare of everything, including ghosts."

Customers were browsing as they walked up and down the aisles. Other workers were right there helping them. I could still hear Grandpa's wheezy laugh a couple of aisles over. The pictures in my head of the Bonner nightmare ran before my eyes. I shivered, feeling a cold draft float over me. Probably just the front doors opening and closing.

"Where is this place, Dad? I've never heard of it."

"It's about forty minutes from town. You head out north and then cut west on an old road. It's gated and not even marked. I think another rancher bought the land and then just left the old cabin."

"I'm going out there tonight. I'll need directions."

"Marc, I can't really tell you how to get there. But I can show you. I'm coming along."

"Well, you don't have to do that, Dad. I can probably find it."

"No, you won't find it alone. I'm going. Besides, you don't really know what is going on out there with this Einstein Posse. It could be dangerous considering what they may have done at school so far. I don't think you're dealing with any brain-dead kids here. This has all been much too sophisticated."

Thinking about what Dad said, I had to agree. It would be dumb on my part to show up out there with nothing but a smile. I didn't have the experience, insights, or skills that Dad had, even if they were forced on him during war.

"You're right, Dad. Thanks for coming along tonight. I'll have dinner ready when you and Grandpa get home, then we can make plans."

"I may not be able to drag pa away from old Mrs. Teeters. They've been at their mating dance for an hour. The old guy does wow the ladies around here, young and old. Who would have guessed?"

CHAPTER TWENTY-EIGHT

S almon burgers and a tossed salad were ready when Dad and Grandpa arrived home. Somehow Dad had pulled Grandpa away from the widow, Mrs. Teeters. Grandpa was still smiling and had a big appetite, so Mrs. Teeters must have infused him with happiness and energy.

In between bites he finally spoke, "I'm going with you."

"What? I don't think that's a good idea, Grandpa. Who knows what we will run into out there?"

"Listen to me, sonny boy, I've been around a lot longer than you have. You wouldn't believe all the things I've been through. I know the Bonner place so I'm going."

It crossed my mind that maybe I was glad I didn't know all the things Grandpa had been through. He had probably made a wreck of many of them. He had survived, though, so I guess he was not as much of a bumbler as he seemed to be.

"Dad?" I looked at Dad hoping he would jump in and tell Grandpa to get lost.

Dad chewed a few times, swallowed, took a drink of water from his glass, and wiped his lips with his napkin. "He knows the Bonner place, Marc. We can't keep him home."

With a triumphant look, Grandpa grinned at me. "So that's that. Let's finish eating!"

After cleaning up the dishes, we each departed to our rooms to get ready for the evening out at the Bonner place. Dad and I met in the kitchen dressed in warm clothes, boots, jackets, hats, and gloves. Flashlights were lying on the kitchen counter by the garage door. I walked over to see if they worked. Behind me I heard a commotion.

"Good God Almighty!" Dad exclaimed.

I turned around to see Grandpa standing in the kitchen. Good, God, Almighty is right! He had a large gray bandanna tied around his head and he was wearing mirrored sunglasses. Camouflage coveralls covered his body and camouflage boots were on his feet. Criss-crossed across his chest were two bandoliers of shotgun shells. He was holding a double-barreled shotgun in his hands. Oh, crap!

"Pa, I really don't think we need the shotgun. Let's leave that here."

Grandpa's face fell. He wanted to play soldier of fortune, and we wouldn't let him. Whew! He probably would have shot one of us out there. I guess he thought a shotgun went well with the history of the Bonner place.

"Well...I'll leave it here then, but we may need protection from these punks."

"Grandpa, I don't want to be naïve here, but I don't think these kids will harm us. They have only hurt some other students directly, and I believe there were some specific reasons for those. We don't want to start a war."

He walked out of the kitchen, turned left, and moved down the hall toward his room. A short time later he returned minus the bandoliers, shotgun, bandanna, and sunglasses. A gnome soldier of fortune, impotent now, with his trademark gray fedora. Looks good to me.

We rode in Dad's truck, Grandpa in the front seat and me in the back. The night was pitch black with clouds covering the moon. It had gotten colder as the day progressed and was about twenty-five degrees now. No snow was in the forecast, but, hey, this is Colorado, so anything is possible. The truck's headlights peered into the evening trying to carve space out of the darkness. It was a losing battle. The darkness seemed to close in on us more and more, trying to exclude us from its domain. Images of old man Bonner blowing off his head ran like a filmstrip across my brain. The dashboard lights barely illuminated Dad and Grandpa sitting in the front seats. They were just dark figures. No one spoke. The hum of the big truck tires on the asphalt and the purr of the engine were the only noises.

I looked out the passenger side window hoping to see something, anything. All I saw was the reflection of my face. I once saw a really old *Twilight Zone* show of a man looking out the window of an airplane; it was pitch black, and all that he saw was his own reflection; that is, until horrible-looking gremlins began to peer at him from outside the window. I glanced away. No gremlins tonight. No gremlins tonight. No...

The truck slowed. Dad turned off the highway to the left onto a dirt road. A fence gate barred our way. Dad put the truck in park and got out of the truck closing the door gently behind him. I could see him moving toward the gate in the beams of the headlights. He opened the gate by removing a circle of wire from the top of the wooden gatepost that was stuck in an identical circle of wire at ground level. Dad pulled the barbed wire gate back out of the way so he could drive the truck through. Returning to the truck he drove through the gate onto the old Bonner property. Exiting the truck again he walked behind the truck and closed the gate. He said he didn't know if any cattle were present here and didn't want to take any chances.

Back in the driver's seat, Dad put the truck in drive, and we moved slowly up the narrow dirt road. I could barely see the two rutted dirt tracks Dad was following. Most of the road was overgrown with prairie grass, going back to its original state. Making progress in what seemed a few yards at a time, we bounced up the track into the mountain above. After what felt like hours, but was only a short time, the headlights flashed off several cars and trucks parked on the grass off to the right of the road. I looked at my watch. It was seven thirty. Whoever had left me the letter was right about a gathering here. Of course, we had a walk ahead of us to reach the old log house. Dad said it was about a half-mile on up the track; the road was washed out and covered with fallen timber and boulders.

Parking in a way that had the front of the truck heading back down the road, Dad put the truck in park, shut off the engine and doused the lights. Now it really was pitch black. We each flicked on our flashlights and stepped out of the truck. The cold air hit me and took my breath away. I sucked in air, and it felt like my lungs were on fire from the cold. Dang! What were we doing out here on such a cold night? This isn't in my job description.

Quietly, we gathered in front of the truck. "The road goes up into the forest about a half-mile further," Dad whispered. "Let's keep our flashlight beams pointed just in front of our feet and move slowly. No talking from here on." Dad started up the road. Grandpa followed him and I brought up the rear. We moved quietly. Occasionally, I could hear one of our boots slipping on a stone. The wind had picked up, which made it colder. At least that is what my face told me. Why didn't I have my face covered?

After about twenty minutes of walking, Dad halted. Moving up beside him I could make out specks of light coming through the trees. There must be lights on inside the cabin, and the light was filtering out through the open windows. I couldn't even see the cabin yet, so I imagined all this in my mind.

Dad and Grandpa moved. Their lights were off now. I flicked off my light and followed. Grandpa stumbled.

"Shit!" he hissed.

"Quiet, Pa!" whispered Dad from the darkness.

We stood there for a moment, two, three, more. Nothing but the wind rustling through the tree branches above us. I heard Dad step forward, then Grandpa. I followed. The light emanated more brightly through the trees. I could now make out the outline of the cabin. It looked like a piece of dark cardboard laid up against a darker background. Dad halted. Grandpa ran into him.

"Oops," Grandpa said into Dad's broad back.

I stood behind Grandpa, waiting. For what, I didn't know. Then I knew. The smell of urine tickled my nostrils.

A splashing sound on the ground nearby entered my senses. Someone was taking a loud, long piss. The splashing stopped. I heard the sound of a zipper, then a loud fart. Clamping my right hand over my mouth, I held my breath not wanting to laugh. The sound of someone pushing through the underbrush could be heard to our right. Then, the outline of a person moving toward the cabin could be seen. We waited.

I felt Dad and Grandpa move forward. We were now within twenty yards of the cabin. Soft white light poked out the windows in front of the cabin. I could see the front door now. We moved closer. Now I could hear the murmuring of voices. It was a low hum. Without sound we now stood by the front door. I recognized some of the voices, male and female. I was beside Dad now. His solid presence quieted my ragged breathing. I felt safe with him.

They were arguing inside the cabin. Something about another plan. I listened.

"What you doin' in my house?"

Dad and I both jerked at the same time. What was that? I looked around the door and into the cabin. Across the way and on the back of the cabin I could see a bizarre-looking face peaking into the cabin. It took a moment for my vision to recognize what I was seeing. My God! Grandpa was looking in the window. The flashlight was held under his chin flashing light upward and distorting his face into a macabre death-face look. An old kid's trick.

"I said, what you doin' in my house?" Grandpa yelled out.

Heads turned toward the back window. They saw the face. Pandemonium broke out. Kids started screaming.

"Bonner! It's old man Bonner!"

"He's got a shotgun! Run!"

"Shut up! Just shut up!"

No one was listening to anyone. They had been sitting, but now several of them were standing and racing for the front door. Dad and I stepped into the doorway. Looks of terror flooded faces. They stopped, knocking each other over and screamed louder!

"Don't kill us! Don't kill us!

"Nooooo!"

"Shut up! Shut up! Shut up!"

I stepped farther into the room. "Enough!" I yelled. "Get a grip, will you! No one's getting killed." The dull roar of voices continued for a moment and then quieted.

"Doctor Thomas?" One of the boys from the gifted program recognized me. "What are you doing here?" He had a totally bewildered look on his face, not quite believing his eyes.

Grandpa had disappeared from the window and came strolling in the front door laughing his wheezy laugh. He was having great fun. I wasn't. Dad halted Grandpa with an outstretched arm. They were both behind me and to the right.

The screaming had stopped as the group realized who had come visiting. They stood staring at us with confused, shocked looks. That soon changed.

"Who invited you?" shouted a voice from the back.

"What's going on? How did you get here?" said another.

"This isn't right! This just isn't right!" sputtered another.

"Doctor Thomas, you are not a member, so you have to leave here now." Qui had walked up to me from a corner of the room. She tried a stare down. No luck.

"Nope, Qui, we are not leaving," I said not averting my eyes from hers. "You guys are not in a place to make demands, so I would advise you to all sit down so we can talk through some things."

Two kerosene heaters blasted out hot air from where they sat close to the center of the room. The cabin had wide pine-plank flooring, and sleeping bags were spread out on the pine floor as if a fun camp out was in progress. Ice chests sat against the right and left walls of the cabin. Overhead, Coleman lanterns were hung from the ceiling, giving off soft light. All the comforts of home.

Counting the boys and girls in the room, ten kids from the gifted program were gathered here. The Einstein Posse? Time to find out.

One by one they sat, taking their places as if in a classroom. "How did you find out about us?" Qui questioned. She seemed to be the leader, or at least she was taking on that role for my benefit.

Sitting on the floor I could feel the cold immediately seep up into my rear. Dang, I need more padding back there. "Well...kids are talking in school about some mysterious group of students who are taking action against other students. The details are vague." I was making this up as I went. I hadn't heard anything from anyone about a mysterious group of students. I didn't want to give away the letter writer, though.

"It seems there has been some retaliation against some school bullies. All of this is aimed at certain males I can name. Fortunately, or unfortunately, depending on who's speaking, this now has gone far enough." Looking around the room at wide eyes I could see the "deer in the headlights" look. They were caught. Out of the corner of my eye

I saw Dad and Grandpa haul over an ice chest and sit down on it. Why didn't I think of that? Oh, well, onward.

"You don't know anything," said Qui. "We're safe." She turned around and looked at her crew sending a stern look of "no one breaks ranks".

"No, Qui. This is over. There are three of us now who know something is going on." I glanced over at my Dad and Grandpa. They nodded. "If I have to I will report what I know to the sheriff, but I would rather one or all of you do that." Shocked looks crossed their faces.

"We can stop you," said Qui angrily. A few heads nodded yes.

"You're not going to do that." I looked into their eyes one at a time hoping to see some common sense there. They began to hang their heads not wanting to make contact with me. Three against ten weren't good odds but, with Dad and Grandpa, I felt safe. Well, maybe just Dad. Who knows what Grandpa might pull.

"It's over, Qui," said Evan Owens quietly from the left. "Most of us didn't want it to go this far. Let's figure out what to do. Doctor Thomas can help us. I trust him and think most everyone else does, also."

Freezing air blew in through the open windows. Our breathing gave off a cold fog. The young group of brilliant students were intent on studying some unseen thing on the floor in front of them. Breathe in. Breath out. In. Out.

"Yeah, Qui, I can't do this anymore," spoke a small girl from the back. Others began to chime in their approval of what the girl had said.

The young, gifted group moved around on their sleeping bags trying to get comfortable. Everyone seemed chilled even though we all wore heavy coats. Part of it was the temperature, but much of it was caused by the cracking of the safety walls they had built around them. They were still adolescents and believed themselves to be invincible. The walls were breaking down and so was their bravado.

"Why don't you tell me about this Einstein Posse?" I had spoken softly, but their heads jerked up as if the question slapped them.

My brain flashed on a vision of old man Bonner killing himself right here in this cabin. I wondered what went through his mind right before he pulled the trigger. I could be sitting right where he was when he did it. The thought made me want to jump up and run. Maybe the place was haunted. The long ago screams of his wife and daughters rang in my ears. I looked around me at the floor and figuratively shook myself forcing myself back to the present.

No one spoke for a time. They looked at each other as if expecting someone else to speak. I saw movement, tuned my head and saw Grandpa stand and begin walking around the cabin. He had his arms crossed, standing erect, with a grim look on his face. I almost laughed, watching him trying to give the hairy eyeball to these young people. These kids were tough intellectually. They wouldn't be intimated easily, but Grandpa was trying.

Qui looked around at her crew, shook her head, and spoke. "I'll begin this, but I expect the rest of you to speak." She was angry, judging, of her crew. "We needed a voice, a place where we could share our frustrations. I guess I took the lead by offering to set up a way to do this. At first it was just a couple of us. Patsy Anderson was the other one who began all this with me. We were both frustrated at what was happening to us at school." Qui hesitated, clearing her throat. She closed her eyes, possibly remembering.

Another young boy spoke. I had spoken to him often, but not in my role as a school psychologist. Bradley O'Hara was a tenth grader who kept a low profile. I didn't work with him at school or hear much about him. "I came into the group last year. I've been in the gifted program for several years, and the jokes and teasing have increased. I got tired of being picked on, because I had a brain and used it. Just because I'm not athletic doesn't mean I'm a loser."

"It was Patsy's idea to name ourselves The Einstein Posse. She came up with an initiation rite and tattoo." This from Jackson Pearson, an eleventh grader.

Initiation? Tattoo? "Tell me about the initiation and tattoo," I asked, wanting them to keep talking.

"The Einstein Riddle is the initiation into the crew," said Qui.

"Tell me about the Einstein Riddle, Qui. I'm not familiar with it," I replied.

Qui seemed the hardest to crack here so I was trying to keep this more and more informal. Her face softened, perhaps slightly opening her emotional door.

"Einstein developed this riddle early in his life. He said 98% of the world could not solve it. It goes like this. There are five houses in five different colors. In each house lives a person with a different nationality. The five owners drink a certain type of beverage, smoke a certain brand of cigar, and keep a certain pet. No owners have the same pet, smoke the same brand of cigar, or drink the same beverage. The question is: Who owns the fish?"

My face must have given away my total confusion. I looked at Dad. His face was blank. Grandpa was pacing again like the macho gnome. "Well...that's an interesting riddle. So, in order to get into The Einstein Posse a person has to solve this riddle?"

Qui smiled. The first one all night. "Yes, we have all answered the riddle. How about you, Doctor Thomas? Want to join us?" There was a tinge of sarcasm but also playfulness; a challenge and an invitation.

Smiling, I said, "I was never in the gifted program in school when I was your age. I was just an average student. Thanks for the invitation, but I already know I can't answer the riddle." I held both hands out palms up.

A young girl in the back spoke up. I couldn't remember her name. "That's okay, Doctor Thomas. The answer is the German." I must have looked totally confused. "Don't worry, I'll explain it to you. Here are some hints: The Brit lives in the red house. The Swede keeps dogs as pets. The Dane drinks tea. The green house is on the left of the white house. The green homeowner drinks coffee. The person who smokes Pall Mall rears birds. The owner of the yellow house smokes Dunhill. The man living in the center house drinks milk. The Norwegian lives in the first house. The man who smokes Blend lives next to the one who keeps cats. The man who keeps the horse lives next to the man who keeps cats. The man who keeps the horse lives next to the man who smokes Dunhill. The owner who smokes Bluemaster drinks beer. The German smokes prince. The Norwegian lives next to the blue house. The man who smokes Blend has a neighbor who drinks water." The young girl smiled at me and said, "Got it?"

"Uh...okay...well, you...uh...I guess I would have to write all this down to, you know, actually get it." My smile was strained. I felt like a buffoon.

"Okay...how about the tattoo?" Maybe I could understand a tattoo better than a riddle. I was totally lost. How in the heck did Einstein get to the German as the owner of the fish?

The gifted students gave me a smirk that was mixed with a bit of sorrow. Finally, Qui pulled up her pant leg and others followed. She pointed to the tattoo on the inside of her left ankle. I looked closely and could see that it was a picture of a brain.

"A brain?

"Yes, after solving the riddle we each got the brain tattoo. It was our sign that we were in The Einstein Posse. Of course, we had to keep it covered since it has all been by invitation only and kept secret."

There was a tattoo parlor off Hettie Road in town. I didn't pay much attention to it, but Steve Montes had mentioned it in a negative way a couple of times. And, all these gifted students had journeyed there. Tattoos were in now. I was out of it.

"Of course," I mumbled. They had done an excellent job, too, because without the unsigned letter I would have never known. I knew I didn't know much about what went on at school, but now I felt I even knew less, like almost nothing. Did someone say kids couldn't keep secrets? I wonder why?

"I'm confused about how you went from Einstein's Riddle to the tattoo to becoming a gang against others at school." I looked around wondering who would tell me the rest of this story.

Evan Owens was watching me. I studied him. "What about you Evan? Want to tell me more?" He studied his hands for a moment.

"Most of us here have been attacked by Arnold Purdy and his gang," said Evan. "They have bullied us for years actually and have gotten away with it. No one was around to protect us from their abuse. I've been punched, stolen from, spit on, had my hair pulled, and been called horrible names. Sometimes teachers saw or heard and did nothing." Evan stopped and took a drink from a plastic cup he had sitting on the floor beside him.

"Patsy had been harassed by Arnold since middle school. She reported him but, once again, nothing happened. He asked her for a date last year but she turned him down. He kept asking, and she kept turning him down. So, he stalked her, sent her nasty notes, started rumors about her being a whore, and showed up everywhere she was to harass her. She withdrew into herself and didn't even want to talk to many of us about it. Qui was the only one she hung with."

Silence once again filled the cabin. The hissing of the lanterns was the only background noise along with the wind and creaking of the cabin. Everyone seemed to be remembering, including me. I had only known Patsy for a few months so didn't have the history these kids had. They lived it.

"I think Arnold and his crew killed Patsy," Qui chimed in. "I was the closest to her, and she never talked about killing herself. We all knew she was hurting but so were we. Heck, I've been depressed, too, but haven't killed myself. Why would she?"

"So after Patsy died you decided to go after Arnold yourselves, because you figured he killed her." I hadn't asked a question. I made a statement deciding to go right for specifics. "Except, you didn't have any proof that Arnold had killed Patsy." Again, a statement.

They all looked like their big plan to punish Arnold didn't have a leg to stand on. Sagging in place, the righteousness of what they had done was draining out of them quickly. "What's the plan now, Einstein Posse?" I wasn't being sarcastic, but I wanted an answer to where they were going from here.

No one had the courage to answer me. Whatever they had in the works for their meeting tonight was probably in ashes now. "Okay, since no one wants to give me an answer as to what you are going to do, I'm going to be the bad guy here and give it to you.

"All of you are involved in breaking the law with Arnold, his followers, and boys in the middle school. You haven't told me you did those things, but I know you did. So, you are all going to turn yourselves in to Sheriff Montes and tell him the truth. If you decide not to go to him, I will do it myself. You have two days before I go to him."

"But..."

"No buts, no excuses, no skating out of your responsibility. Let him investigate Patsy's death by giving him your information." I already knew Steve was investigating, but I wanted them to deal directly with him. It was time for them to clean this up.

"This is confidential, you can't..."

"No, this isn't confidential. There is no confidentiality in this because you haven't told me you've done anything except join a club. So, I don't really know anything. Except, of course, I do, don't I?

"You can think I'm an awful person and never trust me again at school. I'll live with that. But I expect you all to be young adults here, deal with the consequences, and get back on track. I will even go with you to speak with Sheriff Montes if you want. I'm not here tonight because I want to cause you harm. In fact, it is just the opposite. I know being in the gifted program has caused suffering. I wish all the abuse hadn't happened to you. I want it to stop, but you have to let me in on things. Let me help. You're all better than Arnold and his bunch. Enough of sinking to their level. Together, let's do this a better way. They, I mean Arnold and the two others, will be dealt with somehow, someway, as will bullies in the middle school. I'm in on this now whether you like it or not."

I stood, nodded to Dad and Grandpa, and started to walk away from The Einstein Posse. Looking back, I spoke, "Let me know what you decide." We walked out of the cabin and began the walk back down to Dad's truck. The cold and wind stuck me like cold icicles jammed into my body. I was exhausted and confused. Had I done the right thing? It was done, so be it. If possible, it was darker than when we came to the cabin. Low cloud cover blotted out the moon and stars. Our flashlights barely made a dent in the oppressive darkness. I felt like I was walking in a cave and I shivered but not from the cold.

"You did good, Marc. Really good," Dad's voice from behind comforted me. I walked on into the darkness.

CHAPTER TWENTY-NINE

After almost a full day at school, a dull one for a change, I hadn't heard a word from any members of The Einstein Posse. I had seen a couple of them as they entered the gifted classroom down the hall, but that was it. Well, they still had another day. I really hoped they would do this on their own.

The final bell rang, and I loaded up my book bag from my office in the middle school. I was wrung out from the last couple of weeks. My body, mind, and spirit were giving in to the stress mode. I needed to ride my bike or hike somewhere and clear my soul.

As I was walking toward the parking lot and my truck, I felt a presence beside me. It was Qui.

"We're going now. We would like for you to come with us."

Almost before I could process what she said she walked away. I stopped, wanting to check myself to make sure I had heard correctly. Looking toward the direction Qui had gone I saw her get into a car with several other students. The car started, and they drove off. I hurried to my truck, unlocked the door, tossed my bag in the passenger seat and jumped in. I was driving down the road toward Rua Springs before I allowed this to sink in. Hard times were coming for The Einstein Posse, but they would survive.

Steve Montes met The Einstein Posse in the outer office. They must have called their parents, because several of them were there. He asked me to hang out here while he spoke with them in his conference room. Several of them had expressed their gratitude that I was there with them. Other than that, they stayed pretty quiet. I had a sense that someone had already called him and set up this appointment because we had a short wait.

After an hour or so he came out and waved for me to join them. I entered the conference room and took a seat at the table with the ten gifted kids, their parents, and Sheriff Montes. The room was large with room to seat about forty people. About fifteen people could sit around the conference table and the rest could sit in chairs against the walls. The floor had a light burgundy carpet and the off-white walls held several photographs of Colorado scenery; the room was actually a very peaceful, relaxing place. Of course, these kids may not be thinking about that at the moment.

I looked around at The Einstein Posse and their parents, curious as to how they were handling this. They showed stress but also hope. They were all here, and they would all handle the consequences.

"I imagine you know some or all of this story, Doctor Thomas." Steve was being formal. I nodded. "This group of students speaks very highly of you and obviously they wanted you here with them today. That's a good start and will be very helpful as we go forward." Steve wasn't smiling, but I knew there was a softness behind his words.

"There will be consequences for what they have done, and we'll speak to the district attorney about what those might be. They are all prepared to do what is necessary. Also, no more action will be taken against a certain trio of students at school. They know I'm working on finding answers, and they will not interfere. As to what happens now, we will find a time to meet with the D.A. and design a plan. At school, they will be under your supervision, and they expect more protection from the abuse and bullying that has gone on before. They said you would help with that."

Whatever Steve had said to the parents before I came in must have been enough to keep them quiet. They didn't interrupt nor did the students. The room was silent except for the hum of the heat blowing through the vents in the walls.

Steve stood up. "I expect everyone to be available when it is time to meet again. You all go on home now. Remember, you are on unofficial probation now so remember our deal. There are going to be criminal charges that I can't just make go away. I'll keep my part so you keep yours."

We all stood and began to file out of the conference room. I looked back at Steve. He smiled and nodded at me. The kids had come through. I felt pride in knowing them. Patsy's death was still unsolved, but maybe even that would change. Maybe.

That night at home I told Dad and Grandpa about the kids coming through on seeing the sheriff. They were extremely happy and congratulated me. I told them it really wasn't me. The students themselves made a decision to correct their mistakes. That took guts. They just got pushed farther into a corner and decided the only way out was to fight back. Obviously, they did. Now there would be legal consequences. I was still proud of them.

CHAPTER THIRTY

Arriving at school, I checked my schedule before heading to the preschool. It was my day for music again, and I needed to meet with some parents and teachers about completed assessments.

After lunch I was walking through the park toward the high school when two high school boys met me about halfway across. I had noticed that they were sitting on one of the stone benches even though it was very cold and overcast like yesterday. Having so many Colorado blue sky days spoiled me, so when these dreary days come along I feel closed in and somewhat depressed. Some people suffered from SAD, seasonal affective disorder, during these next few months. I didn't think I did, but I certainly didn't like overcast cold days.

"Doctor Thomas? Can we speak with you for a moment? I'm Jimmy Tuttle. I don't know if you remember me."

"Yes, hi Jimmy. Hi, Anthony." I shook hands with Anthony Yankowski and Jimmy. "I have a few minutes. How can I help?"

They stood looking at me and then at each other. Both had on heavy coats. Their shoulders were hunched forward, and their hands were stuffed down in deep pockets. I had a jacket on that barely held off the biting cold, so I wouldn't last long.

"You remember we talked with you after Patsy died?" said Jimmy.

"Yes, of course, you had someone else with you, also, if I remember right."

"Spencer Vaughn. He was with us," said Anthony.

"Okay, shall we go inside and talk?" I hoped they would agree so I didn't turn into a popsicle out here.

"If it's okay we would like to talk out here." Jimmy looked at Anthony for confirmation as he spoke. Diehards. I would have to tough it out in the cold.

"Let's sit here." I pointed to a couple of benches. "Not real comfortable but should work." We all sat.

I watched them struggle with what they wanted to say to me. And, I wanted them to hurry. Darn, it was cold out here. "This seems kind of tough for you guys. Are you in some kind of trouble?"

"No. No, it isn't about us. It's about Spencer." Anthony stopped, looked confused like he didn't know what to say next.

I pushed. "So, this is about Spencer. Is he in trouble?"

"Well, yes, we think so. Uh...we thought maybe you could help," spoke Anthony again.

"Okay, I need one of you to tell me what's up. I'm still in the dark here and actually getting cold." My teeth were beginning to chatter. I had an image of me lying on this bench totally blue, frozen solid. Someone would come by lift me up under one arm and haul me away and stand me up in some meat locker. Stop! These guys looked warm as toast all scrunched up in their big coats. Youth!

"Spencer called us last night and said he needed to see us. We both said sure and met him at the city park in Rua Springs. When we got there he said he couldn't live with the secret anymore and needed to tell someone. He also said it was all his fault."

Secret? What secret? His fault? This was going in an ominous direction, and I had a really bad feeling. "Okay. Did he tell you what was going on?"

The two boys looked at each other. Anthony elbowed Jimmy. "Yes, uh…he said he and Patsy Anderson had been going together."

"What?" I shouted before I could stop myself. "They were going together? You guys didn't know?"

"No," said Jimmy. "We didn't know. Spencer said they decided to keep it a secret from everyone."

"Geez, no one knew? Why did they keep it a secret?"

"He didn't really say," said Anthony quietly. "Spencer said it just kind of happened, and they didn't want to be teased by anyone. So, they kept it a secret. I guess they had been together for awhile. He said Patsy didn't want her mom to know, because she didn't want Patsy dating."

"Well…it's not a bad thing that they were dating. Why was he upset about that?"

Jimmy leaned forward and glanced around checking to see if we were alone. Who would be crazy enough to be out here in the freezing cold spying on us?

"Spencer wasn't concerned about seeing Patsy before, but he said he found out some really bad things about Patsy, and that it was his fault."

"What was his fault?"

"Her killing herself. He said he was to blame," said Anthony, shaking his head back and forth. "He couldn't be to blame. She killed herself, didn't she?" Anthony was looking at me begging for assurance that Spencer didn't do anything wrong.

"Anthony, I don't really know what happened to Patsy. I don't know why he is blaming himself. I really don't, but maybe I can talk to him and help out."

"Well, Doctor Thomas, that's the thing. Spencer is gone, "said Jimmy sadly.

"Gone? What do you mean gone? Where has he gone?"

"We don't know, but he said that it was his fault and that he caused Patsy's death, and he had to go away, maybe permanently. We thought he was joking. He didn't show up for school today and his cell phone is turned off." Jimmy had tears in his eyes as he spoke.

Anthony was barely holding on. They leaned into each other looking for contact, support. The pain was all over them, covering them with grief. My gut was so tight I thought I would scream.

"Did he seem like he was going to hurt himself?" My question shocked them so much they backed away from me.

"You mean…you mean like…kill himself?" Jimmy's voice broke displaying the fact that this was something he didn't even want to consider.

"Yes, Jimmy, that's what I mean. He's blaming himself for Patsy's death. Why? I don't know. But going away like this means he is very serious about escaping from something."

"Oh, Jesus, not another friend! Oh, Jesus, no!" Anthony was crying now, his chest heaving as he tried to suck in air. "You gotta find him. You just have to. Spencer has been our friend our whole life. You gotta do something!" Anthony had his face in his hands shaking his head back and forth.

"I will. I'll get some help, and we'll find him if we can." Their tears and pain were tearing me apart. How would I find him? I didn't have a clue where he might be. "Okay, now I need help from you two. Where would he have gone? What were his favorite places? Let's think about this for a moment." I was sure my nose was frozen. My face was stinging from the cold. I really needed to get inside, but I couldn't leave now.

"We all just hung out in town or at each other's house. You know, we just drove around or watched movies and played games on the computer. We hiked sometimes when the weather was nice. Spencer was into outdoor things, biking, backpacking, skiing. We didn't have any real favorite places. Just all around, you know?" Jimmy was looking at me as if I would spin the dial and land on the place Spencer went. There were too many options.

"Okay. I need to talk to his parents and the sheriff. We'll figure it out." I didn't know how, but I wouldn't tell them that. "Give me your cell phone numbers." I programmed their numbers into my iPhone and had them program mine into theirs. "You head on to class, and I'll get started on finding Spencer." I only hoped we weren't too late. This was bad, very bad. Jesus! Patsy was pregnant, and Spencer was probably the father! Another piece slid into place.

I called Steve Montes as soon as they left. Thank God Steve was available to take my call. After informing him of my conversation with Jimmy and Anthony, he said he would meet me at Spencer's home. I walked back to my office in the middle school and told Mrs. Chang I had an emergency with a student and needed to take off early. She said she would contact the other schools.

We met at Spencer's home west of town. Steve was already there when I arrived. Evidently, he had called ahead because the Vaughn's were waiting at the front door. As I drew near I could see the look of terror on their faces. Mrs. Vaughn was crying, mascara running down her face. She made no attempt to clean her face. Mr. Vaughn looked as if he had seen a ghost, died, and was still breathing. I had met them once before at school early in the year at a function. These people looked nothing like that same couple.

"Have you found him?" Mrs. Vaughn grabbed the front of Steve's coat with both hands. She was on the verge of collapsing. Steve gently took hold of her shoulders.

"Hannah, we've just begun. Let's go in the house and see if we can work on where he might have gone." Steve held her for a moment until she let him go. She seemed to deflate in front of my eyes. The pain was so thick around us that I could almost see it.

Steve stepped toward the front door and the Vaughn's mechanically followed him in. I followed a few steps behind them and closed the door behind me.

The house, a two-story ranch style was basically a box without much character. The interior was dull and cold, lifeless. We sat on couches that had slip covers over them made of dark brown material. Glancing around the room I couldn't help but notice that there were no wall hangings.

No pictures or other art. Curious. The walls were a light brown, so the living room space seemed smaller than it probably was. Table lamps gave off soft light that put everything in shadows, including us, because all the curtains were closed. It felt like a morgue. The place smelled moldy, unclean. A stale coffee smell slid past my nostrils. Did they always live like this? It gave me the willies.

"Doctor Thomas," said Gary Vaughn, "thank you for coming. Spencer spoke very highly of you so I thought maybe you could help us."

The look Gary gave me caused me to flinch. It was as if he wanted to know what I really knew about Spencer and Patsy. It wasn't spoken, but it was there. I felt it.

Steve jumped right in. "Gary, Hannah, when was the last time you saw Spencer?"

They looked at each other for a moment and Gary finally spoke. "Hannah and I had dinner last night about six. Spencer said he wasn't hungry and didn't feel good. He went up to his room. That was it. I left early for an emergency job with IREA. That's where I work, the Intermountain Rural Electric Association. I didn't know Spencer was gone until Hannah called me earlier."

"How about you, Hannah?" said Steve gently.

Hannah had finally begun to wipe her tears with a handkerchief she had picked up off an end table. "Last night at dinner." She was trying to hold back her sniffles with her handkerchief and spoke into it. Her words were muffled.

"Not this morning?" asked Steve.

"Until you called, I thought Spencer had gone to school early. He sometimes does that. After your call I looked outside and his car was still parked in the driveway." She had moved the handkerchief slightly so I could understand her better. Every word was painful though.

"Since his car is still here do you have any ideas about who might have picked him up?"

Gary cleared his voice and spoke in a hoarse voice. "No, he only went out with Jimmy and Anthony. Never anyone else."

"Okay, can we look in Spencer's room?"

Gary stood. Steve and I followed. Hannah Vaughn stayed seated. She was leaning forward with her elbows on her knees and her hands clasped. She didn't move as we walked toward the steps.

Spencer's room was a huge contrast to the rest of the house. His window had no covering. The walls were a light cream color. Spencer had several posters of snowboarding and rock climbing plus several pictures of Jimmy, Anthony, and himself in various outdoor settings. There was a picture of the three of them on top of Long's Peak in the Rocky Mountain National Park. Happier days. The room was very clean for a teenager, too. I wondered why the difference.

"I came up here before you arrived to see if anything was missing. Several things are." Gary moved toward a large closet and opened the double doors. Steve and I followed behind and looked in. "Spencer took all of his backpacking and camping gear. Clothes, pack, sleeping bag, cooking gear, freeze dried food. Gone. He's on the road or gone to the forest."

"Anything stand out as to where he might have gone?" questioned Steve.

"Something. He kept all his maps in here. Some rolled up and some hung on the wall. Notice what he has circled in red on this map?"

Steve and I looked closely at where he was pointing. Rua Springs Mine? The entire map was locations of old mines in the area, but the Rua Springs Mine was circled in red. My stomach fell. I had been there once when I was in high school. Steve had been there, too. My experience was not a good one.

"Did Spencer ever talk about old mines with you?" Steve's voice held an urgency now.

Gary looked at us out of the corner of his eye and then glanced back at the map. "Sometimes. I told him they were dangerous and to stay away, but he didn't listen. He loved their histories, especially the Rua Springs Mine. He has definitely been there." Gary turned and looked at us. His eyes had brightened. Hope had returned. The dead lived.

"I found this history of the mine in his dresser." Gary showed us an old newspaper clipping.

Speed reading the article, I could see why Spencer loved the history. It sounded romantic. Old William Houghton named the mine after his wife Rua, just like the town. He made buckets of money off the silver that was removed until it finally gave out. History. Gary said Spencer loved all of it and historically this was the beginning of Rua Springs.

"It's as good a lead as we're going to get for now," said Steve quickly. "Let's check it out. Marc, go home and grab some gear. Gary, you too. We'll meet at my office in thirty minutes.

Hannah Vaughn hadn't moved since we left her. Gary told her where we were going. She didn't react. I said good-bye to her but got no response. Catatonic was a word that came to mind. Rua Springs Mine. Crap! I didn't want to go back there. First, the old Bonner place last night and now this. My anal sphincter felt like it was up around my throat and closing.

CHAPTER THIRTY-ONE

The final few miles to the mine were surrounded with silence. Everything had been discussed over and over. How did it get to this point? I was emotionally, physically, and, yes, even spiritually exhausted. Everyone was. The death of Patsy had paralyzed part of the community and had brought on the killer beast in the rest.

Steve Montes, me, and Spencer Vaughn's dad, Gary, were in the sheriff's Ford truck heading toward the Rua Springs Mine. It had been closed for decades and marked as very dangerous. But, growing up I made the secret trek to the mine just like most of my school colleagues. It was one of those rites of passage. Fear, thrill, danger, sex, booze, the unknown, secrets, horror stories, and the adolescent belief in immortality. I wanted to look in the mirror and say that I did it and flex my muscles. Pride before sanity.

Gary Vaughn thanked me again for coming along to see if Spencer was actually there. If he was, Gary wanted me to talk him out. Guilt and shame oozed out of Gary's pores. Even in the higher altitude and cold in the air he was sweating rivers. The war raging within him must have been brutal. It was normal that Gary would be afraid for Spencer's life, but this seemed to go beyond that. I couldn't put my finger on what else was happening here. Something was, though.

"About a mile to go to the mine," murmured Steve. He said it so softly I wasn't sure if I whispered it to myself or if he really said it. I could barely make out the sides of the rocky road as we ascended. The tire tracks that were once from wagon wheels were deep ruts cut down to the bedrock over time. With twilight upon us the headlights opened up a narrow view of the terrain ahead. The cocoon of the truck kept out the serenity of the mountain and the so-called terror it might hold. Kids were told stories about monsters in the night to keep them away from the area.

Gary Vaughn was talking to himself again. Softly, he said, "How could he do this? How did he find out?" I wasn't sure what he meant. Do what? Find out what? He mumbled something about a long time ago and that he was sorry.

"We're here," said Steve softly. "No other cars around. Are we really sure he is here?"

"I'm pretty sure he is because of the way he marked his map. Spencer was always outdoors doing something. Hiking, backpacking, skiing. I taught him how to manage as soon as he could walk. He's an Eagle Scout, so he can make it about any place. Getting here wouldn't be a problem for him."

"What is it you really want me to do?" I quietly asked Gary.

"Spencer said he trusted you," said Gary. "I'm not sure of his relationship with you, but he said you were helpful to him and his friends. I heard him say to Jimmy Tuttle one time that he would go to you if he ever needed any help."

"Okay. I want to help if I can," I said.

"This mine is dangerous for sure," stated Steve. "I was up here with you, Marc, when we were kids. I didn't want to go in then and I don't know, but we will. Here's the deal, though. I lead. Marc, you follow me, and, Gary, you follow the Doc. I know kids still come up here to scare each other and to party, but there haven't been any accidents for a long time, and I don't want one today."

Steve slowly inched the truck up to the end of the road, turned the key to off, put it in park, and set the emergency brake. As we sat there in the twilight, the coming final darkness settled around us and started to squeeze. The truck engine continued to tick as it cooled. I felt the approaching night start to clamp its boney fingers around my throat. It was the same feeling I had when I was here the first and last time at age fourteen. How did I mange then? I closed my eyes and tried to control my breathing. Slowly I was able to take in full amounts of air. Breathe in relaxation and blow out tension. Breathe in... Gary cleared his throat. It sounded painful, like a moan. I could only believe both he and Steve were having the same experience I was. When Steve and I, along with several other kids, came up here long ago we never spoke of the experience again. What really happened then? What was happening now?

"Time to move guys," stated Steve in a forced, hoarse voice. "I have headlamps for us." He handed each of us a headlamp. We placed them on our heads and turned them on. "Gary, you follow closely."

We each let ourselves out of the truck and closed our doors quietly. It seemed we didn't want to wake up something sleeping here. The darkness was closing around us now, and Steve and I turned on our lights. Gary switched his on and followed. The fall chill was upon us like a blanket here in the Colorado mountains. I had on an old Land's End jacket, but it still felt like the cold was getting through it. I pulled up the collar, put my right hand in my right pocket and pointed my headlamp toward the entrance to the Rua Springs Mine.

The scree field below the mine was the same as I remembered; so was moving up to it at night. Even moving slowly up, stones of various sizes were displaced and moved left, right and down below our boots. It wasn't steep, but we still had to move carefully so we didn't slide back down. Falling on scree could tear skin off in an instant. We each took a different route up so we weren't in the wake of another. After about fifteen minutes we reached the top and the opening to the Rua Springs Mine was right in front of us. The signs painted on the boards closing off the entrance were the same as I remembered: Do Not Enter, Danger, No Trespassing, and Violators Will Be Prosecuted. I looked at that one and wondered who was watching the mine to prosecute anyone. When I was here as a kid I remembered someone saying, "Persecutors will be violated while inside," and then laughing a deep, low, maniacal laugh. I was surprised that there wasn't more graffiti on the signs.

Steve stopped before the boarded-up entrance and stared at it while Gary and I stepped up beside him. "It looks like one of the lower boards has been pulled off. It's off to the side there. He pointed to the right. "Who knows how long it has been off. Maybe Spencer is in here, maybe he isn't." He looked squarely at Gary.

"He's here," said Gary. "Spencer had a picture of this entrance in his dresser. It had Here printed at the bottom. I didn't find anything else like it in his room. And, remember, all of his equipment plus his headlamp were missing."

"Yeah, okay, we'll check it out to be certain," murmured Steve. He leaned down and started crawling into the opening left by the removed board. "Come on through, Marc. You follow him, Gary."

I couldn't see Steve through the closed opening, but I could see some light filtering through the boards. I got to my knees then down flat on my stomach and began to slither through the opening. Steve's boots were at eye level as I crawled through. His light spotted the floor of the mine right in front of me. I raised myself to my knees and then pushed up so I was standing. I pointed my headlamp down the tunnel and remembered this view from before, thinking this was the entrance to hell. The darkness captured the coming light in the tunnel and squeezed it off as it faded in the distance. Gary was through and standing beside me before I realized I had been frozen in place and had checked out for a few seconds.

"This leads down to flat area that runs off to the left and right. I checked a map before we left," shared Steve. "We stay together no matter what."

My memory was that below us were the "catacombs" named by someone in the distant past. Going right or left would take us into a maze of tunnels where miners searched for silver. Stories, some probably true and some apocryphal, told of miners getting lost in the catacombs and never coming out. After the mine closed for good in the 1920s, those who were brave enough to enter came back telling of strange noises, cries, and what sounded like running water. A slew of stories were told about others who didn't return. Later many of those proved false, because it was discovered a man just abandoned his girlfriend or wife and kids and showed up in another part of the state or country. The only time I was in the catacombs, I didn't venture in very far.

"Spencer is really into exploring the history around the area," said Gary. "He wanted to see ghost towns and old mines. He talked about history and old-time explorers all the time. He didn't talk much about this mine, but I know he explored others with his buddies. We told him what was off limits but knew he would live like an old explorer if he had a chance."

We moved down the old tracks used for the ore cars and into the gloom. Some of the rails were tossed off to the side. There were bits of paper and trash along the way. Remnants of an old campfire could be seen off to the left when I shined my light to where I thought I could smell a long dead fire. The blackened wall and ceiling told the tale.

"Let's take the right fork first and see how far we get," said Steve softly like he didn't want to disturb anything from history. After fifty yards or so we could dimly see the catacombs that went off in every direction but always down.

Our lights were good, but in the distance things were fuzzy, then gray, then black. Most of the tunnels seemed to have very low ceilings so we entered the first one to the left bending over at the waist and twisting our heads back so we could see ahead. Behind me I heard a groan from Gary.

"Damm. Smacked my forehead. Wasn't leaning over enough."

The first tunnel only went in about twenty yards and dead-ended. We turned around and moved back to the entrance and then entered the next one to the right. For an hour we kept moving in and out of short tunnels. We continually stepped around piles of rock that were dumped there or had fallen off the walls and ceilings. Nothing there and no sign of anyone or anything. No trash this far in either. I knew this was a really great silver mine, and old William and Rua had gotten rich off it. The only thing I heard as we moved forward was our breathing and occasionally dripping water. The cold and dampness was probably taking its toll on us. It was closing in on me for sure.

"Looks like these tunnels on the right fork didn't go much of anywhere. Probably either didn't find any silver and at least not much. Who knows," said Steve. "I still can't believe Spencer would intentionally come in here by himself and try to disappear. It doesn't make any sense."

"We've talked to his friends and considered the other places he might have been," stated Gary in a louder voice than I believe he wanted. His voice cracked as he spoke. "This is the best bet and maybe the worst place he might be. I can't give up finding him. He wouldn't take off if he didn't think there was any other option. He isn't that way. Hiding is not what Spence does. He's always outgoing, truthful, never backing down to a challenge. He's hurting so bad he must not think there is anything else to do." Gary stopped for a moment. "Sorry. I can't lose him, too." He said it so softly, and I wasn't sure I heard it right.

"What?" I asked. "Lose him, too?"

"Nothing, sorry for my rambling."

We entered the left fork and began our descent into the darkness. I thought it was strange there were no rails for the ore carts here. No sign they were ever here. The climb down was steeper than the right fork. We moved slowly with our lights shining ahead into the pitch black of the space. Steve and I were side-by-side now with Gary trailing behind us. We had to watch our step because more rubble was on the floor; all sizes and shapes of rocks. The sides of the tunnel were moving in on us and the ceiling was moving down. After some hundred yards the tunnel became so small that we were on our hands and knees crawling forward in single file. We had already explored side tunnels and found nothing.

"Dang, I don't like this at all," whispered Steve back to us. "Maybe it doesn't go anywhere, and we'll have to back out cause we can't turn around. We have what looks like a rock fall up here. I think the tunnel ends, but a cave-in has occurred, brought down part of the ceiling. There are rocks moved out of the top of the cave-in and stacked over along the right wall. These rocks haven't been moved by nature. Somebody moved them. There is an opening at the top that I will check out."

After ten minutes, I heard Montes say, "Oh man, unbelievable." I crawled up the pile of rocks and through the opening, scooted out behind him and saw it then.

"What the..." I exclaimed as our lights shone off in the distance. It was a giant cavern. Our lights barely reached the other side.

"Incredible," said Vaughn as he emerged and stood. "I never heard any stories about this being here."

"It looks like it has water at the bottom so maybe it was a lake inside the mountain," Steve said. "Over there to the left." He pointed with his headlamp. "Doesn't that look like it goes off in the dark? Except it isn't quite dark."

"It has to be Spence," cried Gary. "Who else would be in this crazy place."

I could only hope it was him off there in a side tunnel somewhere. Otherwise... My mind went into hyper-drive. I remembered back to being here before and thinking I would never get out of this mine alive. Thinking about the experience started loosening my bladder and bowels. I squeezed my stomach in involuntarily, living it again.

When Steve and I were fourteen we came here with several other boys. We scared ourselves into the adventure, always trying to see who had the biggest cojones. After exploring some, guys started turning off their flashlights and making horror noises. I got claustrophobic and had to get out. The only problem was that I was leading down a small side tunnel, and the other boys were all backed up behind me. I began screaming that I had to get out. They thought I was joking. I wasn't. Steve realized it was real, and I was in trouble. He started kicking guys behind him to get them to move back. Everyone panicked and was trying to back up and crawl over each other. For awhile it was chaos. I finally got out and vowed never to come back. Except...here I was again.

"Let's head down that direction," suggested Steve. "We need to get this over with. I don't want our lights going out."

The ceiling was still just touching the top of our heads so we bent over as we moved down toward what was left of the water. It was a wide, round cavern but not tall at all.

It reminded me of a puffed up pancake. Who would have guessed this was here right behind where the mining was done.

We reached the floor and moved around the edge of the water to the right. The cave on the right where we thought we saw the light was just ahead. It was the only side cave off the large cavern that I saw from above. Single file we entered the smaller cave.

"Spence!" yelled Gary. "I'm here. It's your dad."

I jerked upright at Gary's voice as it ricocheted around the cave. My heart was pounding so hard I thought I would blow a vessel out of my chest.

"What the hell is the matter with you!" Steve whispered through clenched teeth. "You just can't yell out things without telling us! Man, you scared the hell out of me."

We stood there in the coming silence waiting for the jarring sounds to quit clawing at our ears. Slowly my breathing calmed and quieted. I could hear Steve's teeth stop grinding.

"Don't come any closer!" came a voice from the black void. Once again I was taken by surprise and frozen in place. Gary crashed into my back, and I almost tumbled forward.

"Ahhhh," I hissed as I worked to catch myself from knocking down Steve.

My God, I thought. *We were right! He is here.*

"Spencer Vaughn?" yelled Steve. "It's me, Sheriff Montes. Doc Thomas and your dad are here too. We…"

"I'm here, Spence. It's dad. It's okay," interrupted Gary.

"No, it's not okay and never will be again," came an eerily calm voice from beyond.

"Quiet, Gary," hissed Montes. "Spencer, we need to talk about Patsy Anderson. I know it may have been an accident and maybe you didn't mean to..."

"You don't know anything about it," came Spencer's voice from the darkness. It was harsh and flat, no feeling. Dead.

"I need to come forward and see you. We can work this out. Figure out what to do to help," Steve said in a calm voice.

"No, I'll only talk with Doc Thomas now," stated Spencer. "You and Dad stay where you are."

The echoes of the voices settled into the walls, and it was silent again. Just our shallow breathing could be heard.

"I don't like this," whispered Steve. "We don't know anything about where he is or what he will do. He may blame you, Doc, and try to do something."

"Blame me?" I whispered back. "For what?"

"You worked with Patsy at school. Maybe Spencer thinks you twisted her thinking somehow, and it led to all this."

I hesitated and then said, "Maybe, but there was no indication with Patsy that anything was wrong. And I met with her several times." I paused for a few seconds thinking of how much I had missed with Patsy. Guilt is what I felt now. "He wants to talk with me. Let me see what happens. I'll take my chances with him. Because we were always friendly at school I don't feel any harm here."

Steve looked at me and then back at Gary who was now in silent mode. They looked at me and then each other through the soft light of our headlamps. Their faces and, I'm sure mine, were distorted with the vague light. Shadows glanced off the walls and came back to taunt us. Tight lips, flared nostrils, dark eyes, and slumped shoulders told me we were all wound tight. "Okay, but you have no authority to offer anything. Just work on getting him out of there so we can settle this. If you don't, I'm coming in."

Steve said all this in his sheriff voice. I knew he was right. Gary looked defeated. He was slumped further and looked lost like he had been totally thrown out and of no use. His pain was evident in the shadows of his face. He wanted Spencer to rely on him, come to him, hug him, and together they would make it all right. It wasn't happening that way.

"Spencer? It's Doc Thomas. I'm moving in to speak with you now."

I leaned over and stepped into the tunnel. It wasn't a tunnel carved out by miners. It was natural and carved out by eons of water erosion. It angled off to the right with a low ceiling, but I was able to walk bent over. The walls were very close together, and I had to turn sideways in several places to move forward. My claustrophobia was showing its ugly face. My breathing increased, and I started to panic.

"Spencer, show me some light so I know how far I'm going."

From the left, about ten yards ahead, the beam of a flashlight shone against the right side of the rock wall. I moved forward to the light and then leaned left into the source of the light.

"Move the light out of my eyes, Spencer. I can't see."

After the light was removed from my eyes and moved toward the ceiling, I began to see the outline of the cave. It was about ten feet in height, maybe twelve by twelve. I moved my headlamp around the area and could see that

Spencer had set up a comfortable camp. He must have carried a lot of weight to have all the equipment he had. He had a sleeping bag on what was probably an air bed of some sort. Some plastic frames held food next to a portable stove. Fuel bottles, water bottles, and a battery operated lantern sitting on a cook pot rounded out the rest of his supplies. I smelled what was probably rice and tuna from a recent meal and the faint scent of his body odor. Clothing and a jacket were thrown on the sleeping bag.

"Nice place, Spencer," I said in as cheerful of voice as I could. "You come here often?"

"Funny, Doc. You should be a comedian. Who would have guessed you had a sense of humor."

"Actually, I was being sort of serious. How did you find this place?"

"Don't you want to ask me about Patsy?"

"I figured you would tell me if you wanted to."

"Yeah, I'll tell you." Spencer paused and was silent for several seconds. "I've been to this mine a few times with a couple of buddies. None of us ever talked about coming here to anyone else. I guess someone talked, huh? On one trip here when we were crawling around I came down the left fork by myself. At the end I found the rock pile that we had found before, but some of the rocks toward the top had come loose. I could see the opening at the top and stuck my head in. With my headlamp I could see that the light sort of disappeared into the black. I crawled in farther and it opened into the large cavern. I knew it wasn't from the mine, and I came in to explore and found this place. I meant to tell my friends, but ...well..." Spencer sucked in some air and expelled it loudly. "Sorry, ah, well, you know, this...Patsy."

"Yeah, I know," I said quietly. I sat on the floor near where Spencer was sitting on his sleeping bag and switched off my headlamp. Time passed. He sat quietly and stared at the floor of the cave. I wondered what he was seeing through the stone; perhaps a void that had some sort of meaning for a teenager's existence. Life, death, pain, love. Time stretched. I felt the cold from the floor seeping in from below.

Spencer's voice entered eternity's quiet. It was low, husky, slow. "I didn't hurt Patsy. I would never do that. We, ah, we... I heard what was going around. It wasn't true. Totally not right. I came here after that." He stopped, looked up at me, waiting for a comment maybe. Time moved, shifted. The cold was settling in, making itself comfortable. My eyes made contact with Spencer. He shifted on his bed and looked past me. Searching, evaluating, as if the shadows from the lantern spoke some unknown language only Spencer could interpret.

"Patsy was out-of-control that day. She was crying, trying to hit me. We were in the back parking lot behind the vo-tech building. No one was around since it was early, before classes. Patsy was yelling at me. She asked me why I hadn't told her. I asked her what she was talking about. She kept saying I knew and kept it from her. I grabbed her by the arms and started shaking her, asking her to tell me what she was talking about.

"I had never hurt her before and realized I was but couldn't stop. She kept crying and saying that I knew. I didn't. I was shaking her and telling her to stop, digging in my fingers. She started slapping me, and I grabbed her hands. She broke loose, and I tried to hold her but punched her in the face by accident. Patsy tried to claw my face. Her strength was unreal. I let go. She screamed at me that she hated me, hated herself, and that she would end the pain. She raced toward the shop building. I stood there stunned, shocked, and shaken. I felt sick to my stomach. I didn't have a clue what had just happened. It was horrible, unreal, a nightmare." Spencer paused, looked around living it again and again. It was cold at cave temperature but he had sweat on his forehead. He rocked backward, held it, moved forward, then back and forth again.

I didn't want to break in on his space so remained silent. I would let him continue at his schedule, whatever that was. I was trying to take in the violence of that day and couldn't comprehend what had gone so wrong between them. I didn't really know that Spencer and Patsy knew each other well, except as classmates. Whatever they had was a well-kept secret from everyone. I knew about the marks on Patsy's arms and face but along with Steve Montes and everyone else, that someone had punched her around so they could quietly lift her to the jump rope where she was hung. It had gone from suicide to a possible murder when the marks were found during her autopsy. Now, Spencer's words seemed to finalize Patsy's suicide. It wasn't a murder. Her pain led her to a place of darkness from which she couldn't return.

Spencer cleared his throat, coughed, and moved his right hand across his forehead. He looked at his hand as if it had some answer in it. He studied it further then shoved it under his right thigh.

"I stood in the parking lot for quite awhile staring at where Patsy had gone as if she would reappear and say everything was okay. It was all so crazy. My head went blank, then opened up to the scene again rerunning it; then blanking, then rerunning. I don't even know how long I stood there. Cars started coming into the parking lot so I finally... I decided to go after her. I looked around for awhile and then went to biology class guessing she would show up, but she didn't." Spencer stopped again, seeming to run out of energy. He pushed his fists into his eyes as if he could shut off some silent movie only he could see. He wiped his left hand across his nose and inhaled deeply. So far he had spoken in a soft, flat voice, but I could tell he was working overtime to hold in his gruesome pain.

I wanted to tell Spencer it was all okay, and everything would be all right but that would be psychobabble crap. It wasn't okay and might never be. Any attempt to be someone with empty comments would only hurt. I had heard too many psychologists try to impress people in pain with their own words of wisdom. I stayed quiet. I was just here to listen. Spencer would tell me what he wanted me to hear.

"Doc, Patsy said you were a good listener. I thought I was talking to myself here." He smiled, trying to bring some relief to what was obviously pure torture for him. "You want to say anything?"

"I'm with you here, Spencer. Just know that. I'm here with you as long as you need me."

"Yeah, I know you are, Doc. Thank you," He paused. "I wake up at night thinking she is still alive and just before I feel like I'm gonna be happy, I remember she is gone. I wasn't gonna say this, but I've cried till I'm sick, having dry heaves but nothing comes up." Spencer moved around again as if another way of sitting would bring another outcome to all this. "I didn't know anything was wrong until Mr. Claussen made his announcement. None of it was real. I felt like my heart stopped. Voices rang out all around me. It was impossible. I had just seen her. She said she would end it, but I thought she meant us, our relationship, not this. I couldn't believe it and mostly still can't. We were friends and we loved each other, and no one knew. What we had was so good. I floated when I was around her. I thought she felt the same."

Spencer took in a deep breath, wiped his eyes and nose, and looked at me. "Why did she have to do this, Doc?" He looked down, stuck his hands in his coat pockets, then removed them. "I guess I know though. I know. Now I know, but then I didn't. People think someone did this to her, but I know that's not true. I know we did it. I did it. She did it. There was no way out."

There wasn't any answer about life and death I could give him when he asked me why she did it. I knew all the reasons kids committed suicide and wanted to tell him I understood. But when he said he knew why it happened, my head snapped up and looked at him.

"What do you mean 'you know' Spencer?"

Several heartbeats of silence went by. He reached in his right coat pocket and pulled something out and held it out for me to see.

"This. This is how I know." It was a Lexar flash drive. "She threw this at me when she ran off from me that day. It was the flash drive I had given her as a gift, so I recognized it. See, it has this purple lanyard. I thought she just didn't want my gift. After I picked it up off the ground I stuck it in my pocket and forgot about it until several days later. When I remembered it, I was going to throw it away so I didn't have to remember, but I decided to look at it. I wish I hadn't." Spencer stopped, looked through the wall of the cave again at something only he could see.

Tears were streaming down his face. He didn't try to stop them now. He held out the flash drive, looking at it like it was some kind of cruel joke.

"She wrote a sort of diary beginning from the time I gave it to her. It was just thoughts about what happened during the days at home, school and with us. She liked our secret friendship...until the end. Patsy's writing got stranger and stranger. Being in the gifted program was hurting her more every day. She hated being set apart as a brain and a dunce at the same time. People made fun of her and teased her. Cruel things were said to her. She talked about getting even with some of the girls who teased her. She was angry at being stuck in those classes with the other kids. She thought they were all crazy and said she must be crazy too. She said the pressure to perform was like a punishment. Then, she found something. It..."

Spencer hesitated, looking at me. I could tell it was taking all of his control not to totally fall apart. "This is the hardest part. It has even sent me over the edge. Total cruelty. I couldn't believe God would do this. Patsy crashed with this stuff. I understood why she was so out-of-control with me. Her writing turned to vicious attacks against God, me, and her mom. Whatever was left of the Patsy I knew was devoured by this. Why, Doc? Why did this happen to us? How could God punish us so much? What did we ever do to deserve this? I understand Patsy's hatred of God now."

I kept silent for a few moments and then said, "Spencer, I don't imagine I have any good answers for you. I'm not sure what happened, but it won't cause me to care for you or Patsy any less. I'm staying with you, Spencer, no matter what."

Spencer's face had taken on a mask of death. He seemed haunted by an unknown force that was sucking his life away. His voice was flat again with absolutely no emotion.

"Patsy found some papers in her mom's closet. She said she was looking for some shoes she liked that her mom let her use since they wore the same size. On the top shelf was a cardboard box that seemed like it was ready to fall off, so she grabbed it to tilt it back and a folder fell off the top. It had Patsy's name on it. She said she thought it was her old school records, so she opened it to see how her grades had changed since she entered the gifted program. It wasn't grades." Spencer moved into hyper speed. He acted like if he didn't spit this all out, he would choke on it. He rushed forward. "It was her birth certificate and some paperwork about her birth. She said she looked at the birth certificate figuring she would see her dad's name under 'father', but instead she saw my dad's name.

"She read the rest of the papers, which affirmed that my dad was her real biological father. She knew her dad and mom had divorced around the time she was born, but her mom never told her anything other than they just didn't get along. Patsy later wrote that she came out of her mother's closet screaming for her mother. I guess her mom heard her screaming from outside and came running in to see what was wrong. Patsy was uncontrollable as her mom tried to get her to listen. But all she heard was that, yes, Gary

Vaughn was her biological father. Her mom and my dad had a secret affair that was discovered by Mr. Anderson. He stayed around until Patsy was born and then split." Spencer was now totally deflated and seemed to shrivel up before my eyes.

It all came together like a punch in the gut. The cold air in the cave seemed to be sucked out all at once. I opened my mouth to say something but choked it off in a gurgle. Oh, my, God! The awful truth of all this exploded in my brain. Spencer and Patsy were related? Half brother and sister? Oh no! No, no! This was almost too much to handle. What had Patsy gone through, and what had Spencer gone through and was living with right now! This was way over the top for any adolescent to wrestle with. I couldn't even begin to know where to go with this. "Spencer, I ah…ah…" I caught myself before I showed my shock to him. "I'm understanding now what Patsy and now you are…" I hesitated. Spencer didn't seem to know that Patsy was pregnant. Oh, God! What a horrible shame.

"Did you ever lose someone you loved more than anything in the whole universe?" He looked straight at me. Spencer needed an answer from me and acted as if I hadn't spoken. "Did you?" He hesitated and then with a reed thin voice I could barely hear spoke, "I need to know if you understand." It was as if what he had said about him and Patsy being biological sister and brother hadn't been said or it didn't matter. He wanted to understand what it was like to lose someone you loved.

I turned my head away and then turned back to him. "Yes, I understand, Spencer. I lost someone who was my whole world a couple of years ago."

"Who did you lose? How can you even go on? I can't go on. I just don't think I can." He screwed his fists into his eyes probably welcoming the pain to stop the hurt he was experiencing.

"Spencer, my wife was killed by a drunk driver two years ago in New Mexico. I thought I was going to die, too, but I didn't. There were times I wish I had. I woke up each day wishing I wasn't there. Every day I still feel her loss. It is a hole inside me." I hooked my hands around my knees and felt not only my pain but Spencer's. Screaming at the unfairness of all of it was on the tip of my tongue, but I bit it off. The professional in me still existed enough to stay with Spencer. This was his time, not mine.

"You know, don't you? Somehow I figured you would understand." He swallowed, rubbed his neck. "I hate God, Doc. I'll never forgive him for what he has done to me. What kind of God would allow this to happen? Huh? What kind?"

"I don't know, Spencer. I really don't."

We sat in silence for a lifetime. Spencer, Patsy, me, and my wife, Lilly. Two lives left. Two gone. What did it mean? Or, maybe it all meant nothing. It just is/was. This is it and all there is. God or no God. Which is it? I'm still yelling at God after two years of pain, confusion, and rage. Murder is still in my heart for the guy who killed my wife. Nothing but venom for the system that continued to let a guy off with five prior DUIs. And now, Spencer and Patsy and a love that was but couldn't be and shouldn't be. I hurt so much for Spencer that I was numb with pain. How could I be so numb and yet still hurt so much? The silence hung around us so closely that I was certain I could see it and taste it. Now what? I had to tell him that Patsy was pregnant. Oh, God, how do I say this?

"Spencer, there is something you need to know." I hesitated. His eyes held so much pain that I didn't know if I could go on. I sucked in a deep breath and began. "Spencer, Patsy was pregnant."

His head jerked back like he had been punched. "What? What did you say?"

"I said Patsy was…"

"No, no, no, that's impossible!" Spencer was screaming now.

"Spencer, I…"

"No! Don't you get it! We never had sex!" Spencer was standing now pacing around the cave.

I stood. "But Spencer how did…?"

"Impossible! It can't be! How?" his words trailed off. "Oh, no. Oh, shit. It can't be." Spencer slumped and I thought he was collapsing.

I moved to catch him and he held out his right hand with his palm toward me. I stopped.

"That is what she was trying to tell me. It was another reason she just wanted to die. I didn't get it." He stood in place with tears streaming down his face. "It all makes sense now. Everything crashed in on her. She knew we were related and could never be together. God dammit!" he wailed.

Slowly I moved toward him and he let me envelop him in my arms. I was crying now. We held each other for a long time as our tears flowed. Gradually we quieted and stood apart.

"I'm ready to talk with my dad." It was said with an iron edge.

"You sure?" Dumb question from me. I couldn't imagine any more pain for anyone but more would come.

"Yeah, I'm sure."

I moved from my sitting place on the cold floor of the cave to my knees and then stood bending down to move to the entrance. Leaning out, I looked to the right until I could see Gary and Steve sitting down with their backs to the wall. Steve's light was shining on the far wall unmoving. "Gary? Steve? Can you come in here?" It seemed like weeks since I had seen them.

"Is he okay? Is Spence all right?" blurted Gary.

"I'll need for him to tell you that, Gary," I said

I stepped back into the cave with Spencer and sat against the wall that he was leaning on. Gary ducked down and entered the cave. Steve followed him and stood by the entrance.

"Spencer, I'm so glad..." Gary cried, but Spencer interrupted.

"Don't, Dad!" shrieked Spencer. "Just sit down and listen."

"I'm so glad you are are..."

"Shut up, sit down, and listen to me!" yelled Spencer. Gary froze at Spencer's tone, started to open his mouth, closed it, and slowly sat facing Spencer.

"I know everything, Dad. I know about you and Mrs. Anderson. Everything! All of it!"

"What do you mean you..."

"Cut the crap! Don't lie to me and don't try to deny it! You caused all this! Patsy's death is your fault, Dad. Your fault. Your own daughter, you bastard!" Spencer quieted his words and in an eerie voice said, "I loved her, Dad. We loved each other and didn't know."

"No, oh, God, no. It just couldn't be. No, not you and Patsy. Oh dear Lord in heaven."

"There isn't any Lord in heaven, Dad. It's just you and your lies right here. Right here! You hear me!" screamed Spencer. "Now you can live with your sleazy life and lies."

The sound of Spencer's voice ping-ponged around the cave for what seemed hours. I knew it was only a few seconds though. Gary sat stunned trying not to look at his son, trying to look away, but couldn't. His face was bleached out, collapsing in on itself. The silence stretched, closed in, embraced us. Gary aged before my eyes. Life drained out of him.

Steve Montes cleared his throat. "Spencer, Gary, we need to move on out of here now. We'll come back later for your gear, Spencer, but we have to sort this out now. I need to know what happened and, rather than do it here, we'll go back to my office."

No one moved for a few moments. Spencer looked over at me. I nodded my head once. Spencer stood up and walked past his dad through the cave opening.

Silently we returned the way we had come out through this cave entrance and through the tunnel that led to the large cavern. Our headlamps posted four different pictures on the walls of the cavern. Hunched over and single file we began the trek up the incline toward the small entrance joining this cavern with the Rua Springs mine. The only sounds were of our breathing and the scraping of our boot soles on the rocks below. I was so anxious to get free of the cold and darkness that my brain was almost closed to other sounds. Almost, but not quite.

"Hey!" Spencer's voice slammed into me.

"What?" said Steve.

"I saw a...face up there at the entrance."

"You saw...?

"There!" Spencer's headlamp spot was on the cave entrance. "Jimmy? What are..."

"What are you talking about, Spence? No one is up there, Son," spoke Gary from behind me.

Kaboom! The blast lit up the cave entrance with concentrated bright light and blew us all down the way we had come. A rockslide covered the entrance as rock particles plastered us without mercy. My headlamp lens shattered and angry, sharp rock edges cut into my face. As quickly as it started it was over. I lay on my back near the water's edge sucking in large gulps of air trying to understand what happened. I felt like a freight train ran over me.

"Jesus Fucking Christ!" roared Gary. "What the hell?"

"Is everyone okay?" It was Steve's voice.

"Marc?"

"Yeah, Steve, okay."

"Spencer?"

"I'm okay, I think." answered Spencer. "Just had the wind knocked out of me."

"Gary?"

"Okay, Steve," replied Gary. "What happened?"

"Explosion, I think," said Steve.

I could hear pain in Steve's words. He had been in the lead and I believed hardest hit by the blast.

"I saw him," said Spencer. "My headlamp shone right in his face."

"What do you mean you saw him? Saw who? What are you talking about, Spencer?" asked Gary angrily.

"It was Jimmy. I saw him at the cave opening."

"Come on, Spence, how could you…"

"I saw him, Dad! It was Jimmy Tuttle!" yelled Spencer.

"Enough!" Steve said forcefully. "Let's calm down and figure out how to get out of here."

For a period of time none of us moved. Finally, I heard movement behind me and Steve walked around and stood in front of me.

"Get up, Marc, and no more laying down on the job."

"Yes sir, comandante!"

Grasping Steve's outstretched hand he pulled me up. He grimaced.

"You okay, Steve?"

"Took a blow to the chest. Probably a good sized rock. I'll have a bruise."

Spencer and his dad were standing with us. Two head-lamps were working. Mine and Gary's had taken a direct hit and were dead. Steve checked us over with his light.

"Bloodied, but not beaten." said Steve through a laugh. "Okay, Spencer. What did you see?"

"Jimmy Tuttle. His face was in the cave entrance and then it wasn't. And then the blast."

We stood in silence for a few moments. I was trying to piece together Jimmy Tuttle being here and an explosion. It didn't add up. It was he and Anthony who wanted me to find Spencer.

"He didn't want me to know." Spencer's voice faded into the darkness. "It was Jimmy and Patsy. I didn't quite get it from her diary but now I do."

And so did I. Jesus, one of Spencer's best friends did this. Jimmy used extreme measures to keep it quiet. He doesn't expect any of us to tell the story whatever it really is.

"What are you talking about, Spence?" questioned his dad.

"Nothing. Let's figure out how to get out of here," Spencer said as he scaled the incline to where the opening to the cave once was.

We watched Spencer reach the rock pile in front of the entrance. He moved around it for awhile surveying the extent of the blockage.

"No way out here," shouted Spencer from above us. "The size and weight of the rocks are too large to move. Jimmy did a good job." He began his descent.

Gary dropped to the ground and put his head in his hands. "I guess we'll be here for awhile. Hannah will be worrying by now. I wonder if anyone will ever find this cave or if they will just look in the mine."

"Don't worry, Dad. We won't be here long cause there is another way out." I could see Spencer smiling as he stood above his dad.

Steve and I crowded in close to Spencer.

"Another way?" asked Steve.

"Yep. When I first discovered this cave I scouted all parts of it. On the other side of the cave is a way out." Spencer pointed across the water into the darkness. There is a sharp incline that comes to a small hole. The hole is straight up but I was able to get outside from there."

I wanted to grab Spencer and kiss him. Instead I pumped a fist into the air and yelled, "Yes!"

"Let's get out of here," exclaimed Steve.

Gary stood up and hugged his son saying over and over, "I'm so sorry, please forgive me."

Spencer glared at his dad, nodded his head once, and began walking.

Thirty minutes later after having skirted the cave at water level we reached the incline Spencer had mentioned. After crawling up, sliding down, and dragging each other slowly to the top we finally stood under the small hole above us. I could feel a whisper of fresh outside air on my face. All of us were ecstatic and slapping each other on the back.

"After you, Spencer!" proclaimed Steve as he made a stirrup with his two hands for Spencer to step into.

And then we were out. For a period of time we simply sat on the side of the mountain inhaling the fresh air from the dark sky.

"We're on the south side of the mountain from the mine entrance. Probably a mile or more hike but I think I remember a trail that will take us around." Steve stopped for a moment and took a deep breath. "And then I have a visit to make," he said with a sharpness that would cut a diamond.

I cringed and wrapped my arms around myself. Jimmy was a goner.

In just over an hour we had reached the mine entrance and walked down to Steve's truck. The ride back to Rua Springs for me was a mix of the morose and the ecstatic. A quiet calm before the storm.

CHAPTER THIRTY-TWO

S omehow I made it to school today. Two nights out dealing with school problems had left me emotionally and physically wrung out. I hadn't been for a morning bike ride or hike for a few days. My body couldn't do it. My sleep had been the sleep of the dead, so I couldn't remember a thing about any dreams that may have occurred. In one way that was a relief. Maybe Lilly and Pasty had moved on. But in a strange sort of way, I looked forward to them showing up in my dreams, so I felt the loss.

Steve had called me early this morning after his surprise visit to Jimmy last night. Jimmy admitted he had caused the explosion in the mine to keep Spencer from knowing the truth about Patsy. His dad is an engineer for the highway department and Jimmy had taken a stick of dynamite from his work place. Jimmy had also looked for Patsy on the day she killed herself just as Spencer had. He had found Patsy after she had hung herself. Living with that secret was his personal nightmare.

Jimmy was more distraught and desperate than ever and had followed us to the Rua Springs Mine. He didn't want to hurt anyone he just wanted to continue to keep the secret. Unfortunately, Jimmy had also taken a punch from the blast and his face and hands were bloodied according to Steve. Jimmy knew he had made a terrible mistake with Patsy and was frantic. He knew he had betrayed his friendship with Spencer and believed it could never recover.

Patsy had come to Jimmy for comfort after she learned about her biological relationship to Spencer. Patsy was distraught and Jimmy comforted her all the way to his bed. He didn't know that the one time they had sex had gotten Patsy pregnant. Learning that sent him into hysterics and Steve had called Jimmy's medical doctor for help. Jimmy's parents were devastated. So many lives changed forever. Steve wasn't sure what charges to bring against Jimmy, if any. The punishment for Jimmy was lifelong already.

Several middle school students were speaking with Mrs. Chang at the front desk when I entered the office. The middle school girls' basketball team was playing an afternoon game today, and several girls wanted to attend. Mrs. Chang was advising the girls that they could not attend because their grades were low. They were working hard to convince her otherwise. No go. The girls were being...well...they were being middle school girls so they were honing their debating skills. But against Mrs. Chang they didn't have a chance. It was entertaining for sure. I walked by trying not to laugh.

Later, I collected Donny Packerd, the treatment foster care kid, from science class. I couldn't help but notice that his two followers were sitting elsewhere now. A falling out? Maybe he would say something about it. The sky might fall too.

"Donny, how are things going in your classes?

"I'm not doing so well."

A miracle! He speaks!

"I'm sorry to hear that. Is there something I can help with, Donny?"

"I really miss my sister. I'm worried about her." These were the longest sentences Donny had spoken to me since he'd been here. A breakthrough?

"I would like to hear about your sister. Where is she?" I knew his sister was placed in a different treatment foster home in another town. Donny was obviously hurting though.

He sat in the small chair with his face in his hands rubbing his forehead. "She is in Lamar. I haven't seen her in…a long time. I just wish I could know that she is okay."

"You're worried about her."

Donny was rubbing his forehead so hard I thought he would peel off his skin. "Yeah…I…"

Bang, bang, bang! Someone was hammering on my door. "Doc? Doc?"

Donny and I had literally jumped out of our chairs. My heart was hammering inside my chest just like the hammering on my door.

I opened the door. "What in the world is going on? I'm with someone!" I was angry now.

Mac filled up the doorway with his bulk. "We have an emergency, Doc!"

I must have looked like a fish out of water with my mouth moving but no sounds coming out. "What…"

"Our phantoms have showed up again, but this time we caught them."

"You have?" I stared at Mac, trying to shake off the initial shock.

"Yeah, and you won't believe it, but we have another traumatized boy." Mac started to walk away.

Turning around, I looked at Donny. He was white as a sheet, all blood drained from his face. "I'm sorry, Donny. I promise I'll get back with you as soon as this is taken care of. And, I'll help find out about your sister." I looked in his eyes. He held my gaze. I held out my hand.

"Thanks." He reached out and took my hand and held on for a few seconds. Contact. A first.

"Okay, Donny. We'll work on things together. You go back to class." He nodded and walked past me.

Mac was waiting for me. "You won't believe this." He looked at Mrs. Chang and smiled. "Meet our resident spy." Mac pointed toward Mrs. Chang. "She has been roaming the school at various times keeping an eye out for me." She smiled at him shyly. "Today, she was just leaving the office when she saw two boys pushing a boy into the restroom. She ran back to my office and told me what she had seen. I ran down the hall and entered the boy's restroom. They were binding a young boy with duct tape. I made a flying tackle and downed the two boys, which knocked the breath out of them. Pushing the boy out of the way I grabbed the duct tape and wrapped up their arms and feet before they knew what hit them.

Needing to ask two questions, I wasn't sure which to ask first. "How is the boy and who did it?"

"The boy is Rudy Apodaca. He is traumatized but not like the first two boys. And, once again, he has a reputation for strong arm tactics with other kids."

My face must have betrayed my shock. "Who did it?"

"Two brainy high school kids who came here regularly as tutors in math. One boy has two younger brothers here and the other boy has a younger sister. All the younger siblings had been victims of Rudy, Billy, and Aaron." Mac told me the high school boy's names.

Oh, no! Two from The Einstein Posse. They obviously hadn't listened to Steve Montes and had moved forward on this plan of revenge.

"The younger siblings were duct taped and spray painted with red, but not at the same time so I didn't see a connection." said Mac.

A deputy sheriff entered the office. "Got them, huh?"

"Yeah, they are wrapped up like birthday presents for you down in the boy's restroom."

"Let's go then."

I followed them down the hall to the boy's restroom. Again, Mr. Piño had helped out and was standing with Rudy Apodaca outside the doorway. Inside, the two high school students were sitting on a bench with their heads down. Now was not the time for me to confront them. Besides the roll of duct tape I saw a can of red spray paint rolled up against the wall under a sink. Hmmm... I stepped outside and said hello to Rudy and Mr. Piño.

"How you doing, Rudy?"

"Okay. Those guys weren't so tough. I've seen tougher," Rudy said as he put on his macho face.

"I'm really sorry this happened to you. I'm here to talk with you if you want. You know I'm around, and I'll be here for you just like Mr. Piño."

Teachers had kept their students in the classrooms so they most likely didn't know what happened. The chaos would start later.

The deputy brought the two high school students out of the restroom and walked them toward the front doors. Their hands were cuffed behind their backs. I stared after them. I thought back to the two previous attacks. Gene Oakley was there both times. How come he didn't see these high school kids doing anything?

Early the next morning I was sitting in Mac's office hearing the story of the high school gifted boys. I asked Mac why Gene Oakley hadn't seen anything.

"Well…I found out from the two kids that Gene had a regular routine of going into his closet office and watching movies on his iPad. They had befriended him and knew when he would be gone and took advantage of him. Gene isn't the smartest guy sometimes. These two were here so often they blended in to the walls. Interesting, huh?"

Very interesting! I thought. Smart kids using their own bullying tactics to scare the bullies wasn't the way to solve school bullying problems. It may even make it worse.

"Superintendent Espiñosa has called an open school board meeting to share the details. The lid has blown off, and parents are going ballistic. They don't trust anyone now. I guess I don't blame them." Mac sighed and leaned back in his chair, looking at the ceiling. "I love these kids, Doc. We have to protect them better. Truly we do, but it's a steep uphill battle."

Mac and I sat in silence for awhile mulling over everything that had happened. We were interrupted by Mrs. Chang, our resident spy, who knocked on the door.

"We have two girls fighting in the hallway. I thought you would want to know."

Mac stood, looked down at me and smiled. "Yeah! Let's rock and roll, Doc!"

CHAPTER THIRTY-THREE

The next morning I was sitting in an IEP meeting that had been postponed for over two weeks. One hundred sixty-four. One hundred sixty-five. One hundred sixty... I was counting holes in the ceiling tile sitting in an IEP meeting with Reba Bennett.

"I can't seem to help him!" Reba exclaimed louder than necessary. "He just doesn't get it! I told you all this two weeks ago when we postponed this meeting!"

"Reba..."

"Our plan doesn't work! You promised me you would develop a new plan!"

"No, I did..."

"He needs more help than I can give! Don't you hear me?" Reba was bouncing up and down in her chair. The room was shaking. No, that was just my imagination.

One hundred sixty-nine. One hundred seventy. One hundred...

"Reba, Scott's mother is sitting right here. Don't you..."
George Novak tried to calm Reba, but he couldn't hold a
candle to her.

"I just can't do it! I..."

"Reba," I said softly. "Why don't we try to work this out
together. Scott's mother is here to work with us and she
needs to know we will help Scott be successful. We all need
you to be a part of this team so let's try to look for ways to
revamp Scott's IEP. I know even you want to help Scott." I
wasn't sure at all that Reba wanted to help Scott.

"But...I...you can't..." For once she was at a loss for
words. Good.

I sat back in my chair smiling. Forget counting ceiling
tile. This was way more fun! Yeah!

The school and community rumors about recent events
took off at a blistering pace. Almost all of it was totally off-
base and unbelievably wild. Patsy was pulled off the inac-
tive gossip list because of stories about her. The rumors
said Patsy didn't commit suicide and gangs coming out of
Denver killed her, she was in a cult, she was in some new
religious group that went against God's law; this was punishment because of their rituals. This was part of the ritual.
The best one was that aliens did it. On and on the stories
went, becoming more strange.

Then, they all stopped because the basketball team won
another game and were undefeated. That became more important. Life went on.

Spencer returned to school a couple of weeks later. It
barely caused a ripple. I heard some kids asking him where
he had been. I didn't hear his answer. Later, he came by
my office, though, and said he would like to talk. We made

plans. I didn't see or hear anything from Gary Vaughn or Jimmy Tuttle. I could find out from Steve, but I just didn't have the energy.

Welcome home, I said to myself one day in November when there hadn't been a crisis in school that day. I knew the quiet would end, though. It always did in schools. Kids would continue to be qualified for special education gifted programs and another Patsy would come along. And I would be here when it happened again. Ready to laugh, cry, scream and rage about what kids today have to go through.

Sitting in my middle school office at the end of the day I closed my eyes and began to relax by body by concentrating on each body part to feel peace. As I ended my journey I realized I had let the tension flow from me and drift away. I opened my eyes and smiled. Yes, I said to myself. I will call my dad and invite him and Grandpa to a meal at Mabel's tonight. I tuned on my iPhone, got it powered up, and dialed Dad.

"Hey Dad," I said, when he answered. "How about we go to Mabel's tonight?"

GIFTED

Pronunciation: \'gif-təd\
Function: *adjective*
Date: 1644

> **1 :** having great natural ability **:** TALENTED <gifted children>
> **2 :** revealing a special gift <gifted voices>

— **gift·ed·ly** *adverb*
— **gift·ed·ness** *noun*
(www.merrian-webster.com)

Gifted Definitions:

- General or specific intellectual ability.
- Specific academic aptitude.
- Creative or productive thinking.
- Leadership abilities.
- Visual arts, performing arts, musical or psychomotor abilities.

(Colorado Department of Education-Gifted and Talented Education)

Gifted education (also known as **Gifted and Talented Education** (**GATE**), **Talented and Gifted** (**TAG**), or **G/T**) A broad term for special practices, procedures and theories used in the education of children who have been identified as gifted or talented. There is no standard global definition of what a gifted student is.

While giftedness is seen as an academic advantage, psychologically it can pose other challenges for the gifted individual. A person who is intellectually advanced may or may not be advanced in other areas. Each individual student needs to be evaluated for physical, social, and emotional skills without the traditional prejudices which either prescribe either "compensatory" weaknesses or "matching" advancement in these areas.

(http://en.wikipedia.org/wiki/Gifted_education#Emotional_ aspects_of_gifted_education)

COMMON GIFTED EDUCATION MYTHS

Myth:
Gifted students don't need help; they'll do fine on their own
Truth:
Would you send a star athlete to train for the Olympics without a coach? Gifted students need guidance from well-trained teachers who challenge and support them in order to fully develop their abilities. Many gifted students may be so far ahead of their same-age peers that they know more than half of the grade-level curriculum before the school year begins. Their resulting boredom and frustration can lead to low achievement, despondency, or unhealthy work habits. The role of the teacher is crucial for spotting and nurturing talents in school.

Myth:
Teachers challenge all the students, so gifted kids will be fine in the regular classroom
Truth:
Although teachers try to challenge all students they are frequently unfamiliar with the needs of gifted children and do not know how to best serve them in the classroom. The

National Research Center on Gifted and Talented (NRC/ GT) found that 61% of classroom teachers had no training in teaching highly able students, limiting the challenging educational opportunities offered to advanced learners. A more recent national study conducted by the Fordham Institute found that 58% of teachers have received no professional development focused on teaching academically advanced students in the past few years. Taken together, these reports confirm what many families have known: not all teachers are able to recognize and support gifted learners.

Myth:
Gifted students make everyone else in the class smarter by providing a role model or a challenge
Truth:
In reality, average or below-average students do not look to the gifted students in the class as role models. They are more likely to model their behavior on those who have similar capabilities and are coping well in school. Seeing a student at a similar performance level succeed motivates students because it adds to their own sense of ability. Watching or relying on someone who is expected to succeed does little to increase a struggling student's sense of self-confidence. Similarly, gifted students benefit from classroom interactions with peers at similar performance levels.

Myth:
All children are Gifted
Truth:
While all children are special and deserving, not all children have exceptional academic gifts that require additional or different support in school. Interestingly, most people

readily accept that there are gifted children in performing arts or athletics whose talents are so far above those of others their age that they require additional or different training or coaching. It is important to understand that these same characteristics and differences apply to academically gifted students who need support and guidance to reach their full potential.

Myth:
Acceleration placement options are socially harmful for gifted students
Truth:

Academically gifted students often feel bored or out of place with their age peers and naturally gravitate towards older students who are more similar as "intellectual peers." Studies have shown that many students are happier with older students who share their interest than they are with children the same age. Therefore, acceleration placement options such as early entrance to Kindergarten, grade skipping, or early exit should be considered for these students.

Myth:
Gifted education programs are elitist
Truth:

Gifted education is not about status, it is about meeting student needs. Advanced learners are found in all cultures, ethnic backgrounds, and socioeconomic groups. However, not every school district offers services for gifted students, even though there are gifted students in every district. Because of a lack of state and federal financial support, only affluent districts in many states can afford to offer gifted education programs and services, which leaves many gifted students behind.

Myth:
That student can't be gifted; he's receiving poor grades
Truth:
Underachievement describes a discrepancy between a student's performance and his actual ability. The roots of this problem differ, based on each child's experiences. Gifted students may become bored or frustrated in an unchallenging classroom situation causing them to lose interest, learn bad study habits, or distrust the school environment. Other students may mask their abilities to try to fit in socially with their same-age peers. No matter the cause, it is imperative that a caring and perceptive adult help gifted learners break the cycle of underachievement in order to achieve their full potential.

Myth:
Gifted students are happy, popular, and well-adjusted in school
Truth:
Many gifted students flourish in their community and school environment. However, some gifted children differ in terms of their emotional and moral intensity, sensitivity to expectations and feelings, perfectionism, and deep concerns about societal problems. Others do not share interests with their classmates, resulting in isolation or being labeled unfavorably as a "nerd." Because of these difficulties, the school experience is one to be endured rather than celebrated. It is estimated that 20 to 25% of gifted children have social and emotional difficulties, about twice as many

as in the general population of students. Most gifted adolescent children just want to be normal, to fit in.

Myth:
This child can't be gifted, he has a disability
Truth:
Some gifted students also have learning or other disabilities. These "twice-exceptional" students often go undetected in regular classrooms because their disability and gifts mask each other, making them appear "average." Other twice-exceptional students are identified as having a learning disability and as a result, are not considered for gifted services. In both cases, it is important to focus on the students' abilities and allow them to have challenging curricula in addition to receiving help for their learning disability.

Myth:
Our district has a gifted and talented program: We have AP courses
Truth:
While AP classes offer rigorous, advanced coursework, they are not a gifted education program. The AP program is designed as college-level classes taught by high school teachers for students willing to work hard. The program is limited in its service to gifted and talented students in two major areas: First AP is limited by the subjects offered, which in most districts is only a small handful. Second it is limited in that, typically, it is offered only in high school and is generally available only for 11th and 12th grade students. Coupled with the one-size-fits all approach of textbooks and extensive reading lists, the limitations of AP coursework mean

that districts must offer additional curriculum options to be considered as having gifted and talented services.

Myth:
Gifted education requires abundant resources
Truth:
While, over time, developing an effective and comprehensive gifted education program may be costly and require talented, well-qualified professionals, an abundance of resources is not necessary to begin offering gifted education services. A belief that gifted students require something different from the regular curriculum, followed by hard-work and commitment from community and district personnel, are the most critical components in designing and implementing successful gifted education programs and services.

The National Association of Gifted Children: www.nagc.org

ANSWER TO EINSTEIN RIDDLE

The Situation

1. There are 5 houses in five different colors.
2. In each house lives a person with a different nationality.
3. These five owners drink a certain type of beverage, smoke a certain brand of cigar and keep a certain pet.
4. No owners have the same pet, smoke the same brand of cigar or drink the same beverage.

The question is: *Who owns the fish?*

Hints

- the Brit lives in the red house
- the Swede keeps dogs as pets
- the Dane drinks tea
- the green house is on the left of the white house

- the green house's owner drinks coffee
- the person who smokes Pall Mall rears birds
- the owner of the yellow house smokes Dunhill
- the man living in the center house drinks milk
- the Norwegian lives in the first house
- the man who smokes blends lives next to the one who keeps cats
- the man who keeps horses lives next to the man who smokes Dunhill
- the owner who smokes BlueMaster drinks beer
- the German smokes Prince
- the Norwegian lives next to the blue house
- the man who smokes blend has a neighbor who drinks water

Einstein wrote this riddle this century. He said that 98% of the world could not solve it.

The Answer
Go to: https://udel.edu/~os/riddle-solution.html

AUTHOR BIOGRAPHY

Laren R. Winter spent his career as a school psychologist and now serves as a faculty chair of a graduate program for training school psychologists.

Winter has also worked in private practice as a family therapist and professional counselor. He has directed an outdoor environmental education program, owned a white-water rafting company, worked in churches, and built houses.

Winter is passionate about writing and is hard at work on his next Marc Thomas adventure.

Made in the USA
San Bernardino, CA
24 April 2017